MW01196081

A Killer Getaway

A NOVEL

SIENNA SHARPE

sourcebooks
landmark

For Adam—the only one for me

Copyright © 2025 by Jenna Satterthwaite
Cover and internal design © 2025 by Sourcebooks
Cover design and illustration by Elizabeth Turner Stokes
Internal design by Laura Boren/Sourcebooks

Published by Sourcebooks Landmark, an imprint of Sourcebooks
P.O. Box 4410, Naperville, Illinois 60567-4410
(630) 961-3900
sourcebooks.com

Cataloging-in-Publication Data is on file with the Library of Congress.

Printed and bound in the United States of America.
VP 10 9 8 7 6 5 4 3 2 1

PROLOGUE

I BLINK SLOWLY, WATCHING THE WORLD FUZZ IN AND OUT IN THE CLEAR honey light falling on us through your apartment window. The window is dirty; you're not very good at housekeeping, but I don't care, and after last night I've found out how good you are at other things.

Even though we just had our first night together, I've already planned in my head that after we get married, you'll be in charge of the cooking and I'll be in charge of the cleaning. We'll play to our strengths. If you always leave your laundry strewn around, I'll think it's cute. Promise. Each imperfection will be one more reason to love you, and we will never, ever resent each other.

I'm only half awake. The scene is like a dream—*you're* a dream, one I never even dared have. But last night, you changed that.

The jut of your hip under white sheets, the drape of your arm, the tremble of your breath fluttering the edge of the coverlet. All so easy, and I never thought love would be easy.

Your voice is deep in these early, tender hours as your eyes take me in and you murmur, "Beautiful."

You say it like it moves you. Like there's something sacred about the mathematics that wove my proportions together when I was nothing but a blob of cells. When you speak that single word with all the certainty of an officiant blessing a sacrament, some old, broken place in my heart begins to mend. All my life, beauty has felt like a liability, but at that word from you (and I know it sounds crazy, but…), I heal.

Do you believe that healing can happen in a single moment? I do. I experienced it with you that morning in your Cincinnati apartment above the bakery, with the smell of yeast and sugar in the air around us and the muted grumble of city traffic leaking through the windowpanes.

"Want coffee?" you murmur.

"In a minute," I murmur back, because I don't want either of us to move yet. I want to live in this moment for ever.

Your fingers trail slowly over the line of my jaw, sending shivers like currents of wordless music into my bones. This morning, your touch is as delicate as smoke, but I remember your touch last night. The ferocious urgency that drove us together, tumbling backward on to your unmade bed as you whispered, *Are we doing this?* and I groaned, *Yes*, and our beings cracked open in each other's arms.

That was before.

But of course, there's another scene after.

A darker scene to bookend the light, the sheets now washed in shadows in the hush of a hospital. Still, the jut of a hip. The drape of an arm. The flutter of breath on sheets. A beeping monitor and quiet, muffled sobs that wrench and yank as they come out—my own.

Then, later, me alone in the apartment, with the smell of the bakery in the air and the muted traffic and the sunlight slanting, sitting on the unmade bed alone, not wanting to move. Not because I want this moment to last for ever, but because I'm afraid of what the next moment will bring, and the next after that, and maybe if I stay still enough, I won't have to face a future without you.

It'll get easier, my friends tell me. *Just be patient with yourself.*

But they never held that kind of love in their hands, or felt its perfection and fragility.

They never felt the slick, viscous slide of an entire future slipping away through the cracked shell of a life. In that single moment, I shattered.

I've always hated that old children's rhyme. You know the one— Humpty Dumpty. But it's true, isn't it?

That there are some breakages that go beyond healing.

That sometimes, a single fall can break you for ever.

CHAPTER 1

"A BEVERAGE, MA'AM?" LIKE A FISHHOOK, THE FLIGHT ATTENDANT'S whisper yanks me out of the meditative zone I'd just achieved, back into the chilly, dry atmosphere of the airplane.

"Tomato juice, please." My nerves are fizzing like live wires, but I force what I believe to be a calm smile and close my book. *Crime and Punishment*. Ambitious, isn't it? I have yet to read a word. As Mom always said, go big or go home. God love her, she had no patience for mediocrity of any kind.

The flight attendant rummages in the depths of her cart for a can of V8, and I glance at my seatmate, passed out with an action thriller movie still playing on his seatback screen. Light flickers over his slack face. The plane is full of sleepers. It's a lonely feeling to be the only passenger awake, and more than once since boarding, I've wished I wasn't making this trip. Any minute now, we should see the sunrise burning red on the horizon. The beginning of a day I've been anticipating and dreading for a year.

"Ice with that?"

"Yes, please."

As the flight attendant scoops a noisy volley of ice into a small clear plastic cup, I resettle my restless legs, angled toward the window to avoid my sleeping seatmate's truly heroic case of manspreading.

"Thanks," I tell the flight attendant, as she reaches over him with my can and the cup of ice. He twitches, then his eyes blink awake and he lowers his Bose headphones so they encircle his neck.

"You don't want some vodka in that?" he says as he eyes my drink selection, stretching his muscled arms behind his head in a V shape and giving me an engaging half-grin. "Make it a Bloody Mary? My treat, since I was probably snoring or drooling."

His accent is New Jersey all the way. I put his age around fifty. Successful businessman. Gym-obsessed. Probably drives a Tesla. Divorced? I glance down at his hand and sure enough, there's a pale mark where a wedding band recently moved out. I like to figure out people as quickly as I can. I'm not always right, but I do have an instinct. Which, right now, is screaming yes to the vodka.

"Why not."

I'm not a big drinker. But right now, I could use some help relaxing.

"Get the nice lady some vodka," he says, straining into the pocket of his jeans, presumably for a credit card. "Get me some too while you're at it."

"No card needed, sir," says the flight attendant smoothly. "We've gone contactless. We'll charge it to your seat." She smiles at me. "I'll be right back with your vodka."

"Thanks," I say.

"Reading anything good?" he says, already leaning in to read the back cover copy. "Dostoevsky!" He leans back and gives me an exaggerated up and down. "She's the whole package, ladies and gentlemen! The body and the brains."

I'm not usually one to engage in anger fantasies. It's a waste of both time and emotional energy. Still, something about this guy makes it really easy for me to envision pounding my fist into his crotch. Instead, I tighten my grip on my plastic cup, stare at him, and take a long, savory gulp of tomato juice. I shiver as it goes down.

"OK, woman of mystery," he says appreciatively. The plane gives a sudden shudder, and since I have to divert all my attention to balancing my tomato juice, my violent little vision pops.

"What a tin can," my seatmate murmurs, stretching his thighs out further to the side and grunting. "No space for a big guy like me."

Emasculation, of course, might create more room…

Stop!

"I never fly coach," he continues, "but their first class section filled up. What the fuck, you know? I'm Kyle, by the way."

I force a smile but don't try to make it reach my eyes, as the flight attendant returns with four tiny plastic bottles of vodka and hands us two each. I pour the first into my V8 and swish the ice around to mix it. Is it technically day drinking if the sun isn't up yet?

"Cheers," Kyle says, knocking the tiny bottle in his massive hand against my cup. I sip; he downs his straight away. "You traveling for business or for pleasure?"

"Business."

"Pleasure," says Kyle, twisting the cap off bottle number two. "Well, more like a reset. After the divorce." He waggles his fingers in the air. "You married?"

"No."

"Cheers to that." He clinks my cup again. "Not worth it." He downs his second bottle in a few swift gulps, then calls, "Miss? Miss?"

toward the flight attendant, jiggling his two empty bottles before resuming his chat with me. "I'm the CEO of a really, really successful company, and that comes with sacrifices. She didn't get it. She wanted the goods, you know—the luxury bags, the chef's kitchen, all that shit—but she didn't want to pay the piper. She said I was addicted to my phone, and I'm like, I'm running a company here, sweetheart. You want your five-hundred-dollar extensions, your spa days, your personal trainer, your Swedish au pair—Daddy's gotta run his business, you know? She didn't fucking *get* it, if you'll pardon my French..." For a moment, his eyes stray to his screen, where a car has burst into flames. He laughs and nudges my arm—ugh—but I'm wedged between him and the window and there's no escape route. "Fuck, look, I love this scene, it's a classic."

Some gangster type is standing on the flaming, overturned car, shooting into a line of police officers. Uniformed bodies dance and twitch in the air as the cops burst back like human confetti before falling. I look away. I can't abide violence on screen. After you experience the real thing, the true significance of those final moments of someone's life, you lose your taste for the fantasy.

"So you're not married," Kyle says, turning his attention back to me. "Any interest in grabbing drinks when we land? Don't tell me you have a boyfriend." He laughs, holding up both palms. "Literally, don't tell me, because I don't care. Beautiful woman flying alone? His loss, my gain. We can talk Dostoevsky, maybe you can class me up a little." He shifts in his seat, leaning closer so his breath tickles my skin. "You're a very attractive woman—I hope you don't mind my candor. What's your name, by the way?"

The flight attendant hands him two more bottles of vodka and takes his empties. Her eyes skim over both of us and briefly catch mine. I watch her hesitate, then I nod ever so slightly. *It's OK. I got this.*

"Cat got your tongue?" says Kyle. "What's your name?"

"Lily," I say.

"So, what do you say, Lily? Airport mimosa when we land?"

"I'm going to have to pass."

"And I'm going to have to insist. C'mon. Mimosas as the sun rises. If you're good, I'll toss in some breakfast too. Can't beat that."

"Let's not, and say we did." This time my forced smile is truly more of a grimace, but I'm not sure Kyle is the kind to tell the difference.

"OK, OK," he says, nodding, leaning back a little, his eyes appraising me. "Playing hard to get, I've seen it before." He's still smiling, but I can feel the tension. He's not used to being turned down.

"I'm just not looking for a relationship right now. I hope you don't mind *my* candor," I say.

"This isn't a marriage proposal." His voice is louder, overly jocular. "Just drinks."

I can see a vein pulsing in his neck, and you know, Kyle, at this point, there are a few veins pulsing in my body, too—and it's not the ones you might hope for.

I'm generally coolheaded. I grew up in a trailer park with a mom whose nickname was the Slut of Calumet Heights—no mediocre insults for *our* family—so I had to learn early on how to manage my emotions. That didn't mean I never let my fists fly. But *I* chose when to do it. Not my feelings.

"It's not personal," I say with a shrug. "I'm just not that into it, Kyle."

His neck flushes. "Into what? Drinks?" His laugh is short, aggressive. "Because you had no problem guzzling the one I just bought you." Then he mutters, "What a bitch," so quietly, I could almost imagine it didn't happen. He pushes his headphones over his ears and leans back in his seat, his thighs pressing out even wider.

Not ideal, Kyle. *Not* ideal.

I discreetly send a wish into the universe that his ex-wife is finding her absolute happiness. That she's having multiple orgasms at this very moment, why not.

Then I gently nudge Kyle's arm. He lowers his headphones and gives me a stony look.

"Sorry—random question—you don't happen to be headed to the Riovan, do you?" My voice is perfectly light, perfectly friendly.

"As a matter of fact, yes," he says gruffly.

I figured. The main reason to come to Saint Lisieux is the Riovan, the sprawling, luxurious and exclusive resort where I also happen to be going. I imagine most people on this plane are headed there, too, if not to one of the neighboring islands connected by ferry. Still, it's a good feeling to stick a pin in Kyle and attach him to my mental map. And I know just where I'd stick that pin too.

An image enters my brain of a mini, butterfly-sized Kyle pinned in a display frame. The label underneath: *homo sapiens assholiens*.

"Why?" Kyle adds, with an uneasy edge like he can see what's in my brain.

"I just wondered," I say with a sweet smile. If he has any sort of survivor instinct, it should be blaring an alarm right about now. Lucky for me, he doesn't. "But please—don't let me interrupt your movie."

He casts one more glance at me as he slides his headphones back on, and soon he's chuckling at a car chase scene. Already moving on.

It's always the jerks who move on first. Have you noticed that? You may think I'm bitter, but this is strictly an observation.

As I see how easily Kyle moves between calling me a bitch and laughing at his gratuitously violent movie, something in me clicks.

It's a sensation as physical as my ears popping as I flip from one Lily to another. From Cincinnati Lily—the "30 under 30" business-woman who's revitalizing the city; the fun friend who's always up for karaoke; the "happily single" girl who's a great shoulder for everyone else to cry on—to the other Lily, the one I become for four weeks every summer. I don't think it's strange to have multiple parts to myself; most people do. They're both me.

I down the remainder of my drink in one final swallow, relishing the spice and the burn in my mouth. The restlessness is gone. The booze helped.

The flight attendant is back, collecting trash.

"Everything all right?" she whispers as she holds out the white bag, with a glance at me that says she heard more between Kyle and me than she's letting on, and I appreciate her concern. Really. More of us should be looking out for one another. But she needn't be concerned for me.

I know how to take care of myself.

"Just dandy," I say, as I toss the cup and can into her bag.

CHAPTER 2

THE PLANE TOUCHES DOWN AT SAINT LISIEUX'S SMALL AIRPORT.
Passengers are yawning and stretching in their seats as we bump and
roll down the runway. I stretch too, arching my back until it cracks.
I did finally manage to fall asleep with the hood of my sweatshirt
pulled up. I push the hood back down and rework my ponytail as we
pull up to the gate. I sense Kyle's movements next to me, stuffing his
headphones in his backpack, rattling a tin of breath mints, but I don't
engage, visually or otherwise.

The morning sun slices through the row of oval windows, casting
my side of the plane in furious light, and I drink in the green of the
palm trees beyond the runway as they slide past, a shade of emerald
so intense, I can hardly take my eyes off the sight. Bright flashes of
ocean jab through the gaps in the trees.

The plane comes to a shuddering stop. The seatbelt sign turns off.
Everyone shoots up, but not me. I let them go first. Why get caught in
a crush of people—or smashed against Kyle—just to gain a thirty-
second advantage?

I watch Kyle as he pops open the luggage compartment and muscles down his Tumi roller bag. As he thumps it down, he catches the eye of a woman across the aisle.

"I hate these red-eyes, don't you?" he says, and she laughs politely. It's impossible to miss how the two of them take each other in with one swift, evaluative glance. Both seem pleased with what they see. "I'm Kyle, by the way."

"Serena," she says.

"Here for business or pleasure?"

Ah. He's one of those guys who has a single pickup line.

"Definitely business," she says, standing up and showing off a trim, muscular body in Lululemon leggings and a strappy crop top. She's petite, so as she reaches for her own roller bag overhead, Kyle says, "Let me," and takes it down for her.

"Thank you, that's so sweet," she says.

I wait until the last few people are struggling with their bags down the narrow aisle, then edge my way out of my seat and grab mine.

"Thanks for flying with us," says the pilot, an older woman with a silver bob, as I reach the door. I'm the very last person to leave the plane. "Enjoy your stay."

"Thanks," I say.

The second I step over the threshold of the airplane, a wave of Caribbean heat hits me. I pause at the top of the steep metal stairway that leads straight down to the tarmac, pull my sunglasses from my oversized purse, and slide them on. My roller bag bangs against my ankles as I descend. At the bottom of the stairs, I stop for a second to breathe the island air.

Every year it's the same; the smell brings the memories. It smells so different here—densely alive, with a sweet and salty edge that lingers in your mouth and nostrils. The smell is objectively lovely, but it's also sending me back five years to the first time I set foot on this island at twenty-four years old, with two bikinis, a couple of battered paperbacks and a heart full of dreams. That Lily had nothing—but she had everything.

I don't know if it's the mostly sleepless night or the vodka, but I walk in a slight daze down the demarcated path toward the terminal, dragging the roller bag behind me, its rattle filling my brain with noise, feeling the heat press down, feeling the memories press down. For a second, I could almost be that twenty-four-year-old girl again right now. I could probably even fit into the same bikinis, if I'd held on to them…

Whoosh.

The sliding doors open before me and I'm in the terminal. I've done this often enough that my feet automatically take me to the line for immigration, which is moving slowly in corridored zigzags, with only two officials to handle the planeload of people. I can spot Kyle down the line, absorbed in his phone, shaved head gleaming in the overhead lights, and I have to suppress an eye roll.

I take my place at the end of the line. The air conditioning crawls in chilly tracks over my skin, and I shiver. Forget the bikini. I'd kill for a sweater now.

Hot and cold. Twenty-four and twenty-nine. The Lily with her whole future ahead and the Lily with her future behind… All of a sudden, my heart starts racing. I have an extra hair elastic around my wrist; I snap it against my skin. One thing that's not helpful at all? Getting in my own head.

The line shuffles forward. I rub the goosebumps off my arms.

Why do you keep going back to that place? my friend Nate asked at Murphy's two nights ago, my last hangout with the gang before leaving Cincinnati. *Isn't the pay shit? You're missing peak summer fun! All the singles mingles...*

"You're forgetting all the rich resort singles I'm going to meet," I said with a grin, and my friend Phoebe laughed, slinging her arm around me.

"Now we're getting to the bottom of this weird-ass summer job you're so obsessed with!"

I sipped my drink and played coy as they tossed around jokes about trophy wives and gold diggers, and tried to convince me to catch up with the podcast they're all obsessed with.

They're not a bad crew, Nate and Phoebe and the rest. They're doing their best to navigate the world they live in, swiping left and right, expecting with a kind of sweet naivete that things will be different with their next match. Listening to true crime podcasts to add excitement to their doldrum days. Hoping for that next promotion at the shit company they don't even want to work at; dreaming of that bigger apartment, that next vacation... Coasting on all the mediocre wins that drive their lives forward.

Wow. Harsh much?

They're doing their best, I remind myself quickly. It's not like I think I'm better than them. But we are different at a really fundamental level, and it's impossible for me to spend time with them and not feel that difference. They're still walking through life in a kind of daze; nothing that bad has happened to any of them, whereas—

"Purpose of your visit?"

I jolt my head up.

Speaking of walking in a daze, I don't know how long I was in la-la land, but I'm now at the immigration booth, face-to-face with a man with bags under his eyes and an excitable-looking mustache. His accent sounds mildly French.

"Oh, um—the resort. The Riovan."

"So you're a guest there? How long will you be staying?"

My heart chooses this moment to start drumming so hard it's like someone is playing techno against my chest. I snap the hair tie against my skin. The drumbeat slows.

"Sorry—no. I'm working there. Four weeks. Lifeguarding. I have a visa…" I indicate the passport, which he's paging through. The temporary visa is affixed inside somewhere. I've done this every year, but still, the person behind the desk holds the power of the stamp. I'm acutely aware they could deny me entry for some obscure, official-sounding reason.

The official frowns. Frowns deeper. A little fizz of adrenaline worms through me. *Maybe turning around and going home wouldn't be so bad…*

"Ah. Here we are." He's found the visa. He gives a brisk nod and stamps my passport with all the enthusiasm of an executioner. I'd like to say my shoulders loosen, but they don't. "Enjoy your stay, Miss Lennox."

OK, it is not a good sign that, one, I'm traitorously wanting to go back home, and two, that I'm freaking out about a basic immigration question I get asked every year. But the way he said *purpose*…like he knew…

"Stop," I mutter, making myself walk briskly, *purposefully*, toward the baggage carousel area, where many of my fellow passengers are waiting for the big conveyor belt to spit out their luggage. I didn't check a bag—I'm a light traveler—but I do have to stop at a little kiosk to fill out the customs form stating I'm not bringing agricultural products or large amounts of cash with me.

"So you said you were here for business…" says a male voice, startling me so badly I have to bite back a yelp. Kyle. Unbelievable. I'm about to spin around and say something truly cutting that I haven't come up with yet but I'm sure will come to me in time, when I realize he's not talking to me. He's a few steps away, facing the baggage carousel with his back to me, talking to the petite brunette in leggings from the plane—Serena.

My pen freezes above the box where I was about to check "no" for disease agents, cell cultures, snails. Also…snails?

"Yes!" beams Serena.

"Sorry, remind me of your name…" says Kyle.

"Serena Victoria." She lays a hand on her chest. "I'm actually the new VP of Branding for the Riovan Resort. Well—new-*ish*. I've been here…four months? I was just in New York for a wedding, and now it's back to the old grind!"

"VP, OK, impressive."

She laughs. "It's really not as fancy as it sounds. Basically my focus is digital content growth and customer outreach, and let's just say their last VP of Branding had no idea TikTok even existed, which…" She makes a cringing face and they laugh together.

The carousel beeps, then begins to move. The first piece of luggage comes tumbling down.

"That's mine!" squeals Serena. "It's a sign, right? My luggage never comes out first. Like, someone up there must be looking out for this girl."

"Let me," says Kyle, muscling her massive bag off the moving belt.

"Thank you, that's soooo gentlemanly of you," she says, helping Kyle right the suitcase before snapping up the handle.

"No problem. I'm one of your guests."

"Oh, that's awesome! Are you doing the four-week intensive?"

"I am indeed."

"Well, you're going to love it!" she sings, clapping her hands together into prayer formation, the fingertips pointed at Kyle. "It's totally life-changing. We might expand it to two sessions next summer! I have big dreams for the resort…" She arches her eyebrows and nods. "The market for this kind of transformational experience is so hot right now, you know?"

"I like what you're saying." Kyle nods his head philosophically. "Transformational experience. This is good to know. I was kind of afraid it might turn out to be a glorified weight-loss camp—"

"Oh! No, no, no, weight loss is not at *all* our focus. We are all about *holistic wellness*," she says in an ultra-sincere tone. "Our whole philosophy is that health starts here." She gives her forehead two quick pats, then her chest. "So if you want your body to be at its peak wellness, it really has to start deeper within."

"I'm loving this," says Kyle. "You're speaking my language."

Oh, puke me a river, Kyle, I'd like to say. Instead, I check "no" for snails with a vicious X.

"This"—Serena pinches the almost non-existent flesh at her side—"is just a reflection of what's within."

All of a sudden, I notice a young teenage girl standing next to Serena. She's dressed in a long-sleeve tie-dye T-shirt over leggings. Her eyes are wide; clearly, she's taking in every detail of Serena and Kyle's interaction. Her hair is pulled into twin French braids, and her round body doesn't seem to have hit its growth spurt yet. A tall, slim woman who I assume to be her mother taps her on the arm. "Isn't that your bag, honey? Chop chop! Let's go! We have a shuttle to catch!"

Kyle and Serena, oblivious to their young spectator, keep flirting like their lives depend on it.

"So what you're saying is, I'm the whole package?" Kyle teases Serena, rocking back on his heels to give her the full view of his muscular form.

She giggles and fans her face flirtatiously. "Oh my *God*, Kyle. *Stop.*"

They laugh together for a minute, then Kyle pulls out his phone. "Are you on LinkedIn?"

Serena pulls out hers. "Yeah, but I'm way more active on TikTok— let me give you my personal handle, and the resort handle—and are you on Insta? I'm going to be posting so much amazing content—"

I block out their conversation and sign the bottom of my customs form.

Nothing to declare.

Soon I'm exiting the airport and boarding one of the shiny new Riovan-branded shuttle buses that will take me to the south side of the island, where the resort lies sprawled on an outcrop of rock guarding its private beaches below, like a sleeping dragon.

You can say a lot about the Riovan, but you can't fault it for its looks. Even though it will be a good thirty minutes of bumpy roads before the resort comes into view, I can see it in my mind's eye. It's imprinted there from the first time I saw it five years ago, the same way a flash of searing light imprints itself on the back of your eyelids. A white building on white rocks, overlooking a flawless crescent of crystalline sand and turquoise water that starts shallow, but thirty feet in drops off, the color changing to a deep and dangerous blue-green.

The resort is shaped like a tiara. In the center, facing the water, are the public areas, stacked in a tall building: dining hall, two restaurants, bar, gym, yoga studio, spa. Spreading out like curving wings to either side, to maximize the view of the water, are the guest accommodation and staff rooms. Enclosed in the tiara are two pools, tennis courts, a Zen garden with a water feature, and a cluster of gas fire pits for evening lounging. The first time I saw the Zen garden, I burst out laughing. I'm not sure why. I suppose luxury at that level struck some chord of silliness at the time. Let's just say I wasn't laughing by the time I left.

I find a seat in the back row of the shuttle and rest my head against the top of the bench seat as my stomach protests all of my life choices. Mainly the vodka. In my mind's eye, I see the Riovan like a fortress on the cliffs, waiting for me like it does every year, silent and watchful. Does it know why I come? If it did, would it snap its jaws shut as I crossed the threshold?

I stir in my seat. *Silly.* The Riovan isn't a being. I jiggle my leg as passengers continue to trickle in. Soon we're full up. The mom and her teenage daughter are the last to board. They press into the row right in front of me, the daughter closest to the aisle, and barely have a chance to sit before the bus lurches down the road that will take us to the southeast corner of the island.

"I told you to wear something different. It's hotter down here," I hear the uptight mother say in a low voice.

"I don't like to show my arms," says the teen.

"I don't want to hear it, Skylar," the mom hisses, before reaching into her purse for her earbuds. "I've told you and told you. The solution isn't to cover them up, it's to *firm* them up."

The girl, Skylar, silently turns her head away from her mother and leans into the aisle, giving me a full view of her profile. I'd put her around fourteen. The same age I was when I started dressing in oversized everything.

I watch her for a few seconds. Lean forward.

"Hey."

She twists back.

"I like your shirt," I whisper with a conspiratorial smile. "Great choice."

"Oh, thanks." She seems embarrassed, but pleased. "I made it.

With a tie-dye kit? I got for my birthday? It has, like, um…all my favorite colors in it…" She plucks her shirt out from her body.

I smile. "I like the purple and the blue. They're kind of blending together. In a ring."

"That's my favorite part too! Hey…" Skylar scrunches her nose. "How much would you pay for a shirt like this?"

"Are you selling them?"

"They're really fun to make. And I could customize them with people's favorite colors…"

"Love it. I'd totally buy one."

"Sweetie?" says her mother, one earbud plucked out and pinched between her fingers. "Look forward or you'll get motion sick." She gives me a suspicious frown.

With a guilty little "sorry," Skylar turns forward again.

"I was just admiring your daughter's T-shirt," I say with a friendly smile, even though I'd love nothing more than to give the woman two firm slaps across the face. *You have a great daughter. Don't you dare fuck her up.* "She's quite the artist."

The mom doesn't deign to respond with anything but a thin-lipped smile.

As the shuttle bus bumps over the rough island roads, and the first-timers seated around me ooh and aah as the ocean sends teasing little sparks through the thick vegetation, I close my eyes again and let myself drift.

I don't want to be here. It would be more comfortable to stay in my Cincinnati life, to disappear into the routine of work, the distraction of my friends and their small dramas, the slow, sleepy rhythm of Sundays spent reading the next book on my list of *100 Classics to Read Before You Die* (*Crime and Punishment* is number 48).

But I have to be here.

Call it duty? Compulsion? Vocation? Passion? Maybe. So many labels I could put on it to try and manipulate how others would see it, how *I* see it…but labels are cheap. Reductive. As my mother's daughter, I should know.

The existentialists had it right. (*The Ethics of Ambiguity* is number 25.) We are fundamentally free, which is actually terrifying. We are responsible for our choices. Every. Single. One.

Maybe this is the most profound difference between me and my friends. They don't realize how much power they actually have to quit their sucky jobs, or stop answering work emails after hours, or drink less, like they keep saying they mean to. Whereas I realized the power of choice early on.

Never let anyone treat you that way, Lily.

Whoops—here I am, in my head again.

I choose to doze. A strange half-dream wafts through my consciousness, slowly gaining solidity. The immigration man is my therapist, and as I sit strapped into the chair with motivational quotes blinking *Wellness Starts Here*, Mom is chanting over a loudspeaker, *Don't be mediocre, honey*, which is clearly driving the immigration man crazy because he's screaming, "Purpose of your visit?" over and over, until I do the absolute worst thing I could ever do in this situation.

Admit the truth.

CHAPTER 3

"I'M SORRY, I CAN'T SEEM TO FIND YOUR NAME..."

"Lennox. Lily Lennox." I'm trying to keep my cool, and it's normally not quite this labor-intensive, but today has already been a lot—and it's only ten o'clock. I'm sweaty, tired from my red-eye and the bumpy half-hour ride across the island, and all I want to do is crash in my room for the rest of the day. It was definitely a mistake to let myself doze on the shuttle bus—napping always makes me foggy, and it can be hard to shake. Which just goes to show that choices matter. Thank you Mr. Sartre, et al.

"Is Vic here?" I say. "Vic knows me." Vic is the Executive Manager of the Riovan and has been for as long as I've been working here. It's not like Vic and I are best buds or anything, but after four years reporting to the guy, I can say I know him pretty well. I know his office pretty well too, since I break in every year. He uses a really nice air freshener.

"You're not here... I don't *see* you here..." The blond guy behind the desk in the small Staffing Resources office is young—twenty-two?

He exudes a particular brand of lethargic irritation that says, *I'm not sure if I care enough to solve this problem for you.* He's called Nick, according to his name tag. Even though I assume his job keeps him in this little office most of the day, he looks like he could be a fitness instructor himself; all the staff do. Including me, I'm aware. I know that's why they keep hiring me...though at twenty-nine, I'm at the older end of the spectrum, and trust me, I'm counting the time until I'm told, *Thank you for your application, however, we've already filled the position.* But for this year, I'm still young enough, still on-brand enough.

I wait as Nick types. There's...a lot of typing. I shift my weight and look around the small office. The only change from last year is a big framed poster that I recognize from the Riovan's recent ad campaign. A woman in a yellow bikini is doing yoga on diamond-white sands, her hair blowing sideways, the ocean a luminescent smear of green behind her. Bold white letters proclaim, *Your Best Self Starts at the Riovan.*

I have to work to keep my face neutral, since I don't think the puking face I actually want to make is appropriate.

Still typing. Is he writing a novel?

"Lennox," I say. "That's L-E—"

"Found you." He smiles. "Looks like you'll be in the poolside block—I mean, Vista West. Welcome back, and let me get your key activated." He pulls a plastic key card out of a small drawer.

Um, no.

I coax a smile on to my face. "Listen...Nick? There must be some mistake. I've worked here for...a lot of years. And I always have an oceanside room."

"Sorry, this year you'll be in Vista West," he over-enunciates, like I'm either hard of hearing or an idiot.

Keep smiling. I have a good smile. I've done a lot with this smile.

"I get that this is probably an annoying request. But I've always, *always* had an oceanside room. I know it might take a minute to switch me, but I don't mind waiting."

Nick's face is frozen in a smile drawn so tight, it might start twitching any second.

"Miss Lennox," he says. "Lily. You come here every summer. I get that. That's so great. Retention! Yay. But. This year, we remodeled the East Suites. For guests. They face the ocean and the sunrise, as you are obviously aware." He extends the key card. "B-T-W, there's a fifty-dollar replacement charge for lost keys."

"There sure is," I say without taking the key, still smiling even though my pulse feels loud and erratic in my head. This is not how things are supposed to go. I snap my hair tie. I should let it go. I just got here; I can't die on this hill.

Just take the card, I tell my stubborn hand, which appears to have clenched itself into a fist at my side—

"If it isn't Lily Lennox, our most faithful employee! You deserve an award, girl. So good to have you back!" A short man with gelled hair and a face like an ultra-bronzed Roman emperor is leaning into the office with a tablet in hand.

"Vic!" Thank God. "Listen, I'm sorry to be a pain, but there's a situation with the rooms—"

"I know." He hisses out a frustrated breath through his teeth. "Your roommate hasn't shown up yet! It turns out she went and missed her flight, can you believe it? So, good news, it'll be just you for tonight in the room; bad news, we're going to need you to step in and cover for her." He tilts his head and purses his lips. "I hate to do this, but can you be on the beach at two o'clock? Is that going to be OK?"

No, it's not OK. I'm supposed to be in my usual room, facing the ocean, with twenty-four hours to unwind and acclimatize and deal with all the feelings I know are coming, because I do this every year, and I know the process, *my* process—

"Two?" I repeat with a bit of an incredulous laugh. "I don't even have my gear yet—"

"You can pick that up right away from Supplies. There's a new swimsuit this year, and some really cute branded sweats." Vic's words spatter me like hot oil. I snap the elastic, snap it, snap it harder. "It's all branding all the time this year, we'll go over it later in our staff training—"

"Vic," I cut in—too forcefully, I realize, but I smear on a smile like a hasty layer of icing dragged over a botched cake and forge ahead. "You know I *always* stay in the East Suites—"

"Oh, yes, right, but not this year. We flip-flopped staff to the back—complete redo. We updated the rooms—the guests get the sunrise—and of course we needed new plumbing because of—" He flushes like he said something he didn't mean to. Like a slap, it hits me what he's talking about. What happened last year.

"Because that's the hotel biz, we gotta keep things fresh," Vic finishes in a kind of cheerful panic. His phone rings and he holds up a silencing finger at me. "Yes, hello? Mr. Thorpe, what a pleasure. Yes, the inspector approved everything—" He makes an apology face at me before walking briskly away. I can hear his voice retreating down the hall. "Yes, by the end of the summer it will all be PVCs, as we discussed…"

"What's up with the plumbing?" I ask Nick, gesturing to where Vic just disappeared, trying not to panic over the fact that what happened last year is still something Vic is dealing with. *I fucked it up*, I tell myself. But no, if I had truly fucked it up, I wouldn't be here, right? "New pipes?"

Nick gives me an annoyed shruggy headshake, like he's saying, *How should I know, and why exactly do we care?*

Which reminds me, I shouldn't make a bigger deal of this than it is. So they're still replacing the older hotel plumbing? Fine. That doesn't mean they're still investigating the accident. I remind myself that it's hard to get contractors out here on the island—I've heard Vic complain about it a million times. Also, it's not like they can shut down the entire Riovan to replace all the old metal drainpipes at once. They'd have to do it slowly, so as not to lose revenue.

"Your key," Nick says, and maybe there's not smug satisfaction in his tone, but you know what, I choose to read that into it anyway, because I just need to hate someone a little bit right now.

The key is smooth and cool in my hand. Sweat trickles down my chest. Lily zero, Riovan one.

"What's the number?"

"Room 2-2-0-8," says Nick. "See you at staff training tonight."

CHAPTER 4

THERE ARE LOTS OF WAYS TO GET AROUND THE RIOVAN, AND I'VE learned them all.

With my key in the back pocket of my jeans and the bag of branded gear I just collected from Supplies pressed against my chest, I pick my way over sandy paver stones and grasses, a back way I discovered a few years ago that winds upward through the rocks, eventually looping back down to the West Suites. A rougher path, certainly not roller-bag friendly, definitely less efficient. But more private, and I'm in no mood to run into anyone…especially my past self.

Memories are a funny thing, aren't they? They can be delicate as ghosts one minute, and wallop you like an old-fashioned backhand the next.

I speak from experience about the backhand. And no, my mom didn't hit me, so you can dismiss that lovely trailer-park stereotype. It was one of her boyfriends. I was eleven. "Don't give me lip, girl." What had I said? I wish I could remember. Anyway, it only happened once, but it's not something you ever forget. Mom ended things with him immediately. *Never let anyone treat you that way, Lily*, she said, her mouth aflame with her favorite red Revlon lipstick, her eyes blazing like justice. Even though she was a petite woman, she looked about a mile tall that afternoon.

The sun is beating down, punishingly bright, the heat cut occasionally with a cool breeze off the water, which gleams down below, peppered with swimmers. I'm huffing and puffing. The incline is steeper than I remember, and I have to lift my bag awkwardly between the stones.

Further up the hillside, scattered like white petals along the cliff, are the Riovan's most expensive—and exclusive—accommodation options: the Villas, single occupancy buildings that offer privacy, luxury and a killer view. The type of guests who can afford them mostly keep to themselves. I heard that one time Celine Dion stayed there.

When I finally reach the Vista West wing, with its more modest poolside rooms that used to be the cheaper option for guests, my shirt is stuck to my back with sweat. I swipe my card to gain access to the building. Immediately, frigid air conditioning spills over me.

Inside the elevator, low thumping mood music is playing, and I lift the moist tendrils of hair off my neck. I have no interest in looking at my disheveled self in the mirrored wall, so I lean my head forward and close my eyes for the few moments it takes to rise from the ground floor to the second.

The doors slide open. I orient myself in front of the signage before taking a left. The hallway feels dystopian in its length, door after identical door. Has it always been this long? The wheels of my bag are nearly silent on the carpet. There—2208. I pull out my key card and try to feed it into the slot, but it won't go in.

Did Nick give me a bum key, just to screw with me?

Nope, it's my hand, shaking so hard, the white card is fuzzy at the edges. I need to relax. Unfortunately, there are no manspreaders offering me free alcohol. *Where's a Kyle when you need one?*

"Come on," I coach myself under my breath. There's a loud click, but it's not from my door. It's someone coming out of the room next to mine.

"Hey, are you one of the new lifeguards?" It's a girl with bleached blond hair shaved on one side, long on the other. She's in the lifeguard's red swimsuit, a sweatshirt and a towel hanging over her arm. I can't help but notice that the resort-issued bathing suit this year is cut higher than ever before, displaying not only most of her ass, but her impressive leg tattoo that goes from ankle to left butt cheek.

"Yeah, hi. I'm Lily," I say. Since I'm trying to overcompensate for feeling unstable, my voice comes out sounding a bit too mechanical, so I tack on a laugh. *Great.* Now I sound like a robot ditz.

"Hannah," she says, moving her towel from her arm to her shoulder and cocking a slim hip. "Where're you from?"

"Cincinnati."

"Oh, cool, another Midwest girl. I'm from Chicago."

"Nice to meet you." I pause. "Have you worked here before?" I already know she hasn't, but it's as good a conversation starter as any.

"No, first time." She angles her head. "Are you…OK? You look a little—"

"Oh! Yeah. Fine. I'm just rattled from…" *No! Stop!* "The key card. They're…a little different from last year. I can't seem to get the door open!" And then I tack on another laugh, because at this point, why not.

"Here, let me," she says, and of course, the door opens right away for her. She gives me a sympathetic little grin. "So I guess you've worked here before?"

"Fifth year." I wedge my foot in the door to keep it open.

"Wow! That's commitment."

"You have no idea."

She smiles uncertainly. Am I coming across too intense?

"So…have you met your roommate?" I say quickly. Her expression lightens.

"Yeah, we both got here beginning of June. Her name is Bridget, from the UK. She's on a gap year. She's been working her way through the Caribbean getting jobs at all the best resorts, isn't that awesome? Have you met your roomie?"

"No, she missed her flight. I'm covering for her on the beach in about an hour and a half."

"Well, if you're interested, a bunch of us are pooling our money to charter a boat Friday night to Saint Vitalis—"

That's the next island over. The Las Vegas of the Sea, according to the advertisements. My memories of it from last year are quite vivid—the liquid cling of the little dress Carli Elle lent me, the booming music as the boat skimmed over the water, the way her gold cowboy hat was tipped over her face. She was at the Riovan for the four-week intensive, and though I normally would never think to befriend a guest—especially not a famous pop star who undoubtedly valued her privacy—we'd discovered an unlikely bond in Calumet Heights, where she lived with an aunt for a year after her mom OD'd. *Of all the trailer parks in all the world*, she laughed. The rest is history.

That night, her manager had scheduled her to do a "surprise" performance at the Mambotel. A few key TikTokers had been alerted in advance, and she was hoping to go viral. When Carli asked me to come along, it was a no-brainer to say yes.

The morning after, there was an emergency staff meeting. My head was pounding; I'd only slept for a couple of hours, and I was regretting the second Long Island Iced Tea I'd guzzled on the way back.

Vic was pale, serious. "There was an accident in one of the rooms last night. Rest assured that it's being investigated. Do not talk to the press. Do not talk about it with guests. If anyone asks questions, say, "no comment" or send them to me. Understood?"

For a few days, confusion reigned. The Head of Maintenance was fired. Audrey, the VP of Branding, either quit or was fired. The elusive Mr. Thorpe, owner of the conglomerate the Riovan is part of, made an appearance and talked to the staff about discretion and trust. I'm assuming island officials were bought off and the appropriate palms greased, because within two days, all signs of the accident had disappeared and the investigation was closed.

By the time the story hit the press, it had been sanitized, as is so often the case for celebrity deaths. *Michael Johnson, 54, Manager of Grammy Award-Winning Artist Carli Elle, Found Dead in Hotel Room.* If you didn't know better, you'd assume it was drugs or suicide. A tabloid "exposé" ran a few days later. *An anonymous source says that Johnson, known in the business as "Mr. Mic," scheduled Carli Elle to perform, but declined to accompany his client, in favor of a "quiet night to myself." The source revealed that Johnson had been in a depressive downswing...* They ran some pictures of Carli on *American Idol* where she got her start, she and Michael holding their first Grammy together, and Carli on the yacht on her way to the Mambotel. As luck would have it, I'm in that last picture, kind of behind Carli, laughing. Not ideal, I know. At least my image is blurry and dark enough that only one reporter ever found me. I blocked the guy's number, flagged his emails as spam, and told myself that it was over.

"I know all about Saint Vitalis," I say, unwittingly massaging my temple with two fingers.

"Oh, right!" Hannah laughs. "This is all old hat to you, isn't it? Well. The Mambotel is throwing this massive party. There's a rumor that Adam Levine is supposed to do a surprise show."

"Carli Elle performed there last year," I blurt out without meaning to.

"What? I love her! Did you get to see her?"

"Yeah." *Shut up, Lily!* I chastise myself. *Stop bringing up the very thing you want everyone to forget!* "She was staying at the Riovan."

"Oh my God! Is she as down to earth as she seems?"

"I'd say so."

"Did you ever talk to her? I'd be so tempted to ask for an autograph…"

"No," I lie, though something perverse in me wants to say, *Yeah, and you"ll never believe what she confided in me.* This is not where I make the classic mistake of giving people hints about what I've done because I need everyone to know how clever I am. This is where I shut the hell up.

Hannah pouts. "Boo. This year all we have is that guy from Harvest Moon. Watch out. He's handsy." Ugh. "But you should totally come Friday!"

"Thanks. I'll think about it."

"For sure. Just keep it on the DL… Heading off to party island isn't exactly *on-brand*." Hannah smirks. "But we should be allowed to blow off steam on our day off, right?"

"Totally."

"I'd better get going." Hannah checks her bulky, waterproof watch. "Nice meeting you!"

"Yeah, nice meeting you, too, Hannah," I say as she saunters off down the hall.

OK, OK. Time to go into this fucking room.

"It's not going to be the same as five years ago," I whisper to myself as I nudge the door open. Staff accommodation has always been more bare bones anyway, with plank floors, smaller beds, and furniture pieces displaying their long suffering in dings and loose drawer pulls.

Then I step inside, on to the thick carpeting. The familiar smell washes through my senses: coconut and lemongrass, the resort's trademark scent. A total upgrade from the old staff quarters.

The room is pleasantly shaded, with a gentle light filtering in through the white gauze curtains that are drawn over south-facing sliding glass doors. Two single beds are made up in white sheets and comforters. A small balcony overlooks the pool, and the hum of the AC makes a soothing background of white noise, rippling the edge of one of the curtains.

Well, fuck.

It's exactly the same as five years ago.

The only difference is that instead of two beds, there used to be one.

My knees turn to liquid. I lower myself to the floor, hand on the bed, clutching a wad of the comforter as I go down. My roller bag tips over. I tip over too, forehead to the floor, comforter now pulled sideways off the bed as all the parts of me I've held tightly together during this trip unravel on the plush carpeting of room 2208.

Can you believe we get to stay here for a whole week? Jessica, bouncing on the mattress five years ago, her face lit up with joy.

"Unreal." Me, joining her, but cautiously, perching on the side of the bed.

"Come on! Get in here!" She tackled me from behind, pulling me back on to the soft cloud of the white blanket, wrapping her arms around me and nuzzling my neck. "What's wrong?"

"Nothing," I said. "It's just so...fancy."

"Well, you deserve it," she said, which I supposed was sweet, though perhaps not accurate. As far as I'd seen in my twenty-four years of living, riches and merit had nothing to do with each other.

"I was just lucky."

"Relax," she cajoled as we fell naturally into a spooning position. "We're going to have an amazing week. I still can't believe you won this for us. Thank you."

"I didn't do anything."

"You were caller number one hundred!"

"Yes, I was." I twisted my head and gave her a peck. "I love you."

She nudged my nose with hers. "OK, OK, there's so much to do, we can't just lie around here. There's a seminar on the mind–body connection that I'm totally interested in. I want to meet my personal trainer ASAP, maybe they can give me tips on how to deal with this." She smacked her butt. "Oh, and did you see we each get a consultation with a nutritionist?"

"You're a *chef*," I said. "You know plenty about nutrition."

"Yeah, yeah, but maybe she can help me lose those pesky twenty..."

"Hey, I happen to like the sexy twenty," I pouted, turning around in the bed, surrounding her with my arms and making a teasing grab for her ass, all the while being careful not to press against her too hard in case she felt the little box tucked into my sweatshirt pocket. I hadn't wanted to entrust it to our luggage; it felt safest with me.

A diamond. I'd cleaned out my savings and bought it the week before, an extravagance to fit the extravagance that was Jess in my life. The white rocks overlooking the beach would be the perfect place to propose. I already had a speech written out and mostly memorized. *When you walked into that bar four years ago with your fake ID and*

your knockoff Gucci and ordered a Cosmopolitan, I knew that you
and I would never in a million years be friends…

I keep my forehead pressed to the carpet as sobs ride my body.
I don't often cry; it's not my thing. But didn't I know this would
happen, the second Nick told me I was poolside? Everything in here—
the sights, the smells, the textures—is screaming, *Jessica.*

I pull the comforter the rest of the way down off the bed and wrap
it around my body as I roll on to my side. I keep my eyes squeezed
shut, because if I open them, I'll see one thing and one thing only.

That Jess isn't here.

CHAPTER 5

SEAGULLS CRY OVERHEAD, AND A GENTLE SALT BREEZE TEASES MY hair as I slide on my sunglasses and step on to hot sand, flotation device tucked under my arm, whistle around my neck, dressed in the high-cut red bathing suit. My skin is tacky with suntan lotion and the ocean waves are languid, relaxed. It's a relief to be out of the hotel room and the pool of grief I sank into there. Being on the clock is just what I need to get my head in the game, so covering for my absentee roommate is probably a blessing in disguise. It's going to force me to pull it together and stay sharp, which is extra important today of all days, especially considering what's on the docket for tonight: breaking into Vic's office.

The beach is pretty crowded, and a string of yachts bob out beyond the swimming line, wafting party music. It's mostly resort guests on the beach—you can identify them by their resort-branded white towels—but not exclusively. The resort also sells day passes to people who want to enjoy the beach or the spa. The day-trippers come over on the morning ferry from Saint Vitalis, usually rich party girls looking to detox after a rough weekend at the Mambotel, which you can see at night from the Riovan beaches, a blinking dot in the black ocean.

The scorch of sand on the soles of my feet tempts me to sprint toward cooler sand, but I force myself to keep my pace slow, steady. It hurts now, but in a few days, I'll have my beach feet back. No pain no gain, right?

I pass a long row of lounge chairs filled with women in bright scraps of designer swimwear, out for their afternoon tanning session. Two of them are chatting in low voices.

"...and then suddenly after the last round of quads, I'm puking my guts out on the gym floor."

"Hey, if it works..."

"Yeah, well, I prefer to do that alone in the bathroom, not in front of a celebrity trainer—"

They stop talking to look at my ass. They're not the only ones. I grimace. It'll take a few days to get used to that again too.

Snatches of conversation float past me as I plow across the sand toward the lifeguard chair where I'll be spending the next three hours.

...fine, but I'm telling you, intermittent fasting didn't really work for me...

...who cares if he's crying now? It's called a revenge body for a reason!...

...yeah, she thinks I'm at a work conference in Tampa...

...wait, pounds or kilos?...

Yep. Definitely at the Riovan again.

Part of me wants to look; to link the voices with the faces like a game of matching and start making my longlist. But I force myself to keep walking. Better to wait until after the break-in. It's more efficient that way—and I have an entire week to identify the person

I'm here to find. Normally this first day is all about recovering from travel, anyway.

"Halle-fuckin'-lujah," says the male lifeguard I'm replacing when he spots me. He looks college age, with reddish hair, lean musculature like a dancer's, and freckled shoulders. He immediately starts to climb down. "I was burning to death up there."

There's a small umbrella angled above the high, white lifeguard's chair, but I know from experience that even in the shade it can be brutal up there, especially in the afternoon as the temperatures climb.

"I'm Jason, by the way," he says, swinging forward a hand. "Don't think I've met you."

"Lily. British?" I take his hand, and we have a friendly shake.

"Yep. London. American, I take it?"

"Cincinnati."

He gives me a vaguely confused look, which I'm used to.

"Skyline Chili? Cincinnati Reds?"

"Sorry…"

"Don't worry."

"Ah. Well. See you around then." He starts to go, then turns back. "Hey, a bunch of us are going over to the Mambotel Friday night."

"Already heard."

"Should be a fun night." He points both fingers like little guns. "You're coming, yeah?"

"We'll see, Jason." It's my polite version of no. I have no desire to get drunk with a bunch of college kids. Though I wish them all the best.

He signs out of the clipboard affixed to the chair, then lopes off in the sand. After signing myself in with the barely functioning ballpoint pen, I climb up. The seat is warm, and not that comfortable, which is probably good, because lifeguarding is all about keeping

alert. When you're comfy, it's so easy for your attention to slip...
especially after my breakdown in the room, which eroded the little
energy I had going into today. Still, for the next three hours, I have
to stay sharp.

I re-angle the umbrella, then set the timer on my resort-issued
waterproof watch. Fifteen minutes up here, then I walk the shore,
then back up. At the hour and a half mark, I'll switch places with the
lifeguard on the other end of the beach.

I start my methodical visual sweep of the beach. First, the swimmers who are out the furthest, most of them churning out furious
laps. I count the bobbing heads; fifteen. A few swimmers are cooling
off in the shallower water, and a few more are standing ankle deep,
conversing with one another.

All adults. No little kids here. This isn't exactly the kind of resort
you bring your family to. In fact, Skylar, the teen in tie-dye, is probably the youngest person I've ever seen at the Riovan.

Ugh. The memory of her mother and the way she talked down
to her...it makes my blood boil. I've dealt with her kind before. If I
had a little girl, I would make sure she knew she was beautiful to me.
Period. And if anyone ever made her feel less than—well, I would
know just what to do, wouldn't I?

Never let anyone treat you like that again, Lily.

I shake my head quickly, because being filled with rage, no
matter how justified—and I don't think I'm crazy to say that some
of it is justified—isn't exactly a good state of mind for lifeguarding.
I take a few deep breaths and sweep my eyes over the water again,
feeling its cooling effect almost as if I were physically skimming it
with a palm.

The world is full of injustices, like that mother chipping away at
her daughter. Like Kyle, thinking he had some kind of a right to me.

Like the residents of Calumet Heights, who only called Mom a slut because they were jealous of how goddamn gorgeous she was.

You can't miss it, the injustices happening all around all the time, from bad parenting to misogynistic assholery all the way up the ladder to racism, war, genocide. The way I see it, there are two types of people: those who turn a blind eye to injustice, and those who can't ignore it. The passive observers and those who refuse to be complicit.

And, yeah, I'm the second type.

I adjust my sunglasses and start to sweep the water line again, in the opposite direction. *Swimmer one, check. Swimmer two, check.*

All these people are here for different reasons. I know that. To unwind, to soak up the sunshine, to get that killer beach body—but they all want to be here, at some level. What would it be like to come here because I actually wanted to? With Jess. We'd be celebrating an anniversary, for example. Getting away from the kids—we'd have one by now at least, maybe two. We'd be saying things like, *Oh God, I can finally hear myself think!* and *You think the kids are OK? Is it too soon to text your mom?* (In this world, my mom is still alive, though she sometimes says, *But I'm too young to be a grandmother!* and we all laugh.) Jess and I would lounge on the beach and enjoy the spa, and the scent of lemongrass and coconut would bring back visceral memories of hot sex on the delicious Riovan mattress.

But that's not what I got.

Flecks of brightness burst from the water as it moves, and even with the protection of my sunglasses, I have to squint as I scan. Just a couple more minutes and I'll climb down for my walk along the shore, flotation device under my arm, ready to save whoever might need saving.

It's tedious work, lifeguarding. You have to hone your attention like a knife even as summer heat radiates up, tempting you, always tempting you, *Relax, just for a minute. Let your eyes slip closed...*

My watch beeps. Somehow these fifteen minutes have felt like five times that. Time moves differently when you're waiting for something to happen.

I climb down the chair and make for the cool, firm sand at the shoreline, my eyes tracking over the swimmers, relishing the feeling of movement in my limbs. I count them again, one to fifteen, then again backward.

Did you know that drowning happens quietly? People think that a drowning person will be easy to pick out. Shouting, thrashing, making a scene. But in real life, they're docile. Mute. There one minute, then they quietly slip under. It doesn't even look like they're struggling, until suddenly, they're gone.

Jess went down quietly too. So gently and so quietly that by the time I woke up to what was happening, it was too late.

CHAPTER 6

I SLIP INSIDE VIC'S OFFICE, THEN CLOSE THE DOOR QUIETLY BEHIND ME and turn the lock.

Staff training just ended—a smaller affair for those of us arriving mid-season to support the busy month of July. The focus on branding this year was more heavy-handed than ever, and I had to tune out Serena Victoria's closing speech in which she used the acronym T-H-I-N to remind us of the hotel's values: Thriving, Healthy, Inspirational, Natural. A strange tactic for all her purported "taking the focus off weight loss." After training ended, it wasn't hard to peel away from the group of about a dozen to "hit the bathroom" and let myself into the corridor of offices behind reception. I copied Vic's key five years ago, and thankfully he has yet to change the lock.

His office is dark, the air freshener lovely as ever. I make for the desk, which is a bit of a mess, with his tablet sitting on top of some brochures and what look like loose receipts. At a jiggle of the mouse, his computer monitor leaps to life, shedding enough light for me to see the Post-it note on which his password is scrawled—the same one as previous years but with more exclamation points at the end. Got to love that Vic.

Hunched over the computer, I double-click the folder on the desktop labeled "4-Week Intensive Guest List" and quickly find this year's file.

The file has the guests' basic information—name, gender identity, height, weight, address, employer, emergency contacts. Photocopies of their IDs, signed waiver forms, private health information—not to mention Vic's personal research notes on each, which over the years has proved to be a treasure trove. As Executive Manager, Vic is personally responsible for the satisfaction of each and every guest, but the happiness of the four-week intensive group is his absolute top priority. It should be, since they're paying what for some is a year's salary to be brutalized by trainers and dietitians in the name of wellness.

I hit print.

The printer, a behemoth that sits against the wall, wakes up noisily, sending a rush of adrenaline through me. We have quiet cars now; why can't they design silent printers?

For a few seconds, I'm certain someone will hear the noise, the door will fly open, and I'll be discovered—but as the first sheets of paper start spitting out into the tray, I remind myself that office hours are long gone.

By the printer, I look over the first sheet in the dim light from the monitor, already absorbing information on Melanie Ahrens, 42, who just had gastro surgery...

While the printer keeps churning, I pull out my phone, more from habit than anything else. To my annoyance, there's a WhatsApp notification—a message from Becca, my office manager at Taste of Heaven back in Cincinnati. To my further annoyance, it's a voice message. I told my staff not to bother me unless it's an emergency, and Lisa, my General Manager, assured me everyone understood… Ugh. It's too hard to mentally go back and forth when I'm Riovan Lily. I lower the volume on my phone and press it to my ear to listen. Becca's voice comes through, clear and peppy as always.

"Hey boss, some guy called for you. I know we're not supposed to bug you while you're gone, but it was just, um…kind of weird. He said he had this catering order for a corporate event, but he was only willing to speak with you about it. I said you were out of the office for a while, just like you told me to say, but I could connect him with Lisa. And then he was like, 'Oh, right, Lily's at the Riovan, isn't she?' I was like, 'Excuse me, who are you again?' He said you shared a mutual friend. Michael…" There's a rustling sound. "Jones? Or Johnson? Anyway, I told you weren't available but if I could just take down his name and number, we'd be happy to take care of his catering needs. He just kind of laughed and said, 'That won't be necessary,' and hung up. Anyway, it was such a weird call, I felt like you should know. Oh! And I got his number from caller ID in case you wanted to get in touch with him. It's two-one-two…" I stop the recording, a cold sweat already forming in my armpits.

Forget about aging out of my Riovan job. I'm getting sloppy. Johnson was supposed to be old news, but the second I get here, Vic is still working on the pipes, and now there's this reporter—because that is absolutely what this mysterious Mr. Caller Guy is—claiming some mutual friend crap.

I walk over to the filing cabinet and start opening drawers. What am I looking for? Pipes. Electrocution. Johnson. Carli… *There.* A folder marked East Suite 6605. Michael's room number. I splay the folder out on Vic's desk and start rifling. A bunch of official-looking documents in French… Invoices for what looks like the transportation of Michael's body back to the US, courtesy of the Riovan... Copies of various articles about the death...

"I guess my career is in trouble," Carli said. Last year, poolside, after midnight, following a few drinks, when all confessions are made. The pool was glowing, the moon winking down on us.

After discovering our Calumet Heights connection, I think she felt like she could tell me anything. Nothing like shared trauma to elicit trust.

"What? You've won a Grammy. You've made it."

"Noooo... Michael says I can't book more shows unless I drop two sizes. He's got these pills he wants me to get on... No, don't be like that. All the girls do it...but still, I'm trying my own way first. That's why we're here. I can lose the pounds naturally, and...I lost a friend to pills. So."

"Carli, he is *way* out of line. You should fire him."

"That's not how things work." The tips of her long hair were dyed pink, fluttering over her shoulders like fairy wings as she swished her feet in the pale gleam of the water.

"So, I'm not famous," I said. "But I do run a business back in Cincinnati. And when you get that toxic employee, you have to cut them out."

Her brow furrowed. "I'm telling you, it's not like that in the music biz. Anyway, he knows too much of my shit—enough to ruin my career if I pissed him off. For me to get rid of Michael? He'd literally have to drop dead." She tossed me a glance and suppressed a laugh.

"That bad, huh?" I said, grinning back like I was amused too.

Voices. Shit! Outside the door. The printer is still chugging out pages. I grab the stack that's already printed and dive behind the desk. The pages are warm against my chest.

The door clicks open just as the printer spits out the final page.

At the last minute, I remember the folder I pulled from the cabinet, just lying there on the desk.

They're going to discover me. I will be totally calm. *Hey, Vic, I was just grabbing some info on the guests so I can better serve them…* Oh my fucking fuck, *no* one is going to buy that load of bull—

"Yeah, it's here on my desk…" It's Vic's voice. Someone else is standing in the door. Who? Doesn't matter. All that matters is that they don't find me. I can see the top of the desk from my hiding spot, and I watch him grab his tablet. Somehow, he doesn't notice the folder. "OK, Serena, you were right, I didn't have it with me in training. Dear Lord, getting old is *not* for the faint of heart. Just keep that in mind, sweetie."

"You're not old," comes a cloying voice—Serena's. "But seriously, Vic, if you want me to recommend a cleanse, there's this one that totally targets mental alertness—"

"I have a love-hate with cleanses," says Vic, already back at the door, leaving.

"Speaking of which, have you had a chance to look over the proposal I sent, for the brand partnership with CleanSlim? I just think it's going to be *huge*, our guests are going to *adore* this stuff, and I don't want to keep their CEO waiting."

"I gave it a glance—"

The printer makes a wheezing noise; Vic stops in his tracks at the doorway. Turns.

"What the—?" He crosses the office and plucks up the final page of my printout. "Huh."

My heart slams and slams against my chest. If he turns to the left from where he's standing, he'll see me.

He turns the page over, examines it. "I swear, my printer is possessed." Then, with an "oh well" flourish, he tears it into thin ribbons and drops the shreds into the trash.

"Do you have a second, actually?" says Serena. "If we can go over that proposal together, I can answer any of your concerns—"

"Serena, it's ten o'clock at night!"

She laughs. "I'm a night owl."

"You just want that bonus for bringing on new co-branding," teases Vic. "Not that I blame you..."

The door clicks shut behind them, and Vic turns the deadbolt.

I let my head sink down, feeling the tension burn in my neck.

That was close. Too close. I *am* getting careless. I snap the elastic hairband against my wrist. Then I uncramp my body from its crouched position and retrieve the final shredded page from the trash bin, jamming the slivers into my pocket to be pieced together later. Finally, I return Michael's folder to the drawer.

All these close calls, and it's just my first day here. Surely this doesn't bode well...

But I don't believe in omens.

Vic coming in here was just one minute of bad luck. And actually, flip that around and it was good luck, wasn't it? After all, he didn't see me, and that's what matters. As for the Michael Johnson stuff that Becca called about...some sleazy reporter came across that photo of me and Carli and tracked me down with the goal of squeezing me for a sound bite for some clickbait headline, just like the first time, and if I ignore him, he'll go away, just like the first time...

And how did this guy know you were back at the Riovan?

He didn't. It was a guess. He was fishing, and he just happened to be right. Who cares, anyway? While I don't exactly want to broadcast my presence here, it's also not a state secret.

"You got this," I mutter to myself, as I quietly leave the office.

Finally outside the hotel, with the sound of waves lapping the shoreline below, I run the whole way to Vista West along the dark back paths, intermittently lit, grasses tickling my ankles and the moon impossibly bright overhead, throwing blades of white light onto the ocean. I don't stop until I'm in my room. Breathless, sweaty, but safe.

For now.

CHAPTER 7

THE ALARM CLOCK GOES OFF WAY BEFORE I'M READY, GIVEN THAT I stayed up until three poring over the guest info, scouring the internet, and taking notes. I dress quickly and take the back paths to the dining hall. In the salty morning air, I try to organize some of the guests' names in my head, but it's useless before coffee.

Inside the dining hall, the vaulted ceilings and plush carpeting both expand and soften the sound, blending the conversation, the clink of dishes, and the noise of guests and staff moving around into a kind of underwater vagueness. I make a beeline for the coffee station, tucked into a little alcove above which a decal in scrolling font reads, *Healthy Mind, Healthy You!*

Suppressing a yawn, I pour coffee into an oversize white mug as the heat curls up, giving a foggy sheen to the silver carafe.

The sizzle and smell of the omelet station is directly behind me, and I can hear the soft murmur of a guest ordering—*just egg whites please, and Linda said no salt*—but food doesn't tempt me this early. Don't get me wrong; I'm no food minimalist. I own a catering company, after all. I just need time to get really hungry. Anyway, it's more fun eating when you're ravenous.

"Morning, Lil." Vic has come up behind me, and adrenaline shoots through me remembering last night's close call. Vic likes to circulate during mealtimes, giving out his little encouragements to staff and guests alike. He lays his hand on my shoulder and squeezes. "Sleep well?"

"Yes, thanks," I say, giving him a quick smile before hiding my face in the coffee mug. Mmm, strong and bitter.

His voice redirects with Broadway-level enthusiasm. "Gloria! So glad to have you back this year! Hope you're settling in comfortably? Will you be joining our morning yoga? No time like the present to get THIN, you know! Thriving! Healthy!"

Dear God.

"Inspirational! Natural!" a female voice trills back as I mentally dig, trying to fill in the rest of Gloria's information from the guest roster I studied last night. Gloria…Newman? No, Newland. Pre-diabetic, breast cancer survivor. Fifty-something, recently divorced from an acclaimed baritone whose dick—according to Twitter—apparently needed as much attention as his world-renowned voice. I'm paraphrasing, of course. Poor Gloria.

Mug cupped between my hands, the ceramic nearly scalding my palms, I turn, leaning my butt against the counter's edge, and allow my eyes to rove over the hundred or so people, a combination of guests and staff. They don't separate us. The staff are the brand, as Serena hammered into us during training last night. Only the training, spa, and lifeguarding staff, of course—the ones they make sure are hot enough to be a draw. They make other staff—cleaners, maintenance workers, servers—eat in a dingy little room on a lower level with a view to the parking lot. *Your main job isn't actually to lifeguard, or design a great workout, or give a great massage, though of course we expect excellence there too*, Serena said. *It's to embody the values of the Riovan. Be your ideal self. Show our guests what they're working toward.* I suppose that's why they redesigned the lifeguard swimsuit this year, cut so high it's almost indecent. Where some might call it a great ass (and it is; thank you, genetics), Vic et al. would call it a natural extension of my "fully realized self." I'd laugh if the fury didn't choke me. But I've become really good at swallowing those burning coals as soon as they're lit. I'm no use to anyone if I let rage take over. Cooler minds must prevail. Caffeinated cooler minds.

As I lift the mug to my lips for another deep gulp, a woman waves at me from a table across the dining hall—Nayna, one of the few summer staffers from last year who returned. With the minimum-wage pay, most never come back, but I'm glad she did. Nayna is a truly striking woman. Dreaded hair, golden skin, clear blue eyes. A rootless flower child who runs an online crystal shop. At the Riovan, she runs the spa bar, mixing personalized lotions, shampoos, and aromatherapy oils for guests.

I wave back but don't join her at the table, though I am vaguely curious about the boyfriend she talked about last summer, and if they're still together after he told her he wanted to open their relationship to another woman. But right now it's time to take inventory of who's here, so that I can identify the person I'm here to find: the monster.

I have six days left to find them, if I want to stay on schedule.

It's an exercise a bit like reverse engineering a recipe, which Jessica used to love doing. She'd taste a lobster bisque, for example, squint her eyes tight, and say, *I'm tasting sherry. I'm tasting herbes de Provence. I'm tasting white wine.* I'd jot it all down as she talked her way through it. After she picked apart the flavors, we'd try to recreate it together—well, more like she re-created it while I tried to keep up with the dishes. That was back when food was our happy place, when we were just dreaming up what would eventually become our catering business, Taste of Heaven. A time when dreaming was as easy as speaking and just as cheap. Before the Riovan.

I take in faces slowly as I sip, picking out guests from summer staff from permanent staff. *Which one of you is it?* I've never been a patient person by nature, but I've worked on it over the last few years. It's important not to rush these things.

My eyes alight on Kyle, tucking into an acai bowl topped with sliced bananas. To my surprise, my late-night online sleuthing turned up a juicy little tidbit. His company isn't nearly as successful as he made it sound. In fact, it's in bankruptcy court right now, which begs the questions: Why is he taking a month off during a company crisis, and how can he afford to be here? Not that a guest's financial situation is relevant to my purposes, but still—it's good to know that my instinct was right about Kyle. He's the kind who inflates himself to gigantic proportions, crowding everyone else, taking up more space than he's worth...but there's just air inside. And wouldn't it be satisfying to pop that particular balloon? But there will probably be bigger fish to fry.

I track my gaze around the room to see what other faces I can match with their files. Ooh, at the table by the window, Craig Lancaster, a TV presenter on a gossipy daytime talk show who's always dishing the dirt on celebs. He's apparently on leave due to his heart condition, and is here at the Riovan with his husband of two years, Brian, who must be the man sitting across from him.

At another table, I spot Ana Durango-Carter, a reality TV celebrity who got canceled for saying something appallingly insensitive about her costar's weight fluctuations. And there's handsy Chad

Doyle, lead singer for Harvest Moon, who claimed on Instagram that he left the spotlight for a spiritual journey but really—according to a few clickbait articles and a Reddit thread that I unearthed around two in the morning—has been in rehab in Arizona after being accused of domestic abuse by his model wife. It's amazing what you can find on the internet, given a little time and a willingness to scroll and scroll... and scroll.

A huddle of lifeguards with total bro energy enters the dining hall together, pawing and slapping one another like some kind of bizarre foreplay. I recognize Jason, the freckled Brit, and Kenton, this year's Team Lead. Hannah trails in behind them with another girl I assume to be her UK roommate, Bridget. Bridget is petite and busty with a sculpted, neat little waist and muscled calves. They head en masse to the smoothie station.

Two people clad in black enter next. Instantly a hum vibrates through the room, exploding into smatters of applause. Guests are getting to their feet. Ah—this summer's fitness gurus. Tim and Shayna, smiling, waving, gracious. They used to host that reality TV weight-loss show *Take It Off*. Jessica and I would watch it together in her apartment as she studied for midterms or we dreamed up recipes. Shayna was the tough one who shouted in people's faces as they cried and threw up and literally fell to their knees during the brutal work-outs. "Do you want to die?" she'd screech, leaning over them with no pity in her eyes. "Do you want to live to see your grandchildren? Do you want to change or not?" Jessica thought it was hilarious. I'd pretend to fall, fainting, as Jess shook me and shrieked, "*Do you want to die?*" We nearly peed ourselves laughing.

I have to stop myself from actually shuddering. I can't believe I used to find that shit funny. Chalk it up to being twenty.

Tim was the one who gave the calmer "reality-check" talks. But the crowning moment of *Take It Off* was, of course, the season finale, when the contestants would come in dressed in their old fat clothes and pull them off in front of a live audience as everyone chanted, *Take-it-off! Take-it-off!* Then the contestants would reveal their new, thinner bodies, clad in spandex, as they wept on stage. After some journalist exposed the show's questionable practices, Tim and Shayna disappeared from the public eye. Here they are five years later, out of hibernation, looking untouched by time. Presumably they've been informed that here, we don't use the words fat or thin—unless it's an acronym for something else, apparently. We don't say weight, or size. I used to think that was more virtuous. That was back when I hadn't heard of gaslighting.

I track these two as they move toward the food. Shayna serves herself an assortment of fruit while Tim ladles out some oatmeal and sprinkles it with fresh berries. *Are you the monster?*

They walk up to a table of guests. "Can we join you guys?" says Shayna in a voice like sandpaper. I imagine twelve seasons of berating contestants would destroy anyone's vocal cords. Everyone fawns. *Oh my God, of course! Yes, please—what an honor—*

I watch them settle. Tim, tanned and blond, is in a leather jacket—who wears leather on a tropical island?—and Shayna's dressed in yoga pants and a sports bra, exposing a rippling bronzed midriff. I put a mental star next to both their names in the roster I'm developing in my head.

Two tables over, this summer's mental wellness consultant is holding a court of his own. Pat Burton, author of *The Secret Mind-to-Body Equation*, *New York Times* bestseller, though there are rumors he bought his way onto the list. Chiseled face with a neat silver beard; white hair pulled back in a nub of a ponytail. Single earring, wide-leg white pants, and an A-shirt exposing pale, toned arms. He's surrounded by five older women, all leaning toward him like they're trying to inhale him.

This initial inventory is slow work. I take another long sip of coffee, ignoring the restless pit jiggling in my stomach. Like Jessica's old game with food, you have to give the flavors time to bloom into your awareness. Not rush to conclusions. Open your mind to the possibilities.

"Bacon. Eggs with bacon, please." A voice, rich and masculine, draws my attention back to the omelet station. The voice belongs to an unreasonably handsome thirty-something man dressed in a waffle-weave Henley and joggers that look more suited to a woodsy lodge than a beachy resort. Still, he cuts a fine figure. Wide-shouldered, built like a rugby player, with tousled dark hair and a five-o'clock shadow. I try and fail to match him with one of the pictures from the file.

"I'm sorry, sir, we don't have any processed meats available."

"Isn't bacon…cured?"

"I'm afraid that smoking, salting, and curing are all considered—"

"Yeah, yeah, OK. Got it." He takes a wider stance and stuffs his hands into the pockets of his joggers. He's muscled, but not like a bodybuilder or a movie star. He's more rugged. More natural. And obviously, clueless. "What about sausage? Maybe chicken sausage?"

"Sir," the young chef says patiently, "I'm afraid that sausage is also a processed meat. Have you met any of our nutritionists?"

"You know, it's OK. I think I'll just get some coffee."

"We have a nice assortment of wild mushrooms—" says the chef, but too late, the guest is walking toward me, shaking his head.

I scoot aside to allow him access to the carafe. He's so unlike any other guest I've ever seen. I'm having trouble taking my eyes off him.

"Fuck," he mutters. He poured too fast and spilled.

"Here," I offer, grabbing a wad of napkins and mopping up the spill before it can spread farther. "I got it." As I complete the cleanup, he tops off my mug too. Then, we both lean against the counter, bookends on the small alcove, cradling our respective coffees.

"Don't tell my boss, but I miss bacon too," I admit in a mock whisper.

"Nothing like it."

"Crispy."

"Savory."

"Salty."

"And so very processed," he adds, giving me a sidelong look.

We share a muffled laugh, followed by a strangely charged silence.

Handsome men are a dime a dozen at the Riovan, but there's something different about this guy, and it's not just his shameless penchant for bacon, or his stockier build. I take him in briefly, in stolen glances, and notice the curl of a tattoo peeking out from under the cuff of his Henley. There's an intensity to this guy; a self-possession. Something…powerful. Something raw. A little tingle sweeps my skin. Not a response I should have toward a guest. In fact, not a response I've had toward anyone…since Jessica.

"You're a lifeguard," he says. "Right?"

"What gave it away?" I deadpan.

He grins. "Well. I'm an appalling swimmer, so it behooves me to be friendly with whoever's going to be saving my life." He thrusts out a hand. "Daniel Black, by the way."

I snort with laughter. *Behooves me*? Who the hell talks like that? As he folds his hand around mine and I feel the strength of his shake, I mentally turn the pages of the guest files again. I know I saw the name Daniel Black, but there were a lot of pages, and a lot of names…

"I'm Lily."

His gaze is both direct and disarming. As though his brown eyes could see straight through bullshit. Straight through me. Flustered, I drop my gaze and pull my hand back.

"This is my first time doing a health trip…thingy," he says, his tone low, confidential, a little amused, like we're both in on the same joke. "So…I hope I can keep up. Seems like a pretty intense experience."

I laugh in spite of myself, because that's an awfully casual way to refer to an exclusive wellness retreat that he's paid thirty thousand dollars to attend. Plus tax.

"Yeah, the four-week *intensive* is definitely…intense."

"It's not my normal scene. I guess I gave myself away to the omelet master over there. But, you know, that's the life of a journalist. You go where the story is."

Instantly, my skin prickles. "Oh, you're here doing research?"

"Huge feature on wellness tourism for *Fit Life*. Have you heard of it?"

"No."

"Ouch."

I wave a hand. "I'm not into magazines."

"Not a reader?"

"I didn't say that."

Daniel's eyes crinkle. He sets down his coffee briefly to push his sleeves above his elbows. The man's forearms are rippling with muscle and tendon. Yes, I imagine them braced over me in a compromising position. And yes, I immediately toss the thought into the trash bin, where all such thoughts must go.

"Sorry to have made assumptions. You must get that a lot."

"Meaning…"

"Meaning that you look like a living Barbie doll, and people project their own ideas about what that means on you." He pauses. "No offense."

Fuck, this guy is full of surprises. Gorgeous *and* on point? Unfair.

"No offense taken," I say. "Actually…I appreciate that you said that."

"I bet that makes it hard to trust people. Romantic partners, especially."

"Um…" An alarm blares in my head. *Too close too fast!* But also, how is this guy reading me this easily? It *is* hard to trust people—because there are so few deserving of trust. And for the past five years, let's just say I haven't let anyone get past light flirting with me.

"Sorry," says Daniel, eyeing me. "I guess that's another assumption, isn't it?"

Yes, it is. But it doesn't mean he's wrong.

Mom was gorgeous. She liked to date. People assumed she was a slut.

I was only twelve when I realized I was going to be gorgeous like Mom. I remember the morning it dawned on me. I stood in front of the bathroom mirror in my pajamas, touching my face, my heart pressed tight between warring feelings of exhilaration and deep dread. Beauty made Mom's life harder. It put a target on her back, and that morning, I felt the target on mine, too, as real and physical as my skin, my bones.

Let's just say I did a lot of hiding in oversize clothing when I was a teenager.

And then…

Jessica.

She waltzed into the bar where I was working in downtown Cincinnati with her bevy of college friends and her fake ID, and everything changed. "I'll have a Cosmo," she said in her breathy voice, fixing her big blue eyes on me, and she must have seen something in my wry grin, because she quickly amended her order. "Or... what do you recommend?" For the first time in my twenty years of existence, that night at O'Malley's I was actually thankful for my looks, because they made her notice me.

Daniel's gaze is locked with mine, like he's watching the memories play inside my head. His clear brown eyes don't waver, and I squirm internally.

"Well...you know what they say about assumptions," I say with forced levity.

He grins. "And I'd love to make it up to you. Drinks? Tonight, at the Sunset Bar? Zero assumptions. Just two people talking."

Suddenly, all I can think of is Vic's directive during training last night—the same as every year. *We don't expressly forbid relations between guests and staff—we've learned the hard way that putting a lot of beautiful people together has consequences, ha ha—but we do ask that you exercise good judgment and discretion. And this is your friendly reminder that all guest-related information and activity at the resort is covered in your NDA.*

"I don't know..." I demur. It's not even that he's a guest. It's that I haven't been on a date since Jessica. I should just say no, right?

"It'll be fun," he promises, leaning against the counter, easy in his body, his expression frank.

Fun. The mental trash bin disgorges its own version of what fun with Daniel might look like.

"I..." To my horror, I feel my nipples harden under the thin red fabric of my suit. The white material of the cotton sweatshirt won't do much to disguise that, so I wrap an arm around myself and angle my body away from Daniel. *What are you doing? Just tell the guy no and take a cold shower!*

Across the dining hall, Vic catches my eye and taps his wrist. Right—I'm due at the East pool in five minutes.

"I'd better get to work," I say, pushing off the counter.

"I'll be at the bar at eight."

Damn. Tenacious.

For a second, I flirt with the idea of meeting him tonight. Dressing up a little, doing my hair, having…fun. Yes, there's some rare chemistry between us. Of course some repressed part of me wants to indulge that connection. I mean, the way that man touched me with his eyes alone… But I remind myself that he's not just a cute guest. He's a journalist. It would be plain stupid to talk to him, even off the record. My continued presence at the Riovan depends on a certain amount of invisibility, and the last thing I need is a journalist picking away at the layers.

Invisibility. Huh. A strange callback to my teen years, I suppose, except that this time around, my beauty is the disguise.

"We'll see." I toss Daniel a parting smile as I walk away. "Catch you later, Daniel Black."

"Catch you later, Lily Lennox."

I don't turn around.

Of course the image of him waiting alone at the bar tonight makes me feel a bit guilty. But come on. He'll have no trouble finding someone else to buy a drink for. Whether he's after ass or info for his article, the Riovan is full of potential candidates who will be glad to provide either—or both.

It's only when I get to the pool that I realize: I never told him my last name.

CHAPTER 8

I TUCK THE THICK COMFORTER UP AROUND ME LIKE A FEATHERY
cocoon as I lean against the headboard.

Eight o'clock is finding me not at the bar with sexy Mr. Journalist,
but in bed. Which, to me, is trading up. Honestly, I could go to sleep
right now. After a shift at the beach and a shift and a half at the pool,
I'm beat, my back achy and my shoulders tight—bad posture coming
back to bite me. But my work is not done yet.

In the low light of the nightstand lamp, I pull out the guest roster
and blink a few times. The words are a little blurry—I'm just that
tired.

I've left the patio door open, and a breeze ruffles the curtains,
sending pleasant chills on to my exposed arms. I can't hear the waves
in this poolside room. I miss the sound. Instead, I'm treated to the
splashes of people jumping into the pool, peppered with a few feminine shrieks.

OK, time to focus. I turn the pages as the minutes tick past, flip-
ping to some of the people I remember, like Chad Doyle from Harvest

Moon, who's on antidepressants, and Craig Lancaster, who's really into the sauna. *That can't be good for his heart condition…*

Then, almost without choosing, I flip back to Daniel Black: 6', 170 lb., brown eyes. Now I see why his face didn't immediately connect with his picture. The picture shows a clean-shaven guy with shorter hair in a white shirt and tie, smiling, which somehow is weird. The desk version of the broodier Daniel I met. I scan his health info. Mmm, slightly high cholesterol. Must be all that bacon. Nothing else to note…and Vic's notes are sparse. *Make sure he has a 5-star experience!! This could be great publicity!!! Connect him w/Serena!!!!!*

Wow. That's a lot of exclamation marks.

At a clicking sound, I look at the door. In a panic, I stuff the guest list under the covers just as a girl stumbles in with a roller bag behind her. Roommate. And…she's not looking great. I hop out of bed to greet her.

"Hi, I'm Lily. And you're…?"

"River," she gasps. The door closes behind her. Her dark hair hangs lank around a pale face. "Sorry, I'm—" Her body convulses, and before I can do anything else, she throws up on the carpet. The splatter is pale pink and…chunky. Extra chunky.

"Ooooh," I groan before I can stop myself. There's a panicked squeezing in my gut. Sweat springs up on my skin like a sudden dew.

Jess, are you OK? Me, five years ago in a room just like this one, or nearly, and Jessica puking. It was chunky too. She said she was fine. She must have eaten something that upset her… *Maybe that green smoothie that looked like puke?* I offered, trying to laugh even though the sound of people throwing up has always had a domino effect on me.

I shake myself out of the memory and back to River, who's

grabbing a fistful of tissues from a nearby box, but honey, tissues are not going to cut it...

"Just leave it," I say. "I'll take care of it. Bathroom's here." I swing open the door helpfully.

She makes it to the toilet just in time. As the liquid sound of puke hitting water reaches me, I snap my wrist elastic twice. *She is not Jessica. She is your new roommate and she's feeling like shit. This is not about you, this is about her.* Gathering my resolve, I join her in the bathroom, where she's kneeling over the toilet, arms braced on the seat.

"I'm going to get your hair out of the way," I say gently, sacrificing my wrist elastic in the process as I bundle her hair back.

"Thanks," she moans. "Sorry."

"Don't be sorry. I'm going to call housekeeping, OK?"

I use the old-fashioned room phone on the nightstand to request an urgent visit from housekeeping. Then, I move the guest roster from under the covers to under the mattress. Housekeeping shows up within minutes, thank God, and as the diminutive cleaning lady stoically deals with the throw-up, I lean into the bathroom to check on River again.

"Stomach bug?"

"Food poisoning," she says. "In the airport lounge on my way...I think I ate some—" She vomits yet again, then tilts her puke-flecked face toward me. "Bad shrimp."

My stomach turns, sending a rush of liquid into my mouth, and I force myself to swallow it down. I don't think I'll eat shrimp ever again. Or anything else that's pink. Or food of any kind, really.

"I'm so sorry," I say. And oh, how I wish we had two bathrooms. "Can I...get you anything?"

"Ginger ale? If you don't mind?"

"Of course!" My enthusiasm isn't even feigned; I'm all too happy to escape the room. I hesitate at the door; I'm in my plaid pajama bottoms and the ribbed tank top I like to sleep in, but…I'm not changing into "branded gear" for a ginger ale run. I grab my key card, credit card, and head out.

The Sunset Bar at quarter to nine is hopping, and seeing how dressed up everyone is for their nightcaps, I shift uncomfortably. PJ's might have been…shortsighted. The ribbed white tank is on the thin side; I didn't even put on a bra. Yep. Total and utter mistake.

A live jazz band is positioned at one end of the room, the singer a stunning redhead who's swaying sensuously as she croons, "I've got a crush on you…"

Trying to be as inconspicuous as possible, I sidle up to the side of the long, polished bar nearest to the entrance. Champagne-colored lights hang like warm icicles in clusters all down the length of the bar, making the mahogany top glow like warm honey.

"Hi…" I say, trying to flag down the nearest bartender, but he's in the middle of closing out a customer's tab and doesn't seem to hear me.

I lean on the bar with my arms crossed to hide my braless state and catch the metal footrail with one foot as I take a look around. Little bar-height cocktail tables are scattered throughout the crescent-shaped space. Opposite the bar, a bank of floor-to-ceiling windows faces west. The Sunset Bar is on the top floor of the hotel. Below, fire pits glimmer and the pools glow.

As I try to catch the bartender's attention again, I recognize a high-pitched laugh. Serena, sitting toward the center of the bar. Wearing a tube dress that perfectly matches her skin. Talking to someone whose back is to me…a-*ha*. Daniel.

There are a few customers between us, but still, I stay hunched down, praying neither of them notices me.

"Hey," I say in a loud whisper toward the bartender, leaning forward on the bar as far as I can go, feeling my breasts press against the wood.

He finally looks up and smiles. "What can I get you?" His grin is amused. Yep, buddy, I'm in my pajamas. Take a fuckin' picture.

"A ginger ale. Actually, make that two." I sense I might need one myself before the night's over.

"Can I interest you in a sugarless, organic alternative to ginger ale that's infused with—" he starts, but I cut him off.

"Plain old ginger ale. Sick roommate. And do you have oyster crackers?"

"Uh, I'll have to grab some crackers from the kitchen. Give me a second?"

"Of course," I say.

I glance at Serena and Daniel. Still oblivious to my presence, thank God. Then I distract myself, as usual, by people watching. I spot Kyle tucked into a corner table with a slim blonde—no surprise there. And there's Craig Lancaster at the cocktail table within spitting distance of me, handing a server his credit card, looking positively spray-tanned. And that must be his husband, Brian, across from him. Craig's face has the too-stretched look of someone who has undergone plastic surgery more than once, but Brian looks like a normal dude. He has a kind, puppy-dog face, and a bristly silver-flecked beard. Honestly, he looks a bit out of place. Based on the way he's shifting in his seat, he feels out of place too.

"Why the hell did you order that second beer?" hisses Craig. "I thought you were working on your beer belly!"

Holy shitballs. This guy makes Kyle look like Mr. Rogers.

"Sorry, babe," says Brian. "After that workout with Shayna, I just thought it would be nice to unwind—"

"You. Just. Thought," mocks Craig. "Well, maybe think harder! Because last I checked, I'm footing the bill here."

Their server returns with Craig's card and receipt.

"Want me to add the tip?" Brian offers humbly, reaching for the pen, but Craig smacks his palm down on the pen, blocking his husband's hand.

"Oh, I am *not* tipping the person who served *you* two beers at a *wellness* resort," snaps Craig. "*I'm* meeting with your nutritionist tomorrow. Because we're here to fucking *fix* things."

He marches out of the Sunset, Brian behind him.

A sudden pain flares in my hand. I look down to find my left fist is clenched so tight, my nails are digging into my palm. I open my hand and splay my fingers out on the bar top, letting the cool wood soothe me.

It's OK, I tell my pounding pulse. *This is why you're here.*

My eyes stray back to Serena, who's talking animatedly, clearly shining under the laser beam of Daniel's attention. Her body language, together with the frequency of her laughter, is telling me she's *really* into Daniel. Suddenly, her eyes shift to me, widening instantly with recognition.

Damn. Other than diving behind the bar, there's no hiding now.

"Hey! Lily!"

OK. Now the pajamas are really going to bite me. I'm breaking branding guidelines in front of the VP of Branding. I lift my hand and wave friendly fingers, giving her my most charming and unassuming smile. With a little bit of luck, she'll let me scurry off without an embarrassing public reprimand…

Nope. She's leaving her barstool, clip-clopping over to me in her six-inch heels. She grabs my hand, and there's a reek of gin on her breath.

"Come over here. You have to meet...Daniel...*Black*. He's a very important, erm, writer." She drags me behind her, then pulls up an extra stool, nearly falling out of her tube dress in the process. The bartender returns with my ginger ales and crackers.

"That'll be nineteen seventy-five."

I nearly choke but whip out my credit card and hold it out to the bartender.

"Sorry," I say to Serena, ignoring Daniel for as long as I can even though I can practically feel his gaze burning me up. "I actually need to get this back to my roommate. Food poisoning. Not pretty."

But Serena is already shaking her head, grabbing my arm to pull my credit card back and pulling out a Riovan-branded credit card of her own. "No, no, nooooo. I'll have someone else get it to her. Please, let me..." She presses her credit card into the bartender's hand. "This needs to go to room..."

I sigh and make a "sorry" face at the bartender. "2208. Vista West?"

With a quick nod, he disappears.

"So," says Serena, returning to her perch and indicating the stool on Daniel's other side. "Sit. And tell Daniel...*Black*...all about why you keep coming back to this...*amazing* place. Tell him about how *great* it is here. Hey—hey—Danny—did you know Lily met...Carli *Elle*? The *singer*? Didn't you, Lil? Vic said... Didn't you go to a party on her yacht last year? God, I love Carli!" She starts singing an off-key faux-rap, running her hands down her own body. "*My body is a temple, you're callin' me your goddess, the hottest, your queen, not sorry, not modest—*"

Yep, she's a step past tipsy. Maybe not the best of looks for the VP of Branding?

Daniel and I finally meet eyes. His are twinkling with suppressed amusement. I can't help but wonder who made the first move tonight—him or Serena. He's wearing a simple white button-up and jeans. His five-o'clock shadow has thickened since this morning. Basically, total werewolf energy. *I'm in trouble.*

"Hi," I say.

"Hi," he says back. His voice is warm, questioning. Somehow, that single word conveys so much. I detect both a *Why did you stand me up?* and also, *I'm not mad. Just curious.* Very curious, based on the way his eyes seem to be stripping me down.

A not-unpleasant chill goes over me, and I wrap my arms around my chest, cursing silently. Second time today.

"You two know each other?" says Serena, leaning in and tugging up her tube dress again.

"Not at all," I say quickly at the same time as Daniel says, "Yes, we met earlier."

We laugh.

Our eyes are locked, just like this morning. He tilts his head. I tilt mine. Who's going to talk first?

Don't do this, I remind myself. *You're not here to get close to people.*

Serena leans on the bar and signals for another drink for herself. "Lily…anything for you?"

"No, thanks."

"No, really, you should get something…" urges Serena, already signaling the bartender again.

"I'm not really a huge drinker," I say.

"She likes to be in control," Daniel explains to Serena, his eyes daring me to contradict his annoyingly correct assumption.

What happened to no assumptions? I want to tease, because

something about this man makes flirting easy, but…a Riovan higher-up is sitting right there who could get me fired quicker than she's knocking back those drinks.

"How did you know my last name?" I say instead.

Daniel gives a satisfied smile, like he's pleased I caught this detail. "To be completely honest, Vic was talking about his high standards for the staff and mentioned you by name. He couldn't sing your praises highly enough."

"Well…Vic is an enthusiastic communicator," I say.

"Lovely man," says Daniel, taking a sip of what looks like a piña colada, complete with a little umbrella and a cherry. For some reason, I find his choice of drink fascinating.

"Oh, Vic," laughs Serena, slapping the bar top. "We love him."

"I'm guessing you're interviewing Vic for the article?" I say.

"Absolutely. He's a veritable fount of information about the hotel, its values, its history, all the famous people who've stayed here…" Daniel begins, as I try not to panic. Surely Vic wouldn't bring up what happened last year if he's looking for good publicity with three exclamation points. *Or was it five…*

"We were talking yesterday after the amazing kick-off seminar by that author," continues Daniel, "with the book, what was his name—" He snaps his fingers. "White hair. Earring. Hippie vibes—"

"Pat Burton," Serena fills in. "We *love* him."

Daniel looks at me. "Did you catch his seminar, by the way?"

"Unfortunately, no. Was it good?"

"Mesmerizing," says Daniel with a half grin, and it drives me a little crazy that I can't tell if he's being sarcastic or just plain old flirtatious.

"I booked him," volunteers Serena, her words mushed since she's drinking from her fresh beverage at the same time. She sets her glass down. "He's a…" She swipes her lips with the back of her hand. "Friend of a friend."

"Must be nice to have those kinds of connections," says Daniel, raising his piña colada half an inch off the bar top before setting it back down, without drinking. "Cheers to that."

"Oh, networking is…*everything*. Believe me."

Damn, she's sloshed. I don't want to be a killjoy, but she really should be focusing on hydrating right now, not imbibing more gin. Even with Daniel sitting between us, the smell is rolling off her, as strong as car fumes. I move to breathing through my mouth.

"Can I get you some water, Serena?" I say.

"Sure," she slurs.

Now it's my turn to flag the bartender, who understands immediately and gives me a thumbs-up. I make a discreet throat-cutting sign—I'm pretty sure it's time for the VP of Branding to be done for tonight. The bartender gives me a subtle nod, with a concerned look back at Serena, who's slumping down farther on the bar, now trailing a single finger in a lazy circle in the wet ring her glass left on the wood top.

"Out of curiosity, did you know the previous VP of Branding?" says Daniel, angling himself a little more toward me. "Serena was saying she's only been in the position for a few months…"

"Of course. Audrey Lawali."

"Wasn't she VP for under a year?"

"They turn over often."

"Why do you think that is?"

I shrug.

"So, about the last one," Daniel persists. "Audrey. Serena said something about her getting fired… Do you know anything?"

"What exactly is your article about?" I say with exaggerated caution, glancing at Serena, who's still lazily tracing circles in the moisture, apparently oblivious to our side conversation.

He laughs. "Sorry. Not for the article. Just my natural curiosity."

"I'm a lowly lifeguard, Daniel," I say in a quiet, amused voice. "Whatever happens in the upper echelons is beyond my pay grade. Now, if you want to ask about our rigorous lifeguard protocols, or my favorite sunscreen, or my feelings about the new swimsuit..."

Under his intent gaze, another wave of goose bumps goes over me, and something perverse must be operating through me, because I uncross my arms and turn fully to face him. My tank top can't be hiding much. His smile widens, but to his credit, he keeps his eyes on my face. Good man.

"Well, Lily Lennox," he says, rubbing his thumb in little motions over the center of his lower lip. Which is remarkably full, for a dude. Pillowy is the word that comes to mind. "What are your feelings about the new swimsuit?"

"Have you seen it in action?"

"Refresh me." That thumb is still rubbing his lip. My eyes keep drifting to it.

I laugh. "Let's just say it doesn't leave much to the imagination."

"Shame," says Daniel, and I swear this man could make love through eye contact alone. "Imagination can be a powerful drug."

My breath catches; I am officially turned on.

"I, for one, stay away from drugs."

"Good girl," he says, his voice barely audible, for my ears only, and suddenly I imagine the Sunset Bar emptied of people, mostly dark, with just Daniel, me, and the warm glow of the champagne chandeliers. His breath, hot in my ear—*Good girl.* If I braced my feet on the middle rung of the barstool, it's the perfect height for—

Trash bin! Now!

But instead, the image sharpens, and heat surges between my legs as imaginary Daniel steps between them, his eye contact unwavering as he fingers the bottom edge of my tank top and—

His eyes break away from me and the vision shatters, leaving an uncomfortable pulsing still working its way through places in my body that haven't felt any pulsing in years. Damn it—I'd forgotten how fucking good it is to feel this way—

No! Intimacy is dangerous!

"I'm afraid we have a situation," Daniel says, and for a second I think he's talking about the next-level attraction simmering between us, but there's a loud snort, and I follow his line of sight.

Ah. Serena. You wouldn't think such a mighty snore could come from so petite a frame, but the universe likes to have its little jokes.

I slide off my barstool to approach her and jostle her arm. "Serena? Hey, Serena? Wake up…"

Her head lifts infinitesimally. "Hmm?"

"Hey. Good, you're awake…"

She immediately slumps back down onto her arms.

"Please tell me you didn't buy her an irresponsible number of drinks," I say with a touch of crankiness, because it's pretty clear now that I'll have to attend to Serena's needs instead of Daniel attending to mine. Damn it, Serena. Not that I actually would have done anything with Daniel, of course…

"I'm afraid she's the one who bought me drinks." Daniel stands, giving a sorrowful look at his unfinished piña colada. "Come on. We should get her back to her room."

I scrunch her shoulder. "Hey. Hey. Serena? What's your room number?"

Her eyes open and a sleepy smile drizzles over her face. "It's… four-zero-zero…zero." She draws the zeros in the air. "Why?"

"Bedtime," says Daniel. "Don't worry. We'll deliver you safe and sound."

"Awe, you guys are the sweetest." She loops an arm around me, and Daniel positions himself under her other.

"On three," he says.

"Three?" says Serena with a slur to her voice. "Heeeey, awesome! I've always wanted to do a threesome! It'll be sooo fun… You guys are soooo hot… I'm up for anything, seriously…"

My cheeks burn. I don't look at Daniel, but I can feel him shaking with laughter as we lug the VP of Branding back to her room.

CHAPTER 9

SERENA'S ROOM IS NOT JUST A ROOM, BUT AN EXECUTIVE SUITE, AS the brass plaque proclaims, one of a dozen located in the central building of the Riovan opposite the spa, which is closed. Behind the spa's glass door, the reception desk is lit by a security light at a weird angle. Eerie. Not a fan. Though I do wonder if Serena has a key... The saunas are back there, and it could be useful to have off-hours access.

Serena rummages in her clutch purse.

"Voilà!" she cries, pulling out a matte black key card with a golden swoop on one side. "Threesome tiiiiiime!" She swipes the card, and Daniel opens the door.

My plan is to help her straight to bed, but she pulls away from both of us and lurches inside, leaving Daniel and me hesitant at the threshold. "Wow, the floor is moving!" Then, she jumps face-forward on the bed. "The fun is over here, guys!" She smacks her own ass.

The tickle of laughter in my throat wars with the mortified heat blazing in my face. This might be the most bizarre—and inappropriate—interaction I've ever had with a superior in a place of employment.

I step inside the room, but Daniel braces an arm on the door frame. "Do you think we should…"

"Have an amazing threesome?" I complete, looking over at Serena, who is now in doggy position executing a sloppy twerk. I tilt my head and pretend to consider. "While intriguing, I'm afraid I'll have to pass."

We both laugh. Daniel gives an incredulous headshake. "Not in my cards when I signed up for a wellness retreat…"

"It'll make your article extraspicy." I put on a fake reporter voice. "*When the VP of Branding offered me a night of kinky sex with her and her subordinate, lowly lifeguard Lily Lennox*—wait, that's too many Ls—" I suppress a laugh. "But seriously—you won't write about this, will you?"

"Rest easy. I'm not here to take down the Riovan."

I feign wiping sweat off my forehead. "Phew." But actually, his casual remark is drawing feelings to the surface like blood to a cut.

Taking down this place is exactly what I wanted a journalist to help me do, five years ago.

I called reporters from any and all English-speaking news outlets. Leaving voicemails, sending emails, begging them to do an exposé on the Riovan…and what did I get back? Just a handful of terse *Thanks for your inquiry. If we would like to discuss further, we will contact you at the information you provided.* Most ghosted me.

No one cared enough to tell my story.

Would Daniel care? What if I told him everything, tonight, right now?

But that's impossible.

I look at him and wish with all my might that this was happening five years ago. Or even four. What if he'd shown up the first year I was lifeguarding? I would have told him everything, and he could have written the article that would have incinerated this place. Then I wouldn't have had to do what I did—

"Hey—you OK?" he says, with those eyes that apparently see everything.

"Fine." I force a smile. That ship has sailed. The last thing I need now is to be featured in an article that draws attention to me in any way. I had my moment of shouting and waving my arms at the world. That didn't work; now it's about staying under the radar. "Just preparing myself to deal with…" I jerk a thumb backward toward Serena. Right on cue, there's a loud groan from the bed, and this one is not the sexy kind. She's going to be very sick, very soon—I can feel it.

"Escape while you can," I joke, even though I'm spiraling a little. What-ifs always get you on the way out, don't they? Like airport shrimp.

Daniel gives Serena one last look as if considering if he should stick around, but I say, "I got this."

Looking relieved, he says, "Good luck," then heads off down the hall. I wait a couple of seconds to see if he'll turn around. He doesn't. I close the door behind me.

Alone now with my drunk superior, I take a moment to survey her room. King-size bed made up in the resort's signature white. Modern art, a pink velvet chaise longue, a brass bar cart, fully stocked not with alcohol, but what appears to be protein powders and supplements. And a whole row of windows overlooking the dark ocean.

A noise makes me jump. Serena, snoring, now curled on her side.

"Hey, wait a second, sleepy lady," I say in a loud voice, as I draw the curtains over the dark windows. "Don't nod off yet. We need to get some water in you." I make for the bathroom, hoping to find a glass. Holy shit. A steam shower, a soaker tub, and its own sound system. There are a hell of a lot of switches on the wall. I flip one, but instead of the lights coming on, spa music starts playing. I flip it back off. The next one, thankfully, turns on the lights above the vanity. There's a clean glass on the sink; I fill it up with water and bring it back to Serena.

I prod her shoulder. "Here, sit up, time for a nice drink."

"Ooooh," she groans but manages to prop herself up. She downs the whole thing in three gulps. "I feel so weird." She clutches her middle and turns wide eyes on me. "Oh, no."

Here it comes. I pull her up, and we barely make it to the bathroom before she pukes into the toilet.

"Dear God," I breathe as my stomach clenches too. Two pukers in one night; just my luck. Time to switch to mouth-breathing, permanently.

"Oh, it's OK," she says as she heaves again, releasing the tiniest bit of liquid. "At least I'm getting thinner!" Her laugh is ghoulish, interrupted as it is by a fresh round of stomach emptying.

I can't even pretend to laugh at her joke. Assuming it was a joke. Instead, I fill up the glass again, because she's going to have a hell of a hangover tomorrow.

"Seriously," she says from the toilet, still slurring her words. "I *hate* fat people. Don't you? Like, swear to God, if I ever got fat? I might as well just—"

And just like that, I'm ready to bash her face in.

Thankfully, her next round of puking cuts off her sentence, or I might have done just that.

It's not just the smell of her that's toxic, it seems.

I wasn't always like this. Growing up in Calumet Heights, I saw a lot of people with short fuses. It's easy to get that way when you're always on the brink of disaster. I learned the hard way that you don't throw the punch right away. First, you think it through.

For five damn years I've been thinking it through here at the Riovan. This is not the year that I crash and burn.

I lean down to hold back her hair as her body convulses.

She's half a head shorter than me. True, she works out, but she's also drunk off her ass. If I plunged her face into the toilet, I'm pretty sure I could keep her down…

My body is producing adrenaline like it's going out of style. And adrenaline makes you stronger too… My grip on her hair tightens, but then a voice, soft and warning, says, *This is not how we do this, Lily.*

Serena seems to be done throwing up, for the moment. I release her hair and step back. She rolls to the side of the toilet, one arm draped on the seat.

"Thank you," she slurs. "*God.* The only thing worse than barfing is when it comes out the other…" She laughs suddenly. "The cleanse company… What's it called… Clear… Clean…"

No idea what she's talking about.

"You sound like you're doing better," I say mechanically, "so actually, I should probably get going—"

"Wait. No. You're…I need your opinion." She yanks a piece of toilet paper off the roll to wipe her mouth. "You're…gorgeous. Obviously, or we wouldn't have hired you! What was I saying?"

"How about we get you to bed?"

"No, no, no, don't go, Lily! You're like my…big sister. You remind me of her…"

"That's nice, but I—"

"It's a laxative, but you'd never guess it from the"—she

hiccups—"label. So good, right? You do this…cleanse! And you shit it all out. I'll tell Linda to put it on everyone's"—*burp*—"diet plan, and they'll drop a size without even trying."

Right. The co-branding opportunity she was discussing with Vic. Disgust starts to twist my face, but I fight my expression back to neutral.

"That's a terrible idea."

"Really?" Her brow wrinkles. "But people…they're paying thirty fucking thousand dollars to do the intensive, Lily! If they don't drop fucking…a *lot* of pounds, OK? They won't come back or"—hiccup—"tell their friends." She slumps deeper on the wall, her tube dress riding up—and down. "We need the fat people to keep coming, and we need to make them…not fat. Seriously. That's a top-down company…directive. Because that's our brand." Her hands lift in a magician's flourish and she whispers, "That's what…we *do*."

"Stop!" I slam my fist on to the vanity counter, breathing hard. Not smart, short fuse, but I've reached a bit of a limit. Then I crouch down and tap her cheek, just a sharp little tap with my palm, even though I'm tempted to slap it. Hard. "Stop saying fat. Serena…fuck! You wrote the guidelines! Remember? We don't say fat. Thin. Weight. Size. Get it together!"

Her eyes are wide, surprised. Shocked.

My first thought is, *Now I've done it. She's going to fire me.*

My second, *Fine. If she fires me, I kill her.*

Third thought, *No! If she fires you, you appeal to Vic…*

Then her mouth curves up and her eyes crinkle and she laughs.

"Oh my God! That's *right*! The *guidelines*… What a bunch of bullshit, right? You and I both know that what people want is to be skinny!" She burps. "Can we just be real…Lily? You're legit. We can talk, like…honestly. One of my performance metrics? For my job? Is pounds lost per guest." Both her arms fly up, fingers pointing to the ceiling. "And Clean…Clear…Slim…whatever it's called. Not only is it gonna help those pounds melt off. There's a huuuuge commission in it for me too. Hey, you should help me! If we can get more, erm…"

If she says "fat people," I swear to God I'm going to—

"*Guests* here, and enrollment climbs, I get a lot of money, and…" She sighs and leans her head back against the wall, exposing her neck. Her thin, vulnerable neck.

OK. Time for me to go.

Call me soft, but I don't fancy rotting for thirty years in the Saint Lisieux prison for Serena. I've researched it, and let's just say that conditions are less than ideal. Their version of a toilet is a hole in the floor, and the number of prisoners they cram into each cell can't possibly be up to fire code. Extradition would be marginally better, but still, one could hardly call that living one's best life.

The voice in my head whispers, *Then again, is* this *your best life?* I shut down that intrusive thought as fast as I think it.

"Hope you feel better tomorrow," I say and make for the door.

This time, she doesn't try to stop me.

Outside, in the silence of the hall, I stop. Brace my hands on the textured wallpaper with its ivory bamboo pattern. Let my head hang. Everything in my brain is fizzing, my whole body shaking. I slam a fist into my palm once, twice.

Every year, I come back to the most triggering place in the world. I come looking for this, don't I? For that one person to pull my trigger…

Not true. That's not how I do it. I'm not reactionary. I'm purposeful. I get on the plane. I switch into Resort Lily mode. I come here coolheaded and survey my options, and make a plan. I'm sensible and self-controlled.

I don't explode.

Why does it feel different this year? Why am I feeling so off-kilter? Is it the poolside room? It threw me down memory lane, and I haven't managed to recover? Am I that fragile? I think of my mom that day, standing tall in her Revlon lipstick with the cast-iron skillet in her hand. So strong. *I want to be like her.* She seemed like an avenging goddess. It wasn't just lipstick. It was blood. Splattered on her and splattered on me, like some ancient sacrifice.

I reach for the hair tie at my wrist, but it's not there, so I slap my own face, as hard as I wanted to slap Serena's. Then again, for good measure.

I have to be detached, like last year. And the year before that. And before that. Invested and detached. Present *and* removed. Here, but not here. That's just how it has to be, or nothing gets done.

"We have to stay calm, Lily, or nothing gets done." Mom. Sitting on the couch, her arm around me, as we looked down at the boyfriend. Trevor. Handsome. Mom had a weakness for beauty. "We can't panic. Cooler heads must prevail."

She was looking at the body appraisingly, like she was shopping for a new pair of shoes.

"We'll wrap him in the shower curtain," said Mom, her hand mindlessly rubbing my shoulder. "I'll borrow Ed's truck. After dark, we'll just go for a drive."

I rub the stinging spot on my face. Serena's name now has a huge star next to it on my mental roster.

I give one final glance at her door, then call the elevator.

The gym is open 24/7. I've never been into working out, but desperate times, etc., etc.

It's two levels down. I let myself in with my key card. The gym is dark, but I don't turn on the lights. I glance at the wall clock—nearly midnight.

I choose the treadmill at the end of the line. The lonely one at the edge. The screen wakes up at my touch. I've never used one of these, but thank God it's intuitive. I program it to a nice jogging speed and hop on. I'm not a runner, but I feel like I could sprint a marathon. Twice. I increase the speed. I add some incline. Increase the speed again. My legs burn. My heart burns. My feet pound the rubber. I'm breathing through my teeth, trying to wrestle my feelings back into whatever place they normally go.

I'm not supposed to be feeling all this emotion.

I increase the speed again. My legs are a blur beneath me.

I go. And I go, and I go, and I go.

CHAPTER 10

THE LATE-NIGHT RUN-A-THON MUST HAVE REALLY DONE SOMETHING, because on Friday at breakfast, though my muscles have become throbbing, mean little pain-pretzels, I am mentally back where I need to be: coffee in hand, mind wide open, taking stock in the dining hall as the sun rises over the water. My hair tie was still buried under the covers along with my roommate when I let myself out of the room at 7 a.m., but I've replaced it with another. It doesn't fit quite the same, but we are bending, we are flexing, we are fine.

The smells of breakfast float through the air—frying eggs and hot veggie hash and, best of all, coffee. My stomach rumbles. The special is sprouted wheat English muffins with avocado butter, which I'd love to see Daniel's reaction to—is he into *anything* healthy? (and why do I hope the answer is no?)—but Daniel isn't here.

Personally, I have designs on the omelet station—wild mushrooms, a sprinkle of chives, a dollop of goat's cheese. Heaven. I check my watch and make a deal with my stomach: five more minutes of brain time to absorb whatever I can, and then it's food time.

From my spot nursing a mug of black coffee in the alcove, I note Craig and Brian holding hands at Shayna's table and looking angelically happy as they listen to Shayna, whose face is moving expressively. Did Craig apologize to Brian? Probably not. The Craigs of the world don't think they need to. The Brians of the world never insist that they do.

I note the reality TV star, Ana Durango-Carter, sulking alone with her phone, with only a teensy beige smoothie to comfort her. Skylar and her mom are serving themselves oatmeal, seemingly chipper. As I watch, Skylar's mom gives her daughter a tender look and tucks a tendril of her hair behind her ear. So there is some love there… though that doesn't excuse the dysfunction.

There's Serena at a corner table with sunglasses on, taking teensy sips of a dark-green smoothie. When my eyes land on her, I feel perfectly calm, and this is good. No visions of drowning her in her own pukey toilet this morning.

My plan for today is simple—find a way to get into one of Shayna's yoga classes. I want to see if she feels like the woman I knew from the show. The problem is, she's so popular that all her classes are booked for the next two weeks.

I should also sign up for one of Pat Burton's seminars and try to see if this guy is a harmless (if narcissistic) hippie, or something less savory. I didn't see him on the schedule for today, but there's a "fireside chat" tomorrow I could squeeze in…

I continue my slow perusal of the room.

Kyle, shaking his legs out by the juice bar as one of the juice mixologists feeds kale into the machine. The juice mixologist is cute, and I can tell by the angle of Kyle's body that he has noticed. I wonder what Kyle will ask her since obviously she's here for business, not pleasure.

Chad-the-Handsy, slouched in line behind Kyle (will he make a grab?).

Gloria, in earnest conversation with Pat Burton.

The acoustics of this room make it impossible for me to overhear anything unless I'm next to someone, but I make no move toward any of the people I'm evaluating. Right now I'm just reading the vibes.

Picking my target, as you can see, isn't exactly scientific. Yes, there's a roster that I study. Yes, I try to make observations. Yes, I try to be analytical in my final choice, and methodical once the target is determined. But there are a lot of guests, and a lot of staff, and studying them all to determine the perfect ranking would be an impossibility.

So much depends on chance—where I am at what time. Who else happens to be around. The odd conversation I happen to overhear, like Craig's nasty little attitude last night. Or Serena's drunken co-branding rant… Neither of which I would have been privy to if my roommate hadn't eaten bad airport shrimp.

So if Serena or Craig ends up being my final target, in a way, it wasn't my uberscientific analysis. It was the shrimp.

That's not to say they won't deserve it, and as long as I'm sure they do, I don't need a perfect method. I don't need to suss out the ethics of chance, or ruminate over whether something deeper like fate or destiny might be at work. In the end, I can't worry about what I can't know. Besides, there's no perfect in this world. Only our best, and I'm doing mine.

There's movement to my left. Daniel? *Quick, think of something witty to say. About sprouted wheat.* How do you flirt about wheat? I turn my head, smiling.

Oh. It's Vic.

"Hi," I say, noting his odd expression. Uh-oh. This is not Chipper Morning Vic.

"Lily. We need to talk."

"Something wrong?" I say lightly, as my heart pitter-patters like a nervous bird.

It's Serena, I just know it. She wants me gone after I saw her drunk and basically shouted at her. She ratted me out for breaking branding guidelines, and now Vic has to do her dirty work.

"I hate to interrupt your coffee moment, but—let's talk in my office."

Well, fuck. I'm about to get fired.

I take my coffee with me as I follow him. My brain whirls around various strategies like a washing machine on spin cycle. Should I appeal to my tenure? Her drunkenness? His mercy? We pass reception, into the hush of the administrative office area.

Damn it, Lily! I shouldn't have yelled at Serena. Or slammed my hand on the counter. *See what your short fuse just did?*

We've reached his office. He closes the door. The air freshener I normally enjoy is way too strong this morning. My nose tickles like someone is physically plunging the smell up into my sinuses.

"Sit, please." He looks genuinely distressed, so I sit, even though I'd prefer to stand.

He leans back in his chair with a sigh. The desk is between us.

"There's no easy way to do this." He puffs his cheeks, blows out air.

As tense as I am, it is strange to see him so worked up about talking to me. I've seen Vic fire people before—he's used me as a witness a few times over the years—and the man is a smooth wall of politeness. He's so good at it, I've witnessed people *thank him* for firing them. This Vic is…not that Vic. Does the man actually have emotions? And does he maybe actually kind of…care about me? I remind myself firmly that I don't need him to care about me. Just rehire me every year. And not fire me today.

"I know what you're going to say," I butt in, because his hesitancy is driving me crazy, and I might as well take the bull by the horns. "I was way out of line with Serena last night. It was a weird situation, but you're right, I didn't handle myself in a professional manner. I get that she's probably really upset about that. But you have to understand that she was really, really...*really* drunk." Three *really*s might speak to Vic, I hope? I'm about to launch into the pleading portion of my entreaty when Vic laughs with...relief?

"Thank *God*, you get it!" He leans back in his chair, looking like a weight has lifted. "Between you and me, Serena is out of control! Lily, that girl is going to send me to an early grave. I'm pushing forty, and in she comes with this chihuahua TikTok energy. And then she gets drunk with a journalist we're trying to impress?" He shakes his head and points a finger at me. "I owe you. You bailed me out, big-time. Unfortunately, now I have a huge favor to ask."

"Uh..." I'm too stunned by my reversal of fate to say much more.

He leans forward on the desk. "You and I both know about this big party at the Mambotel. It's not on-brand, but whatever, we're in the Caribbean. The problem is Serena. She has it in her head that she's going to go along *with the staff*! I told her right up front that this is not very vice-presidential of her, but you know what she told me? The Mambotel is a 'TikTok gold mine'!" He makes air quotes. "She's going to 'highlight its proximity to the Riovan' as part of our summer marketing push!" He pauses and purses his lips. "It's not a bad idea, honestly. I think it could add some voom to our website. We've always had a good relationship with the Mambotel. They're the yang to our yin. But—that's not the point! Serena. I need you to keep an eye on her tonight. That journalist, Daniel—you met him, right?"

I nod.

"A little birdie told me he's going to be there too, and we can't have another last night tonight. You get me?"

"Loud and clear. But…why me?"

"I trust you. You've been working here for years. You're a lifeguard. You…" He spins his hands. "Guard lives."

"*And* as a lifeguard, I've already been invited," I say with a little smile. If Vic, the executive manager, went along, it would be plain old weird.

"You get it," he says. "But I know this isn't your job. If you're not comfortable—"

"I can't do the early pool shift if I'm out partying all night."

Vic's face melts into a relieved smile. "I'll have Kenton reassign you."

"And I want in to Shayna's yoga class."

Vic's brows shoot up. "O-kay…"

"Her classes are booked for the next two weeks," I explain. "And I…really want to work out with her. I used to watch her show. I guess you could say I'm a fan."

Vic types at his computer for a moment, frowning. "How about tomorrow? Four p.m.?"

"Perfect."

"Glad I can return the favor." Vic holds my gaze for a moment. "Why do you come here every year, by the way? That journalist was asking." He tilts his head. "Which made me realize…I don't actually know."

"Why was he asking about me?" I shoot out without thinking.

But Vic waves a dismissive hand. "Oh, I mentioned that our focus with guests is brand loyalty, but some of the staff have become quite loyal too. He asked who, so I told him about you. And Nayna—and a couple of our trainers. I told him the Riovan is like a little family to me, and I'm the proud Papa."

Ew. There is nothing paternal or loving about Vic, but I'm not about to break it to him.

"So—what is it, exactly, that brings you back?" he says.

My mouth moves of its own accord, about to spit out something obvious like the beaches, or the weather. It would be so easy to give Vic some bullshit about how it's a dream job, and who wouldn't pay to work in a place like this, blah blah blah—but I really have known Vic for a long time, and something in me wants to be honest.

"Because this is the last place I was happy."

There's a beat of silence. It's not like we're about to get all emotional together. That's not Vic and that's not me. Not to mention I'd sooner kill the guy than hug him. But there's a moment. Then Vic says, "What happened to him?"

"Her," I say, with a humorless twist to my mouth. "She left me."

Vic gives me a compassionate frown. "You deserve better."

I stand up and recover my coffee mug. It's cold now. "No. She did."

CHAPTER 11

FIREWORKS EXPLODE IN THE DARK SKY, RED AND GREEN AND PURPLE lights falling like shattered streamers, adding their glow to the fairy lights and tiki torches that encircle the chaos of a thousand people partying hard on the Mambotel's expansive beach.

I'm sipping a Shirley Temple in one of the open-air bars as I watch Serena try to assemble the staff into a line for a picture in the sand with the ocean and the fireworks behind them. Watching Serena, after all, is the reason I'm here—and not just for Vic's sake. Magical, isn't it, when purposes align? And if I run into Daniel while I'm here…*I'll stay away.* Because, if I recall it accurately—and I do—during my last interaction with Daniel, I ended up joking around about a night of kinky sex.

The forty-minute chartered boat ride over to Saint Vitalis was a party in and of itself. Serena is all about the pregame, to the amazement of the staff, who really got into the whole "our VP is drinking with us" mood. I did quietly suggest, "You might want to slow down there, boss."

"Don't worry," Serena reassured me with a confidential smile. "I've got it under control."

"Yeah?"

She laughed. "I know, I know. Got to keep up good appearances for the brand." She lowered her voice. "Actually, Vic ripped me a new one today. He's totally bent out of shape about Daniel Black and his big article…" Her furrowed brow melted into a smirk as she raised her Manhattan. "But I know how to work journalists. Anyway, I've been thinking about his 'big article' too…"

"Ha-ha," I said, deadpan, suddenly unable to summon a smile.

By the time we docked at the Mambotel's marina, I had accumulated some useful information about Serena. She has a mild allergy to shellfish. A phobia of enclosed spaces. She's a graduate of the University of Maryland, and her parents work in PR firms in DC. Her top viral TikTok video wasn't one of her (many) sexy coastal bikini shots, but a video of her slipping on some rocks.

With a few flicks and swipes of her fingers, she pulled it up, and I leaned in to watch. The video wasn't long; just ten seconds or so. It was of Serena on the edge of the jetty. The ocean was lively, splashing up around the rocks and misting the air with rainbow sprays. Based on the angle, Serena had wedged her phone in the crevice of a rock so that she could record herself posing with the waves spraying up around her, but four seconds in, she slipped and fell on her butt. Tried to get up and slipped again. The next few seconds were a slow-motion replay of her falling, but zoomed into her bug-eyed expression. I had to admit, it was some smart editing.

"Two million views," she said with fake morosity, martini glass in hand (Manhattan long gone). "My friend actually posted it, and I was going to take it down, but…I guess people love to see that I'm actually human, or something. What are you gonna do?"

What are *you going to do, Serena?* I think, as I watch her try to arrange her tipsy staff for the perfect shot. Whether it's the inebriation or the mad energy of the party, everyone's having a little trouble following directions.

"Let's rearrange you and you." Serena shouts to be heard above the music as she switches Hannah and Kenton in the line. "And then, can you guys all move three steps forward?"

The Mambotel's beachfront stage, the beating heart of the party, is crammed with musicians dressed in shiny shirts who are all a little too into it, especially the smiling male singer whose hairy chest is mostly bared under what looks like an ice-skating costume: tight black pants and a blowsy shirt with ruffled sleeves that shimmer as he shakes a huge set of green and red maracas.

"Oh, la-la," he sings with exaggerated diction, his smile fierce, his maraca shake gleefully aggressive. Three ladies in towering fruit hats shimmy to his left. "Sing ta-ta…"

If his Ts get any sharper, he's going to cut someone.

Behind the lighted stage, the Mambotel itself is huge. Sandy-colored and brightly lit, with searchlights coming out of its center like a bouquet of light, roving the sky in sinuous circles.

The mood is crazy here. The party has the chaotic energy of a Chuck E. Cheese birthday party, but with way more skin on display. The smells of firework smoke, ocean salt, and marijuana make for a heady combination. Mambotel employees circulate around the crowd taking drink orders, dressed in exaggerated costumes: hugely oversize sombreros, grass skirts with coconut bras, the stripper's version of a flamenco skirt, even the odd pirate costume. Culturally insensitive? Obviously. Effective at drawing a crowd? Hell, yes.

Two open-air bars flank the stage, and both are doing brisk business, judging both by how long I had to wait to get my beverage as well as the giant sixty-dollar fishbowls of electric-blue drink with plenty of straws, meant for friends to share. They're everywhere, and from what I've already heard, they're strong.

I'm quite happy with my Shirley Temple, heavy as it is on the grenadine, watching Serena and my fellow staff members struggle to take a photo.

I haven't spotted Daniel yet. As a guest, he wasn't on the chartered boat with us—but I'm keeping my eyes peeled. Just for the purposes of reporting back to Vic, of course.

"Um, you? On the right," Serena barks suddenly. "Could you actually get out of the picture?"

A girl places a hand on her chest and mouths, "Me?" It's one of the massage technicians, a curvier girl dressed in a hot-pink bikini top and harem pants. Even though she is gorgeous, I know exactly why Serena doesn't want her in the shot.

"It's not personal," says Serena brightly, "but these are for the website, so everything has to be 200 percent on-brand. No offense."

I see the moment the girl realizes what's going on. That she's the one curvy body in the otherwise perfect line of sculpted muscle and tiny waists. Her face flushes, and she crosses her arms over her body and steps sideways in the sand, away from the group, her shoulders caved in.

"Great. That's it," says Serena, holding up her fancy phone to frame the shot again.

There's no visceral feeling of hatred rising in my chest toward Serena tonight. All I experience instead is a mental click as I file this moment away, taking note of the details: how casually Serena just humiliated this girl. How this was done in full view of the rest of the staff. How Serena doesn't even seem aware of what she's just done. Some narcissists, I've found, are strangely innocent about their own toxicity, oddly oblivious to the trail of hurt they leave in their wake.

Leaving the bar area, I stride toward the massage tech, drink in hand, sand shuffling up around my ankles.

"Hey. You want a drink? My treat?"

Her attempt at a smile is even sadder than a frown. "Oh, that's really nice!" Her accent is full Minnesota. "I'm Brianna. You're one of the lifeguards, aren't you?"

"Lily. Nice to—"

"Lily!" Serena's voice cuts into our little moment. "There you are! Get in the picture!"

I hesitate. I don't want to piss Serena off by refusing her—I do need to get closer to her, if she's going to be my next target. I'm also not going to waltz in and replace Brianna.

"No," I say, waving a hand but smiling. "I'm good."

Serena stomps her foot playfully in the sand. "I'm not taking this until you're in it! Come on! You look great, we need you!"

I feel a light touch on my arm. Brianna. "You go ahead."

I give Brianna a questioning look. She nods vigorously and gestures with both hands, like she's trying to sweep me toward the action. Fine. At this point, resisting will just be a bad look.

"Arms around each other!" coaches Serena as I join the line. That's the moment I spot Daniel, maybe thirty feet away from us, dressed in shorts and another white button-up, fending off a Mambotel employee dressed as a pirate who seems to be trying to coax a drink order out of him with a prop sword.

I flip my attention back to Serena's phone and smile as she clicks away.

"We're having fun! Perfect, yes! Hold your drinks up! Now put them down in the sand. OK, now everyone jump in the air! Now let's pretend we're dancing, big smiles—we're getting some video, this is so good, who's got some moves?"

As Jason from London breaks it down in a twerky chicken dance, I recover my drink from the sand—yep, ruined—and slink back away, looking for Brianna. I still owe the girl a drink. But she's disappeared. Is she OK? Maybe she's in one of the porta-potties. They're set up at both ends of the beach. I have no way of knowing which way she might have gone. I should be sticking close to Serena, but I'll go back in a second.

It's not long before I'm away from the stage. On this quieter section of the beach, people are sitting around fire pits in chill circles, smoking joints and passing beverages. Fireworks are still popping off above the water here and there. A cool breeze stirs the hem of my dress.

Suddenly, I spot not Brianna, but *him*. Alone, sitting in the sand by the shore. His back is to me, and the murmur of his voice tells me he's on the phone.

I slip off my flip-flops and hook them around my finger, then walk toward him quietly. It can't hurt to say hello. Right? *Oh God.*

The sound of the waves is hypnotic. Rhythmic. Relentless. And the sound of Daniel's voice is even nicer—decisive, deep—

I'm finally close enough to make out what he's saying.

"...why here? Why any of this? If we can't answer the why, we can't hope to stay one step ahead—" His head jerks around—he must have sensed my presence. "Lily. You scared the—" He smacks a hand to his chest, exhales, then laughs as he lowers his phone.

"I didn't mean to sneak up on you." I gesture to his phone. Based on the angle he was holding it, it looks like he was recording a voice memo. "Sorry to interrupt."

"Don't apologize."

"Taking notes for your article?"

"Yeah."

I make quotation marks with my fingers. "'Why any of this?'" I mean it to be playful, but he looks uneasy. "Sounds serious."

"Yeah, well…you know…" He gestures at the dark ocean in front of us, where a tiny glinting light represents the Riovan. From here, it feels like I could pinch my fingers and snuff it out.

"The intense-wellness culture deserves our curiosity, you know?" he says. "What drives people to drop all this money on their bodies?"

"Easy." I sit next to him with a light laugh, stretching my legs out in the sand. "The Riovan makes its money from people who desperately want to love themselves. The market is huge, because people are taught to fear their own bodies, and fear breeds hatred."

I'm impressed that I said that. Though…maybe not my smartest move, revealing to an investigative journalist that I don't actually think the sun shines out of the Riovan's ass.

He grins. "Can I quote you on that?"

"Hell, no," I say with a grin of my own.

"Well, at least satisfy my curiosity. If that's what you think of the Riovan, why come back so often?"

Ah. The same question he asked Vic. But I have no temptation toward honesty tonight; Daniel gets my standard response.

"Sun. Sand. A break from Cincinnati."

"Low hourly pay."

"Trainers who can help me fine-tune my goblet squat."

He laughs. "What the hell is a goblet squat?"

I give him a coy smile. "Do you need me to show you?"

"Under different circumstances, I'd be tempted to say yes."

"I don't think poorly of the Riovan, though," I say quickly. I got a little too negative too fast, and I have a cover to maintain. "I'm not *anti*-fitness. It's just…never mind. Ignore everything I've said. I get philosophical when it's late."

He nods affably. "So what do you do in Cincinnati when you're not lifeguarding?"

I hesitate. Then again, he could find this on Google. "I run a catering business."

"An entrepreneur. Hey, I bet you serve bacon," he says with mock longing.

I have to laugh at this. It's a good feeling, laughing. It makes my body feel awake, alive.

"Bacon-wrapped dates with blue-cheese sauce," I count playfully on my fingers. "Bacon and spring greens risotto. Bacon and maple doughnuts. Bacon cheddar biscuits—"

"Stop!" he begs. "I can only take so much temptation. So, Ohio State graduate?"

"Uh…I'm more of a school of life kind of girl."

"That fits in with my theory about you."

"You have a theory about me?" I shouldn't be loving that so much.

He smiles self-deprecatingly. "I have a theory about everyone. It's a journalist thing."

OK, that's fine, we're fine.

He continues, "I see you as a maverick. And by that, I don't mean a rebel. I think you're a very ethical person. It's just…I feel like you're the kind of person who has their own moral code." His eyes challenge me. *True?*

I keep my expression neutral, but my heart is beating fast. Really fast. *Is this a smart game to play?*

"What else?" I find myself saying.

He tents both hands at his mouth, hiding a tiny smile. "You're old beyond your years. I think you saw a lot growing up, and it's made you guarded." A flash of firework lights his face briefly. "You're independent. You're not afraid of being alone. But…I think you're deeply lonely."

Fuck. How can he have seen…all of this? Who is this guy?

"So," he says. "This is the part where you tell me I'm totally off base."

I should shut this down. Say something trite, stand up, rejoin my group. Brianna! Where is she?

"No…you're right," I say, absentmindedly looking over my shoulder, as if I'm expecting Brianna to be lurking nearby. "I…I did have to grow up fast. My mom died of breast cancer when I was young. I got a lot of unwelcome attention. I had to figure my shit out real fast." I throw a quick glance at Daniel. *Are you happy now?* "Whatever. It's in the past."

I wait for his reaction, but he's silent. Saying nothing is probably one of those dirty journalist tricks that gets people to talk even more. Won't work on me, bud.

"And the lonely part?" he finally presses. "Was I wrong about that?"

I dart another glance his way. His eyes are hooded. Is this a come-on? Maybe. Do I care?

My heart is beating fast. I shouldn't be saying anything more about myself. I come back to the Riovan year after year because I do my job and I don't draw attention to myself. My invisibility is my reentry ticket, and revealing shit about myself could really screw things up down the road.

"I did have someone," I say quickly. "We were in love. I was going to marry her."

"What happened?"

Of course he would ask that. I went there.

The question is, do I want to keep going?

I peel my eyes away from Daniel and look out at the ocean. The reflections of the fireworks in the water seem more melancholy than festive here on the darker, quieter area of the beach. I remember lying back with Mom on a picnic blanket every Fourth of July. We'd hold hands as we watched the sky bloom into a living garden of light. Fireworks blaze so powerfully, you can't look away. They overwhelm your senses with light and sound. And then, they're over, and the sky is black and empty again.

"She's gone," I say. To Daniel. To the ocean. To myself. My heart is thundering. I swallow. Do I make it sound like we broke up, like I did this morning with Vic? Something about Daniel is suddenly demanding more from me. And the scary thing is, I want to respond.

"There was…an accident. I…I blame myself."

He's silent for a moment, as if waiting to see if I'll offer more. I don't, even though I want to. The story is pressing on my heart, pressing for release. Instead, I wrap my arms around my torso, like that will help me keep it all in. *Oof.* It's not just thinking about Jessica. This stark summation of my life I've just given to Daniel? It's a story without a lot of fluff. A life that was mostly hard. It feels…depressing. Depressing as hell.

It also doesn't escape my notice that within minutes of talking to Daniel, I've revealed the two biggest events of my life: losing my mom and losing my girlfriend. What's scariest is that, far from taking it all back, I want to give him more.

That's the thing about starting; it's hard to stop.

"Her name was Jessica," I say, and as I utter her name, my throat squeezes painfully. I place my palms in the sand, as if trying to find an anchor in something bigger than me. Something stable. Instead, I think of the grains of sand, and how once they were rock, strong and stable, now mere specks, remnants of what they were. So small, who could even distinguish one from the other?

"I've always liked the name Jessica," he says.

"Yeah. Me too."

The waves lap the shore. The music from the Mambotel pulses in the background. Down the beach, two pirates perform a choreographed sword fight to cheering onlookers. I think, *What a strange world.*

Daniel and I sit quietly, side by side. He says nothing, but he says, *I'm sorry*, and I say nothing, but I say, *I know.*

CHAPTER 12

SATURDAY IS BUSY, THE POOLS AND THE BEACH CROWDED WITH DAY-
trippers from Saint Vitalis. We go there at night, they come here
during the day.

I sleep in until ten—we didn't get back from the Mambotel until
3 a.m.—and, after reporting back to Vic that Daniel and Serena
didn't even cross paths, I get busy with lifeguarding duties, starting
with a supply inventory for Kenton, the Lifeguarding Team lead.

As I walk through the supplies room and tick buoys and oars
and life vests off the inventory sheet, I'm narrowing the list in my
head. I have my longlist, of course, but I like to get it down to three
by the end of the first week, which is approaching fast. Of everyone
I've considered, Serena is an obvious first choice. Craig, an iffy but
possible second. The third slot, however, is really giving me trouble.

Kyle, however high he may rate on the international scale of assholery, doesn't have the particular flavor of poison I'm here to find. Ana
Durango-Carter is so private, she's hard to get a read on—not to
mention she has issued a public apology for her insensitive comment

about her costar. Perhaps she's learned her lesson? Skylar's mom is kicking around in my mind, but that small tender gesture at breakfast and the look of love I saw in her eyes is making me lean toward *no*. I have considered Shayna for slot three. But my biggest impressions of her are still from *Take It Off*—i.e., years out of date. Ugh. Usually I'm in a much better position by now.

It's Daniel. I have to face it: He's a distraction. I've spent way too much time thinking about him when I should be focusing on my potential targets.

During my lunch break, as I pick at a microgreen salad alone at one of the window-side tables, a brief, dangerous thought slides into my brain. What if I let myself pursue things with Daniel—or at least, explore the possibilities? What if, instead of putting on the brakes every time I see him, I give myself permission to—

What, you little fool?

There is no "possibility." There would always be pieces of myself I'd have to withhold, and I'm smart enough to know that doesn't work long-term. The choices I've made are not compatible with a normal, healthy relationship. Not now. Not ever. And I know myself well enough that a fling with Daniel wouldn't be enough to satisfy what I'm feeling. It would just make me want more.

As I wrap up my afternoon shift at the lap pool, I resolve to distance myself from Daniel. I can ice him out, like I've done with every other person who's demonstrated even the mildest interest in me for the past five years. The hot city council member who gave me the contract to cater his meetings and was a dead ringer for Ryan Gosling. The barista girl with the blue hair. That pitcher for the Cincinnati Reds.

Right before dinner, I head to the yoga class I signed up for yesterday, and even though Daniel joins at the last minute two rows behind me, I focus fully on Shayna's surprisingly soothing instructions. As I wrap my right leg over my left and intertwine my arms for eagle pose, letting myself feel the satisfying amount of effort it takes to maintain balance, I determine that the next time Mr. Black comes around, no matter how werewolfish his energy, no matter how much he makes me want to reveal my deepest, darkest self, I will be stone cold.

Shayna, I notice, is lovely to everyone and gives modifications for a heavy-set woman with a leg injury with the gentlest of touches. No yelling, no body shaming; nothing but calm, steady encouragement from the former queen of breaking people down on national television. I find myself grimacing in my downward-facing-dog position as I hear her say, "You're doing so good, Traci," to the woman in question.

Forty minutes later, when class ends, I'm covered in sweat. I'm rolling up my yoga mat when she approaches me.

"Hey, I haven't met you before."

"Lily. One of the lifeguards." We shake. Both our palms are sweaty.

"You're welcome in my class anytime."

"I used to watch your show," I blurt out. "*Take It Off*?"

"Yeah, a lot of people watched that show," she says with a dry, raspy laugh. Do I detect a hint of regret? I press on.

"You really helped a lot of people lose weight."

"Thanks," she says, but her expression doesn't seem pleased. "Let's just say I wish we had prioritized the long-term health of the contestants. Losing all that so quick...it wasn't sustainable."

"You were such a badass, though," I prod.

"I'm glad you enjoyed it," she says, and I recognize a forced smile when I see one. "But I'd do it all differently if I had the chance."

"Well..." I say lamely, vaguely registering out of the corner of my eye that Daniel is leaving the studio. "I guess hindsight is twenty-twenty."

"I guess it is."

I return my yoga mat to its place, then take a long drink from my water bottle.

Ugh. I hate that I like her.

No. You hate that you're losing your biggest potential number three and you're not sure who should take her place.

Of course it's great that she's showing signs of having changed. It's not like I was hoping she'd embarrass Traci or anyone else for my sake. It's not like I was hoping she was still the monster from years and years ago. But I leave her class feeling the weight of that empty third slot like an iron around my neck.

In the evening, I sit in on Pat Burton's "fireside chat," *The Mind as a Muscle*, and even though I notice Daniel one row in front of me, and he turns around multiple times to catch my eye, I look stubbornly forward.

Could it be Pat? But by the time he's giving his closing remarks, I'm just not seeing it. He definitely loves the sound of his own voice. His "deep" observations, such as "habits are the tools we use to train ourselves for the race of life," felt like poorly disguised clichés. His boot-straps story of his rise to success was ick, and honestly, the whole "manifesting" thing he's obsessed with is just a way to pretend you have control over the things you don't. It's self-deception at its finest.

But none of these qualities makes him deserving of the slot.

So Shayna's a no. Pat's a no.

Who, then?

To comfort myself over the missing piece in my mental plan, as Pat moves on to Q&A, I start sketching out a few potential plans for the two I do have. Very loose, but this is how it starts. Serena could fall down a staircase. She's known for her lack of coordination all over TikTok, after all…and she sure drinks enough that it would be easy to chalk up to inebriation. I could help with that part too. Not to mention, I know just the stairs. A memory sparks—the long yawn of the steep descent to the basement indoor pool. The wet cling of the moist air. The echoey slap of his flip-flops as he headed down, AirPods in, head bobbing, completely oblivious to my presence. The muffled yell—the noisy tumble of his fall—then, the sharp silence—

I shiver the memory off. *Not now.*

Craig. Craig is easier. He loves the sauna, but he can only spend a few minutes in there due to his heart condition. What if he lost track of time? How could I facilitate that?

There's applause; I guess the Q&A is over.

"Hey, Lily—" Daniel says as we both rise, but I simply work my way out of the row and walk away, as if I didn't even hear him.

Men, I've noticed, are quite insecure, even the ones with bristly, masculine five-o'clock shadows. A single freeze is usually enough to put them off for quite a while, if not forever. Daniel will be no different.

And this does not make me sad.

Sunday morning, I line up behind Craig and Brian at the smoothie bar (Craig orders for Brian; another small humiliation for the file). And who gets in line behind me but Daniel. It definitely feels like he's following me.

Don't flatter yourself, I remind myself harshly.

"Morning," he says behind me, so close I can feel the warmth of his breath on my neck. Goose bumps race down my arms, my back.

Admit it, Lily Lennox. You're into this guy, and he's forcing you to remember that sex exists.

Annoying, really. I've done just fine without it for five years.

But have you?

Everything in me wants to turn around. *Stone cold*, I remind myself, and even though my heart pounds like it's trying to get out of the jail I've shoved it in, I don't acknowledge him.

It sucks—in fact, it *really* sucks—but on the other hand, it's reassuring that I'm sticking with my earlier decision. *See? I'm still in control.*

What makes it even suckier is that Daniel has insights about me that no one else has ever had, not even Jessica. I know in some deep part of me that he could really get me—if I let him. Yes, Jess was the love of my life, but I try not to wear rose-colored glasses about anything—not even her—though it's tempting, isn't it, to cling to the fairy-tale version scrubbed of all the shit? The truth is, it *was* a fairy tale. *And* there was shit. Both are true. With her, I was my most authentic, naked self; for a while, in the safety of her love, I experienced a freedom I have never since felt. Right before the end, though, we stopped truly seeing each other. The curiosity Daniel has about me? The way he looks at me, like he's on a mission to figure me out? Jessica and I stopped doing that. Instead of seeing each other, we just saw our own hurts. And that made us feel alone. Even together, we felt alone.

I think back to our return from the Riovan. We got back to Cincinnati in the afternoon and took a taxi home. As soon as I unlocked the door, Jess stomped off to the bedroom and started unpacking her bag. Doing that silent, angry cry, where tears just spilled down her cheeks. It had all started at the airport during our Miami layover. I bought a bag of M&M's, and she snuck a handful. I didn't realize until she started crying that she'd made a commitment at the Riovan to do a thirty-day junk-food ban, and was pissed at herself for breaking it within the first few hours of leaving.

"My nutritionist said I'm fat because I make lazy choices," she said, angrily—but at herself, I could tell, not the nutritionist.

"That was a horrible thing for him to say, Jess," I said, both shocked that someone would say something so appalling to her and stung that she hadn't told me about this interaction before. If she'd told me while we were still at the Riovan, I could have gone to bat for her and raised hell with a manager. "I hope you told him to go fuck himself."

"He's the expert, Lil. And maybe his delivery wasn't on point, but he was right."

I reached over and rubbed her shoulder. "No, babe. He was a dick to you, and I totally would have kicked his ass if I knew. No one gets to talk to you like that, OK?"

She pulled her shoulder away from my hand.

Wait—was she mad at *me* now? I was on her side! Anyway, her "screwup" was just a couple of minuscule pieces of chocolate. Now that I knew about her commitment, I could support her.

I sat on the bed, feeling frustrated. Jessica's back was to me. The ring was still in my pocket. The moment to propose had never come, and now it felt like it was slipping further and further away with Jessica's dark mood.

Couldn't we be mad together at the nutritionist?

"It was just a few M&M's," I said.

"Your body is a history of your decisions," Jessica said fiercely. Where had I just heard that? Oh yeah, one of the seminars at the Riovan. "Every decision is important, Lily. Especially the small ones. That's what I realized this week, and I've already fucked it up."

"I'm sorry you let yourself down, or whatever," I said, determined to get back on track. I'd been looking forward to a cozy, snuggly evening watching a movie. We could have salad for dinner. Kale chips, or a bulgur bowl. Whatever Jessica wanted. "I'm sorry I, like... facilitated that, by buying those stupid M&M's. I get that—"

"No," she said, whipping a dirty T-shirt toward the laundry hamper and missing. "You don't get it. You can eat whatever you want and you don't gain any weight. You don't even work out, and...!" She turned, face raw. Her hand swept up and down through the air, like she was saying, *Look at yourself.*

I wrapped my arms around my torso as an all-too-familiar wave of shame broke through me. A shame I hadn't felt since meeting Jessica, but which was also familiar as dirt. It used to cling to me like a second skin. When I moved, it moved with me, like a shadow self. During the foster-care years, I heard it again and again, in not so many words. *Beauty means trouble.* My looks were not to be celebrated. They were a liability. A target. A vulnerability and a weapon. I know that's why my first foster family only kept me for two months.

"She's too much of a handful," I overheard the mom, Dana, explaining to the social worker on the phone as she folded laundry. I had the door of my bedroom cracked so that I could listen. "She's not a bad girl, but...it's just not a good fit right now. I have to think of the whole family." Like her husband, Scott, who couldn't keep his eyes off me. Like their teenage son, Tim, just a year younger than me, who was clearly in puppy love with me. I'd seen my name written over and over again in his notebook. *It's not my fault!* I wanted to scream. *I didn't do anything! I'm sorry I was born this way!*

When Jessica waltzed into that bar with her college friends the night we met, it was like she gifted me with a new self. She erased all the old feelings. Jessica made me feel like my beauty, my body, were finally on my side. My beauty didn't just get her attention. It opened the door to love.

On the bed, watching her unpack, a hurricane of feeling raged through my body.

"I've always loved you just how you are," I exploded. "How dare you throw the way I look in my face!"

Jessica was never cruel, but that afternoon, her laugh sounded cruel to me. "You have no idea what it's like to live in a body you hate."

I went so cold in that moment. The words *Yes, I fucking do* burned in my mouth. I swallowed them like an ice chip. They hurt going down.

I'd only given Jessica the barest sketch of my tumultuous childhood. It was understood between us that I didn't want to talk about any of my *befores*—not the trailer park, or Mom's death, or foster care. Jessica and I were living in our happily ever after, and that is where I wanted to stay.

So maybe, in retrospect, it was my fault that she didn't understand how for so long I felt that my body was the enemy, attracting danger, marking me as trouble, chasing me from one family to another. How beauty made me the predator and the prey. How for years and years I hated my body, just like her.

But in that moment, I wasn't thinking clearly. I wasn't thinking logically. All that mattered was that my Jessica, my love, my safe place, was suddenly telling me that it must be so easy to be me because of my beautiful body, when I'd spent most of my life wishing it away.

The words I had swallowed surged back up like bile.

"Yes. I. Fucking. Do."

Even to my own ears, my whisper sounded like steel, and for a moment, I felt dangerous.

We stared at each other, Jessica still crouched and tear-streaked by the messy guts of her luggage, me sitting on the side of the bed with clenched fists, the engagement ring cold in its tiny box in my sweatshirt pocket. The ring I'd meant to propose with—but Jessica kept putting me off when I suggested we take a romantic walk. *We can do romantic walks in Cincinnati! We only have a few days here, Lil. I want to take advantage of…* The trainer. The nutritionist. The life coach. You name it.

"You look like a goddamn Barbie doll, Lily. I'm fat. OK? Look at me! I'm disgusting!"

"I thought our love went beyond how we looked."

Jessica stood, rage and tears mingled in her face. "I'm sleeping at my parents' tonight."

It's only now, all these years later, that I see how she may have heard my comment. *I thought our love went beyond how we looked.* I meant it as a reassurance. That even though of *course* I was attracted to her sexually, our bodies and how they looked were never at the root of our love. Now, I think she heard it as me agreeing that she was disgusting. If I could rewind time, I'd overcome that cold feeling that had taken hold of me. I'd wrestle it back with all my strength. I'd stuff my own pain aside. Then I'd burst up from the bed and enfold her in my arms and topple over with her on the mess of unpacking. I'd pull out the ring and thread it onto her finger and whisper, *You're beautiful. Period*, over and over, until she believed me.

"May I take your order, ma'am?" says the cheerful smoothie mix-ologist, snapping me out of the memory.

I roll my shoulders and plaster a smile on my face.

"Spinach and carrot juice, please, with a touch of jalapeño."

"And would you like to add any protein powders to that this morning?"

"Why the hell not," I say. As he puts the veggies through the whirring juicer, I can't help but think of that bag of M&M's at Miami airport. It's not like things would have turned out differently without it. There would have been another bag of M&M's, or chips, or whatever, at some other time. The problem wasn't that we live in a world full of snacks. The problem was that we live in a world full of Riovans.

Even in the flames of my anger after what happened to Jessica, when I was soliciting every news outlet on God's green earth to help me take down the Riovan, part of me always knew it wouldn't be enough. Knock this place down, and another will rise up. The problem was too big for me—a Medusa, a cancer, growing faster than I could ever hope to excise it.

"Enjoy," says the mixologist, handing me a cup full of muddy brown-orange vegetable sludge.

When I walk away with my beverage, I notice Daniel is no longer behind me—in fact, he's left the dining hall.

Good.

Sunday during my beach shift, storm clouds roll in late in the morning. The other lifeguard signals to me and I give a thumbs-up; time for storm protocols.

It's a familiar routine. I switch the safety flag to red, then make for the shoreline, blowing my whistle and waving at the half dozen swimmers still in the water.

"Everyone out of the water, please!"

People gather up towels and beach bags, looking nervously at the sky. I don't blame them. It's hurricane season, after all.

As the wind picks up and the waves roll in with climbing intensity,

I put up the DO NOT SWIM warning sign. That's when I notice a straggler who seems to think it's time to bodysurf. *Yeah, bud, that's how you die.* I blow the whistle in two sharp bursts, then shout, "Hey! Time to come in!"

By the time the first fat drops of rain hit the sand shortly after, the last guests are running toward the hotel, including the errant bodysurfer. My fellow lifeguard is beating a retreat with his gear, and I signal to him that I'll be right behind him. Alone on the beach, I linger for a moment, relishing the roar of the waves and the pelt of the raindrops, letting the wind rip through my hair.

The first night I planned on proposing to Jessica, a storm came up suddenly, just like this. The rocks would be slippery, wet. Too dangerous. I put it off.

There's always tomorrow, I thought.

But the next night, she wasn't herself. "I'm hitting the gym," she said when I suggested a walk. "My trainer set a really aggressive goal for me, so."

"But didn't you already work out this morning?"

"Yeah, well, some of us have to work harder at it than others," she said, with a hint of bitterness that I now know was a warning sign of what was to come. But at the time, I brushed it off, reminding myself that she'd been up at six for the sunrise yoga and hadn't stopped since; she was just tired and cranky. I'd give her some space. We had four days left. There were parts in our life that were tight—money, our small apartment, our shared closet—but time was not one of them. We were rich in time.

"OK," I said. "Well, have a good workout. I'm going to hit up the sauna, if you want to join me later."

I yelp with surprise at a sudden masculine voice behind me.

"Need help?"

I whip around, snapping my reverie shut, again becoming aware of my surroundings—and the man standing inches from me, dark hair blowing in the wind. Daniel. A sharp jolt of irritation makes my lips tighten. Why is he popping up everywhere I go? I'd ignore him again, but with only the two of us on the entire beach right now, it's a bit harder to pretend I don't see him.

"No, thanks. I got it," I say, as I bend to grab my towel and fling it over a shoulder.

"Look. Lily—" He runs a free hand through his hair, which is already wild. He's barefoot, sweatpants rolled up past his ankles, in a soft gray hoodie that the wind is sticking to his muscled body, with that stupid five-o'clock shadow that I want to run my stupid palms over. "Did I say something wrong?"

"What do you mean?" I say without looking at him, as I climb the lifeguard chair to detach the umbrella, which strains against me as I try to close it. Even I can hear how fake my question sounds.

"I mean, did I offend you somehow?"

It physically hurts to ignore him, but hey, short-term pain for long-term gain.

He raises his voice above the wind. "If I did something, or said something, at least give me the chance to apologize."

I'm so tempted to look down at him, but avoiding eye contact is key. I focus on pushing in the metal peg to detach the umbrella. Of course, it sticks. My ponytail whips around my face, a flurry of raindrops stinging my cheek. ·

"When you shared about Jessica—" he shouts up, and something about hearing her name on his lips makes me snap.

"It's not that!" I shout down at him.

The peg snaps inward; the umbrella detaches. I slide it off the pole and muscle it down. The wind screeches in my ears.

"Then what is it?" he calls up.

"I'm just busy!" I start making my descent, umbrella tucked by my side. "I have a job here."

"No! Something is wrong!" he shouts over the wind. "Why won't you tell me what it is?"

I focus on getting the clipboard off the chair. *Stupid, stubborn man.* "Get inside, Daniel! The storm!"

"You know what I think?"

"Nope," I yell, focusing now on getting everything bundled together in my arms. Umbrella. Clipboard. Flotation device. Towel. Self-possession.

I take off across the sand, the wind beating at my back, Daniel running alongside. The palm trees by the hotel are nearly bent double. The rain comes in swift flurries, then stops, then starts again.

"I think you're attracted to me, and you don't know what to do with your feelings."

I laugh sharply, stop for a second, and give him the incredulous look he deserves. My ponytail lashes furiously at my face. "Just because you're hot doesn't mean every single woman wants you, Daniel!" I resume my forward march.

"Don't do that!"

A gust of wind whips some sand up. I lift an arm to protect my eyes.

"What?" I yell.

"This," he says. I don't stop walking, but in my peripheral vision I can see him gesturing with his arms. "This…*game.* You want me to leave you alone? OK! You hate my guts for some reason? I can handle that! But that's not it. So what is it?"

A ferocious gust of wind nearly sends us tumbling into each other. He steadies my elbow, just a brief moment of contact. Enough to make me want more. Everything about Daniel makes me want more. More of his attention. More of his body. More from myself... and my life.

My throat is tight.

What is it? It's that Daniel isn't just a guy I could have fun in bed with. A one-night stand wouldn't be enough to get him out of my system. No, this is someone—

"Watch out!" yells Daniel. There's a rough hand on my arm, yanking hard. My knees hit sand; the wind catches my towel, and it flies through the air like a drunk bird just as a folding chair hurtles past my ears, so close that I can hear the whistle of the wind through its metal rods. Both Daniel and I watch as the chair bounces across the sand before vaulting into the water.

"Shit," I breathe, still crouched. The angle of Daniel's body momentarily protects me from the brunt of the wind's force. Adrenaline pumps through me. "That was close."

"Let's get inside," he says, and before I can object, I'm tucked under his arm, and we're running toward safety in tandem. As we approach the hotel and the fence that encloses one of the pools, I can see staff running around, securing the rest of the chairs.

Daniel yanks open one of the poolside doors into the hotel, fighting the wind. We tumble into an empty hallway by the laundry room. As soon as the door closes behind us, the silence rings in my ears.

"Thank you," I say, and then suddenly I'm looking into Daniel's eyes. Damn it, I've been avoiding eye contact for a reason. The chill of the air conditioning sizzles coldly on my wet skin.

"So. What did I do?"

The rain beats against the glass door. My muscles are clenched like a boxer before a round, and my back teeth grind together. Daniel Black is the most maddening individual I have ever met.

I throw down the gear. "Why can't you let it go?"

"Because if I did something wrong, I have to own it."

Well, fuck. I know how that feels.

"There's something between us," he says.

"Exactly," I say, relieved he said it first. "Unfortunately, I'm not into flings."

"OK."

"What do you even want from me? An island romp?"

"Is that what you want from me?" A tiny grin appears on his lips, and I can read what he's thinking. *So you are attracted to me.*

"How could you know what I want?"

"I'll know if you tell me."

I put my hand on my forehead and release a growl of frustration. "Fuck, Daniel! I don't know how to…"

Be myself and hide myself at the same time.

Remain guarded when he makes me feel so safe.

I've already revealed so much to this guy that I never planned on sharing. If I let myself get closer, what the hell else will I spout out? What if I slip up?

"What are you scared of?" Daniel says.

I sink back against the wall with a sigh of defeat. I don't want to fight this. I don't want to fight *him.*

"You."

He holds my gaze for a moment, then nods. He takes a step closer, so close I can smell the salt on his skin. He lifts a hand and grazes my jawline with it, sending shivers down my body.

"Am I really that scary?"

My heart pounds. With my eyes, I say, *Yes.*

With his eyes, he says, *Why?*

I try to send back, *It's not you. It's me,* but I'm not sure if he gets that part because then he leans in. It's like the past few days of orchestrated avoidance on my part have been a mere delay, a tiny hiccup as we rush toward what feels like the inevitable conclusion. My eyes slip closed in surrender, and our lips meet. His mouth searches mine, and I feel my body arching against the wall, our hips grazing. He cups one hand against my face, the other at the small of my back, guiding my body closer to his.

I don't know if the kiss lasts five seconds or five minutes, but when I pull back, I'm breathless, shaking, somehow pulled out of time and place, like I'm not at the Riovan anymore but somewhere both undefined and more real than wherever it is I've been living for the past five years.

In other words, the opposite of detached.

I was right. This isn't just someone I could spend a fun night with. This is someone I could fall for. *Fuck.*

My mind is chaos, bumping along like an empty can tied to the back of the speeding car that is my body.

"What are we doing?" I whisper, my hand reaching up to run against the grit of his stubble, like I've wanted to do since I saw him that first morning at the coffee alcove. God, it feels good. I like him rough, and the entire surface area of my body is wondering if he gives it rough too.

His eyes probe mine. The corner of his mouth lifts. His voice is hypnotic as he murmurs, "You tell me, Lily Lennox."

I lean into his neck. His spicy, sweaty smell overwhelms me, and just like I knew I would, I want more. I lean into his ear, and against my better judgment, from some hungry place Daniel Black has opened in me like a cavity of desire, I whisper, "How close is your room?"

CHAPTER 13

THE STORM LASHES AGAINST THE WINDOW OF DANIEL'S ROOM. IN THE
dim light, it feels like we've left the world behind and entered some
liminal dream space where anything might happen. He turns the
deadbolt on the door, then walks toward me slowly. I don't break our
gaze as I step out of my sweatpants, now dressed only in my bathing
suit. My heart is drumming in my chest. It's been so long. Do I even
know how to do this?

He stops a few inches from me and strokes my jaw with his
thumb. Daniel's breathing is even, his movements controlled; this is
a man who is not in a hurry. I might not even know that he wanted me
right now, except for the erection pushing against his pants.

"Are you sure?" he says.

I nod, mute.

"If at any point you want me to stop—" he says.

Without breaking eye contact, he peels down the top of my bathing suit. His eyes say *Still OK?* and I send back *Yes*.

Outside the window, the furious ocean rolls onto the beach in punishing waves. The wind beats at the glass, and our bodies are cast in gray light.

His gaze drops and tracks over me, taking in the fall of my breasts, still without touching. But my body responds as if he was, my breathing growing heavy, my nipples contracting, a dull pulse pounding between my legs.

Daniel tilts his head, his gaze returning to mine. "What do you want, Lily?"

I lick my lips. What do I want? A lot, suddenly. His tongue on my breasts. His mouth between my legs. His dick, as deep in me as he can get it. But all I can manage to say is, "You."

The same way I just answered his question, *What are you scared of?* Maybe it's always the thing we're afraid of that we also want the most.

My head is swimming with heat. I'm very, very wet. Which I hope Daniel will discover very, very soon. I feel greedy for the moment his fingers discover how vigorously my body responds to him.

"Come here," he says. He peels off my bathing suit the rest of the way, and we fall on to the bed together. He pushes me onto my back and straddles my hips. I run my hands up his muscled torso, taking him in—his solidity, the tattoo on his arm I can now see is a dragon with the tail curling around his forearm. Slowly, I trail my finger over its lines.

Bracing his arms on either side of me, he leans in and gives me a look that says, *You like what you see?* I sigh my agreement. Then, his mouth is on mine, warm and wet. He kisses me with a slow, deep urgency. I can feel the promise of the weight of him hovering just above me, and I want it so bad, all of him, crashing down on me. Instead, all I get is the brush of his chest, feather-light on my skin. I arch my back so that my breasts push into him harder. *I need you now.*

He cups my neck with one hand as his kiss deepens, and then his hand moves down me, taking me in by touch—the swell of my breasts, the plane of my stomach, the tender, sensitive flesh between my legs—

Ah. His fingers slip into just the right place, and I groan. Daniel in bed is just like Daniel out of bed. Deliberate. Focused. There's a wordless communication that somehow flows between us, and I know based on his microadjustments as he explores my body with his fingers, with his mouth, that he's reading my every sigh, my every movement, learning from my reactions, zeroing in on what I want.

It doesn't take long until a searing pleasure is burning between my legs, a sensation so close to pain I can hardly take it. Daniel's strong, patient fingers and his capable tongue bring me to the edge.

As the burning becomes nearly unendurable, I cry out, "I can't—" because the feelings are so strong, and my body isn't used to this anymore, but he says, "You can. Let go," and that's what sends me over.

"Ah—" I gasp, and it's all I can do to smother a scream as I fall into a release that feels like a sun flare ripping through me in wave after wave, destroying everything but hot sensation.

It's only after I'm whimpering in the aftermath, legs trembling, that Daniel takes his pants off and rolls on a condom. He lifts himself above me, powerful arms braced, and plunges in, angling our bodies just right so that each thrust hits that spot.

"You're going to make me come again," I whimper.

"Good," he says with wolfish pleasure, as my body opens for him like a cloven fruit, my hips pushing up so that he can thrust even deeper. I'm no longer in control of anything, least of all myself. All I want is to be taken over by this—by him—by this devastating feeling that is more powerful than I am, that demands my utter surrender.

I cry out as my eyes squeeze shut, my body arching under his.

I have a moment of panic as I sense another mind-erasing crush of pleasure about to take me. I could fight it. Try to stay in control. But I let go, and in the release I'm gone, nothing but hot waves drowning me again, pushing me under to where life is nothing but this single moment of feeling.

Afterward, we lie on his bed, the sheets cluttered around us, my body still thrumming. I'm on my stomach, he's on his side, idly stroking my back.

Even the storm outside has calmed somewhat, as if the weather is somehow responding to the two of us.

I find myself...wordless. Utterly content to just lie here, being touched. Time feels slow, generous, like it's opened up a pocket of eternity for the two of us to rest in for as long as we want. Daniel apparently doesn't feel the need to talk, either, and I know without asking that we're experiencing the same thing: the present. A rare thing when I'm mostly either grieving the past or planning for the future.

Daniel's fingers are light and agile on my skin as they dance over my spine. I stretch with a satisfied moan.

"What's this?" His fingers stop their stroking.

I crane to look. Ah—that little area on my left forearm.

"Just some old scars."

"Cooking oil?"

"No." I rub the spot—just a sprinkling of white dots, like a constellation. Almost invisible now, unless you're looking closely. "I don't cook."

"Wait. Your catering business—" he begins.

"I know, I know. Jess was the chef. I ran the business side. You know, the contracts, the bookkeeping, the advertising. The boring part." I pause. "Obviously we have a new head chef now."

His finger makes little circles over the scars. "What's the story, then?"

"Always the journalist."

"Or maybe you just fascinate me."

I laugh and roll on to my side, pulling the sheet up around me. "It was the early days of our catering company. Jess got a deal on an industrial-sized coffeemaker on eBay. But every time we tried to use it, we tripped the breaker. We didn't have the money to hire an electrician, so I watched a few YouTube videos and…" I realize I'm smiling. Which, considering it's a memory of Jessica, feels…different. Good. "I went into the electrical panel to bypass the breaker, and it was filthy. Like, so dirty. So I got a wire brush to clean the lug. The brush accidentally shorted out to ground, and there was a huge spark, and basically I got showered with molten metal."

"Holy shit," says Daniel.

"I know. It ruined my favorite Beatles T-shirt. And it also got me between the electrical gloves and my sleeve."

He grins. "I had a sense that you were the handy type."

"I wouldn't call myself handy. It's more like I do what has to get done." I pause, taking in Daniel's incredible body. Solid, with a smattering of dark hair across his broad chest. And I realize that I barely know a thing about this man. I wag a playful finger. "You're really good at getting me to talk, mister, but you don't talk much yourself, do you?"

"Occupational hazard."

"Tell me something about you. Are you handy?"

His grin turns mischievous. "Well, didn't you think so?"

"No, really!" I swat him. "Do you own a tool box? Can you use a wrench?"

He grins again but then clears his throat and knits his eyebrows like he's decided to behave.

"Um, let's see. I've replaced a faucet. Caulked a bathtub. Do you want the whole CV?"

"Plus references." I laugh, and so does he. "Here's a better question. Why journalism?"

He rolls on to his back, and now it's my turn to scooch over and prop myself above him, trailing my fingers down his chest, swirling my fingertips through the hair.

"The short answer? Conviction. The world needs people who are willing to tell the real story."

"No rose-colored glasses," I say.

"No." He loses his gaze in the ceiling.

"You say that like you're sad."

He readjusts his body, putting his hands behind his head, which highlights the musculature of his arms.

"I made a mistake, once upon a time," he says. For once, instead of looking at me, he looks somewhere to the right of my face. "I… let something drop that I should have pursued. I listened to my boss instead of my conscience. People got hurt. I blame myself." His eyes flick back to mine, and though normally I'm good at reading emotion, I can't quite read him.

I squint. "Did this 'matter of conscience' happen at your current job? *Fit Life*?"

"Before *Fit Life*. But you know? I learned from it. I realized that the truth isn't just about me and my conscience, or me being able to sleep at night. It's about all of us. It's a responsibility we have to one another. Any time we betray that responsibility, the ripples are far-reaching. I promised myself I'd never compromise again." He stops short for a second. "And I haven't."

"Well." I lay my palm flat on his chest and feel the solid beat of his heart. "I guess the important thing is to learn from our mistakes, huh?"

He gives me a long look I can't quite interpret. I try to reverse engineer what I'm sensing from him. Curiosity? Guilt? Or is he wanting me to pardon him? But how can I, when I don't know the details? I'm about to probe further when he breaks our gaze and sits up.

"I'm going to start up the shower. Want to join me?" He hops out of bed and heads for the bathroom. I can't help but admire his ass. Wow. Seriously. What a great ass.

"Sure," I call out behind him. "Give me a second."

I hear the shower turn on. Then Daniel, singing loudly and off-key.

For a moment, I just sit there, cross-legged on Daniel's bed, drawing the sheet around me like a robe. I'm not ready yet to step out of this pocket of eternal present. I want to keep feeling it all—all these things that will end as soon as I move. The buzzing in my body. The aftershocks of pleasure that are still warming me. The calm beauty of the rain, now pinging brightly against the windowpane. The way the gray shroud of the sky is brightening; I never knew gray could be so dazzling. And Daniel, of course—the second most unexpected thing that's ever walked into my life.

I feel myself smiling. I met Jessica at a bar. Daniel in a coffee alcove. It's silly, but could it be my thing? Finding love by the beverages? *Hah.*

I'm squirmy with happiness. How could it have been so good on our first try?

And how much better could it be on our second…

This is too good to be true.

I just met Daniel, and yet somehow he makes me feel…

Safe.

Being with a man is different—and I need different. This relation-ship, or whatever I should be calling it, feels new. It's nothing to do with Jessica—though Daniel also doesn't seem afraid of that part of my life. He is neither intimidated nor put off by the fact that I was in love with a woman, or that she met a tragic end. In fact, I don't think anything could scare this man.

Though, speaking of tragic ends...I conjure the list I've been working on in my mind. Serena, Craig...I shake my head, to clear it. What if, instead of doing what I came here to do, I...let go? Daniel's voice comes back to me. His decisive command. *Let go.* And I did.

Is this where my path forks? Could I abandon the plans that brought me here and leave with Daniel at the end of it? What would it feel like, to get on a plane in three weeks and never come back to the Riovan?

I open my hands on the bed and contemplate them. The natural curl of my fingers, not fully open, not fully closed. From here I can choose to flatten my palm, or make a fist. Both require effort. What takes more strength? To hang on, like I've been doing for five years? Or...to let go?

Daniel hits a high note on "Stayin' Alive," bringing laughter bubbling up in my stomach.

I leave the bed, the sheet trailing behind like the train of a ball gown, and enter the steamy bathroom. For a second, I just enjoy the sight of Daniel from behind through the foggy glass enclosure, scrubbing his armpits.

"Need any help in there?" I say as I let the sheet drop, slide open the glass door, and step inside.

"Hey, hot stuff," he says, as I take the washcloth and scrub his back like it's the most natural thing in the world. Really, it's because it allows me to keep gazing upon the marvel that is his backside.

"Can I return the favor?" he says when I'm finished, and I oblige. His firm scrubbing up and down my back feels soothing, and based on where his hand lingers, I'm pretty sure our feelings about each other's backsides are mutual.

"Maybe we should get room service," he says as we towel off afterward, our bodies flushed from the hot water and the mutual scrubdown. I'd nearly forgotten how handy it is to have someone to reach those impossible-to-access spots on my back. "They have a really good pho...though it is meatless." He grimaces.

"Pho sounds perfect."

He rubs the towel over his hair, which stands on end, and jerks his head toward the shower. "Hey, fun fact: Did you know that until recently the hotel had metal drainpipes?"

I stop cold, towel gathered around me. "Really?" I carefully secure the towel around my chest.

"Yeah. Metal drainpipes from the eighties. They're switching them out for PVCs."

"Hadn't noticed, but hey. Updates are good." Mechanically, I bend to flip my hair down, then wrap a second towel around it, turban-style. Pho doesn't sound so good anymore.

"That death last year," he says. "Michael Johnson."

The name hits me like a sucker punch, and for a second, I'm really and truly out of breath.

It's OK, I reassure myself. It was no secret, and Daniel's writing an article about the Riovan. Of course he'd come across that unsavory tidbit.

I straighten. Force myself to breathe normally. Make my face neutral despite the racket of pounding in my chest.

"Yeah, the music producer, right?" I say casually, like I'm going with the flow here. At least...I'm pretty sure I say it casually.

"Manager," he corrects. "For Carli Elle. Serena said you knew her, right?"

"Carli, yeah, she's great."

"Too bad her career hasn't recovered from losing Michael."

I make a noncommittal noise, even though this is news to me. I squash the little surge of guilt. Better a career hiccup than a parasitical manager who makes you hate yourself. And yes, I'll die on that hill.

"You were working here last summer, weren't you?" says Daniel. "When he died?"

"I was."

"Must have been intense."

"Yeah. It was such a shock. There was a big staff meeting—" I don't have to pretend to shiver. "Vic was worried about negative media attention. They basically ordered us not to talk about it." I look in the mirror and lean in, pretending to examine a spot on my skin.

"Well, I have a theory about it," he says, also casual, like he's recapping a football game.

"His...death?"

"Yep."

I try to make light. "You have a theory about everything."

He walks up behind me. I force myself to meet his eyes in the slowly unfogging mirror.

"Well...less of a theory," he says. "More like something I've wondered about, and now that I know you're an amateur electrician, I might as well ask you." He swivels a finger in his ear.

"Shoot," I say, even as I leave the bathroom, the oppressive post-shower humidity, the oppressive closeness of Daniel. I make for my clothes, the red bathing suit like a fallen rose petal on the floor, and the white sweatpants next to it.

My eyes catch on the bed where, ten minutes ago, I was sitting cross-legged and happy, thinking that my life might be taking a new direction.

Then I moved, and the small eternity shattered, just like I knew it would.

It doesn't have to be ruined. Maybe Daniel is just venting his curiosity.

I should play it cool.

I should get out of here.

Daniel, a towel tied around his waist, follows me. "How hard would it be to bypass a breaker for a specific room in a hotel?"

"Um...no idea?" I crouch to pick my clothes up off the floor even as a fresh wave of panic washes through my body. *Not hard,* I think, *as long as you know where to find it.*

There are electrical panels on every floor, in the utility closets by the ice machines. The doors are locked, and so is the panel itself, but I'm good at getting hold of keys I'm not supposed to have.

"So theoretically," he continues, taking a seat on the side of the bed and leaning back on his arms, "if someone wanted to murder Michael Johnson by electrocution in the bathtub, what would you say their first step would be? Bypassing the breaker, right?"

Fuck, fuck, fuck. I want to rewind to the part where I was admiring Daniel's ass.

"Sorry... Why would someone want to kill Michael Johnson?" I think it's OK that I sound flustered here. Who wouldn't be? The papers all reported an "accident" that, reading between the lines, could be taken as suicide. Any normal person would be upset at the suggestion of murder.

"Who knows," says Daniel. "Show business is cutthroat. I'm sure he made some enemies on his way to the top. You were here when it happened, though. So what do you think?"

Is it just me, or is Daniel looking at me really intensely right now? Then again, he's always looking at me intensely.

I bat his question off with a laugh, because the best way to cover up the depths is with a shallow little distraction.

"I'm a lowly lifeguard, remember? You're the journalist. What do *you* think, Daniel Black?"

He grins. "Only bad journalists reach their conclusions at the beginning of their research."

"I thought he was high when he died." I step into my bathing suit and start pulling it up. For some reason, I feel more naked in this moment than when I was literally naked just moments ago.

"Oh, he was. But the cause of death was definitely electrocution."

How the hell does he know that? It was clear as day when you looked at the body, of course. But Vic paid off the Saint Lisieux police, just like I figured he would. And it's not like Michael's family wanted the details leaked either.

"Are you…sure?" I force another laugh. "That's not the story I heard."

"Did you hear his Bluetooth speaker was found floating in the bathtub?"

"No…"

Daniel snorts air out of his nose and shakes his head. "The thing is, there's no way that little speaker had enough voltage to kill him." He pauses. "Actually, how much voltage would a speaker like that have?"

"I don't know," I say faintly. Definitely under five volts. Not enough to kill. I looked into it.

"I'd say under five volts," he says. "Not lethal. Then again, I'm not the expert."

His pause tells me he's waiting for my response.

I've never had a heart attack before, but this is probably what it feels like. My heart squeezing out painful beat after painful beat. Spikes in my lungs that light up with pain every time I breathe.

If this was a normal conversation, at this point I'd probably ask the next question in the logical progression. *Then what do you think killed him?* Followed by the inevitable *Who?* But I'm not leading this horse to water. He might just drink.

Bathing suit is on. Pants are on.

"I'm going to have to take a rain check on the pho," I say, unwinding the towel from my hair and rubbing it through my wet locks before tossing it on the bed next to Daniel. My voice sounds calm, I think. I shake my hair out and run my fingers through it. "I just remembered I need to go return the supplies I left downstairs…" The ones I foolishly dropped in the hall to go have sex with a man who is suddenly way too interested in talking about the obscure details of a death I was definitely behind.

But he doesn't know it's me.

He can't know it's me.

I never talked to Michael Johnson in my life—not even during his albeit shortened stay at the Riovan. I didn't know him at all, and I certainly didn't benefit from his death. As far as Daniel's concerned, what motive could I possibly have? And how the hell did Daniel know about the Bluetooth speaker? I still remember the moment I tipped it into the water. *Plop* it went, interrupting Marvin Gaye's "Sexual Healing" as the device shorted out and bobbed in the bathwater like a dead fish next to its dead owner.

Daniel's words ring in my head. *If someone wanted to murder Michael Johnson…*

That is how everyone would see it, isn't it? As murder. But that's not how I think about it. I chose to end Michael's life, but "murder" is such an unsavory word. It brings to mind red meat and bloody knives and the smell of sweat. It sounds...unhinged. Like a wild animal thoughtlessly ripping into its victim, responding to the urges of the moment, with no forethought or compass, just hunger and opportunity. That's not how it is with me. Yes, I kill, but never thoughtlessly. I play by the book. I make my choices carefully.

Carefully? some part of me is screaming. *If you were careful, there wouldn't be a journalist asking you questions about Michael's death a full year later!*

Calm down, I try to coach myself, but it's a bit too late for calm. *Need to go. Need to go now.*

"I can call down for the pho while you return the—" Daniel says, and I can tell he's trying to read my mood.

"No," I interrupt, and yes, I am aware that I sound a little manic right now, which is all the more reason to leave. "I really have to go, Daniel."

"Oh, OK. You sure?" he says, and his expression is innocent enough. Even a little disappointed. "Did I...upset you? I didn't mean to."

I look at him, sitting there on the bed, still leaning on those beautiful arms with the sculpted muscles, his fingers splayed out. The fingers that were just inside me about a million realities ago.

"Sorry, I just—" I shake my head like I'm trying to shake off an insect. "Is this for your article? Because I thought it was about wellness tourism."

"No, you're right," he says. "I guess it's just idle curiosity."

"Yeah?" Because it didn't sound very idle. Finding out the real cause of death that the press didn't even get hold of? Accurately estimating the voltage of a Bluetooth speaker? Idle, my ass.

Then again…maybe this is what journalists do for fun? Research and analyze and pick at things until they unravel? *Pick at Lily until she unravels?*

"I'm sorry if I was insensitive," Daniel says, standing, rubbing the wet back of his head. "You know. Bringing up a violent death when you've…"

My mind can't help but fill in what he might say.

Killed so many people.

Taken a murder vacation every year.

"…had so much loss."

Yes. Loss. He's not wrong.

"It's fine," I say, but I'm already heading toward the door. I pull it open; Daniel catches it. Wraps his fingers around the edge of the door and leans toward me.

"Hey. Lily. I had a good time."

Mechanically I say, "Me too." The hall is long, and even though I'm facing Daniel, I can feel it yawning behind me, begging me to sprint down it as fast as I can.

"Did I ruin it?" he says softly.

"I said it's fine." I force a smile and finally meet Daniel's eyes. *Ruthless.* My read is instantaneous. There's a new, hard-edged ruthlessness in Daniel's gaze.

Or maybe it was always there. Maybe I've just never noticed it because of the haze of desire I've been looking at him through…

Then I blink and it's gone, and in his eyes is actually just the same probing intensity as always. *Am I just being paranoid?*

"I'll take you up on that rain check, you know," he says with a parting grin.

"OK," I say.

Then, *Click.* The door closes, severing us.

I breathe out in a long stream, then force myself to walk. My whole body feels strange, sick and dizzy. The buzz of pleasure in my blood has turned sharp and lurching.

What the hell was I thinking? Cool? Analytical? I just fell on Daniel like a hungry predator...thoughtless, starving, opportunistic.

How close is your room? Seriously?

I knew better.

And that's what scares me.

CHAPTER 14

THE RAIN HAS STOPPED; THE WIND HAS GENTLED TO A PLAYFUL BLUS-ter. I head straight for the beach, filling my lungs with clean, sharp gulps of air. Somehow, it's past six o'clock, and the clouds are shredded ribbons of pink and orange, like gashes in the gray dome of the sky. I hit the sand and pause to cuff my sweatpants before making for the shoreline, my strides long.

I need space. Space to move, to breathe, to feel that I'm not actually trapped.

Back in Daniel's room, at first, I relished the feeling of being hemmed in; the heady scent of his skin, the sticky heat melding us together, the tight wrap of his body, holding me down. But now—

I walk fast, toward the shore.

See? I'm not confined. It's just a feeling, a brief panic. I can go where I want, as far as I want, as fast as I want... *It's not like Mom.*

On the other side of the plexiglass, she no longer looked like an avenging goddess with the remains of her just sacrifice at her feet, but a pale, small woman swallowed by the orange jumpsuit. Fragile, with her bloodless lips and her limp hair and her roots showing. Stripped of power, stripped of choice.

"I'll be out before you know it," she promised through the black phone as we pressed our hands to the glass. Almost meeting. But not quite. "I'm gonna find a real good lawyer, and it's all gonna be fine."

It was not all fine.

I didn't lie to Daniel. Mom did die of breast cancer, but in prison. She'd been diagnosed shortly before the Trevor incident. She hadn't told me yet. And who knows if that's why she cracked. Some instinct that she wouldn't always be around to protect me. That she had to do what she could, while she still could, consequences be damned.

Go big or go home, Lily. At least she practiced what she preached; she went big. She did not come home.

Trevor. It's hard to separate the real man from the stereotype he's become in my head. Tall. Gauntly muscled. Handsome face, hungry look in his eyes. Always out of money. Always drinking. Greasy nails from the mechanic's shop where he worked. Funny as hell one minute, angry as a devil the next. He sure could make Mom laugh. But he could just as easily make her cry.

It took a couple of weeks for the cops to come knocking, but come knocking they did. Everyone in Calumet Heights knew Mom had been seeing Trevor; she wasn't the most private person. And trailer parks don't hold secrets, especially not when it concerns the so-called slut that everyone loves to hate. Even neighbors who had been friendly to Mom's face were more than eager to join the witch hunt. One woman claimed she had seen us loading him into the borrowed truck. Another implied this may not be Mom's first time killing—she had always been high-strung. Unhinged. And then, of course, there was the hard evidence. Traces of Trevor's DNA in the bed of the truck. In our carpet. On the skillet.

As my life fell apart around me, I obeyed Mom's instructions and repeated ad nauseam the two statements she made me promise to stick to, no matter what: *I don't know* and *I don't remember*. My only defense against a justice system that, I was quickly realizing, was not just at all.

In the years that followed, as I bounced from family to family in Ohio's foster-care system, and Mom died, and I grew taller and curvier and failed in school, that horrible afternoon when Trevor's body crumpled at Mom's feet became an obsession. Trevor had received justice. But Mom had not. Could it have played out differently? It turned and turned in my head like a never-ending carousel.

What if, instead of Mom reacting so instinctively, we'd arranged an "accident"? What if we'd bleached the truck…ripped out the carpet…chopped him into pieces and got rid of them one by one…

I killed Trevor and disposed of him in a thousand different ways over the next years as I suffered through another sleepless night, or rode the bus to school, or spaced out during another test I knew I'd fail anyway. Each time, I mentally followed the progression of each manner of death step by step. The pros, the cons, the risks. In the infinite realm of possibilities, there had to be one perfect kill, one that left no evidence behind. One that left me and Mom together.

I started to sleepwalk. Lose weight I didn't have to lose. My collection of C and D grades dipped into Fs. But it just didn't seem important to find the slope between two points or remember the dates of Civil War battles.

In a way, those obsessive nights were a waste of time. You can't outsmart the past. Can't redo it, can't save yourself from mistakes already made and paid for. In another way, they prepared me to make my own plans, now. And maybe I've taken a foolish pride in how good I am at it; at choosing the perfect death for the best victim that raises the fewest questions. But now I'm wondering...*was* Michael the smartest target? For such a high-profile person, was bathtub electrocution the best way? Should I have pushed him off the yacht instead? Facilitated an overdose that mightn't have raised any questions at all? An injection might have been cleaner. It's not like I was any stranger to that method—I'd used it before, with Sophie Coste, who went into very convenient liver failure. For Michael, I could have secured some heroin on Saint Vitalis, no problem, and...

I've reached the shoreline. I stop, letting the wind flatten my sweatpants against my legs, and look out at the water. The waves are rolling out the last of their passion, drawing their nearly spent energy up on to the sand for one final release, then sighing their way out. I let my memories of Mom and my lingering what-ifs sigh their way out too. It's the present I need to be worrying about, and this very real journalist who is way too interested in a death that does not concern him.

How? How did Daniel know all those details about Michael's death? Why does he care?

I set off walking again, arms wrapped around my body, stepping over broken shell bits and piles of seaweed the storm cast up, avoiding the occasional beached blob of jellyfish. As I pick my way through the debris, following the wavy, ever-changing line between water and sand, my mind launches fragments at me. The bobbing orange Bluetooth speaker. The little craters pockmarking Michael's chest.

That night by the pool wasn't the only time Carli and I talked about Michael. One night, I saw her head for the sauna, so I followed her there. As luck would have it, we were alone.

As we sat in the heat together, she opened up again, just as I'd hoped she would. She was going to get on the pills Michael had been touting. It wasn't as sketchy as I might think, she explained, because a legit doctor was involved; he helped a lot of celebrities. Michael had promised it would boost her career, and he hadn't led her astray yet.

"I know it's a grim reality. But chunky doesn't sell." She shot a half grin my way. "Unless you're Lizzo." She leaned back against the wall, sweat rolling down her face. "God, I love her."

"There's room for more than Lizzo," I said, scraping my hair into a top knot to get it off my neck.

She made a noncommittal noise, and then we were silent. I knew better than to lecture her.

We sat there in the heat, and I knew in that moment what I had to do. I had my target.

"Well, I'm going to hit the shower," she announced after a while. Before leaving the sauna, she stopped in front of me, dipped her face, and kissed me on the lips. Short, salty. Somehow whimsical.

"You're sweet," she said, tucking a stray curl behind my ear.

"And you're beautiful," I said. "Just like this." If only she could see it. She leaned in for another kiss, this one slow, savoring, and I cupped her cheek. I pretended to enjoy it. It was only polite. But I didn't actually feel anything toward her.

Because I wasn't really kissing Carli Elle, famous singer, half-dressed and sweat-drenched and—under any other circumstances—a more than desirable lover. I was kissing Jess. I was telling Jess she was beautiful.

It's always about Jess.

"Hey," Carli said at the sauna door, as if an afterthought had just struck her. "I have a performance at the Mambotel next Friday. Want to come with?"

"Sounds amazing," I said. It clicked. That would be the night.

Carli had already told me about Michael's legendary nightly

baths, which she laughingly described as "his religion." Scalding hot water, Epsom salts, and R&B. He had one every day, without fail.

Me being on Saint Vitalis with Carli for her performance wasn't quite an alibi, but at least I'd be off the island when his body was found...in the bath. It was almost poetic. Dead in his religion.

The sand is damp, cool, firm under my feet as I come to a stop. I've reached the end of the beach, where a jetty of white rocks makes a natural wall, extending pretty far out into the water. On the beach side of the rocks the water is calmer, but the other side is lively.

I stand there at the edge, not sure whether to turn around and walk the beach the other way, or risk the slippery rocks for the spectacular view at the end of the jetty.

Maybe you just fascinate me. Those words of Daniel's keep coming back, like airport shrimp. They felt so good at the time. Being an object of desire always feels good—I suppose it feeds the hungry little narcissist that lives inside each of us, and God knows I'm no exception. But now, it's all too easy to hear Daniel's words from a darker viewpoint.

I glance behind me. But I'm not ready to go back to the hotel.

Up we go, then. I find my footing on the first flattish white rock, then climb. These are the same rocks I was going to propose to Jessica on. The same rocks Serena went viral for slipping on. The waves are still crashing to my left, but I know how to be safe, and anyway, it's worth the risk. It's out of view of the hotel, and I need that feeling of breaching a barrier, of space and more space, of expansive water and sky that are bigger than me.

Barefoot, I hop from rock to rock, pausing in between to recalibrate. I've already been so reckless with Daniel, and I can't afford any more recklessness, especially on these rocks where I could break my leg and fall in the water and fucking drown. That would be rich. Not to mention Daniel would interpret it as a sure sign of guilt. *I was on to her, so sadly, she took her own life… At least I gave her the orgasm of a lifetime before she passed.*

Hah.

Puddles have settled into every crevice of the rocks, and the mossy patches of growth are slick. My foot skids slightly as I hit a slimy spot. It's really not hard to see why Serena fell. As the waves crash up from the left of the jetty, the water sprays my ankles.

Traversing the rocks takes all my focus, giving my mind a welcome respite. I finally reach the last rock. Now, only the ocean is before me, gray and furious.

I sit with one knee drawn up and the other leg hanging down, not even caring that the wetness is soaking into the seat of my sweatpants. I close my eyes and breathe. I taste salt on my lips and remember Carli's kiss.

It was a hair dryer, by the way. Not the speaker.

As I said, Michael liked to take baths with his Bluetooth speaker playing, which did bring electrocution to mind. Fortunately, the Riovan had old-fashioned metal drainpipes; that was a must. The Epsom salts would help—saltwater conducts electricity well—but even so, the battery voltage from Michael's speaker wouldn't be enough. However, 220 volts would do it…

I happened to be in my own bathroom washing my face as I was thinking about this, and my eyes landed on my roommate's hair dryer. I picked it up and examined the tag. *Do not remove this tag! Warn children of the risk of death by electric shock!* A little picture showed a bathtub and a hair dryer with a red line over it. A little advertisement meant just for me. *Here's how you do it!*

I frowned as I turned the hair dryer over in my hands. Of course, if I threw the hair dryer into his bath, it would trip the breaker. But if the breaker had been bypassed…

The next day, a bunch of us lifeguards went over to Saint Vitalis for some shopping on our day off. Everyone else bought shell jewelry, straw hats, and boho maxi dresses. I bought a maxi dress too, to wrap my other purchases in.

It was easy to clip the Ground Fault Circuit Interrupter off the end of my new hair dryer and rewire it with a non-GFCI plug that would not act like a circuit breaker.

The evening of Carli Elle's performance, I went to the electrical panel on Michael's floor, unlocked the protective door marked RESTRICTED ACCESS, unscrewed the panel, and donned the electrical gloves I'd bought at the little hardware store on Saint Vitalis, along with my other supplies.

I identified the breaker that went to his room and flipped it off.

Using the screwdriver, I revealed the black wire that routed to the bathroom plug.

I pulled the black wire and stuffed it into the main 240-volt lug at the top of the breaker box. Then, I tightened it and replaced the cover.

The charge was now coming straight from the lug, which still had a breaker, of course, but the hundred-amp one that would be located somewhere by the entrance of the hotel. Way back where the whole box comes from…so it wasn't going to trip easily. Nope. It would keep delivering killer electricity.

I'd got a key to Michael's room the day before, from the front desk. "Carli Elle's manager locked himself out of his room," I said. "He's, uh…naked." They were more than happy to give me a key, and I was more than happy to pretend to run up with it.

Forty minutes before Carli Elle's yacht was due to leave for the Mambotel, I let myself into Michael's room. Right away, I heard the music filtering out from the bathroom door, which wasn't all the way closed. Marvin Gaye.

I still had my electrical gloves on. First, I put my extra key card on the dresser. I didn't bother wiping it down for prints; I'd collected it yesterday and, presumably, delivered it to naked Michael in the hallway, so if anyone even checked it for prints—which was unlikely—my prints made sense. A lack of prints, to my estimation, might be more concerning to authorities. Then, I pulled the hair dryer out of my backpack. I walked softly over the carpet. Through the crack in the bathroom door, I could taste the steam. I could smell his bodywash. I could see Michael's head lolled against the edge of the tub as he rolled it from side to side with the rhythm, his mouth puckered a little in his enjoyment of the music.

Couldn't blame him. It was a good song.

I pushed the door open, plugged the hair dryer in, turned it on, and heaved it into the tub. No hesitation. No big showdown. No chance for last words on either of our parts.

There was a sputter and a crackle and a smell. It was so fast; he was dead.

Still, I leaned over the body and looked, just in case. His eyes were bugged open. Tiny, charred craters marked his chest. He smelled like barbecue. I haven't had the stomach for barbecue since—a pity, really, since Taste of Heaven does a really good job with smoked ribs.

Still wearing my electrical gloves, I unplugged the hair dryer and pulled it out of the water. My pulse was regular, my head cool. I'd planned it well, and nothing would go wrong.

I took one final look at the man as "Sexual Healing" echoed around us—the last song he'd ever hear.

"You shouldn't make women feel like shit about their bodies," I said out loud.

He didn't answer.

Then I kicked his Bluetooth speaker into the water for good measure.

It only took ten minutes to set the electrical panel to rights. Back in my own room, I changed into the slinky dress Carli had lent me for the evening, swiped my lashes with a little mascara, and headed out, backpack slung over my shoulder, already weighted with rocks to make sure it sank along with the screwdriver and gloves.

"Have fun!" said my roommate, who was curled up in bed with a novel. "I'm totally jealous!"

"I will! Thanks!"

As the boat pulled out of the marina, I asked Carli, "Isn't Michael coming?"

"We can't wait any longer," she said, giving her phone a frustrated check. "He probably fell asleep in the bath."

He sure did, I remember thinking. *And he ain't waking up.* It would make a killer song. In a parallel universe, I'd tell Carli what I did just so she could write it.

Somewhere between Saint Lisieux and Saint Vitalis, I tossed the backpack into the sea.

Carli slayed that night.

I did wonder if she might remember our conversation by the pool. The way she said, *He'd have to be dead.* If the possibility would cross her mind that I had done it. But she left the Riovan the next day, undoubtedly to avoid the attention that would surely come after her manager's untimely death, and I never saw her again.

Sure, a newshound found me because of that picture. And there was that random call Becca WhatsApped me about. But no one ever asked me questions about Michael's death. Not the Saint Lisieux police. Not hotel management.

No one until Daniel.

CHAPTER 15

AS I LIE AWAKE AT 2 A.M. WITH ONLY MY ROOMMATE'S WHIFFLING snore for company, it's as though I regress mentally to my teen years, playing Trevor's death over and over in my head. Except this time it's Michael's. A useless exercise, but tell that to the 2 a.m. brain. Around 3 a.m. I doze off but keep waking up from dreams where Daniel is killing me as he fucks me. Dark? Absolutely. But given everything that happened yesterday, it doesn't take Carl Jung to interpret that one.

Then, from 4 a.m. to 5 a.m., my brain decides I need to review every single interaction I've ever had with Daniel Black. That is more useful.

A few salient facts emerge.

He didn't know what a goblet squat is.

He didn't know that bacon is a processed meat.

He doesn't like green smoothies.

By the time my alarm goes off at seven, it's utterly obvious that he can't possibly be a journalist for *Fit Life*. From the very first morning

I saw him, Daniel has seemed like a fish out of water, hasn't he? Since then, he's shown me over and over that he doesn't belong.

Then why is he here?

As I pour my coffee, I come to a swift decision: I have to talk to Vic. If Daniel really is digging into Michael's death, Vic should know. After all, Vic and I share a common interest when it comes to matters of deaths at the Riovan: cover them up.

Very possibly, it's our only commonality—but an important one.

"Do you have a minute to talk about Daniel Black?" I say, leaning into the door frame of Vic's sunny office thirty minutes before my morning beach shift. It's supposed to be a beautiful day, as poststorm days usually are. Blue skies and bright sun—the opposite of the never-ending sleepless night I'm just emerging from.

Vic removes his fashionable, clear-framed reading glasses and sets them on the desk.

"Tell me Serena didn't pull another Serena," he says, sounding preemptively exhausted.

"No, nothing like that." I come in the rest of the way, close the door behind me, and sit across from him. Lean on my elbows. "He's been asking me questions about that death last year. You know…the music producer?"

Vic groans and leans back in his chair. "Michael Johnson," he fills in. "Carli Elle's manager."

"Right. I just wonder," I say carefully, "if Daniel might be here under…false pretenses?"

"Why can't people leave well enough alone?" says Vic, snapping his head back up in real exasperation. "I do *not* need another branding crisis this year!"

"Sorry," I say humbly.

It hasn't escaped me that every time I kill, I am leaving a bit of a mess for poor Vic—but maybe part of me enjoys that little twist of the knife.

The first year, Vic was person of interest number one on my target shortlist. After all, who could be more toxic than the manager of a toxic place? I even planned his death, involving a modification to his nightly Old Fashioned that would interact with his medication regime. Ultimately, I had to bow to practicalities and hit the brakes. He was too high up to kill. His death would risk too much attention. Not to mention, Vic seemed to both like and respect me—which made him my ticket back into this place.

I've come to understand that Vic is both oblivious and impervious to the Riovan's toxicity. He doesn't see the harm he's doing; he's too self-obsessed. You can just feel it when you're around him—that Vic loves Vic with every ounce of Vic's heart. Sometimes I want to shake his bronzed shoulders and say, "Wake up and smell the shit you're calling roses!" But I've concluded the exercise would be useless. People like him can't understand the rest of us—the ones with cracks where the poison can leak in.

"No, you did the right thing, telling me," Vic says, shaking his head. "These journalists."

"Daniel seems to think it wasn't a suicide," I say, trying to sound innocently surprised. "But it was…right?"

"Of course it was," he says, with so much conviction I almost believe it myself—and I'm the killer. Good old Vic. Just as stubbornly oblivious as always. "Any more questions, you send him my way."

"Will do."

Vic's gaze floats to the window. His mind seems suddenly elsewhere. "There was a death the year before that…do you remember?" His eyes slide back to mine.

I shake my head, even though my mental file spits it all out. Brett

Teubler. Staff nutritionist with a convenient allergy to penicillin. It wasn't as hard to get hold of the antibiotic as you might imagine.

"A staff member died," says Vic.

"Oh…that's right. B…Brent?"

"Brett. We kept it quiet. It was a freak medication mistake, but…" Vic's forehead almost wrinkles. "Never mind."

"What?"

"Well, it's silly. Blame it on my superstitious abuela, but sometimes I can't help but think this place is cursed. Did you know it used to be a sanatorium?"

"No," I say with an involuntary shiver. However involved I've been in the hotel's present, I've never looked into its past.

"Yes…the place was originally built in the 1890s. Rich French families used to send their daughters here to have abortions, whether they wanted to have them or not. And sometimes the servants too, if…well, you get the picture. My abuela used to say, *Victor, evil calls to evil.* I can't help but think…" His brown eyes meet mine. "Every year I've worked here, someone has died."

I force myself to breathe normally, blink normally, keep my face calmly compassionate, but say nothing.

"Do you believe in curses?" says Vic.

"No," I say.

And I'm not interested in dwelling too long on the idea, since that would make me the curse. We wrap it up, but I leave my tête-à-tête with Vic feeling sobered, thinking about those girls who were sent here, possibly against their will. Their bodies were a source of shame. The professionals had to intervene.

I guess a hundred and thirty years later, nothing on this island has changed.

As I pass through the hotel lobby, a pile of magazines on a low table catches my eye. On top is a copy of *Fit Life*, with a muscled couple on the front in wedding garb holding up cake-topper figurines that look like mini Hulks. *Dax & Deirdre: Our Body-Building Wedding!*

Are you serious?

I pick it up. Start to leaf through. OK, Daniel Black. Prove to me that you actually work for these people. There's an article titled "Smoothie Your Way to Waistline Goals!" by Natalie Yoon. "Cold Weather Running Tips: Burn It Up All Winter Long!" by Peter Torsney. "Ten Remedies for Joint Pain," "Your Best (Gluten-Free) Life…"

And there it is. I almost don't believe it; I'd convinced myself he wouldn't be in here, but his name is plain as day under his article titled "Has Body Positivity Gone Too Far?"

I start reading.

We've all heard that big is beautiful. I'm here to tell you today—it's not. When did our culture become so dishonest? We've become brainwashed with body positivity messaging, and the world needs to wake up and smell the roses. It's killing us. One pound at a time.

It's like I'm frozen in place. I read to the end.

Motherfucker.

No. He can't have written this. Not the man I met last week who was so charming by the coffee, so sweet when I trauma-dumped at the Mambotel. Not the man whose bed I leaped into just yesterday.

Could they have made him write it?

But even as I try to find an excuse, I remember Daniel's words. *I promised myself I'd never compromise again.* It sounded so lofty when he said it to me…and all that stuff about his responsibility to humankind or whatever... Is this judgmental piece-of-shit article his way of fulfilling his duty toward truth?

I rummage through the stack on the table and pull the previous month's issue. I rifle through the pages, scanning for his name. Oh, no. This one's worse. "Sex with Big Girls: The Honest Take."

I don't want to read it. But more than that, I don't want Daniel to have written it.

I'm told that gentlemen don't kiss and tell...then again, I've never thought of myself as a gentleman. I'm a journalist, and I'm here to tell you the unvarnished truth.

I can barely stomach what I read next. It's crass. Misogynistic. Pure poison. Everything I hate most about the world we live in.

This isn't a guy who's removed his rose-colored glasses. This is a guy who's picked up the fun-house glasses from the pits of hell and is looking at the whole world through them while shouting loudly about what he sees. And getting paid for it, to boot.

You want a toxic target to fill in that final slot? a voice in my head says. *You've got one.*

Shit fuck, fuck, fuck shit.

I storm out of the lobby, throwing the magazine into the nearest trash bin where it belongs.

I may have to kill Daniel Black.

CHAPTER 16

I'M SEETHING DURING MY ENTIRE SHIFT AT THE BEACH AS THE SUN shines and the salty waves roll, and the guests lounge and swim and gossip. I seethe through lunch as I load up a plate at the salad bar and wolf it down to lessen my chance of running into Daniel before I have a plan. And then I keep on seething during my afternoon shift at the lap pool.

It's exhausting to seethe for so long. Then again, this isn't something I can just bounce back from.

That gut instinct I have about people? It's usually right. But this time, somehow, it was one thousand percent wrong. As I sit in the high white lifeguard's chair with the pool laid out beneath me, so organized with its neat, bobbing lane dividers, I snap my elastic against my wrist once, twice, thrice.

"Don't you people clean this pool?" comes a voice to my lower left, startling me out of my reverie. Craig Lancaster, holding a dripping wet leaf between his fingers, his face twisted with disgust, water streaming down his lean body.

"I'm sorry, Mr. Lancaster," I say, automatically slipping into my best customer-service voice. "We do clean the pools, but sometimes—"

"Whatever. Don't want to hear it." He flicks the leaf away and stomps off, but I still hear him mutter, "Thirty fucking thousand dollars and I'm swimming in filth."

Anger bunches in my throat. *You're the filth, you toxic asshole,* I want to scream, and you know what, maybe I just will—

No. I force my hands to release their sudden death grip on the chair's arms.

What's happening to me this year? My emotions have been stronger. Less predictable. And now I'm having unpremeditated sex with men who write articles like the diatribe I just read in *Fit Life? What the fucking hell, Lily?*

I watch a slim woman cut through the water with a perfect breaststroke, her feet whipping together and propelling her body in a beautiful glide. When she turns in the pool, I recognize her—Skylar's mom. My eyes quickly find her daughter, reading a graphic novel on a lounge chair, pale legs extended and a bucket hat drawn deep over her eyes. Focused—like I need to be.

OK, Lily. Here's what we're going to do. Daniel is now on the list. Yes, killing him jumped into my mind earlier, but that was knee-jerk. This is me—yes, seething, but also very much logical and in control, adding his name to my official mental roster in an official capacity.

A traitorous voice wheedles, *Well, I probably won't have to kill him… Surely there will be someone more toxic.* Ugh, how am I already trying to find an exit door for the man? He deserves the same consideration as anyone. This isn't about the way he made me feel seen for the first time in years, or the way he set me on fire like he'd known my body for years instead of minutes. Nope. This is a matter of fucking *principle.* This is for Jessica.

A couple more guests slip into the pool's open lanes. A sloppy crawl, a choppy backstroke. Skylar's mom leaves the water shortly after they begin, her lithe body dripping as she saunters over to where her daughter is, chooses a lounge chair, and promptly goes to sleep. Skylar catches me watching and gives me a little wave. I wave back, then make a heart sign with my hands. She makes a heart sign back. I return my eyes to the swimmers.

Skylar's mother has problems. It's not like I've forgotten her comments about Skylar's body. But in the end, her toxicity levels would have to be exponential to justify me taking away someone's mother. Not an impossible standard—I did it once. I still think about Jade—the daughter in question. She was older than Skylar at the time—eighteen—but still so young, which did give me pause. But at the end of the day, I figured that processing the sudden death of her mother would be less damaging than hearing that woman scream things like, *No one will ever love you if you look like this—you get that, don't you?*

Was I right? I guess I'll never know. But I'd like to think I gave Jade a chance at the best possible future. What she does with it is up to her.

But back to the matter at hand. Tomorrow is the official start of week two. The week that I consider my shortlist.

Daniel. Serena. Craig. Three names; right on track. Next step? To let them coexist for a while in my mind as I consider how I might kill each of them. Week two is about sketching out plans. By the end of the week, it'll be one name and one name only. Week three, I fine-tune and execute my plan. Week four is about making sure I get away with it before going back to Cincinnati.

Experience has taught me that I don't have to rush to make a decision between the top three. The decision always happens naturally, if not scientifically. If I've done the prep work, let the observations settle like sediment, put in the active thought time, one name will organically rise to the top. There will be a moment this week—like that evening with Carli Elle in the sauna—when something sparks and the decision is made for me.

Because that's how it feels. That a light flips on all by itself, illuminating the way forward. It's not a denial of my agency—I don't want Mr. Sartre to turn in his grave on my behalf, God rest his existentialist soul. It's more an acceptance of the kismet involved.

At the end of my shift, my roommate River relieves me. As I sign out on the clipboard, she says, "Hey, a bunch of us lifeguards are having a euchre tournament. We might take over our room tomorrow, if that's OK."

I freeze my smile into place. Tomorrow is my day off, and I was going to hole up in the room with my laptop, log into the Guest Services Portal using Vic's username and password, and start piecing things together. But…you know what? It might do me some good to get out of Dodge. Get a little space, a little perspective. I'll rent one of the Riovan bikes and head to Brisebleue—pronounced Briz-bloo—Saint Lisieux's only town. There are legendary daiquiris at Island Vibes, the only bar in Saint Lisieux's only town, and you can always overhear some Riovan gossip since a lot of the local staff drink there.

"Sounds great," I say.

"You're welcome to join!" says River. "Do you know how to play euchre? It's supposed be a Midwestern game. Hannah taught us. It's really fun, once you get the hang of it!"

"Nah," I lie. "I never understood it."

In fact, euchre was the card game of choice in Calumet Heights. I could whip everyone's ass, no questions asked…if I were here to play games.

But I'm not.

CHAPTER 17

NEXT MORNING, I DRESS QUICKLY IN A TANK TOP AND CUTOFFS AND apply some sunscreen, rubbing a little extra into my cheeks, where a few new freckles have appeared. I head to the dining hall to grab a quick breakfast. Then, with my laptop and water bottle in my backpack, I head down to the Adventure Rentals outbuilding.

"Thirty-five dollars for twelve hours," says the man behind the desk, where bikes, kayaks, and paddle boards can be rented by the hour or for the day. I fork over some cash, exit into the muggy morning air with my sky-blue bike, and I'm off.

The road starts off at an incline, climbing from the coast to a rocky plateau before dipping into the rainforest. I'm sweating within minutes.

Honestly, it feels good to sweat from effort rather than boiling in the lifeguard's chair, unable to move. I'm not one for predictions, but this is going to be a good day. A productive day. I'm going to make my plans and figure out what the hell to do about Daniel.

It doesn't take too long for the Riovan to disappear behind me.

There's a whippy little wind for a while, and I have to move to the shoulder of the road as a Riovan shuttle bus passes me, but soon the rainforest looms, a deep, saturated emerald. Here, the road splits. The paved road leads to the airport, and the dirt road leads to Brisebleue. It seems telling. The paved road toward departure, as if the road itself is trying to remind me how much easier it would be just to leave. The rougher road is for staying.

The coffee and steel-cut oats from my hurried breakfast slosh in my stomach as I bump down the rutted incline that takes me off the main road. A moped chugs by, Riovan-bound, shared by two cleaning ladies, as evidenced by their uniforms. They give me a friendly wave. The one behind is holding the driver around the middle, and the driver is laughing. Even though they're only in my field of vision for a few seconds, I can feel the warmth between them like the sun on my neck. The comfort, the security of their friendship. A little curl of envy moves through me. I used to have that...and for a few hours, I thought I could have it again with Daniel. And now I have to consider how I could kill him. *Unfair.* It's very tempting to feel sorry for myself. I flick these feelings away. A good day, remember?

A few other mopeds pass me, then a battered-looking Jeep with four guys in maintenance jumpsuits, and a few people on dilapidated bicycles—more workers headed to the Riovan. How do the locals feel about the resort? It provides employment, sure, but it also privatized most of the nice beaches for the tourists to enjoy.

What if I had got my way? What if, at twenty-four, I had succeeded in shutting the Riovan down? Would the locals have been cheering, or pissed that their jobs were gone?

Either way, I know I was naive to even think it was possible. But I was reeling from losing Jessica, and I wanted to see the place burn, no matter the consequences.

I seriously must have solicited every news outlet, starting with the *New York Times* and the *Atlantic* and going down the list from there. Surely, someone would want to run the story of two lovers who went away to a wellness resort and came back the opposite of well. Ruined. My strategy was top-down. First, the big publications. By the time I made it to the *Tampa Advertiser Monthly*, something in me had hardened. I can't even call it disappointment. It was…well, no one gave a shit. The worst thing in the world had happened to Jess, to me, and no one cared; no one but me—and Jess's family, of course.

Maybe the subject wasn't serious enough for the *New York Times* or clickbaity enough for the *Tampa Advertiser*, or maybe no one was interested in trash-talking the powerful conglomerate that owns the Riovan. Whatever the cause, my efforts were dead in the water. I had to let it go, but I had no idea how to do that.

I wasn't new to death. Mom had already died—but cancer isn't personal. Jessica's downfall? It was absolutely personal. Toxic people fanned the flames of her normal insecurities into the raging bonfire that ultimately consumed her.

I booked a ticket to the Riovan for what I thought was my final visit, to scatter the metaphorical ashes, to face the place that had taken Jessica from me. I wanted closure, a way forward.

And though I certainly didn't find closure, a way forward did open.

A final moped buzzes past, its engine wheezing as though it were on its last legs. The young woman riding it waves at me, and I wave back. Then, as if that were rush hour and now it's over, the road gets really quiet, except for the protesting rattle of my own bike, my breathing, and the birdsong in the trees—so bright and clear it almost sounds artificial.

Even this early in the morning, it feels hotter in the rainforest—humid and close, cloying.

There's the distant roar of a waterfall, and if I didn't have to get shit done today, I'd be tempted to park my bike and see if I could find it.

That would have been a fun adventure to have with Jess.

I press on.

When I taste salt in the air again and a cool breeze licks my face, I know I'm almost there. The edge of the rainforest comes suddenly, and I'm shooting out of the green back into open air, going down a little incline. Ahead is Brisebleue, a scattering of buildings on a flat area that, when it rains, becomes a mudfest. Beyond, the ocean, huge, gleaming, bigger and bolder on the northern side of the island than it looks from the Riovan, as if we only get the diluted version down there. This isn't a place of gentle bathing and lounging; here, the ocean challenges the shore, lashing it with determined violence.

Soon, my bike is hopping over the rutted dirt road that becomes Brisebleue's main street. I have to swerve to avoid a pair of wild chickens, and a fruit vendor throws a halfhearted "Mangoes, good price" at me as I bump past, bike rattling like a jar of teeth.

The town is mostly shacks, as if someone dumped the leftovers of a construction project in a pile and everyone grabbed what they could. There's the salt-bleached motel, called simply "Motel," with a reputation for bedbugs, a grocery store that seems more of a convenience store, and a handful of open-front operations selling clothing, incense, auto parts, and pharmaceuticals, each with a rotating postcard rack out front.

Brisebleue may not be traditionally touristy, but it does get its share of backpackers and surfers. Back in the early 2000s, a surfer named Dino set a Guinness World Record on a wave nicknamed La

Mort Bleue—the Blue Death—and surfers have been coming ever
since, looking for that killer, once-in-a-lifetime wave…and willing
to stay in questionable accommodation for the chance.

I dismount my bike in front of Island Vibes. The bar-restaurant
features a weary tiki theme, but I respect the attempt to bring some
charm. The owner, Randy, is an American expat who worked for
Microsoft, cashed out big on stock options, and retired early. His
wife passed away from ovarian cancer—we connected years ago over
our mutual losses—so he figured, what the hell. He moved to the
Caribbean and fulfilled his longtime dream of owning a restaurant in
paradise. That was fifteen years ago, so now at almost seventy, Randy
spends most of his time on the beach while Sean from New Zealand
runs the day-to-day.

I lean my bike up against the side of the building. The front of
the restaurant is open to the elements, with a grass-roof awning that
provides shade over the outdoor seating. Inside, ceiling fans are running and it's marginally cooler.

My eyes take a minute to adjust to the dim interior. A table of
men are drinking iced coffees. A woman eating eggs on toast is speaking earnestly in French into her phone. I check my watch as I approach
the bar—ten o'clock. Too early for lunch, but that's OK. I'll do some
research first and order one of their ridiculously sugary Thai iced
coffees to tide me over.

"Lily?" comes a voice from the shadows behind the bar, and I
turn to find Sean standing up with his tousled blond surfer's hair and
permanent case of sunburn. He's wearing a tank top that displays
muscled arms, and a hemp necklace with a charm dangles from his
throat. He wipes his hands on a dishrag and graces me with a wide,
pleased smile that highlights his dimples.

"Sean!" I greet him, slipping on to a barstool. "Long time no see."

"You're back, huh?"

"Every year."

"What can I get you?"

"Iced coffee. I'll be here for a while, though, so I hope you have something good for lunch."

The menu is tacked above the bar, but it's never current.

"We've got a poke bowl you'll love. The fish is primo. Caught this morning."

"Looking forward to it." As long as it's not too chunky and pink. I lean on the counter as he prepares my iced coffee.

"How's business?" I ask. When you're in the food trade, you know how up and down it can be.

"Solid." He turns around and hands me the chilly plastic cup, rattly with ice floating through a milky brown sugar-colored liquid. Damn, my mouth is watering. "Actually, I'm buying Randy out."

"What? Randy is officially retiring?"

Sean's forehead furrows. "He has prostate cancer."

I exhale. "Is he seeking treatment, or…"

"It's metastasized, so…he's gonna let it run its course."

Oof. In reality, I barely know Randy. I see him once or twice a summer. Why does this feel like such a blow?

"Cancer is such a bitch," I say.

"Sure is," says Sean. "But you know, he misses Brenda. He says he's ready to go."

I nod empathetically, but I don't relate. I miss Jessica, too, but I can't imagine myself being ready to go. I have too much unfinished business.

"Oh, hey," says Sean. "We're having a big retirement party for Randy on Friday. You should come." He reaches for a stack of blue paper by the register and hands me the top sheet. Randy's smiling face is at the top, in black and white. Beneath, in Comic Sans font, the page reads: *Randy's Retirement Bash! Trivia, Half-Price Drinks and More From 7 p.m.! Don't Miss It!*

"You might take a few, get some Riovaners up here," Sean suggests, handing me some more copies. "I know Randy would love to see Vic. They used to hang."

"Sure, no problem," I say. I promise to put them up in the staff break room and other public places, and to personally hand one to Vic.

I choose a table under a fan, where there's lots of light, and connect my laptop to the Wi-Fi. It takes a minute, so I trail my eyes over the pictures Randy has hung on the wall—a younger Randy with a surfboard under his arm. Various celebrity surfers at Island Vibes raising the famous daiquiri in salute. A faded shot of Brenda, Randy's wife, from the 1970s, pregnant and smiling, here on Saint Lisieux. They came here together as a couple a few times over the years.

Like me and Jessica.

It's strange how I've never noticed this similarity. Randy and I both came here with our romantic partners; we both lost them. I guess the similarity ends there, since he came back permanently to follow a dream. I just dip in once a year to chase my nightmare.

Finally, the Wi-Fi connects, and I turn my attention to my laptop screen. The Riovan Guest Services Portal loads slowly, in calming shades of blue. I tap in Vic's info, and after a short wait, I'm in. The first two years, I had to break into Vic's office for this part of the process too. Thank God they moved to the Cloud.

In spite of Island Vibes's less-than-lightning-fast Wi-Fi, it's an easy system to navigate, and it tracks absolutely everything for everyone staying at the resort. The courses they've signed up for. Appointments with nutritionists, counselors, coaches, chiropractors.

Scheduled spa services. Also, their allergies. The medications they take. I type in Daniel Black, then take a long sip of sweet, cold coffee while I wait for the page to load.

Ah. He's sitting in on Pat Burton's seminar today, *Mindful Healing*. But other than that...not many services. A massage at the spa later on today, and that's it. Huh.

The Riovan costs an arm and a leg, so most people pack their schedules. Jessica sure did. Why doesn't Daniel want the full experience for his article? Surely the magazine is paying for this. If all you're doing is hanging out on a warm beach and hitting on the lifeguard, you can do that without leaving the good old U.S. of A.

Whatever. I'm not here to figure out why toxic assholes like Daniel Black do anything. I'm here to figure out how to kill them. And what do you know? Under allergies, Daniel has a nice big red warning: lethally allergic to sesame. Wow. Why are my shoulders suddenly supertense? I should be feeling great about this. Killing someone is rarely this damn simple. I stare at the screen for a long beat, imagining myself slipping some sesame oil into Daniel's food. It would be so easy—ask him on a date, and when he's in the bathroom, boom. I could do it without breaking a sweat. So why am I suddenly sweating?

I roll my shoulders, then shake myself. *Moving on.*

Craig is up next. I type his name into the search bar and pull up his file with a click. He has that heart condition, which I already knew about—unstable angina pectoris. I looked it up a few nights ago, and his risk of sudden heart attack is definitely higher, which is good to know. That could appear "natural" for sure. He's on anticoagulants and takes aspirin regularly. The nutritionist has him on a low-fat diet—no surprise there—and there's a note that he is absolutely not able to do intense physical activity. As I peruse his schedule, I notice that he has a standing appointment for one of the individual sauna rooms every day he's here. An appointment that only lasts five minutes. A little internet research tells me that, in his condition, staying in the sauna for much longer could be lethal. That, or dousing him in really cold water right after his session. That could set off a heart attack. Though I struggle to picture myself storming in with a bucket of ice water. What if it didn't work? That would be awkward. Dumping him into a cold pool would be better, but if he passed out in the heat, how would I carry him from the sauna room to the pool? Things to think about.

Finally, I look up Serena. As VP, her information in the system isn't as extensive as a guest's, but it does display the services she's booked with her 50-percent management discount. She's seeing a life coach once a week. She has a lot of cosmetic treatments lined up—a weekly facial, the Seaweed Body Wrap, a mani-pedi. Everything I might have expected. Even though I've already imagined staging a "slip" on the stairs, it's a little disappointing that there's not something as obvious as, say, Daniel's allergy. Damn it—why couldn't *she* have the sesame allergy? Still, there's always a way. Let's see… Could I somehow poison her body wrap? Though a poison absorbed through the skin doesn't feel like it would be fast-acting enough. I make a mental note to research this further, but…maybe an accident is my best bet with her after all? The thing is, even though a push *sounds* simple, it's risky. I've only pushed someone once, and it's definitely not my favorite method; too much can go wrong. However, if you can pull it off, it does leave the least evidence behind. High risk, high reward.

"Hey, you want that bowl of poke?"

I snap the laptop shut and smile up at Sean, who's looking amused. I glance at the clock. Wow—two hours have gone by.

"You know I do," I say.

"Coming right up. Any allergies?"

I almost laugh. "Nope."

I look around the place as Sean disappears into the kitchen. The light has shifted. Everyone who was here earlier is gone, and a sparse lunch crowd has taken over. A couple of teens holding hands across a table. An old man drinking a beer with half-closed eyes and ignoring his sandwich. Two loud Americans—a guy in board shorts, a girl in a bikini—sharing nachos. The scent of the spiced meat wafts over, and my stomach growls.

My phone vibrates against the table with an incoming call just as Sean returns with the poke bowl, a mountain of rosy fresh tuna pieces sprinkled with bright-orange roe. Perfectly fanned avocado slices, and a sprinkling of sesame seeds like a wink from the universe.

I gesture my thanks as I pick up my phone. It's a WhatsApp call. As soon as I see who it is, my gut clenches and my heart races. There's no question; I have to answer.

"Hi Beth Ann," I say into the phone. Already, I sound stiff and cold, not like myself at all, but I don't know how to be any other way with Jessica's mom. We never shared a lot of love. Maybe she could tell how hard I was trying to impress her back when Jessica introduced me, our first Thanksgiving together. Maybe she didn't like that I had no family, no mom, no "roots," as she called them. Or maybe she just didn't like that her daughter was with a woman.

Now, of course, she has all the reason in the world to openly hate me. I'm the person responsible for her losing her daughter.

"Lily?" Her voice already grates—breathy and gentle and *nice*.

I can understand her hatred. I'll never forget that horrible dark night in the hospital waiting room as she shrieked at me. *I can't believe you left her alone in the apartment! What were you thinking?*

I had no answer. She was merely voicing the same things I'd been shrieking at myself.

"What's going on?" I ask. Of course, there's a fierce little hope at the reason she might be calling—but I squash it.

"I hope I haven't caught you at a bad time," she says. "I know you're out of the country right now."

"This is a fine time," I say, using all my self-control to keep my voice calm. For the love of God, woman, just tell me why you're calling. "What can I do for you?"

"Well...this is maybe a little awkward, but..."

I bang my fist silently against the table and watch the poke shake.

"There's a picture."

What?

"And Don was wondering if perhaps you have it. Maybe in a box with some of Jessica's old things? It's from her college graduation. She's in her cap and gown, and Don and I are on either side. We'd just like to have it back. If you don't mind looking for it. Jessica's birthday is coming up, you know, and I'm making a little collage for the party."

It doesn't escape my notice that there is no invitation for me.

Not that I'd want to go.

Jess isn't here anymore. It makes me feel sick inside to envision Don and Beth Ann in party mode, putting on a celebration and waxing sentimental over old photographs.

Beth Ann talks on. "One of us could pick it up from you, or you could mail it. We'd just really like to have that picture back."

"Sorry. I don't remember that picture," I say, leaning my forehead on my clenched fist and squeezing my eyes shut. *You kept what was supposed to be mine*, I want to scream at her. *And now you're shaking me down for a picture? Don't you understand that I have nothing left?*

"Well, perhaps you could check…" Beth Ann lets her voice trail off.

"Yeah. OK. I'll let you know," I say, and then I disconnect the call. I won't check. And I won't let her know. *Fuck you*, I think. I remember Jessica's stories about how her mom would put them both on "little diets" in advance of swimsuit season. Early on in our relationship, Jess rolled her eyes and laughed as she told me these stories, like it was just another annoying eccentricity of her trim mother, along with her obsessive flossing and consummate vacuuming. But I've never forgotten.

I rip the paper off the disposable chopsticks, target a piece of tuna, and, for a few minutes, just allow myself to enjoy the food. The velvety texture of the spicy mayo, the juicy sweetness of the diced mango. The crunch of tempura flakes and the bursting salty pearls of roe.

By the time I'm dredging the last bite of rice through the sauce at the bottom of the bowl, I'm ready to dive back into my research. Sean comes to take away my bowl.

"Hope you enjoyed it."

"It was perfect. Hey—you hear all the Riovan gossip here."

He nods, that amused smile already back on his lips.

"Has anyone been talking about that death last year?"

Sean's eyes crinkle in thought. "Actually…yeah. An American from a magazine was here just a few days ago. Daniel something. He was asking what I knew about the guy. I said, I heard he was some big shot in the music industry, and there was an accident of some kind."

Oh shit.

Sean continues. "Daniel said, did you hear what kind of accident, and I said no, my impression was the staff wasn't in the know either. Management kept a tight lid on that one. My educated guess?

Drugs. It's always drugs with these celebrities." Sean nods slowly, as if the motion of his head were jogging his memory. "But then, he started asking about the hurricane. Yeah, he was really interested in the hurricane."

Wait—huh? My expression must show my confusion, because Sean keeps talking.

"Yeah, ten years ago, wasn't it? Hurricane Alberta. Destroyed everything." He swipes flattened palms through the air. "The Riovan rebuilt in six months, but Brisebleue…" He shrugs. "We never really recovered here. I mean, Randy had some savings, add in some sweat equity, we brought Island Vibes back within a year." He gives me a half smile. "I was the plumber, the electrician, the dry-waller, you name it. Learned a lot that year. But that guy, Daniel—he was curious about local resentment, you know? And Randy's story. Why he chose to build here instead of closer to the resort, where he'd get more business. If there was…I don't know. Bad blood between us and the Riovan. At that point, I'd had enough of him, so I told him he'd have to talk to Randy."

Well, now I'm even more confused. Yesterday, I thought Daniel might not be a journalist. Then I read his *Fit Life* diatribes. Now he's asking questions, and it's not just about Michael's death, but a hurricane from ten years ago? The topics seem not only unrelated, but too serious for the kind of stuff *Fit Life* publishes—or the kind of refuse Daniel seems to enjoy writing.

I smile at Sean, even though my pulse is drumming. I can't seem to fit the pieces together where Daniel is concerned. And if I'm going to kill him, I'd better make damn sure I know who I'm killing.

"Thanks, Sean."

He hesitates before leaving. "You OK, Lily?"

I give him a fond smile. It's sweet that he seems to actually care.

"Peachy," I say. I check my watch. "Is it too early for something strong?" After that call from Beth Ann, I could use some help.

He seems pleasantly surprised. "Not at all. What'll it be?"

I smile back, but I'm already opening my laptop back up and typing Daniel Black into the search bar.

"Surprise me."

CHAPTER 18

I TURN THE BIKE IN AT THE RENTAL DESK JUST AS THE SUN IS DIPPING out of sight to the west. My legs are a little achy, and my eyes hurt from staring at the computer screen for so long.

Outside Adventure Rentals, I stop on the path leading back toward the hotel. In front of me is the main building, the windows of the Sunset Bar reflecting the last of the light. Should I grab some dinner? Or head back to my room in Vista West for a shower? Shower, I decide, and walk decisively toward the lesser-known path I used my first day here.

It's a beautiful night. The ocean is laced in pink and yellow reflections as I head toward Vista West, its windows cozy and welcoming. In the dome of the sky, the first stars are poking through the velvety blue. A cool ocean breeze dries the last of the sweat on my body as I take the familiar stone walkway. The solar garden lights are just popping on for the night.

It was a productive day. I now have mental blueprints of how I could potentially kill Craig, Serena, and Daniel. Not perfect plans, definitely not finalized, but a solid start. As for Daniel, my online research was interesting, though like everything about this man, I'm not yet sure what to make of it. He's been on staff at *Fit Life* for five years. I tried to find out where he worked previously, but even with a long series of searches featuring all the key words I could think of, I got nothing. It's like he poofed into existence only to write toxic waste. I couldn't even find a photo of him, just one of the watercolor caricatures that all the staff at *Fit Life* use in their bios. Besides capturing his hair color and five-o'clock shadow, the caricaturist did a pretty shit job with the resemblance.

I stop in my tracks on a sandy rock, suddenly remembering. That call the anonymous guy I assumed to be a journalist made to Taste of Heaven; the one my office manager Becca contacted me about. Pulling out my phone, I quickly find her voice message and press play again.

"Hey boss, some guy called for you… I was like, 'Excuse me, who are you' and got his number from caller ID. In case you wanted to get in touch with him. It's two-one-two…"

On a whim, I type the numbers into the WhatsApp keypad, hit *Dial*, and switch it to speakerphone. It rings once, twice. And then: "Hello?" A voice I'd know anywhere. My whole body is pounding. "Hello? Lily?" He sounds out of breath.

I hit disconnect on instinct. Which is silly; my picture on WhatsApp already gave me away.

Almost immediately, my phone vibrates in my hands; he's calling back. I hit decline. He tries again, I decline again. Then, a message from him pops through. *Lily? You OK?*

My thumbs hover over the screen as I process. Daniel Black was looking into me before we even met. That first morning in the coffee alcove—he already knew who I was. *Oh God.* As that first conversation replays in my head, I remember my exact thoughts about him: too close, too fast. Why didn't I listen to that instinct? And then he asked me out for drinks at the Sunset Bar. *Zero assumptions*, he promised. *Just two people talking.*

Liar. Fucking *liar*. He came here to look into me. That has to be it…right? He's got it into his mind that I killed Michael Johnson, and he seduced me into confessing that I know something about rewiring electrical panels, and now…

What? An exposé? Lily, the killer lifeguard? He can't prove anything, can he?

A tiny flicker of doubt stirs, muddying my line of thinking. Why did he go to Brisebleue and ask about the hurricane? All that stuff Sean said about local resentment—how does *that* fit in?

There's no way he's doing this story for *Fit Life*. *Fit Life* is what you read in the lobby of your doctor's office; it's not investigative journalism.

Ugh, ugh, ugh. I do not want to be dealing with this complication right now. My body aches from the back-and-forth bike trip; my head feels foggy from the long hours of research staring at the screen. It would be nice to give myself the gift of a simple good night's sleep. But I have to figure out what Daniel wants from me—how much he suspects or knows—if he may have even followed me here, as I'm starting to fear. And this problem is far too urgent to leave for tomorrow.

I start to type. *Hey, sorry for the dropped calls—weak Wi-Fi! Dinner tonight at the Sunset?*

Daniel's response is nearly immediate. *In the middle of something. How about tomorrow? 8?*

Tomorrow. Ugh. I want answers now.

I pick some dry skin off my lip, considering my next move. Yes, I have questions for Mr. Black. I suppose they can wait until tomorrow. But he's not going to roll over for me either. It's not like I'm going to say, "Why are you really here?" and he's going to tell me. I need a more direct method.

I thumbs-up his message, swipe WhatsApp shut, and pull up my web browser. Soon, I'm logged back into the Guest Services Portal. The platform isn't supermobile-friendly but I'm able to locate Daniel's schedule pretty quickly anyway.

Ah. He's in the middle of an evening gym session with Tim from *Take It Off*. It wasn't on his schedule earlier… I note that it lasts until eight thirty. Hence him sounding a little winded.

I wonder why he's suddenly so interested in working out.

But I do know that it gives me, starting now, exactly thirty-nine minutes if I want to break into his room.

CHAPTER 19

"HI," I SAY IN A FRIENDLY TONE TO THE WOMAN BEHIND THE RECEPTION desk. "I'm so sorry to bother you, but—" I lower my voice and lean forward over the counter. "We have a journalist staying with us. Daniel Black? And he, um…just locked himself out of his room. Could I grab a key for him?"

The woman's brow wrinkles. "We'd be happy to issue him another key if he can come down himself—"

"He's naked." I make a cringe face. "Vic is really keen on keeping him happy, so I'm supposed to run Mr. Black a key as quickly as possible. Oh—I'm Lily. I work here too. Sorry, I should have said."

Still, she hesitates, possibly because I'm a sweaty mess and not looking on-brand.

"Look," I say, with an edge to my tone. "I'm not trying to be difficult, but this is urgent. Do you need me to get Vic?"

Immediately, the resistance melts off her face.

"Of course not, no need to bother Mr. Salinas. Let me just activate a new card for Mr. Black—"

Key finally in hand—and multiple minutes wasted, ugh—I take the elevator to his floor, slicing the card back and forth along my palm because the ascent feels unusually slow. Can't they build faster elevators? Time is money, people! Finally, the doors open. Two guests are waiting. I smile, they smile back. I walk down the hall slowly, knowing their eyes may still be on me. As soon as the elevator doors close fully and I'm free from watching eyes, I sprint.

My lungs are heaving as I finally reach his door and jam the key card in. Inside the dark room, my eyes immediately find the bright green digits of the bedside clock—*shit*. Only twenty-two minutes to spare. *Move, Lily!* I flip on the lights.

First: dresser drawers. All empty; he hasn't even unpacked. I push open the mirrored closet door where the room safe is. His luggage is on the floor—a hardback Tumi splayed open, with a mess of clothes spilling out. At least that makes it easy to search.

I rummage through the clothes, looking for anything—identification, papers, notes.

Nothing.

He has a backpack leaned up against the TV console, a laptop open on the desk, and a pair of reading glasses on the nightstand. I go through the backpack next. Water bottle—almost empty—some pens, an unused legal pad, a sleeve of tissues, a battered pair of sunglasses. Onward.

The laptop springs awake at a touch of my finger to the mouse pad, but of course it's password-protected. Even though I already know it's a waste of time, I make a few random attempts—DBlack123, DanielB, DanielB1. When it warns me that I have one attempt left, I stop.

The nightstand drawers are also empty, save a hotel notepad, a laminated TV guide, and a room-service menu.

The bathroom is messy. A towel on the floor. Personal hygiene items scattered across the sink. Aftershave—mm, smells like him—and immediately, I'm mentally on his bed again, naked under him, the smell of sweat and desire rolling off him, my hands clawing at his back—

Trash bin! Trash bin!

Back to the present. Cheap razor, a beard trimmer, a toothbrush, Colgate toothpaste. I note toothpaste smeared in the sink, hair clippings on the counter, some Q-tips in the trash. I return to the bedroom area and check the clock. Ten minutes left, and I've found nothing of worth. Certainly nothing magazine-related... No notes for his article, though of course those would likely be on his phone and laptop. No press ID... Would he keep them in the room safe?

The default number, I happen to know, is 1-2-3-4. Most guests change it, but... I punch the numbers into the keypad. It pops open—ha!

Inside the safe, there's finally something. A microphone. A ring light. Some cash, US dollars and euros. And finally, a US passport. I reach for the passport and open it. Daniel's face stares back, utterly serious. Almost scary-serious. My eyes immediately fall on his name.

Daniel Aleksy Lukiewicz.

What the...

I'm reaching for my phone to take a picture of his passport when I hear a voice outside the door—Daniel's. Shit! He's back early from his workout!

Tossing the passport back in, I shut the safe, but there's no time to close the sliding closet door. I make a wild scan around the room for the best hiding place, then dive under the bed, already feeling the sting of a rug burn down my leg. It's a tight, tight fit—I have to keep my head turned to one side. I've barely wiggled my feet out of sight when the door clicks open. The clearance is so low that if he sits down on the bed, he might actually crush me.

"Did you get the coroner's report I sent?" It sounds like Daniel's on the phone. "No. I'm not sure yet... I'll shoot over my notes. See what you think."

And then, he sits on the fucking bed.

The pressure is immediate, and intense. I can feel my spine bend and my lungs compress. His feet are inches from my face. One lifts, then a sock is flung. Then, the other sock.

"I know. You think I haven't thought of that a million times?"

The voice on the other line is a muffled blur but sounds animated.

"No. It can't be a coincidence. I'd bet my career on it. I *am* betting my career on it. One person, every year, at the same time of year..."

Oh, fuck. He's not just looking into Michael's death. He knows there are more.

In fact, I might be next. If he shifts, or bounces a little, he might snap my spine, and then it's adios Lily.

He chuckles. "Nah, you're right. Just remember I'm here under Daniel *Black*, OK?" Pause. "Yeah, let me know about that advertising slot. It feels like exactly what we've been waiting for."

Sweat is beading on my forehead. My lungs are pancakes.

"Could be huge," he goes on. "Listen, I just got back from a workout. Let me call you after I hit the shower."

He gets up. Sweet relief. Painfully, slowly, I allow my lungs to fully inflate again.

He must have disconnected his call. I hear the clunk of the phone being set down on a hard surface.

I listen to him pad around the room. His feet come in and out of my line of sight, then one lifts—ah. His workout shorts are coming off. Then a pair of black briefs. In spite of the circumstances, I have a sudden and very specific vision of the two perfect muscled mounds that comprise his ass. A grunt tells me his shirt is next, and it's also suddenly very hard not to remember how good his torso looked when it was inches above mine. Some quiet thwacks tell me he's throwing his clothes on the bed. Then, the creak of the bathroom door and, finally, the sound of the shower—my exit cue.

I wait until I hear him singing, loud and off-key like last time. This time, it's Cat Stevens's "Peace Train," a song that's always made me inexplicably sad, even though I think it's supposed to be hopeful.

Forget about "Peace Train" and peace your way out of here! I chide myself and army-crawl out. I scrape sweaty tendrils of hair from my eyes as I make for his laptop, just in case he happened to drop his password in as he roamed about the room; still locked. Fuck. Do I have time to go back into the safe…

The shower turns off. Nope. Also, who the hell takes a two-minute shower? Can he even be clean?

Then a thought hits me like a freight train.

I could kill him.

I could kill Daniel in this very room.

He's stronger, too strong for me to overcome without the element of surprise…but I'm creative…

No, you're thinking crazy.

I move with swift steps toward the door. I open it as quietly and as quickly as I can and step out into the hall, where—

"Fuck!" I breathe, just as a surprised maid with an armful of towels says, "Merde!"

She was obviously just about to knock when I flung open the door.

"Um…" I give a guilty smile. "He's in the shower. You might want to come back?"

She hesitates, then extends the soft pile of towels to me. In accented English, she says, "Would you like to take them inside, miss?"

"Ah…not a good idea." I shut the door behind me the rest of the way. Unfortunately, the noise of the door clicking into place is somehow gargantuan.

Daniel must be out of the bathroom, because from inside the room I hear him say, "Hello? Who's there?"

"Please don't mention me," I say, with barely enough time to register the puzzled expression on her face before I'm fleeing down the hall.

I round the corner just in time to hear the woman say, "Towels, sir?"

"Oh—yeah. Thanks. I forgot I ordered these."

"You're welcome."

I don't return directly to my room. Instead, I head to the beach to clear my head.

Daniel's name is Lukiewicz, not Black. Fine. He's not the toxic *Fit Life* reporter—great. He's only *posing* as the toxic *Fit Life* reporter, which—what the hell? Then again, I guess that means I didn't sleep with some toxic asshole, so that's a plus! But—killjoy—he's looking into the deaths I am responsible for. And I can't imagine it will take him long to realize that the dates of my yearly employment coincide, always, with the demise of someone. *Or maybe he came here already knowing that.*

Why is he investigating—and why undercover? Is he…FBI? Interpol? But what was that about an advertising slot?

I pull out my phone and type his name—his *real* name, this

time—into my search engine. It only takes a little scrolling to find a hit...nope. Broken link. But the next one is a LinkedIn hit, which is very promising. I open my LinkedIn app and switch to private mode so he can't see I'm looking. And there is his headshot, looking almost as serious as his passport picture.

His work history is very conveniently spelled out...except that it ends over a year ago, with his last job at—oh, shit! The *Pacific*, one of the most illustrious news magazines in the English-speaking world.

I have no idea what to make of this. Did he get fired? Is he trying to get his job back at the *Pacific* by writing some big exposé...about me? *If that's the case, you're out of luck, buddy*, I think grimly. I'm not ending up in prison like Mom. It's not that I'm unwilling to accept that my actions may have consequences, but frankly, none of the people I've killed are worth going to prison over.

I've reached the shoreline. I take a seat on the sand, run a hand through my hair, and tilt my face into the cool breeze coming off the ocean. I've answered some questions, but...now there are even more.

The most pressing question: Am I his prime suspect? Or, God forbid, his only suspect? He didn't say my name during his phone call. That's good. But I don't know who he was talking to, and maybe he keeps his cards close.

I lean my chin on my knees and watch the waves roll in, allowing their rhythm to return calm to my speeding heart. The moon makes a long reflection, like a path made of light.

For some reason, Jessica feels near to me right now. As though the moon-path were connecting me to the place where she's gone, and at any moment, I might see her walking through the glimmer toward me. I wish I could buy her a ticket on Cat Stevens's peace train. Send her home.

She's not at peace, I know it, even though medical science would tell me otherwise. I'm not a spiritual person, but in my heart, I know she's in stasis. Still with me, trapped here, still needing all the things I failed to give her…

I swallow the lump in my throat. I don't even know what the lump is—some burning wedge of grief and anger.

I'm shaking. Maybe from cold.

I could still kill Daniel.

But that's not the playbook, is it?

He's not toxic writer Daniel Black; that's just his cover. I only kill toxic people. I don't kill to protect myself.

I'm shaking harder; I draw my knees close to my chest and wrap my arms tight around them, working my finger under the elastic on my wristband and tugging it rhythmically without letting it snap.

Is this how I go down?

It can't be; I can't let it be. Tomorrow at dinner I'll figure out what he knows. And if he truly is on to me…I'll deal with it then.

Does Jess know what I do for her?

Maybe she would hate it. I don't know. I can't speak for her; no one can. But if she can see me down here, doing my best, I hope she understands that this is my way of leaving some kind of legacy from the pain I fear she's still in.

I pull out my phone. It's late, but I don't care. I dial Beth Ann.

She answers on the second ring. "Hi, Lily! Did you find the photo?" Her voice is breathy and eager.

My mouth is dry. When I start talking, I know I sound like a robot.

"When you called earlier, I thought maybe you were calling to talk about the—the other disagreement we've had."

There's a weighted pause.

Beth Ann's tone takes on a chill I know all too well. "Don and I have made our desires quite clear on that point."

Fury knots in my throat. "I was going to marry her."

"Thank God you didn't."

"What's the point?" I spit. I'm nearly hyperventilating. This is why we don't talk. Because I can't stay unemotional with the woman who set herself against me—against us. Against her own daughter. "Just tell me what the point is! I don't understand!"

"The point is to do the right thing, even when it's hard."

"But it's not right, Beth Ann! It's—"

"We gave you Taste of Heaven free and clear," she cuts in. "We didn't ask for a cent from Jessica's part of the business. We have been more than generous with you. We gave you what was yours, and all we're asking is for you to respect what's ours."

My teeth are clenched, distorting my words. "I. Can't. It's wrong. It's *wrong*."

"I'm sorry you feel that way, Lily, but this conversation is over."

She disconnects.

With a growl of rage, I throw my phone. It lands somewhere in the sand. Then I bury my face in my knees.

I rub my finger, hard. The finger where my ring would have gone too. I bought a diamond ring for Jessica and a simple band for myself. I didn't propose at the Riovan, but I thought there would be chances back in Cincinnati. Then she spiraled so fast...by the time I realized she needed professional help, a proposal didn't feel right. We checked her into Restore30 for their thirty-day program. When she came out, I should have proposed then, right away. Instead...fuck. And now, here I am.

I feel like a widow, but I was just the girlfriend.

Finally, I get up. Recover my phone. Brush it off.

My whole body feels numb, but I force myself to walk back to my room. River is in the shower, thankfully. I huddle in my bed under the covers without taking off my clothes. I'm still filthy and sweaty from my day at Brisebleue and my painful minutes intimately bonding with Daniel's floor, but I don't have the energy to move.

Maybe when River gets out I'll hop in the shower. Maybe I'll feel some sharpness return, some sense of being in control, but right now I feel completely hollowed out.

Maybe I'll…

CHAPTER 20

I SIT UPRIGHT IN BED, HEART THUNDERING AS HARD AS IF I'D BEEN running, sweat rolling down my body.

The green numbers on the hotel alarm clock say 2:36 a.m. The room is black around me—and sweltering. I throw the bedcovers off my legs and take a minute to just breathe.

I was having a dream about Beth Ann vacuuming incessantly outside my door... I look over at River, whose mouth is open, emitting a rhythmic rattle. *Right.* Snoring roommate.

Well, there's no getting back to sleep in this heat. Is the AC off? I cartwheel my legs over the side of the bed and pad over to the digital thermostat by the bathroom. Ninety-five degrees Fahrenheit? That can't be right—and yet I can feel the confirming thickness in the air, like I'm inhaling hot soup.

When a sharp, rapping sound comes from the door, I muffle a yelp, adrenaline jolting me more awake than I'd like to be at this hour. I put a hand to my chest to try and help my heart recover. Anger follows. Who the hell is knocking at this time of night? Daniel?

I walk over to the door ready to give someone a piece of my mind but first put my eye to the peephole. I nearly reel back in shock as I take in the distorted face looking at me, hair in disarray, eyes wide, mascara smudged.

Carli Elle?

My fingers make a frantic fumble to unlock the chain and deadbolt. I fling open the door.

The hallway yawns back at me. No one there. The hall lights flicker, then dim.

"Carli?" I say softly, as a gust of chilly air raises goose bumps on my body.

Using a foot to keep the door propped open, I step out into the hall. There she is, all the way at the end of the hall, walking quickly away from me. The lights are flickering and buzzing like a beehive.

"Carli!" I call out. Damn it—if I go back inside the room to find my key, I'll lose her. There's only one thing to do. Letting the door close behind me, I sprint after her, to the corner she disappeared around, just in time to see her slip through a doorway.

It's a lot chillier out here, reminding me that I'm dressed only in my sleep tank top and a faded pair of polka-dot PJ shorts. I shiver. I reach the place where she disappeared—the ice-machine room—and step cautiously inside. No Carli. The buzz is louder here. Something must be going on with the building's electrics. The vending machine has an OUT OF SERVICE sign taped to it. There's only one place she could have gone from here: the door marked RESTRICTED ACCESS, where this floor's electrical panels are.

The handle gives—unlocked. Not good. I push it slowly open, her name on my lips, ready to release a torrent of questions.

Empty. It can't be. I turn, then turn again. There's literally nowhere else to go. But someone has been in here. The electrical panel is open, a cable pulled out. And on the floor lies a pair of black electrical gloves, curled like dead, dark fish skins…and a hair dryer.

I pick it up with a shaking hand. The GFCI cord is cut off. Shit. And yet…it can't possibly be the hair dryer I threw into the ocean. That one sank. No one could have possibly found it.

What the fuck is going on? A copycat crime? Some sick reenactment?

I drop the hair dryer and return to the hall, just in time to hear the click of the emergency exit door across the way.

I follow, muscling the door to the stairwell open. It's echoey in here, all cinder blocks and no carpet. The floor is cold against my bare feet. I can hear quick steps somewhere beneath me.

"Carli!" I shout and take the steps two at a time, my voice taking on monstrous proportions in the empty stairwell. At the bottom of the stairs, I push open the heavy door that takes me outside the hotel.

The air is clammy, sticking to me like a skin as I run after the dark figure. Above, the sky is pulsing with heat lightning, illuminating Carli's shadowy figure as she runs up the cliff. The natural stone path is harsh underfoot. To my left yawns a killer drop. The hungry, dark ocean rumbles its menacing presence somewhere down there, just waiting for someone to fall into its throat.

"Carli! Stop! Let's talk!" I shout. And then, a light in a window flips on, bright and cold, stopping me in my tracks. It's one of the Riovan's luxury villas, the building appearing out of the dark like a slap, as if it weren't there a second ago and has simply materialized. I squint. There's someone there. An outline. A man.

"Daniel?" I say.

Suddenly, I understand.

Carli hired Daniel to investigate me. To find evidence. To bring me down.

"Aah—" I yelp, as something wraps around my throat. The pain is horrible; my breath is cut off.

An angry voice says, hot, into my ear, "You ruined me." It's Carli. I claw at the thing around my neck. It's a wire. It's cutting into my skin already. I can smell my own blood and feel its wretched pulse as it oozes around the wire like a rising swamp.

"Ca—" I gasp. I crash to my knees. My lungs are in shreds. I feel her pulling tighter, now bracing a knee against my back. She wrenches my head up with her force, and I can see Daniel's silhouette, still unmoving. Can he see us?

Help, I want to cry. But I have no voice.

"You thought you could do whatever the hell you wanted," says Carli. "But you had no right. My career died with Michael. And it's your fault!"

My hands keep working uselessly at the wire. They're wet with blood. I've got to explain, make Carli see that Michael was actually destroying her—but my vision is swimming with spots.

"No more playing God, Lily Lennox. You're a murderer." She's speaking through a smile now. "Time to taste your own medicine."

My lips move—*No, you've got it all twisted around*—but no sound comes out.

I fix my vision on the bright star of the villa. The silhouette, unmoving.

I fall.

I blink awake. The sky is fresh with a pink sunrise, the ocean happily splashing against the cliff.

I prop myself up slowly; my whole body hurts.

My fingertips brush my throat. I'm alive.

It was a dream.

But why am I outside, on a stone path? I gingerly sit up, feeling the knots in my back. Holy shit, I sleepwalked.

"Motherfucker," I groan as I work myself to standing, my joints and muscles clamoring their protest.

I should feel relieved that it was all a dream. But sleepwalking is freaky business, especially when it takes you to the edge of a fucking cliff.

As I stretch the kinks out of my back, I register someone watching from the nearby luxury villa a little farther up the path. Not Daniel idly observing my murder, thank God. A woman in a robe, standing in the sliding door. In sunlight, the villa is stunning, its clean modern lines contrasting with the natural edges of the cliff. The whole wall facing the ocean is made of glass. The woman straightens as she notices me and shields her eyes, clearly wondering what I'm doing here.

"Hi," I call out, feeling the need to put her at ease. "Beautiful morning."

Her response is to disappear back inside. The path leading to the luxury villas is private; I'd better leave in case she's calling hotel security.

I head down the pathway, taking care where I place my tender bare feet, and head back to the hotel. First stop, front desk, because my sleepwalking self didn't grab a key.

The first time I sleepwalked was with the Miller family, back when I was in foster care. I liked them. They had a girl my age, and a boy two years older—Shari and James. They played board games on Saturday nights as a family, went on long Sunday bike rides, and genuinely seemed to like one another. But one night, I was dreaming that I had accidentally killed James with a skillet and I had to run away before they realized what I'd done.

When I woke up, people were screaming at me. I was confused, overwhelmed, and I remember bursting into tears, because I didn't understand why I was in the driver's seat of the family's Honda Odyssey. Thankfully, I hadn't actually tried to drive it yet. The minivan was just idling in the garage, and the family woke up because the carbon monoxide detector went off.

I was reassigned to the Loetz family within the week.

The Loetzes weren't into board games. They were a self-described "boring" family, which meant that they and their adult son, who lived in the basement, watched a lot of TV. They knew about my sleepwalking, so every night, the dad locked me in my own room "as a precaution," with a toddler potty from their bygone baby days in case I had to go in the night.

One night, I dreamed that they were poisoning me through the vents so that I would be weak enough for them to take out. I had to escape. That time, I woke up in their kitchen, crouched on the counter and armed with two knives, with the husband shouting, "Put the weapons down, Lily!" as the wife held up throw pillows like shields. I dropped the knives and started shaking and crying. Apparently, I had escaped out of the window, jumped one story down, and headed straight for the knives. They had security-camera footage and replayed the whole thing for the social worker.

"I'm sorry," I remember crying. "Please give me another chance." The Loetzes weren't as nice as the Millers, but I didn't want to move again. It was the nicest bedroom I'd ever had, with a window seat and a desk and a reading lamp that you could turn on by touch. "I didn't know what I was doing."

There were a few more episodes, though not as dramatic as the first two. Thankfully, a shrink put me on benzodiazepines, and the sleepwalking stopped as suddenly as it had started. I haven't sleepwalked since. Until last night.

I need to get my hands on some benzos.

"Can I help you?" says a friendly voice. I'm next in line at the front desk. I lower my voice, feeling self-conscious about my situation. And my appearance. The tiny polka-dot shorts and tank top are the opposite of "on-brand."

"Hey. I, um, locked myself out of my room." Thank God it's not the same woman as last night.

"OK. Happy to help you. Room number?" says the young woman, whose name tag reads Carolina.

I give her my information; she gives me a key.

I really, really have to pee at this point, so before returning to my room I make for the restrooms down the hall. The women's restroom is a cavernous affair with marble sink countertops and golden fixtures. A few women are chatting at the sink while they wash their hands, and the smell of coconut and lemongrass is overpowering. "The jungle excursion was booked, but she got me a spot!"

"Do you think we need bug spray?"

"Oh, good idea. Let's check the gift shop—"

A couple of stalls are occupied, but I keep my head down and disappear quickly into a free one. For a while, I just sit there on the toilet as I relieve my bladder, head hanging, listening to the sounds of people coming and going with brisk morning energy.

I hate the feeling of impotence sleepwalking gives me. As if I were a loaded gun in the hands of a stranger...and the stranger is myself.

Self-pity really isn't my thing, but a little voice edges in anyway.

Why are things always so hard for me? My childhood, the loss of my mom, losing Jessica—and now this mess with Daniel, the only person I've felt drawn to in years, who's trying to make a case that links all the deaths together, to a single killer. Which he may or may not already believe is me—a question I intend to answer tonight at the Sunset.

"Hey, what's wrong, honey?" says a voice I recognize, pulling me out of my pathetic little pity party It's Serena, her voice echoey in the bathroom. There's a sniffling.

"It's my mom," says a second voice. A younger, more childish voice, which I also recognize immediately. Skylar. "We're going on the waterfall exploration tour today. So I put on my bathing suit? And she said I'm f-f-f-…fat."

"Oooooh," Serena croons. "Hon, growing up is so hard." She clicks her tongue compassionately, and for a second, I think—maybe Serena is about to redeem herself.

If she's kind to Skylar, I decide spontaneously, I'm not going to kill her.

"I just don't look…pretty enough," says Skylar, gulping back her words in a way that tells me she's trying not to sob.

"Trust me, when I was your age, I had exactly the same struggle," says Serena.

"R-really?"

"Of course! I was overweight as a kid, too! But don't worry. We all have the power inside us to make a change."

"N-not m-me," says Skylar, sniffing again. "My mom says I have n-no self-control."

"That was probably hard to hear," says Serena. "But listen…you don't have to do this alone! Sometimes we all need a little help! Actually, we're working with this amazing company now. It's called CleanSlim, and I'll give you a complimentary package. Would you like that?"

"Really?" Skylar's tone is so sweet, so grateful. "What is it?"

"You just mix it into your smoothie, and all the baby fat will fall right off. Promise!"

Oh. My. God. Serena is giving a laxative to a teenager.

"Can I have some now?" says Skylar.

Serena laughs. "Actually, I do have some on me…" There's the sound of a zipper, then the crinkling of plastic. "I keep this with me to give to prospective customers. How lucky that we ran into each other! Now, don't tell your mom. Just surprise her with the results! Wouldn't that be fun?"

"Yeah," says Skylar. "Will it work that fast?"

"You do have to keep at it, but you'll start seeing a difference within the week, promise."

"Wow. Thank you!"

I hear Skylar leave the bathroom, and then Serena humming to herself and washing her hands.

For a minute, I brace my hands against the sides of the stall and push as hard as I can, feeling the blood throb in my body. I don't even have to try to conjure up the violent scenarios. I see myself killing Serena in six different ways within as many seconds.

One thing is sure: I've got my mark. This is it. Now I have to calm down and bide my time and do it smart, like I always do.

When I emerge from the stall, Serena is tweaking her makeup at the mirror.

"Lily! Oh my God, I didn't realize you were in here!" She does a bit of a double take. "Rough night?"

"I locked myself out of the room," I say with a wry smile, as I imagine killing her in two more ways. The faucets have sharp edges. "Not ideal." I take in Serena's sweat-drenched athletic top and flushed face. "But you look like you've had a workout already."

"Oh, it's just my morning hike. It's important to build those habits in, you know?" She uncaps a highlighter and sweeps it over her cheekbones, turning her face from side to side.

Morning hike. My heart pounds.

"Where do you hike around here?" I say innocently. Or do I sound guilty? Shit, I have to play this right. Thankfully, however I sound, her focus is on her mascara now, so she takes it in her stride.

"I have this whole circuit that goes around the hotel and ends on the rocks by the ocean, you know that gorgeous jetty? It's the perfect spot for a posthike meditation session. No one is up that early, so it's just the sky and the water and…" She laughs and pops the mascara wand back into its tube. "Little old me!"

I feign a laugh. "Wow, you must get up really early, then." I make some attempt at redoing my ponytail, even though it's useless. I need a full shower and change of clothes.

"Five thirty," she chirps, smacking her freshly moisturized lips. "It's perfect, because then I'm hitting the rocks just as the sun rises. Soooo pretty! Well—see you around, Lily." She hesitates at the bathroom door. "Hey, do you happen to know if that journalist is single?"

I give her a wide-eyed "what journalist?" expression but follow it up quickly with an "Oh, yeah, him…no, I think he has someone back home."

"It figures," she says with an exaggerated pout. "All the good ones are taken."

"Yeah. Pity. But there's always that other guy…Kyle?"

She screws up her face like she's having trouble remembering, then visibly flinches. "Yeah, ew. Too old. Too *needy*. But hey, great talk!"

She swishes out of the bathroom, leaving me momentarily alone.

I look at myself in the mirror. My hair is wild, frizzed from sleeping outside. My polka-dot shorts look extraratty and faded in the daylight, and my tank top has fresh sweat stains. But no matter how disheveled my outward appearance may be, inwardly, things are sliding into place.

It's the same sweeping feeling of certainty like all the other years, when I realized it had to be Michael Johnson. Brett Teubler. Sophie Coste. Carlos Dulatre. A gut-level feeling that's almost like a déjà vu—as if I had already made this decision in some previous, parallel life, and I'm just remembering, *That's right, it's this one.*

Serena. On the jetty. At sunrise.

Not on the stairs, like I was thinking before, but the very rocks where she recorded herself slipping already. Obvious. Perfect.

It'll be a shove. Nothing with tools or electrical panels—nothing that will leave evidence behind. No doubt she's a strong swimmer, so first I may have to bash her head on the rocks. When they find her body—bodies always wash up—they'll see the trauma on her head, but it will be easy to assume she hit it going down. The viral TikTok will resurface, a sign of what was to come, a dark omen people will be eager to believe. *The irony*, they'll say. *Such a loss for the Riovan.*

I wash my hands, dry them with the ultrasoft paper towels, and toss the damp, crumpled mess into the trash.

I smile to myself. This is a good plan. Despite the tumultuous start to this year's trip, everything is falling into place like it always does.

As long as Daniel doesn't interfere.

His presence is an added risk, that's for damn sure. But I'm here for a reason, and I'm not about to let Daniel Lukiewicz stop me. I'll just have to be more careful than ever—and that starts with figuring out exactly what he knows—or thinks he knows. Tonight. At the Sunset.

While we eat and drink and flirt, I'll pretend everything with Daniel is fine. I'll put him at ease with a piña colada or three. And

I'll find out once and for all what the hell he's up to, using whatever means necessary—such as the low-cut top I have in mind. I won't even feel bad about using alcohol and sex. In my playbook, the ends always justify the means.

CHAPTER 21

"TRY THIS." MY ROOMMATE RIVER HAS BEEN TOTALLY INTO THE FACT that I'm going on a date. She's leaning into the bathroom where I've been getting ready, exuding innocent excitement, holding up a tube of lipstick.

"Ooh, thanks," I say, taking it from her.

"So is this, like, a summer hookup, or is there potential?" says River, crossing her arms as I turn the lipstick upside down to examine the label. The shade is called *Not Tonight*. I frown. Is that foreboding or auspicious?

At least I know I won't be sleepwalking tonight. I have the benzos in my purse. They weren't even hard to get—the Riovan pharmacy is fast and loose. I told the pharmacist what I wanted and picked the pills up between lifeguarding shifts. I paid in cash and gave a fake name; no one even asked for my ID. Easy peasy.

"I don't know," I say cautiously, uncapping the lipstick. "I'm still feeling him out."

"He's cute, though," River says. "We've all kind of, erm…noticed him. Don't you think he looks like Wolverine from the first X-Men movie?"

"Oh?" I say, as if I didn't have that identical thought the first time I saw him. "Yeah, I guess I could see that."

"Maybe you could bring him to that party."

"What party?"

"The one at Island Vibes on Friday. Didn't you see the flyers in the staff room? Everyone's going! I mean, half-priced drinks, hell yes. And it's supposed to be really, like, *authentic* up there."

"Oh, awesome," I say, but my mind just isn't there.

I make the first stroke of lipstick along the upper outline of my lip, following the curve and dip. Then the lower lip. The last time I wore lipstick was…

Jessica, of course. She holds so many last times. It was the welcome-home date I planned for when she got out of treatment. We dressed up, her in a teal wrap dress, me in a retro A-line with an electric guitar print, and walked around the Botanical Garden. My first thought had been dinner, but a date focused on food all of a sudden didn't feel so safe.

It was really sunny. I forgot my sunglasses, and my cheeks soon hurt from squinting. We held hands. Had her hand in mine always felt so small, so delicate? We admired the flowers and took a million pictures. I had a million questions for her, but I held back, and she didn't offer much. Until the end of the day when she smiled and said, "Thanks, Lil. That was…almost perfect."

"Almost?" I said, already doing a lightning-speed mental review of the day. "Did I…do something?"

"It's more like what we didn't do…" She bit her lip and grinned. "Can we get some kimchi fries from Fufu's? I'm starved."

I started laughing, and then crying, and then we were hugging, and I thought, *She's back. She's really, really back.*

I step back from the mirror to survey the results.

"Yes!" River claps her hands, making her adorable top-knot bob. "That is *the* perfect color on you!"

She's not wrong. The blood-red shade makes my skin look alive, golden, the few tiny freckles across my nose and cheeks shining like sand-sprinkles in the sun. I look...*like my mom.*

The vision is so sudden, it feels like my heart stops beating. I freeze. I don't want to break eye contact with myself, in case Mom goes away.

"You OK?" says River after a minute.

"Oh..." I force a laugh, look down, breaking the moment. My heartbeat returns to its usual rhythm. "I was just thinking that I look like my mom."

"Well, your mom must be gorgeous, then," says River generously.

I don't bother to correct her *must be* to *must have been.*

"Thanks," I say.

"Have you decided what you're wearing yet?" says River. "Because I have this vegan leather miniskirt? I think it would look amazing on you."

"I'll try it on," I say, enjoying this small, innocent connection with my roommate. Ignoring the voice that says, *If River knew what you were really doing here, she would literally run screaming away from you.*

The skirt is perfect and goes with the halter top I'd been planning on, and before I know it, I'm ready for battle.

I do one final check in the bathroom mirror.

Somehow, the little curl of a smile hiding in the corner of my lip isn't mine; it's Mom's.

It's like she's sending me off, looking at me the same way she did when, as a kid, I waited for the school bus to take me into the big, bad world. She'd say, "Be brave, sunshine. You've got this. And if you don't, I've got *you*."

Except she doesn't have me now.

The tiny smile drops from my lips, and it's just me again, staring back at myself.

No one does.

I spot Daniel at the far end of the Sunset, sitting at a tall table by a window, leaning back in his chair. It takes him a minute to notice my approach. When he does, he sits up straight and smiles slowly. *Excellent.* This is the reaction I was hoping for. My halter top with the plunging front shows just enough cleavage to entice—a deep shadow, the promise of soft curves. Chandelier earrings graze my shoulders. My hair, still slightly damp, is gathered at the back of my head and secured with a tortoiseshell clip. And the miniskirt is about half an inch away from public indecency.

I don't even feel bad about using my body to bring his guard down.

"May I?" Daniel rises to pull my chair out.

The Sunset is hopping tonight, but our table feels pleasantly removed from the chatter and clink. The band is playing Brazilian jazz, the singer—a brunette tonight—crooning in Portuguese. The energy in here is...expensive. Not a single pirate hawking electric-blue fishbowls in sight.

I sit, very aware of the way the miniskirt rides up.

"Thank you," I say sweetly.

Daniel settles in across from me, resting forward on his elbows. The table is small. If we both leaned in at the same time, we could kiss across it. I'm grateful for the lipstick. It feels like armor.

A server brings two glasses of water right away and hands us each a slim drink menu and a more substantial dinner menu. I cross my legs. For a minute, we study our drink menus in silence.

"I don't know why I'm looking," laughs Daniel. "I already know what I want."

"So do I," I say, setting the menu down.

It doesn't escape me that he doesn't volunteer his choice. And I don't volunteer mine.

Daniel settles back in his chair, propping his elbow on the backrest; I settle back in mine. He studies me, his lip twitching toward what might become a smile. Is he thinking of our afternoon together in his room three days ago? Because I'm not. I'm very actively not.

The server returns. Daniel orders a mango jalapeño frozen margarita; I order a whiskey, neat.

"Has anyone told you your drink choices are girly?" I say, as I peruse the dinner options.

"Have to feed that feminine side."

For a while, we study our menus in silence, and then the server is back with our drinks. "Are you ready to order?"

"I'll have the steak fries. Medium rare," says Daniel.

"I'll take the halibut, please."

The server whisks our menus away, and we're alone again. Daniel stirs his orange concoction with the tiny straw, then sips. I swirl my whiskey but don't drink any.

I crook a finger at my lips, taking care not to disturb my lipstick. "I read some of your articles."

He gives me a blank look.

"You know. In *Fit Life*. They have some copies in the lobby." I wait, curious to see how he'll respond. Will he own it? Or reveal he didn't actually author them? There's a small shift in Daniel's expression, from blank surprise to studied neutrality. I steeple my fingers. *Your move, buddy.* The jazz pianist does an impressive run in the background, and the room explodes into clapping, but my attention on him doesn't waver.

"I'm flattered you sought out my writing," Daniel finally says, when the applause has died down.

I can't believe he's not defending himself! Unless…is it possible he doesn't know how awful they were? Maybe he borrowed the real Daniel Black's name without reading the guy's most recent work. If one can call that shitsmear of words on paper "work."

"I had no idea you'd slept with that many women," I say, shaking my head as if in wonderment.

Daniel stops mid-sip with his margarita, and I feel a surge of triumph. *Now we're getting somewhere.*

"Not that I'm judging you," I add. Unexpectedly, I'm having the teensiest bit of fun right now. "Anything for journalism and the pursuit of truth, right?"

Daniel sets down his margarita slowly and dabs his mouth with a cloth napkin. I can almost see the thoughts racing through him. So the man *is* capable of being rattled.

"I found you in the hotel's system," he says suddenly.

Now it's my turn to choke on a little bit of my drink. I could ask, *How did you get into the hotel's system?* Except that it's not hard to imagine how easy it would be. Daniel has already interviewed Vic. Assuming this interview took place in Vic's office, an observant person such as Daniel couldn't have missed Vic's Post-it note with his username and password, stuck to the side of his computer.

"Yeah," Daniel continues, raking a hand through his hair, almost like he's nervous. "I was doing some research and…I came across your name."

"I told you I work here every summer," I say evenly.

"I mean, I found you as a guest. Your reservation with Jessica. Five years ago." He leans forward. My heart is thundering. "I didn't realize the two of you were here together."

"Yeah, well." Enough swirling of my drink. I knock back a big, burning swallow.

Daniel leans across the table, and even though my guard is up, I have to admit that he doesn't seem coldly questioning. He's calm and curious. In the deep, probing, rough voice I've loved all along he says, softly, "Why do you keep coming back, Lily?"

Wouldn't you like to know, I think. Instead I say, "You already asked me that."

"At the Mambotel," he acknowledges. "Sun. Sand. A break from Cincinnati."

Shit, this guy is a memory machine.

I purse my lips as I consider my response. "That wasn't a lie. There's just…more to it." I make a sweeping gesture. "This is where happy memories of Jessica live." Not quite the truth. Those "happy memories" are mixed at best. Still. Let him think I'm here to relive the joy.

The server is back with our food. Daniel's fries are thin and crispy, and I'm suddenly ravenous. My halibut is a milky, buttered fillet over barely wilted spinach greens. I'm very tempted to steal a fry off Daniel's plate, but I don't.

"You said you're a reader. What are you reading?" he asks, his focus now on the sharp knife he's using to cut into his steak. I avert my eyes as pinkish blood oozes out of the thick piece of cow. I have the sudden urge to become a vegetarian. Or pescatarian? The halibut is very good.

"*Crime and Punishment.*"

"Really?" He sounds impressed.

"Don't get too excited," I say drily. "Spy novels are much more my jam."

He laughs, and a warm feeling spreads through my gut. I guess I like making Daniel laugh, whatever his last name may be. *And whatever he may think I'm doing here.* Which I don't have a 100 percent grip on. But there's still time...

I take a bite of silky halibut. The fish is so fresh, so flavorful, that all it needs is the simple seasoning of butter and salt.

"Well, since you're reading about murder," says Daniel, "why *do* you think people murder other people?"

"Is this your go-to date question?" I say, giving him a cute, bewildered look, even though a warning alarm is blaring in my head.

He grins. "Just a thought exercise."

I gesture with my fork. "Love. Money. Jealousy. Hatred."

He lifts his knife. "You forgot revenge."

I hesitate for a second. Should I stay on the defensive, or...?

"Are we talking about Michael Johnson?" I say. Let's just go there. Why not.

He laughs, almost like he's pleased I called him on it. "Maybe."

"Do you know how I got your number?" I say.

He tilts his head with an expression that says, *Where is this going?*

I continue. "When I called you on WhatsApp last night."

He nods slowly, his eyes scouring me. "I left my number with your office manager at Taste of Heaven."

My heart starts racing.

"You wanted to talk to me about Michael then too. Why?"

He half shrugs. "I was scoping out potential angles for my article before coming here. You know, preliminary research. I've always thought the story on Michael seemed incomplete, and you were in that picture with Carli Elle. I figured I'd follow up on that lead, see what you knew."

"Your article for *Fit Life*."

"That's right."

I stare at him for a second. "You knew who I was that first morning we met."

"True."

"But you didn't let on."

"Also true."

"Did you sleep with me just to get an interview?"

He gives me a look of amused intensity. "Not *just* to get an interview."

I should be furious right now. Instead, I'm strangely turned on. Heat is crawling up my thighs, and I can feel my pulse quickening. I shift in my chair and resist the urge to fan myself with a napkin.

I have to focus. I still don't know for sure if he's on to me.

"So," I say. "You're an ends-justify-the-means kind of a person."

"Aren't you?"

"Anyone who's ever done any good in this world is."

"Is that what you're doing here?" he says. "Sun, sand, doing good?"

"Absolutely." I raise my whiskey, then knock the rest of it back. "I'm literally here to save lives."

"Well, that's a good thing. Because people seem to die here every summer."

"Really?" I say, as if it does concern me, but not that much, even though my pulse is throbbing in my veins.

OK, I'm a person of interest. That's becoming clear; why else would he bring up the deaths, if not to analyze my reaction? At least he doesn't seem to have a handle on my motive, which is not money, jealousy, hatred, or revenge. I'm here to do a calculated good in the world. To pay a tribute, to leave a legacy. To cut poisonous people out of the world like the tumors they are and save the people it's not too late for.

I almost wish I could explain this to Daniel. But no matter how I explained my playbook to him, or proved how much good has resulted from my actions here, he'll just see a monster. An unhinged violent female who thought she was above justice. *Just like it was with my mom.*

"One death per year for the past four years," he muses. "It's an awful track record for a wellness resort, don't you think?"

Shit. I'm losing control of this conversation.

"And—sorry—are you implying that I know something about these…deaths?" I say, trying to sound cutely confused.

"Do you?" he says, raising a flirtatious brow.

"Of course not!" It's not hard to sound upset. "What do you want from me, Daniel?"

"You asked me that already."

"Yes." Frustration makes my tone tight, edgy. "The afternoon of the storm. And you didn't answer."

In fact, he turned the question back on me, and then I lost my mind and practically dragged him to his room.

"I want to get to know you," he says, leaning forward. There's a shift in his energy, and suddenly he's brushing one of my fingers with his. My frustration melts, and the heat in my thighs climbs higher. OK. I see what's happening. He's changing tactics. He seduced the story about my electrical expertise out of me, and now he thinks he has a winning ploy. But even though I see his game, and how easily he's playing me, I don't remove my hand.

"But why?" I say, wrinkling my nose so that I look confused—I hope. "Because you think I can provide useful content for your article? Or…" *Because you think I'm the killer.* But it wouldn't be smart to say the last part. As much as I want to get to the heart of things, playing stupid is a better cover.

His finger nudges my hand over, so my palm is now facing up. Gently, sensuously, he strokes a finger down the center, sending a shiver through me. Fuck, he's good.

"You don't like all my questions, huh?" he says in a husky voice.

Dear God. Sex was supposed to be *my* weapon. I should move my hand away and be very cold right now. Yep. I should do that.

"Maybe I don't want to talk about murder, Daniel," I say, as he continues to play with my hand. "Maybe I've had enough death in my life."

"We don't have to talk about murder anymore."

"Oh?" My voice is a hoarse whisper. "What should we talk about, then?"

He gives me a look. "I was going to suggest that we don't talk anymore at all."

I bite my lip, lipstick be damned, because the sensations he's awakening just by touching my hand are driving me crazy. Each light stroke of his finger sends waves of electricity down my body. The heat between my legs is getting sharp, the tight fist of desire inside me so intense as to be painful. All my body wants now is release…

Am I about to let him play me?

You're smarter than that! the reasonable part of me screams back.

Then again, if I go downstairs with him, I'm back in his room, which could prove useful. This conversation has made it pretty damn clear that I'm a suspect. But suspicion doesn't send people to prison. Evidence does. He has theories, obviously. But no proof, no foul. Does Mr. Lukiewicz have anything substantial on me? That's the question now. My previous search of his room was rushed. If I get a second chance, maybe I'll be able to find out if he has anything incriminating on me. And maybe even...get into his laptop.

"Are we done here?" he says softly.

I nod.

He flags down the server to get the check.

CHAPTER 22

I ROLL ONTO MY BACK. WHERE AM I...?

Oh.

Daniel's bed. Light is angling through the center of the mostly drawn curtains. So, I spent the night here. And the sensation of the sheets against my bare skin tells me I'm not wearing any clothes.

I stretch a little in bed, then draw the sheet around me as memories of last night crash through me. The way we didn't even speak as we rode the elevator down from the Sunset, but his finger kept stroking the sensitive skin on my palm, then my wrist. The way he studied me while he touched, the way his lip curled when my breaths shortened. The way that, as soon as we were in the privacy of his room, he turned me against the wall and slid his hand under the miniskirt, pulling aside the thin fabric of my damp, lacy thong and touching me with relentlessly even strokes until I was arching back, palms on the wall, gasping his name as his fingers drew up wave after wave of unbearable heat.

And that was just the first ten minutes.

I move onto my side, expecting to see Daniel next to me, but his side of the bed is empty. Pushing up slowly, I spot him across the room, sitting at the hotel desk in sweatpants with his broad—and remarkably shirtless—back to me. He's tapping away quietly on his laptop with a steaming paper cup of coffee next to him. My clothes are still cast about the room—the lavender lacy thong, the miniskirt, the top.

I rub life into my face. *Shit.* I didn't mean to stay until morning. I was trying to wait until he was asleep so that I could quietly search the safe again…but I must have fallen asleep.

I guess I was too exhausted after letting him pleasure me again and again. I kept thinking after he brought me to climax that it was his turn, but no. He'd just start on me again, in a new position. I lost count somewhere around six before he finally rolled a condom on and put me out of my delicious misery.

That memory brings a shiver down my spine…and a little farther down too.

"Sleep well?" Daniel swivels in his chair. He's adorable this morning, hair askew, five-o'clock shadow bristly—and he's wearing reading glasses. Unbelievably, nerdy Wolverine is even hotter than regular Wolverine. *Kill me now.*

"A little too well." I check the clock. Eight twenty already? "I have a shift in forty minutes."

Still enough time to do some searching…

"You snore," he says, a sparkle of mirth in his dark eyes.

"You kick," I retort.

"Mea culpa," he says, and don't ask me why it's hot that he's speaking Latin, but not all of these things can be explained with logic.

In any case, time is ticking—again—and I need to get him to leave.

"You wouldn't by chance want to go get me some coffee?" I make a cute pout, gathering the sheet tight at my chest and definitely aware of the plump rise of my cleavage.

He takes off his glasses and grins. "I'll brew you some right here."

I twist my lips. "Room coffee?"

"It's actually excellent. Trust me." He rises from his chair and makes for the minicoffeepot.

"Or you could be a gentleman and pick us up some breakfast..." That would take him at least twenty minutes, right?

"I ordered room service. Should be here any minute."

Fuck. Has he thought of everything?

I crawl out of bed, helping myself to Daniel's shirt from last night and securing it with a couple of buttons. It hits just below my hips. I pad over to nerdy, coffee-making Wolverine and wrap my arms around his bare back from behind as he tears open the packet of coffee grounds.

Damn, he feels good. Warm, solid. I can feel his muscles moving in his back as he continues to set the coffee.

"Ew, you stink," I murmur. He doesn't. This is a lie.

"Really?" He lifts an arm and gives himself an inhale.

"You need a shower, Mr. Stinky Man. Now."

He pushes the coffeemaker's *On* button and swivels in my arms so he's facing me, before issuing a growly invitation. "Join me?"

I smirk. "If you're lucky, smelly-head. Go." I smack his ass, noting the surprised flicker in his eyes followed by a very sexy little smirk. "Go get clean."

He locks his arms around me. "Are you sure you don't want to get dirty again first?"

"Not before breakfast," I say, with another firm smack on his very toned rear end.

"OK," he says, gripping my hips like he's trying to cement me in place. "I'll shower, but don't disappear on me."

"I'm not going anywhere," I whisper and lean up for a peck, morning breath be damned.

At the bathroom door, he turns. "If room service comes while I'm in the shower, there's cash on the dresser for a tip."

"Take your time!" I shout as he disappears. The shower turns on. I make a beeline for his laptop, which is miraculously still unlocked. I take a hasty seat. The chair is still warm from Daniel, the Word doc he was typing in just there for the taking.

OK, Mr. Lukiewicz. You gotta give me something...

I read quickly. *The Riovan cuts an impressive picture on the beautiful coast of remote Saint Lisieux... The water on sunny days is a crystalline blue...* Blah blah blah. The document is just notes about the hotel. This is actually very good. He *is* a writer of some kind. If he was Interpol, or FBI, I'm guessing he wouldn't be spending his precious time writing atmospheric copy about the resort.

I minimize the Word doc and start scrolling through his folders. Playlists... Article Proposals... Travel Receipts... Photos...

Episodes?

I click on that one. Inside are ten numbered folders—for Episodes one through ten, I assume. I open the first.

There's a Word document entitled Carlos Dulatre. Blood starts rushing through me like a spring flood as I double-click.

The memories are immediate, flying at me like a spray of gravel to the face.

It was four years ago. Carlos was my first true target, a Riovan fitness instructor, and he deserved it. It was my first year as a lifeguard. That year, the Riovan was filming promo videos of real customer testimonials for their new-and-improved website, and I happened to walk in on Carlos encouraging a young woman to vomit before her recorded weigh-in.

I made an elaborate plan to kill Carlos. First, I'd flirt my ass off and get him to promise me a one-on-one late-night workout session. I'd ask him to demonstrate a bench press, and while I was "spotting" him, I'd make sure he had an accident. The barbell would "fall" onto his neck. They'd find him the next morning, and everyone would assume he'd misjudged his strength—and been stupid enough to think he didn't need a spotter.

Unfortunately, the flirting didn't work. Turns out Carlos was not only gay but had it out for seasonal employees like me. "Private training is for paying guests," he said when I proposed a private session. His lip curled, like I disgusted him. "Sometimes you people forget that you *work* here."

Later, as I headed to the basement pool for some relaxation of my own, there was Carlos ahead of me on the stairs, a towel slung around his neck, AirPods in, moving his head to the music. We were alone. I didn't think twice. I jumped down a few stairs, and before he had time to turn around, I shoved him.

The stairs were slippery. It was a long way to the bottom. And he landed head first. The Riovan installed a dehumidifier and antislip strips on the stairs the next season.

Daniel's notes are surprisingly thorough, spanning from Carlos's childhood all the way to his death. My name is nowhere in the file— but the Episode One folder contains a hell of a lot more than this single document.

I open an audio file, the first of many. Maybe it's risky to play audio with Daniel so close, but he's singing "Ring of Fire" loudly. Should be safe.

A female voice, tinny in the computer speakers, says, "Yes, I loved Carlos. He had so much positive, go-getter energy. He made me feel like I could do anything. I was devastated when I heard about his accident."

"You appeared in a promotional video for the Riovan," says Daniel's voice. Deep, self-assured, and somehow soothing to listen to, in spite of the dark subject matter. "Can you tell us about the experience of working with Carlos while filming that promo material?"

"Sure. He'd been working with me for two weeks already. I had this weight goal, for my wedding. And the whole video was supposed to showcase my last weigh-in, and like, that moment of me hitting my goal." There's a weepy pause. "I couldn't have done it without Carlos."

I hit stop. Oh. My. God. Daniel tracked down the woman who vomited. And…she's speaking fondly of Carlos. My stomach turns.

I open the next audio file. Daniel's voice, again.

"So Carlos was in his third season at the Riovan when he died."

"He was very dedicated to our customers." I'd recognize *that* voice anywhere. Vic. "No one cared more than Carlos. Their goals were his goals. Frankly, sometimes guests do come here with stretch-goals. Some might have written them off as unrealistic, but Carlos always had the mind-set that anything was possible. I think he really inspired people to give their all."

"Is there any reason you think someone might have wanted to kill Carlos?"

"Kill him? No! It was an accident."

"I have in my notes that the Riovan installed antislip treads on the stairway where he died. Would you say that conditions were unsafe, prior to that update?"

"No. Our liability-insurance carrier did ask that we make updates after the accident, but that's standard. We were absolutely up to code. Accidents happen, sad but true."

"So you don't suspect foul play?"

"No. I'm sorry."

"OK, no problem. Let's pivot. How well do you know Sean Williams? Expat? Runs Island Vibes?"

There's a short silence, but I can hear Vic bristle anyway.

"I thought this interview was about something different. Please turn off the recording."

Good job, Vic.

I click into other episode folders, noting Word docs and audio files that I don't have time to dig into, all carefully labeled.

Episode Two centers on Sophie Coste. Three years ago, she was here with her eighteen-year-old daughter, Jade. She was awful. She berated Jade all the time about her appearance and her supposed lack of discipline. The moment I chose her as my target? When I heard her say, in the pool locker rooms, those words that have haunted me ever since; the words no mother should ever say to a daughter. *No one will ever love you.* Better no mother than *that* mother. A steroid injection took care of her. Jade flew her body back to the States. No matter how often she comes to mind, no matter how much part of me craves the knowledge that she's out there living her best life now, I can't allow myself to look her up. It's one of my rules. I do my part by removing the poison; the survivors have to do their part after that. I have a clear understanding of where my scope of control ends: when the bad guy is dead.

Episode Three, Brett Teubler, staff nutritionist. He was doling out unregulated weight-loss pills like they were candy, brought over from a supplier on Saint Vitalis. His penicillin allergy, carefully noted in the file, was his downfall. You can get a lot of shit on Saint Vitalis, no questions asked.

Episode Four brings us to Michael...so what the hell are all these other episodes about?

Ah. Episode Five. Suspects. My hand is shaking as I double-click on the eponymous Word document. And there it is. My name, right at the top. My body floods with adrenaline, urging me to run, but I force myself to stay still. This isn't a surprise; not really. I knew after our date last night that I was a suspect. But that doesn't make it any easier to see it spelled out in black and white.

Lily Lennox (29yo)—came with her girlfriend Jessica five years ago (what happened to Jessica?), returns once a year, always during the death. Motive—???

I read as though I'm ingesting the words in a speed-eating competition. As with Carlos's file, Daniel's notes on me are surprisingly thorough, from my childhood to present. I skim descriptions of every encounter we've had at the Riovan…without the sex. And then, at the bottom, a big:

End goal—to take the place down? But why like this?

But good. There are more pages—i.e., more suspects. Next up is Victor Salinas, Executive Manager. Well, that's convenient. I can't say I feel guilty that he's on Daniel's radar for the things that I've done. Actually, for all the destruction Vic and his policies have wreaked, wouldn't there be some kind of poetic justice if Vic went down for the deaths? Though I can't imagine he'd ever be convicted—what proof could Daniel possibly have?

Next, Sean Williams from Island Vibes. I don't have time to read all about Sean's childhood, though I catch phrases like *radical conservationist* and *anti-Establishment*. Instead, I skip to the bottom of Daniel's notes on him.

Motive—revenge for inequitable recovery after hurricane?

The shower turns off.

I close all the files and shoot up from the chair, shaking. I need the laptop to go into lock-screen mode, or he'll realize I was messing around. I can hear Daniel moving about the bathroom. As I splay my fingers to hit Control-Alt-Delete and force it to lock, I notice a logo in the center of the desktop that, in my frenzy of opening and closing files, I hadn't yet registered. A white circle with an old-fashioned stylized black mic in the center, and a spray of blood.

I stop, fingers poised above the keys.

I know that image.

It's the logo for *Who Killed Me?*, the true-crime podcast that broke out big with its first season last year. I haven't listened to it, but my friends sure have. Shit fuck. I can see it now. All across the Anglosphere, people tuning in eagerly to Season Two. *Suspect number one is Lily Lennox, the "30-Under-30" catering queen whose knife skills are doing double duty…*

I've never listened to these kinds of podcasts—true crime isn't my thing. Contrary to what you might believe, I don't want to fill my head with murder and death and all things dark. But now I'm seriously regretting that choice. If I'd listened, I would have recognized Daniel's voice right away.

The bathroom door opens. I'm out of time. I lock the screen and spring from the chair just as he emerges from the steamy bathroom. Did he see me practically jump away?

Daniel opens his mouth to say something as I line up the lies. *I wanted to check the weather. The radar. The stock market. My phone is dead.*

But a knocking interrupts us. "Room service!"

As Daniel tips the guy and sets the tray of food on the desk, I scurry about the room, recovering my various articles of clothing.

By the time he's lifted the silver domes off the piping hot plates of omelets and greens, I'm zipping up the back of my miniskirt.

"Sorry, I have to go," I say.

"I thought you were going to stay."

"I'm out of time."

"You need to eat."

"I need to not get fired."

"Lily—" He runs a hand through his damp hair.

I interrupt whatever he was going to say with what I intend to be a quick kiss on the mouth, but he pulls me in, lengthening the kiss. The smell of his pine bodywash envelops me. The warmth of the shower is still on his skin. But I can't let myself get drawn into that warmth anymore. I push him away and leave without another word.

As I walk down the hallway away from his room, chilly with air conditioning, a single thought keeps repeating in my head: I slept with a man who wants to expose me as a killer.

It felt like he cared, and I let myself believe he did.

But it's all a game to him.

A game that could end me. I realize this. If I kill this year, Daniel will have one more death to lay at my feet. Would it be stupid to proceed with my plan, knowing that my name is literally in his suspects file? Should I catch the first plane out of here instead? I hate the thought of fleeing—of abandoning all my carefully laid plans. But it would be stupid to put more ammunition into the loaded gun that is Daniel Lukiewicz…which, by the way, is pointed at me. And yet I also despise the thought of letting go, of letting him win…

My brain is a muddle, and for all the possibilities and variables that are battling to make sense in my head, all I can really think right now is, *Fuck.*

CHAPTER 23

SWEAT TRICKLES DOWN MY TEMPLES. I SWIPE IT AWAY, BUT THE trickle just starts again, like a leak I can't plug. My thoughts feel liquid too, dribbling out no matter how much I try to stuff them away. I need to focus. Whatever I am, I am a good lifeguard… I have a responsibility to these swimmers, but no matter how much I snap my elastic, I can't seem to keep a correct count of how many people are in the water—

I could kill him.

The brightness on the beach is intense, even behind the protective wall of my sunglasses. Everything feels washed out, not quite real, as if someone poured bleach over the world.

But if I kill him, everything changes.

I snap my elastic.

Focus on the swimmers. One, two, three… No, wait—one—

"You know, the bass player at the Sunset?"

Two women are shuffling through the sand past my lifeguard chair. From up here, they're just broad straw hats and slick, reflective legs.

"Wait, hot band guy?"

"You wouldn't believe what he can do with his tongue…"

"You *didn't!*"

"I did!"

There's a man swimming far out—not too far yet, but almost… He's the older man who likes to do his laps along the perimeter of the swimming area.

Killing Daniel would solve everything.

Except then, I'd be a true murderer. Up until now, I've merely been a killer.

Could I live with myself, if I kill for my own gain?

Could I go back to Cincinnati and run my business and go out with my friends and sleep at night if I killed a guy who wasn't toxic, just inconvenient?

My thoughts jump track like a wild train. Because there's another solution: to not kill anyone this year. Not Daniel. And not Serena either. Not while a true-crime podcaster is literally up my ass. A death at the Riovan while I'm still here will just add fodder to his growing files. I can skip this year. Make up for it the next. By then, he and his little podcast will have moved on to greener pastures.

Jessica, I think—a mental plea to someone I'd love to talk this through with. I wish she could tell me what to do. What she wants.

Jessica, it's so bad. Not only is Daniel an investigative reporter on my trail, but he's the host of last year's breakout podcast, and I'm set up to be the main course of Season Two.

I try to imagine how she might tilt her head or scrunch her cute nose.

At least the sex was good, I can almost hear her say. Ha. We loved our dark humor.

The thing is, I've always known the risk. The consequence for what I've done is prison for life; I've never fooled myself about that. But I've always assumed I was going to be smarter. *Said every killer ever.*

There's always someone who comes for you. *Isn't that the lesson of* Crime and Punishment, *stupid?* The dance of Raskolnikov and Porfiry? I haven't finished yet, but I can already feel it's not going to end well for Raskolnikov. And part of it is his uncertainty, his waffling, which is exactly what I'm doing right now. I want to slam that book over my own damn head.

But maybe I can still convince Daniel I'm innocent. Especially if he really wants to believe it. Which he has to…right? Even though I'm the first name on his list, part of him must not believe I'm truly dangerous, or he wouldn't have slept next to me all night, helpless, knowing I could have killed him… Yes. Either he doesn't believe in his heart of hearts that I actually killed anyone, or he thinks I'd never kill *him.*

I like that first option. People who want to believe something are much more persuadable. *But how?* How can I erase his suspicions? Talk alone won't do it. Sex won't do it…

I take a swig from my water bottle.

The sun beats down full force. The shade of the umbrella protects my shoulders but not my legs. The waves sing their bright way onto the shore. People lounge and swim and bake.

Damn it, I wish Daniel *had* written that horrible article. I wish he *was* the appalling Daniel Black, staff writer for *Fit Life* and all-around shit human. Then I could kill him and be done with this whole mental dance. If there's one thing I hate, it's indecision.

My wrist is red from all the snapping, but I snap again anyway, viciously, as if I can cattle-prod myself out of this uncertainty.

The blue of the water cuts. So bright—

A flicker, far out, like a visual snap against my awareness... what was that? I lean forward, shading my eyes. Another flicker— something pale—a hand. It disappears.

I leap down from the chair, my training kicking in without the need for processing or thought. My feet hit hard on the sand; I grab the flotation device under my arm and sprint, already fitting the whistle to my lips.

I blow my whistle; a path clears. I keep my eyes on the spot where I saw the hand. The lifeguard at the end of the beach blows his whistle too, a signal that he's heard my call for help. Swimmers are starting to leave the water as I plow into the ocean, the waves splashing up violently around me. I run through the shallows, then dive forward. Strong arms, Lily, strong crawl forward. Eyes on the place where you saw the hand. But it's a lot of blinding blue, and not much else. I reach the area and dive, opening my eyes in the murky underwater. Tendrils of dark seaweed make the ocean floor shadowy. I turn, go up for breath, then back down, one hand on the flotation device, scanning.

There. I release the flotation device and dive down to the pale starfish shape that the body makes, arms and legs extended. It's an older man, his limbs pale and weightless in the water, eyes closed, mouth open: not good. *C'mon, Grandpa*, I think, as I hug my arms around his torso and kick my legs in firm scissor swipes to bring us both to the surface. *Today is not a good day to die.*

Our heads shoot above the waterline. I gasp air in, but he doesn't draw breath. I have to get him to shore, ASAP.

Anchored on the flotation device, I kick with all my strength toward shore, keeping a firm hold on the chilly, limp body of a man who might already be dead.

Three lifeguards meet me in the shallows, and together we lift the man out and lay him on the sand. I crash to my knees and begin CPR.

Firm pulses on the chest, rocketing my strength into him, willing life to return. *C'mon. Live. Live.* I press my mouth to his. His lips are cold. I pinch his nose and blow breath into him, emptying my own lungs, willing it to fill him up with what he lost. Then, I knot my hands together and begin the pulses again.

He coughs up water. His eyes flicker open, a milky blue.

The jolt of relief feels like someone punched me and leaves just as fast.

"You're gonna be OK," I tell him, my voice surprisingly steady for the swell of feeling that's expanding in my chest. I push the feeling back. Time to stay neutral, strong, in control. "You had a little scare, but you're gonna be OK."

Then, paramedics are arriving with a stretcher and I'm stepping aside, and my supervisor Kenton is there, serious and in charge, with a clipboard and a pen, dressed in his Team Lead T-shirt. He asks me questions about the event, which I describe mechanically. After he completes the necessary form, he puts a kind hand on my shoulder.

"You did good, Lily. I'll take your shift from here; you go recover. I'm sure that was emotional."

"Thanks," I say, gathering my bag and water bottle and towel.

Was it emotional? I don't know how I feel. There's been no space to feel.

As I walk through the sand back toward the hotel, to my surprise, guests are making a spontaneous human corridor and breaking into whooping applause, like I'm a one-woman parade. Now emotion comes, making a thick knot in my chest, painful and raw.

You don't know me, I suddenly want to shout out. I cross my arms; my hands are shaking. *If you did, you wouldn't be cheering.*

And yet, as people cry, "Bravo!" and "Well done!" it feels…

strange and wonderful. To have done something so universally, innocently good that, for a few moments, everyone agrees I'm the hero.

The passageway of applause takes me all the way to the end of the beach, and right before I step onto the cement walkway that will lead me back to the Riovan—

Daniel. In a row with all the other faces. Beach towel over one shoulder, pumping his hands together in firm claps like everyone else, eyes sparkling, a broad smile on his face, radiating unreserved approval.

As I catch his gaze, he nods, like he's saying, *Well done.* The moment slows down, the seconds expand, and…I know in my gut this is one of those pivotal moments when something either happens, or it doesn't.

If I have a chance at convincing Daniel of my innocence, of my moral purity, this is my moment.

I meet his eyes fully and smile back, willing him to see the hero in me.

The hero who just saved an old man's life.

The same hero that kills.

I've been saving lives all along, I send to him wordlessly. *I am good. And see? I'm doing good.*

And I'm going to keep doing good…

…next year.

This year has become too dangerous. I won't kill Serena or Craig—or anyone.

Scrapping all the effort of the past week feels like a small death. All the hours spent scouring through guest files, researching each candidate, trying to piece together the complex puzzle of a perfect death—it fucking sucks to just throw that away. I know more than most that life is short—shorter than we're ever ready for—and it's hard to accept that I just wasted a piece of my life, no matter how small, on plans that won't come to fruition.

On the other hand, in some small part of me, it also feels good not just to have reached a decision…but to have let go.

Anyway, in the grand scope of things, it's OK. I force myself to remember: There's always next year.

All good things come to those who wait.

CHAPTER 24

"LET'S RAISE A GLASS!" CRIES VIC. THE BAR AT THE SUNSET IS MOBBED with lifeguards, spa techs, trainers, and more. Vic put the word out among the staff that drinks were on the house, and let's just say that everyone showed up thirsty. "To our very own hero, Lily Lennox!"

"To Lily!" everyone shouts, followed by a staccato rainfall of glasses knocking against each other. We all drink. The whiskey makes a trail of fire down my throat.

The band strikes up "For She's a Jolly Good Fellow," and everyone sings along, not just the staff at the bar, but guests as well, standing at their tables, beverages aloft, the sea of glasses catching the light.

I smile on them all.

It's strange to be the center of attention when I normally seek to avoid this kind of notice, but it hasn't escaped me that Daniel is right over there at a table of his own. The more he can see me in a positive light, admired and respected, the less likely that he'll assume I'm a killer.

"Lily, what you did today was exemplary," says Kenton, grasping my shoulder as soon as the song ends, his expression sincere. He has to lean close and shout to be heard over the eruption of whistles and whoops around us. "You're a credit to the team."

"Thank you," I say, also shouting. "I'm just glad Herb is OK." Herb Tulaine was the name of the man. He got whisked away to the small island hospital, and I'm hoping we'll hear an update on him soon.

"So proud of you," says River, sidling up to me and giving me a sweet side hug that I return. Something about her fresh innocence touches me. Some of the other lifeguards—Hannah, the English chick, a few more—chime in with, "Yeah, awesome job," and "Way to go out there, Lil."

"Thanks, guys," I say and notice my whiskey glass is empty. I turn around and set it back down on the bar. Even though I'm not intending to drink anymore—I really shouldn't drink at all while on benzodiazepines—Vic immediately gestures to the bartender. "Another for the lady!"

The kitchen is bringing out free snacks and placing them up and down the bar—bowls of salted nuts, hummus with pita, chips and guac. I snag a soft wedge of fresh pita and drag it through the hummus. Wow. It's probably the best hummus I've ever had. Immediately, I'm trying to break down the flavors. Chickpeas and tahini, obviously, olive oil and lemon and garlic—

"The woman of the moment," teases the bartender, interrupting my reverse engineering as he thunks another whiskey in front of me, sparkling amber in its cut-crystal glass. "Anything else I can get you?"

"Nah, I'm good," I say with a grin as I take a tiny sip.

"There's some fresh oysters in from Maine…"

"Too salty," I laugh. "I'm a West Coast oysters kind of girl."

He laughs. It's the bartender from that night when I got the ginger ales for River. He's cute, and I feel like he's trying to flirt. But he doesn't hold a candle to Daniel.

I smell him before I see him—pine and salt with a little earthy layer of pure man. *Speak of the devil.*

"Big morning for you, huh?" says Daniel, leaning his forearms on the bar next to me. A warm wave travels through my body. He's drinking something pink and frothy, as per usual, and I nudge my shoulder into his.

"You could say that." Maybe it's the buzz of whiskey, but in a strange way, I feel relaxed about the whole Daniel problem. This morning I felt our natural enmity. Now, I'm feeling our alignment, our similarities. We could really understand each other, I bet. If we trusted each other enough to open up. After all, we're both here trying to do what's right. We're just working off different compasses.

No, stupid! a sensible though annoying voice in my head pipes up. *These soft nice feelings? It's 100 percent booze! This man is still a threat!*

But…is he? Really? He's so…*nice.*

And since I'm not killing anyone this year, he won't have anything on me.

"I was just getting to the beach when I saw you jump down from the chair," says Daniel, looking at me intently. "I watched the whole thing."

"Well." I pick up my whiskey and give Daniel a long look. *See? I'm a good person.* "I was just doing my job."

His lip lifts in the familiar subtle smile. "Yeah. I know. It was actually really cool to watch you in action."

I raise an amused eyebrow. Contrary to the sensible voice's possibly valid concerns, I'm feeling really good about this interaction. He's looking at me differently, I can feel it, and maybe there's some wishful thinking involved, but I'm daring to hope I've fallen right off his suspect list in one fell swoop. Which would mean our cat-and-mouse game is over, and I don't have to grill him anymore or be grilled…just enjoy him, and his newly refreshed vision of how good-hearted I am. Maybe tonight could end in his arms. Maybe soon we'll be laughing about him ever suspecting me… *Yeah, remember when I thought it was you?* Oh, it'll be so funny…

"Excuse me, young lady," says a wavering voice, and when I turn to see who's talking, I nearly swallow my whiskey down the wrong tube. I come up spluttering.

"Oh—hi Mr. Tulaine! I'm so happy you're back from the hospital!"

It's the man I saved, looking pale and tired, but alive. It's great to see him upright. He thrusts out a hand, and I grasp it. He keeps hold of my hand, sandwiching it between both of his.

"I can't thank you enough."

"It's what I'm here to do."

"I would be dead if it weren't for your quick actions on the beach."

"It's just my training," I say. "It's what any of us would have done."

"My family thanks you too. In fact, they insisted I get you on FaceTime…"

Before I can object, he's pulling out his phone and dialing and holding up a screen that pops suddenly with a bouquet of happy faces. At the center is a round-faced woman with sparkling dark eyes.

"I want to reach through the screen and hug you!" she cries through a smile. "Thank you for saving Pappy's life! You have our eternal gratitude! Anything we can do for you—anything—you tell us, OK? You want a place to stay in Tampa, you've got one."

"That's so kind," I say, smiling back at all the faces. I can feel their genuineness, even through the grainy picture. "But it was nothing. I mean, I was just doing what I'm here to do."

"Well, it wasn't nothing to us," says the woman, with a tone of kind reproof. She puts a hand on her heart. "It was everything."

After Herb hangs up, we exchange a few more pleasantries, and he insists that we exchange numbers so that we can stay in touch. Finally, he retreats.

Daniel leans in. "Can I confess something?" His arm goes around my waist, and his voice is soft in my ear. "I think I may have misjudged you."

"Oh?" I say, my heart immediately picking up its pace. Does he mean what I think he means? Is this confirmation that I'm off the hook in his mind? But before I can inquire further, Serena comes crashing into me with a vice-like embrace, forcing Daniel to step back.

"Let me steal you!" she says and leads me without much choice to a table where the remains of her dinner are still sitting—a salad, it seems. She indicates the chair opposite her, and I sit.

"Listen, Lily, I love what you did this morning, and I totally want to do a TikTok with you tomorrow!" She frames her hands in the air like she's seeing the shot already. "We'll do a quick recap of what it felt like to save the old guy's life, and you can be all humble like you've been this whole time—I *love* how you keep saying, 'It's just my job,' that's *so* appealing to people—"

"His name is Herb—" I try to interrupt.

"And I'll post it to my account. Of course, if you're on TikTok I'll totally tag you. You'll get a huge boost in your followers, trust me. This is going to be one of those win-win-win scenarios—"

As if I cared about any of that.

"I don't know, Serena. I think I'd prefer not to, if that's OK with you? It just seems...I don't know." I wince. "Exploitative? Of his privacy?"

She reels back as though I insulted her. Which...maybe I just did?

"It's an uplifting, sweet story, Lily. Anyway, this is your final year at the Riovan. Why not leave one last mark, you know?"

Excuse me?

For a second, my vision really does go fuzzy, like a temporary loss of consciousness.

I can't have heard that right.

"Sorry...last year?" I finally manage.

Her lips make an O, like she's just realized what she said. She leans across the table, her hand wrapping around my forearm and squeezing, her look suddenly all compassion.

"I am *so* sorry to tell you this way. Me and my big mouth! Vic was going to have this convo with you next week, and I totally just blurted it out."

"You're not rehiring me next year?"

"I'm sorry, but...no?"

"Why?" It comes out aggressive, but I'm feeling aggressive. From warm and relaxed, and possibly even ready to slip back into bed with my podcaster enemy and explore whatever new sexual heights we'd be sure to achieve, my chest is lurching in painful, jagged beats. What the fuck is happening? I just saved a life! How dare they—how can they—take *away* all of this! *Jessica,* I think, *Jessica, you have to help me,* but she's the one who needs my help. She's not at peace.

I'm sorry, Jess. The words gush out of my heart like hot blood. *I'm sorry I wasn't your hero. I'm sorry I let my guard down when it was your turn to need saving... I'm sorry I couldn't put your pieces back together.*

I picture Jessica, perched on a wall like Humpty Dumpty in that old children's rhyme I've always hated. The part where he "had a great fall?" That's passive voice. Which disguises the actor. Yes, I failed to catch Jessica, and I'll be sorry for that every single day for the rest of my life. But before that? Someone fucking shoved her.

I can't be done here, just like that. Serena can't take this away from me—from Jessica—

"It's nothing personal…" Serena says. "It's a business decision."

"Based on what?" I say, not even caring to hide my anger.

"Our branding image."

"You just wanted to do a TikTok with me two seconds ago!"

"That's what makes this so awkward." She leans back and sighs. "But you have to understand. You're turning thirty next year, Lily!"

I take a swig of whiskey and then slam my glass down.

"Yep. Thirty. Just…put me in my grave."

"That is *not* what I meant."

"What did you mean?"

Her voice is pitched high in frustration. "That most of our lifeguards are college age."

I pinch the bridge of my nose and squeeze my eyes shut.

"This is so…" The booze and the emotion and the benzos are making it hard to think clearly. I lower my head into my hands and take a deep breath, then another. Serena says nothing.

I don't believe everything happens for a reason. Hell, no. Open your eyes—there's too much chaotic tragedy in this stupid world. But what I've been doing here for the past five years? It's forcing meaning out of a meaningless tragedy. I've made my loss into something. I've squeezed a legacy out of the pain that Jessica went through. And now, Serena is going to take that away.

Serena, who just said…

Why not leave one last mark?

I lower my hands to the table and lift my face, slowly.

Serena is still making a concerned expression, even though in reality she doesn't give a shit.

Yes. I think I will make one last mark.

"Sorry." I smile slowly, with an embarrassed little laugh, as though I feel bad for my outburst. "I didn't mean to freak out on you. You know what? I'd love to do that TikTok."

"Oh!" She seems taken aback, but in a good way. "OK. Amazing! And Lily—you've done so much for the Riovan. I know it, and Vic knows it too. Thank you for understanding. It's not personal, you know!"

"Of course!" I smile even wider. "I get it. It's just business." *Just like what I'm going to do to you.* "So we could do the video really early tomorrow morning? Maybe shoot it on that jetty? It's so pretty out there…"

"Ooh, I love it!" She shimmies in her chair. "Yes, that would be perfect."

We make our plans to meet before sunrise, and I return to the bar with my nearly finished drink, still buzzing, but not in the soft, golden way from before. I scan for Daniel, but he's disappeared. All for the best. I can't worry about him right now, in case it gives me cold feet. Nope, we're all systems go. I'm off to bed now. I need my wits about me for tomorrow.

I leave the Sunset with no fanfare—everyone is having so much fun, they don't notice my departure, and that's just fine with me.

As I take my usual rocky path to Vista West, inevitably, I start thinking about Jess again. This is my last year in the place that destroyed us. Earlier today, on the beach, after saving Herb, I thought I could wait another year to kill. Now I see I was just repeating an old mistake. I waited to get engaged when I should have proposed right away. Waited to get married when I could have just whisked Jessica to Vegas. If I'd taken my shot, Jessica could have been mine—legally, in the eyes of the doctors, her family, the world. But I hesitated.

How could I tell myself earlier that good things come to those who wait? It's bullshit. I can't believe I was about to make the same mistake that ruined my life and Jessica's five years ago. But I'm recentered now.

All good things to those who *take* them.

I repeat it like a mantra, whipping it into my brain over and over as I snap my elastic until it's all I can hear, all I can feel.

All good things to those who take them.

All good things to those who take them.

Time to take one final life.

CHAPTER 25

I WAKE BEFORE DAWN.

The room is gray, as though the reality has been sucked out of it, and for a few seconds I just lie in bed, listening to River's snores and the whoosh-whoosh of the air conditioner pumping out chilly air.

Today, I'm going to kill Serena Victoria.

A spike of panic in my chest follows this thought, as if I've been impaled through the heart, fixing me to the mattress.

Then the sharpness softens, washing out like a wave into a deafening numbness, like the drone of a bee swarm.

My pulse slows, my body calms. That's when I move, swinging my legs out of the bed and padding to the bathroom.

I turn on the sink, splash water on my face. Pull my hair back. I don't need makeup; we won't be doing that TikTok.

Back in the bedroom, I quietly pull on a pair of joggers and a tank top, marveling that these are my legs, going into the pants. These are my arms, poking through the sleeves.

I remember this feeling all too well. I've always imagined it's like putting on a space helmet. Protecting yourself behind a glass visor from an atmosphere that could kill you if you tried to breathe it in.

I first had it back in fourth-grade theater club. Mr. Arnold, the theater teacher, gave me a small but heartfelt talking part in *Hello, Ohio!* I practiced my lines night and day, so excited for my big debut. The night of the performance, I walked out on stage. The lights were hot. I could feel the eyes on me, and, like someone flipped a switch, my body turned to lead. There was no way I could move, much less say my lines. And then, a buzzing washed through me, a white noise like a crashing ocean that deadened everything else. I walked to my spot on the stage and said my part. I could barely hear myself speak the lines above the buzzing, but I could feel the vibration of the words leaving my throat, their tickly whisper as they left my lips, the muscles in my face working to do the facial expressions I'd practiced over and over.

It was a triumph. Mr. Arnold had tears in his eyes. Mom gave me flowers and hugged me and said, "I had no idea you were so gifted! My budding actress!" The principal even shook my hand.

But all along, I kept to myself the disappointing truth: that I hadn't enjoyed the moment. Hadn't even really been there for it. It had been...*nothing.*

I didn't sign up for theater again.

Outside the hotel, the early morning air is chilly and moist. I shiver and briefly wish I'd brought a sweatshirt as I head to the path leading to the beach where Serena and I planned on meeting.

I see her taut silhouette in the distance, standing still facing the beach, dressed in dark, form-fitting athletic wear. I wonder what she's thinking. If she has any instinct that this will be the last time she sees the sun rise.

"Hey, Lily," she says once I'm near. Her voice is perky, as if she's been up for hours, and she's carrying a big thermos. "Ready?"

"Let's do it," I say, and she leads the way.

She's shorter than I am, but her pace is quick, her step bouncy. Full of life.

Not for much longer.

"Want some of my morning wake-up blend?" She lifts the thermos toward me without stopping her brisk walk, but I wave it away.

I could use a pick-me-up and really wish I'd stopped for coffee, but my temptation to share Serena's brew is short-lived. Who knows what toxic powders she's mixed in.

"So I was thinking we go for spontaneous," she says. "You talk, I record, and I can edit later."

"Sounds good."

We walk in silence for a while, toward the jetty. The sand is damp with morning dew, and our sneakers leave clear footprints. The water is dull, but soon it will be spiked with light, and Serena will be dead.

"Hey, are you going to that party? At Island Vibes?" says Serena.

"No. Are you?"

"I'm thinking about it. I don't know. A lot of people are going, but the place looks kind of…junky? On the other hand, half-priced drinks!"

I don't answer. She doesn't know it yet, but this is a decision she won't have to make.

I'm not like the killers in books who give long speeches to their victims, who really want to make sure they know why they deserve to die. I couldn't care less whether she knows or not. What matters is to do it quickly and leave the scene even quicker.

I won't return by way of the beach; I'd be seen. Instead, I'll cut up the hill and head for the cover of trees farther inland. I'll circle back around to the hotel the long way, go to my room, change into my bathing suit for my ten o'clock shift, and pray that the footprints disappear under the tracks of other morning walkers. Then, I'll do my job and make sure no one drowns, and act surprised when her body is found, whenever that may be.

"Hey, slow down..." I call out, as I suddenly realize Serena's quite a bit ahead of me. I wouldn't say I'm out of shape, but the pace petite Serena is setting is formidable.

She's strong. Quick. In shape.

But I'm taller, and I have the benefit of surprise.

"You're dragging," she sings out in a teasing tone and lifts her thermos again in invitation.

"No, thanks," I say.

"You know, I didn't used to be a morning person either...but I'm on these pills, and they are seriously amazing."

"Pills?" I say, even though I'm not surprised.

"Well...antidepressants."

I stop walking. The rim of the sun is lighting up the water, and I feel the first hint of warmth in the breeze that brushes over my cheek.

"You're on antidepressants?"

Her expression scrunches. "I shouldn't have blurted that out. Please don't mention it to Vic. I don't want him to think I'm, like..." She jiggles her hands and pulls a face. "Unstable."

We keep walking, now abreast.

Part of me wants to say all the reassuring things I know are true. Struggling with depression is nothing to be ashamed of. It's brave to get help. That's what those medications are there for.

Instead, I stay silent, trying to reel back in the soft emotions her confession elicited, trying to return to the dead, droning removal she just cracked through.

"It's from growing up poor," Serena blurts out. *Huh?* "Like, I have massive imposter syndrome, working here. Sometimes I just spiral, like—how long is it going to take everyone to realize I don't belong?" She laughs. "Did you know I had to practice to get rid of the twang in my accent? I'd watch the news and literally repeat everything the news anchors said, so I could sound smart and polished and professional. And my mom—she got so overweight, she literally couldn't fit in a normal vehicle. She was homebound for years, and eventually she just…died on the couch watching TV." Serena shivers. "Anyway, I've worked really hard to be here—and that's why these bonuses I was telling you about are so important to me. It's me proving to myself I'm not going to end up like my parents did." She pauses and gives me a nervous side-glance. "Sorry! I don't know why all this stuff is spilling out!"

Probably because some part of you knows you're about to die.

"It's OK," I say in a neutral tone. Nothing more. Even though my heart is tugging at me, I force myself to actively wall up what she's said. I don't want to relate. Don't want to see the similarities between her story and mine.

We reach the rocks.

Stay focused.

She climbs ahead of me. I reach the top just seconds behind her, panting.

"You OK there?" she says.

"Fine," I say, wiping away a trickle of sweat at my hairline.

"OK. Let's get you sitting on that rock there at the end…"

We jump from rock to rock, all the way to the end of the jetty. I stand on the very last rock. The one I'm about to push Serena from. The ocean is lively, crashing up against the left side, then sucking at the rocks as it retreats, only to batter it again. *That's the side I have to push her off.*

She's positioning the camera, but I can't let her press *Record*. Can't let there be any evidence we were here together.

"Wait! I'm not ready," I say. "Could you—um, come over here? There's something in the water."

"What is it?"

Still looking at the water, I twist my expression as if I were seeing something disturbing.

"You'd better come check it out."

She blows out her breath in exasperation but picks her way toward me.

This is it. This is it.

Even if she is struggling with depression, that doesn't make her less of a monster.

She's next to me, leaning over a little.

Blood pounds through my veins, filling my head with its rhythm.

Now. Now, I tell myself.

I step back, giving myself a little room to lunge forward. The more upfront force, the better.

Serena is fixated on the water. "I really don't see what you're talking about, Lily."

I lunge—

A blare cuts through the soundscape, jolting me back again.

Serena straightens up and looks at her phone, totally oblivious to the fact that I was one second away from sending her over the edge onto the sharp rocks and into the vicious current.

She frowns at her phone, then lifts it to her ear. "Vic?"

Damn it.

I cross my arms around my body. The wind is extra-icy up on the jetty. I'm close enough to hear the frantic tone of Vic's voice. Serena's frown deepens as he talks, and I hear Vic's final words loud and clear. "*Get back here right now!*"

Serena disconnects and looks up at me, her face drained of color.

Stricken. "We have to get back to the Riovan right now. There's been an emergency. It's that girl."

I don't even have to ask what girl. She swims into my mental view, in her tie-dye shirt and her whimsical braids.

"Skylar," I say.

"There's an ambulance on the way," says Serena, but I'm already running down the jetty, jumping from rock to rock, back inland. I scramble down the rocks on to the beach, and the second my feet hit sand, I run flat out. The jolt of Serena's footsteps is right behind. The buzzing is gone, the numbness a distant memory. I'm fully present. I can feel the cut of the wind and the painful, anxious thumps of my heart. I don't know what happened to Skylar, but I can guess. Teenagers aren't supposed to be dosing themselves with potent laxatives.

All I can think as I run is, *Not like Jessica. Don't let this be like Jessica.* Down the beach, back to the place that takes, and takes, and takes.

CHAPTER 26

MY LUNGS ARE ON FIRE AS SERENA AND I CRASH ON TO THE SCENE playing out in front of the Riovan.

The hotel's circle drive is a chaos of activity, people and vehicles and flashing lights, but all I can see is the stretcher bearing Skylar, carried by two paramedics. They have an oxygen mask over her face. I run up to them. I have to make sure she's alive—

A forearm shoots up like a guardrail, blocking me at chest level from getting any closer.

"Mademoiselle," says a man in a navy-blue uniform with reflective strips on his jacket. "I'm going to ask that you stay where you are."

"You don't understand." I clutch his arm. Tears fist in my throat. "I'm her—"

He waits with a look of beleaguered patience.

Her what?

I shake my head as a hot fog fills my vision. I remove my hand from his arm. Stumble back.

"Sorry."

I have no legal standing here. No legal standing with Jessica either.

The medics load the stretcher bearing Skylar into the back of the ambulance. She's so small under the blanket. I know without asking that it was the stuff Serena gave her that did this—the CleanSlim. What else could cause a perfectly healthy teen to go into a spontaneous health crisis? In her eagerness to drop weight and please her mother, Skylar could easily have taken way too much—

The ambulance lights are flashing silently, in bursts of red like a pulsing heart, just like the lights flashed that night. It was after midnight. It was cold. I was still in my suit from the conference, and my nice eggshell silk blouse. They let me ride with Jessica. She had an oxygen mask on too. I worried the hem of my blouse. The silk was splattered with blood. *I'll have to get it dry-cleaned*, I remember thinking, incongruously.

"Is she going to be OK?" I kept asking, in the ambulance and then when we arrived at the hospital, but no one would tell me. Her eyelids looked so delicate. *Open*, I wished at them. *Open*.

I feel a hand on my arm, and my entire body jolts.

"Lily, why don't you head back inside—"

"Vic," I say, spinning around, seizing his upper arm and shaking him. "It's that brand...CleanSlim—Skylar took it."

"Sorry—what?" He seems genuinely confused.

"She was crying in the bathroom... They didn't see me—I mean, Serena or Skylar. I was in a stall. I think Serena thought she was alone. Skylar's mom was on her about losing...losing—" I gesture toward the ambulance, aware I'm not telling Vic the story right, but my head is a hot scramble. I make an erasing gesture with both hands and shake my head. "Sorry—what I'm trying to say is, Serena—"

"Shh," he says, grabbing my shoulder and giving it a few firm pulses. "I can see you're upset, Lily, and understandably so. You've been through a lot in the past twenty-four hours. Let the medical professionals do their job, and you and I can talk later about…whatever you're trying to tell me."

"You don't understand—"

"Sorry, I can't talk now," he says firmly, his attention tearing away from me as he waves at someone across the drive. "Eric! Thank God. Over here—" And he's off.

I crouch down, suddenly light-headed.

"What's wrong with my daughter?" Beth Ann is shouting.

No, it's Skylar's mom shouting.

What's wrong is that you've infected her with the idea that she has to be thin to please you. She wanted to make you happy. And now look what you've done.

I hear Serena's voice and register that she's standing next to Skylar's mom by the open back of the ambulance. "All our thoughts and prayers are with you," she's saying, loud and saccharine above the running engine. Does Serena know what she's done? Does she know this is her fault?

The ambulance doors slam shut.

My chest is seizing up, my breathing short. I crash my head into my hands.

I failed. Again. I should have found Skylar, after what Serena told her in the bathroom…should have made sure to take away those powders…or talk to her mom, or Vic…instead, all I could think of was my target list. When I could have done so much more.

Have I done anything at all of value, these past five years? I always had it in my mind that I was saving the victims. What if the people I sought to protect are still ruined?

I haven't looked them up. Not Jade, whose mother I injected with steroids. Not Carli Elle, whose career apparently took a free fall. I've always told myself it's because I understood where my scope of control ended. I removed the bad guy; the rest had to be up to them. But what if I didn't really help any of them?

That's why I haven't looked.

That's the truth.

Not because of some bullshit about scope of control.

Because I'm scared.

Scared that what I've done here, the things that can't be taken back, were all...

For nothing.

"Hey." A hand rests on my back, its pressure solid. Daniel.

"I fucked up," I gasp out with a shallow laugh. I don't even care what Daniel thinks. "I—fucked—up—" I can barely fit the words in between my frantic spurts of breath.

"Hey. Hey. It's OK, Lily. Just breathe."

The ambulance bleats out a siren, and tires screech as it peels out of the circle drive. Vic's voice comes from somewhere above me.

"Is she OK?"

"I think she's having a panic attack," says Daniel. His hand doesn't move from my back.

"I'm fine—" I say. "I know I have to be at the pool."

"She's in no condition to lifeguard right now," says Daniel.

Vic crouches down. I still don't look at him. He smells like magnolia.

"Lily? I know it's been a lot between Herb Tulaine and this little girl." His voice is appeasing, but I know I'm losing standing in his eyes. Businesslike Vic has never appreciated meltdowns. For five years now I've given him strong, capable Lily. I shouldn't care that my image is crumbling in his eyes; fuck that. I'm not welcome back next year anyway.

"You just take it easy, OK?" Vic is saying. "Don't worry about your shift. We'll cover for you. You take care of yourself."

The problem is, I've forgotten how to take care of myself.

It's about taking care of Jessica—trying to rebalance the scales— trying to force something good out of a nightmare and set her free somehow. Trying to save the victims that can still be saved...

But maybe I haven't done that at all.

Maybe I've just pretended to.

Maybe this hasn't been for them, but for me.

Daniel is helping me stand, wrapping his arm around me. The world is tipping under me, but his grip is steady. "C'mon. I got you."

The comforter is a cocoon around me, holding me and my grief wrapped tightly together as I lie curled on Daniel's bed. Loud, painful sobs peel out of me, as though someone were yanking them out, stripping me down.

I want it to stop, but I'm past the point of no return. If my grief is the predator I've been running from all these years, it's finally caught up.

Pain is all there is. It feels like I'll never move again.

Then, strong arms wrap around me.

Daniel; he's lying next to me, holding me.

He doesn't flinch as I spasm and cough and choke on my tears.

He doesn't say anything either. Just stays, solid and unmoving and warm and real.

An eternity later, my body begins to ease, each breath slower and deeper than the last. Finally, after a ragged exhale that feels like it expels the last of the poison, I feel myself return from wherever I just went.

It still hurts. But the violence is over, for now.

We lie quietly as my body remembers how to breathe, how to be. Daniel's arms are braced around my torso, one of my hands wrapped around his wrist, and little by little, our breathing syncs, as if we've found the same frequency of existence.

I don't know how long we lie here.

Or why I start speaking.

"She slit her wrists in the bath."

Daniel doesn't flinch. The curtains are semidrawn, and a fierce blade of light lies across our bodies, jagged and brilliant.

Daniel's notes: *What happened to Jessica?* I'm not surprised he couldn't find out, between HIPAA laws and Jess's family's private-mode social media. I'm going to tell him. I need him to know. I need someone to know my side of the story. What it felt like to live through that horrific night.

"But we think she actually...changed her mind. Partway through." My throat squeezes.

I hate this part. Hate it. Just because I've never spoken of it out loud since then doesn't mean I haven't relived it over and over in my head.

"She got out of the bath and tried to get to her phone to call for help, but she was dripping wet and weak from blood loss, and she slipped and hit her head on the kitchen counter." I suck in my lips and breathe out through my nostrils. Even though I wasn't there, I'm seeing it play through my mind as if I were. Like I've done ever since it happened.

That night, I was at a networking event for young entrepreneurs in Cincinnati while my girlfriend was attempting to take her own life.

I was hobnobbing while she decided she didn't want to exist anymore. I was talking about loans and grants and marketing software and customer "touch points" while she was walking through unimaginable pain, because she was that desperate for an exit.

Fuck.

I wipe the tears with the back of my hand. I had wondered about leaving Jessica alone for a whole day. She'd only been back from her program for about two weeks. Technically, she wasn't supposed to be alone at all for the first thirty days. But she seemed OK, and when I suggested that she spend the day with her folks, or that we call in a friend to be with her, she was adamantly against it. "I'm not a child, Lily," she said. "I don't need a goddamn babysitter." And I had so much on my plate. In her absence, I'd been running Taste of Heaven alone, and I was in over my head. I'd been feeling like Jessica tossed me to the sharks, and the conference was a chance to not be so alone; to talk to other young people who were ambitious and overwhelmed, just like me. I sat in on lectures, forums, and panels. I took pages and pages of notes: books to look up, city resources available to us, recommendations on a better ERP system for tracking our inventory. I was feeling excited, invigorated, capable; like a real adult, dressed in my suit and brand-new eggshell silk blouse.

After the closing awards banquet, where the mayor made an appearance, I went out for drinks with a few people I'd met—the owner of a new gluten-free bakery, a tattoo artist, and a beautician who was working on her business plan for a beauty school in an under-resourced neighborhood. We lingered at the bar until eleven thirty, laughing and talking and promising to stay in touch.

"If I'd gone straight home…" I say, and Daniel pulls me even closer, knotting his hands together around my torso like he's a human seat belt.

"But I didn't," I make myself continue. "I stayed out."

I unlocked the door just after midnight and kicked off my shoes. The apartment was dark, with just the lights in the kitchen and the bathroom on. "Jessica?" I called softly, walking toward the kitchen. Shit—why was the floor wet? Ceiling leak, I thought immediately—we'd had one a few months prior when the dishwasher in the upstairs unit broke. But no, the ceiling looked fine.

Then I saw her. First, just a pale foot, peeking out from behind the island. I darted forward. It took me a second to understand what I was seeing. My girlfriend on the floor behind the kitchen island, naked, wet, bloody, a huge gash on her head and ribbon cuts up her forearms. I didn't shriek. I didn't cry. I dashed to the couch and grabbed her favorite fuzzy blanket, then ran back to wrap her in it.

"Jessica, can you hear me? Jessica?" I said as I propped her up, trying to get the blanket around her cold body.

She was limp. Her lips were blue. I hoisted her up in my arms. Her head lolled back; she was deadweight, but I managed to get her to the couch.

For a second, curled there on the couch, it seemed as if she were snuggled up. She always fell asleep during movies; I'd seen her in that position a hundred times.

Sitting there on the couch next to her, one hand on Jessica's knee, I pulled out my phone and called 9-1-1. As I spoke the words to the operator, "I need an ambulance right away," I remembered my mother and her sense of otherworldly calm during crisis. *We'll just go for a drive.*

I trusted my mother in that moment. Trevor's corpse was laid flat on our carpet, but she had a plan. And in a strange way, I felt her with me that night as I wrapped a body for the second time in my life. One in a shower curtain, one in a blanket. One who deserved it and one who didn't. The parallels felt comforting, because nothing made sense. The one thing in my life I'd wanted to succeed at was loving Jessica, and making her safe in that love, and I had failed. *Just like my mother.* Who hadn't protected me from Trevor, after all. She only struck Trevor after Trevor struck me.

But I don't tell Daniel all of this. I just say, "When I found her that night, she was already gone."

Then I cry again, but it's different this time. More like I'm choosing to release something pent up rather than being attacked by something outside myself.

And then, somehow, in Daniel's arms, I fall asleep.

When I wake up, I'm disoriented. The light has changed; the blade of sunlight is gone. What time is it?

"Hey, sleepyhead," says Daniel, swiveling in his chair. He's on the computer at his desk again, though this time, fully clothed. The air conditioner is humming. It's after two o'clock.

"Skylar," I say.

"I called the hospital ten minutes ago. No updates yet."

I exhale. I feel heavy with worry over Skylar, but also, somehow grounded.

"I know your name isn't Daniel Black," I say as I sit up, drawing the comforter around my shoulders and leaning against the bank of pillows.

Daniel doesn't even flinch; in fact, he goes extrastill.

I'm still too. My heart doesn't pick up speed. There's zero adrenaline in my body.

Something happened to me when I told Daniel the story of that night—the night that split my life in two.

It's not that I'm suddenly liberated from my grief. It's not that I'm happy or healed. No; I can still feel the familiar tight center of pain around Jessica, who I know is in limbo still, waiting for me to save her, which I can't do.

I don't feel afraid anymore. That's what's changed. This cat-and-mouse game I've been playing with Daniel suddenly seems silly, childish. Unnecessary. I'm ready to face what Daniel knows and what he plans to do with that information, fully confident that whatever I do next—flee, lie, kill—will be clear to me when the time comes.

I've made plans, and they've gone to shit.

Now I'm trusting my gut, and whatever happens will happen.

"I know you're a podcaster," I continue, "and that you've been investigating me."

He shuts his laptop, then comes over to the bed. He sits on the side, one knee up, and braces himself on his arms. We don't touch.

His gaze, as always, meets mine without hesitation. "I wanted to · tell you at the Sunset last night."

For a second I don't know what he's talking about. Then I remember his arm slung around me; his confession. *I think I may have misjudged you.*

"What were you going to tell me, exactly?"

"That I did come here to look into the pattern of deaths. There's been one every July at the Riovan for the past four years. I did come here thinking you might be behind it. But—" He shakes his head with a mirthless smile. "Yesterday, I saw you save a man's life, and then this morning, your reaction when they loaded that kid into the ambulance, and then hearing your story about losing Jessica—it just confirmed how wrong I was about you." He reaches forward, and I allow him to take my hand. "Lily, I can't apologize for looking into you. I'm here to find the truth, and I can't be sorry for that. But I never wanted to hurt you."

This is the last thing I ever expected Daniel Black-Lukiewicz to say. His hand is warm, but my hand in his feels cold. I should feel relieved, like a tremendous weight has been lifted.

Instead I feel…what?

"I understand," I say. "You're here for truth and justice, and you did what you had to do. I can respect that."

"And you're here to grieve the woman you loved," he says, meshing his fingers with mine, his eyes full of compassion. "I see that now."

"Yes," I say, surprised at this insight. I've never thought of what I do here as grieving, but it makes sense.

"Here's the thing," Daniel says, his voice low as his fingers twine with mine. "At first I got close to you because I needed to figure you out. I mean—I was attracted to you from the start, but in my head, it was strictly in service of the story. And then, somehow, along the way, I—" His eyes on me are so intense. "I fell for you."

Oh.

His words hang between us.

Daniel Lukiewicz is in love with me.

And honestly, it's a bit of a mindfuck for the person you thought wanted to see you in handcuffs to declare their love.

My heart should be singing right now. I should be laughing, crying happy tears, kissing him. Because isn't this what I wanted? Not a fling, but someone to love me?

Now my pulse quickens, just a little, like a bird on a branch poised for flight.

I could forget about killing Serena and leave here with Daniel.

It's not the first time I've had this thought, but before it was a pipe dream, a silly fantasy. Now, it's an actual possibility. I could start fresh with Daniel. Sell Taste of Heaven. Give up my apartment. Leave the city where I first found love and so horrifically lost it...

Slowly, I pull back, withdrawing my hand from Daniel's. I lift both knees under the blanket and wrap my arms around my legs. The Riovan may let me go without a second thought, but not Jessica. She won't let me go so easily.

It'll never work, Daniel and me. Where would we go?

Not Cincinnati. That's Jessica's territory. But I can't give up all the places that were hers either, can I? The business we dreamed up, the apartment, the bakery downstairs with the croissants we'd get on weekends. I can't give her up. He can't come, and I can't leave.

Daniel's expression doesn't register hurt—he's too stoic for that—but he leans back as well, patiently waiting for me to respond.

I've fallen for you, too, I want to say. Can he see that in my eyes, even though I'm not speaking it aloud?

But there's a deeper reason this can never work: He doesn't know me. Before, during our cat-and-mouse, we were on equal footing. Both of us lying about our reasons for being here, and both of us trying to get the truth out of each other.

Now, I've won. I finally know the truth about him.

But he doesn't know the truth about me.

I *want* Daniel to know me—to know what I've done, every detail of it—and love me anyway.

And that is impossible.

"This is my last year coming here," I say. "I've been told I won't have a job here next year."

"What?"

Now it's my turn to quirk my lips in a mirthless smile. "I guess you could say I've 'aged out.'"

I watch Daniel take this in, and I'm thankful he doesn't say something obvious, like, *How dare they?* Or, *What do you mean, aged out?* He's not one for cheap talk. Instead, he nods slowly.

"I'm sorry to hear that."

"I can't be in a relationship with you, Daniel."

He leans forward, intense. "I'm not asking for that. I know I'm probably coming on too strong, too fast. But Lily, if there is any part of you that wants to explore this with me—" His face is set. "We'll do it how you want. Long-distance, if that feels safer. Or, after I wrap up my work here, I can come to Cincinnati. Just to visit. Or I can rent a place. I can run the podcast from anywhere. We can take it slow. I just—never felt this way about anyone before. You're the most alive person I've ever met. When I'm with you, everything feels more real. It's beautiful, and it's fucking with me in the best of ways, and I don't want you to walk away without knowing the full extent of how I feel. I want you in my life. Whatever that looks like for us. Period. I've never been so sure of anything before."

You don't know who you're talking to! I want to scream, and then I want to shake him. *You don't really know me!* Or maybe it's myself I want to shake.

I want this, just as bad as him, maybe even more. And I can't let myself have it.

It would hurt too much to have it, just to watch it break.

I force myself to unwrap the comforter from around my shoulders and immediately shiver. The room is freezing. I slowly work my way off the bed, Daniel tracking my every movement.

"Maybe people just die," I say.

I can tell by his expression I've lost him. He's still sitting on the bed; I stand above him and lay a hand on his cheek. It's bristly and warm.

"Maybe the Riovan deaths aren't part of some pattern, Daniel. Life is chaotic and strange. I know you want to tell a story. Have you considered there isn't one?"

"No way," says Daniel, his eyes suddenly fierce. My hardheaded Daniel Not-Black.

Maybe I'm off the hook for now, in his mind, as a suspect. But he's not going to let this go, is he? I guess Daniel and I have that in common too—stubbornly hanging on.

He's hanging on to his story, and I'm hanging on to my plan.

I am going to kill Serena tonight.

A girl is hospitalized because of her—a sweet, insecure girl whom Serena merrily sent toward destruction.

I'll do it at Island Vibes, during the chaos of Randy's retirement party. I'll convince her to come; I know I can do it. She's already debating it, I just have to push her over the edge—metaphorically speaking, this time. I can sell it as a TikTok opportunity. Positive media that she'll surely want after today's disaster—positive media that Vic demanded she come up with. Plus, half-priced drinks!

The location is actually ideal. It gets her away from the Riovan. Now that I think about it, maybe it was a blessing in disguise that I didn't kill her this morning on the jetty. Not only will this break the pattern of the past four years of deaths, but it will dilute suspicion, because Sean and Vic, Daniel's other suspects, will both be there.

I don't feel bad about this. Vic deserves it, and Sean will be just fine.

With my hand still caressing Daniel's cheek, feeling that delicious wolfish stubble that I love and trying to memorize how it feels against my palm, I say, "Let's not force things."

What do you mean? his eyes ask me.

I tilt my head. "Let's just let this be what it was."

Now I can see the pain in Daniel's face—tattooed in the creases of his forehead, written in his eyes. It's almost unbearable to look at. His eyes say, *So this was just a fling to you.*

I try to send back, *Just a fling.* One final lie.

"Let me take you to dinner," he pleads in that husky, podcast-perfect voice of his.

I shake my head, but allow my hand to run up through his hair.

"Don't worry, Daniel," I say softly. "You'll forget me soon enough."

Or at least, that's the hope.

CHAPTER 27

DUSK FINDS ME IN THE BACKSEAT OF A JEEP WITH KENTON AT THE wheel and a girl named Kim from concierge services next to him. I'm smashed between Brianna the massage tech and a lifeguard named Sergio, who's already pregaming pretty hard with a vodka-filled water bottle.

When I biked through the rainforest to get to Brisebleue a few days ago, I remember the birdsong, the saturated smell of life, and the deep silence. Tonight, all of that is drowned out by the smell of exhaust and the roar of six engines, because it's not just us, it's a whole caravan of Jeeps. To everyone's surprise, Vic authorized the use of Riovan-branded vehicles to help transport the staff across the island for Randy's retirement party.

"We could use some team building after our two big scares," he said during the "team huddle" he called before dinner, meaning of course Herb and Skylar. Skylar, he reported, was severely dehydrated but was stable and expected to be discharged the next day. "People forget how hot the sun is here! You have to drink extra water."

Which meant Vic hadn't taken my rant about Serena's involvement seriously at all—either that, or he was covering for his staff, his hotel, just like he did with Michael Johnson's death. Nothing worse in Vic's mind than liability and negative publicity. I can't say I'm surprised.

"What a relief!" crowed Serena.

It was easy for me to sidle up to her when the huddle was over and whisper, "We should celebrate tonight, right? Blow off some steam?"

"Oh my God, fine, I'll come," she said and then poked me playfully. "But you're buying me a drink!"

A small price to pay. A drink for a life.

I couldn't help but say one more thing to Serena. "Those powders you gave Skylar in the bathroom. The CleanSlim—"

"It's perfectly safe!" she snapped back, but the red flood in her cheeks gave her away. She knew she was guilty.

"Does anyone know Randy?" Sergio is saying between gulps of water. "Like, is he anyone's friend or just some rando?"

I ignore the question, but Brianna speculates politely.

Being part of a Jeep entourage is not ideal. I wanted my own set of wheels to get to and from Island Vibes. It would be smart to have autonomy on the night I'm killing someone. But when plans were being made and Vic was assigning drivers and doing a head count, opting out of the plan would have drawn more attention. And maybe it's better this way—moving with the group, blending in. Not to mention, would I really have biked back to the Riovan alone, through the rainforest, in the pitch dark of night?

"I've never seen such a gorgeous shade of green!" Brianna exclaims, holding up her phone and snapping picture after picture as we tear down the dirt road behind the lead vehicle. "Are you guys seeing this?"

"Heads up—monkey!" shouts Kenton from the front seat, and Brianna yelps with delight, swiveling her camera.

As we pass under a tree, I spot it, hunched over on a branch— sandy-colored fur and an ink-black face, looking at us with a sage expression.

"It's a vervet monkey," says Sergio. "I read about them. They're actually not native to the island…"

He continues his little animal-kingdom lesson, with Brianna oohing and aahing, but I tune them out. Close my eyes. Feel the wind breaking over my face. I quietly slip my hand into my crossbody purse and feel the little sandwich bag. I crushed a dozen of my benzodiaz-epine pills into a powder. At the party, I'm going to mix them into Serena's drink. According to the internet, the effect on Serena could range from light drowsiness to a "coma-like state."

And then, I'll drown her.

She'll be drunk and woozy. I'll suggest we get some air. And I'll lead her to the beach. The way the ocean hits the northern side is different—the waves are wilder, the currents stronger. Completely understandable how a drunk girl might lose her footing and get pulled under. I'll call for help when it's done; I might even perform CPR once I'm sure she's dead, to prove I tried to save her. The story will be simple: *Serena wanted to go for a swim. I told her it was a bad idea, because she seemed really drunk. I even tried to stop her, but…*

In case they do a toxicology report, I have a few more uncrushed benzos in my pill bottle that I'll slip into her purse, to make it seem like she took them regularly. There's no name on the label; it could just as well be hers as mine.

I don't like the thought of holding her down in the dark water. I prefer a quick death. The thrust of a needle. A shove down the stairs. The toss of a hair dryer. I know she'll struggle, and I'll have to remain steady, and it will be more drawn out than anything I've done so far. But this is the best plan I've been able to come up with since this morning's ruined attempt.

The first sign of town is the thumping rhythm in the air. Whatever music they're playing, someone has turned it up to the max. And then, we crest a hill and there it is, Brisebleue, sparkling and magical with the dark beach just beyond. Main Street is lined with strings of lights, and the soft brushstrokes of dusk have erased all the daytime grime.

We park and climb out of the Jeep. I'm wearing a short one-shoulder dress with a ruffle at the bottom. Not my style, but when River saw what I was planning on wearing—shorts and a tank top, the most practical outfit for what I planned on doing—she tossed me one of her dresses and wouldn't let up until I'd put on lipstick too.

"You never know if Mr. Black will be there," she teased.

"Oh, I don't think this party is his thing," I returned, but still—all three of his suspects in one place? Of course he'd be here, if he knew about it. Chances are low he'll find out about the party, though; I only put up flyers in the staff break room, and there's no way Sean invited him. Not to mention, I may have just broken his heart, so with any luck, he's being a cliché for once in his life and drinking his sorrows away via a series of sugary cocktails. At the Sunset. Alone.

For Randy's party, Island Vibes has set up picnic tables in the street. A DJ presides from a crude wooden stage outside the restaurant, and at least a hundred people are milling around, eating nachos, drinking cocktails, and dancing. It's the perfect amount of chaos. No one will notice when Serena and I slip away.

I quickly lose my Jeep entourage as I press toward the restaurant, where I know Randy will be holding court. Whatever happens tonight, I do want to say goodbye to him.

I find him behind the bar, wearing a silly straw hat, mixing the drinks while Sean deals with the food. I've already decided I won't let on that I know about Randy's cancer. Sean gives me a subtle salute, and I give him a chin-up gesture.

"Hey, Randy," I say warmly, leaning my elbows on the counter. "Great party."

He comes all the way out from behind the bar to embrace me. He smells nice, like beer and spiced ground meat from the nachos. I'm aware that technically we don't know each other very well, but once you bond with someone over a similar loss, you don't forget that.

"What are you going to do with yourself in your retirement?" I say when we pull out of the hug.

"Oh, you know. Not chemo." He gives me a look. "You know about the cancer? Everyone knows."

"I wasn't going to mention it, but…"

"It's OK. I'm not sad. I've been lucky enough to have two great lives. My life with Brenda, and then my life on the island. Some people don't even get one good life!"

"That's an amazing attitude."

"It's not an attitude. It's the truth. Luck struck twice. Now it's my turn to bow out, and who am I to complain?"

I squeeze his arm. "I hope it's a fun night tonight, celebrating what you built here."

"It's Sean's now," he says loudly, getting Sean's attention and an answering smile. Then Randy mock-whispers, "Poor bastard." We all laugh, then he says, "You enjoy yourself tonight, Lily. You won't be young forever—take it from me. Flirt with someone. Get buzzed. You know, live a little."

"OK," I say, laughing lightly to satisfy his image of me. A young, single woman in a ruffled dress without a concern in the world. Just here to party, like everyone else. For a second, I wish I was her.

Then I spot Serena.

Leaning against a wall with a cocktail in hand, dressed in a skin-tight tank top and high-waisted shorts, talking to a guy with surfer vibes. And her cocktail is almost empty.

"I'll be back in a sec," I say, excusing myself from Randy. I go up to Serena and reach for her glass.

"Hey, boss. Can I get you a refill?"

Serena smiles at me. "Hell, yes! Another strawberry daiquiri. Let me give you my credit card—"

"No! This one's on me, remember?" I say with a smile. She knocks down the last little bit, and I take her empty glass.

Randy makes the drink, and we chit chat a little more about the food biz and how supply chain works on the island. Then, I excuse myself and head to the restroom. There's just one all-gender room behind a thin bamboo door with a barely functioning lock, but it'll do. I mix the powder into Serena's thick drink quickly, then rinse out the sandwich bag and bury it in the trash under some crumpled paper towels.

As I approach Serena, I can hear the surfer talking in a loud, annoyingly confident voice.

"Yeah, so my time in Bali was nuts, I met this chick who believed that—get this—her tattoos were spirits, and they, like, spoke to her—"

"Here you go," I interrupt, handing the drink to Serena.

"Thank you, God, you're a lifesaver," she says, and easy as pie, she guzzles down nearly half of it in one go.

"Hi, I'm Thomas," says the surfer guy, bestowing me with a charming smile and reaching out a tanned paw to shake my hand.

"Hi, Thomas."

"So…have *you* been to Bali?"

"Sorry, I was just—" I gesture vaguely behind me, already walking away.

It'll take some time for the drugs to have an effect—and I'm not spending it talking to him.

I head outside and walk the length of the street. I pick out a familiar face—Kyle, of all people, dancing in a bit of an ick way with a woman who seems legitimately into him. *To each their own.* I wonder how he heard about the party. Doesn't matter. Kyle may have been the subject of my first little violent thought on the way here, but he's nothing to me now. Not even deserving of the energy of a violent thought. Not like Serena, who I'm about to hold underwater as she fights, because she will definitely fight, no matter how drugged…

The nachos smell amazing, and two servers in Island Vibes aprons keep bringing them out, but I don't have the stomach for food right now. Instead, I keep looking at the dark horizon beyond town where I know the ocean lies waiting. In the brief pauses between songs, I can hear the waves. It sounds like they're shouting.

The DJ has people dancing the Electric Slide when I head back inside the restaurant. It's almost too simple; Serena is slumped in one of the chairs. Thomas, who's nowhere in sight, has clearly moved on.

"Hey." I jostle her arm. "Hey, let's get you up."

"Ooo0-eeee," she says, grimacing as she pries open her eyelids. "I'm feeling…"

"Yeah, that daiquiri was strong, huh? Let's get some air."

"OK," she says.

I loop my arm through hers, and she leans on me as we leave the restaurant. I scan for familiar faces but see none. Good. I keep walking, leading Serena toward the beach. I won't look behind us to check if anyone is watching. This is an innocent walk.

"Where are we going?" Serena finally says, as we take the first step off the harder path and onto cool sand. The air is noticeably colder here.

"Just a little walk on the beach."

She comes along like an obedient pet.

The waves are loud. The water is dark, with occasional flashes from the moon, which is playing peek-a-boo with some ragged clouds.

"Take off your shoes, you don't want to get them wet," I say when we're a few feet away from the water. That will make it look like her swim was intentional. I kick my shoes off too. She unburdens herself from her purse and turns toward the waves. Quickly, I move the pill bottle from my purse to hers.

I'm still calm. I imagine the adrenaline will kick in at some point. Just not yet.

Serena steps out of her sandals. "Ooh, are we going swimming?"

Could she make this any easier?

As I settle our shoes and purses together, she prances into the water all by herself, laughing as the waves splash up around her knees, then her thighs.

I follow, still keeping a little distance, as if I really were watching out for her. I don't turn to see if anyone has followed us, but just in case, I say loudly, "Don't go any farther! You're too drunk, Serena!"

"I feel fiiiiine," she says, tipping over a little bit. Then, a wave hits her just so, and she kind of sinks sideways.

Now.

I take two big steps forward.

"Serena!" I cry, still playing to an imaginary audience.

From a distance, it might look like she was falling and I was trying to catch her.

But my hands find what I think is her back, and I push down.

There's no final moment of us making eye contact, or me seeing the fear in her face, or any of those silly cinematic moments.

Just her tipping and me bearing my weight into her back from above, and then grabbing her by the neck and the hair and holding her down.

The ocean thrashes around me, alive and hungry. Waves come up against my body; water splashes my face, stinging. Salty.

Her legs kick desperately, her feet graze my thighs, but since she's underwater, everything is gentle, more like a caress. I feel her body convulse, like it's trying to spasm its way toward air. My own lungs feel desperate, and I realize I've been holding my breath too. Living through what she's living through, as if my body were trying to stay connected to the gravity of what I'm doing.

She manages to get her head up out of the water and gasp in one swallow of air, but her face isn't to me, just the slick wet back of her head. I force her down again.

"Hey!" I hear behind me, in the distance.

Daniel. I'd know his voice anywhere.

Now adrenaline spikes, but I stay still, keeping my grip on Serena firm as her head bobs from side to side, still fighting, still trying to find air. I don't turn to look at Daniel.

He wasn't supposed to be here. He was supposed to be nursing his wounds with a piña colada or three at the fucking Sunset. And yet, his presence here feels inevitable, like the finale to the dance we've been doing since that first morning by the coffee.

And while there's dread, there's also relief.

Finally.

No more hiding.

Let him see who I really am.

That's where this has all been leading.

I'm here for truth and justice, too, Daniel, I'll tell him when I pull Serena's lifeless corpse from the waves and he says "Why?"—which of course he will. Every good finale has a why, when everything is laid bare, and I suppose Daniel and I deserve no less.

The truth (I'll say) is that Serena peddles harmful substances for profit and almost killed a child this morning. The justice (I'll tell him) is this: her death.

And then, Daniel's body is rocketing into mine with all its solidity and strength. I lose my grip on Serena just as a monstrous wave sends me tumbling under. For a second, I'm submerged, sucking in water, with black above and black below, but then my feet find the sandy bottom, and I push off, coming up spluttering.

"It *was* you!" Daniel shouts. "I can't fucking believe it!"

He's already a good distance away from me. He's hooked his arms under Serena's armpits and is dragging her to shore.

"You're too late," I shout, making for shore too, dress streaming water, hair like a wet snake down my back. "She's already dead."

CHAPTER 28

"NO!" SAYS DANIEL, AND THE SECOND MY FEET HIT SAND, HE'S SURG-ing forward, grabbing my shoulders, hurting me. Serena is immobile on the sand, a waterlogged blot. "I saw you bring back Herb. Bring her back!" He shakes me with each word, as if he can shake his conviction into me.

"Don't you get it?" I say, with a sob that's also a laugh. "I killed her, Daniel! I want her dead!"

"This isn't justice for Jessica," Daniel says, his voice raw, wild. "All these deaths? This is revenge!"

"No. It's justice."

"This won't bring back Jessica!"

"You think I don't know that? I'm saving the people it's *not* too late for, Daniel."

"It's not too late for Serena!"

He releases me and, with a fierce expression, springs toward her. He's down by her side, pushing the wet hair out of her face, pressing her jaw to make her mouth open, clearly preparing to try to bring her back himself.

That's not how you do CPR, I want to tell him. You have to start with chest compressions.

And then I'm remembering.

Catapulted back to that night, that horrific night when my life split in two, when my heart cracked open, forever broken. The night that became the pulsing, living center of all my regrets and rage.

I didn't run to the couch to get the fuzzy blanket first, to wrap Jessica in.

No. The first thing I did was CPR.

It's too awful to remember. I suppose that's why I snipped it out of the story.

I saw her foot, pale. Her body, bloody and wet on the kitchen floor. I was CPR certified, and my training kicked in. Down by her body (too cold, too blue), my hands plowing into her chest with violent, downward strokes. Live, live, live. Blood on my eggshell blouse. My lips pressed against hers in the mockery of a kiss.

When she started breathing again, I was so hopped up on adrenaline, it almost didn't register.

Then I wrapped her in the blanket and called 9-1-1.

You saved her life, they told me later.

Except they were wrong. First, I failed to protect her from herself. And then, by bringing her back, I condemned her.

"How could you leave her alone in the apartment?" Beth Ann shrieked in the hospital waiting room. They'd taken Jessica back for emergency surgery. She had a brain hemorrhage; they had to operate right away. "You broke the rules!"

Jessica told me she was fine. She said she didn't need a goddamn babysitter. She said, go to your networking thing. Don't worry about me. So I did.

But I couldn't say that out loud. It sounded childish. Insufficient. So I said nothing and let Beth Ann shriek.

I almost didn't mind her shouting. I deserved it. The first thirty days posttreatment, Jessica wasn't supposed to be alone, and I had flouted the rules, thinking she knew better; thinking I knew better.

Something is scratchy and rough on my knees. The sand. I've knelt by Jessica.

No, it's Serena.

"She doesn't deserve saving," I say.

"And you're willing to go to prison for this?"

I turn to look at Daniel, and the memory I was wrapped up in slips off like a coat, leaving me cold and shaking.

Daniel is an eyewitness, and if Serena dies, I have no doubt he'll testify against me.

I've always told myself I was going to be smarter than my mom. I would also kill the bad guys, but I would get away with it. I came here this year to do one thing. And I did it. But with Daniel here, everything has changed. Is Serena's toxicity worth getting locked away for? What is the value of her life weighed against mine?

What was the value of Trevor's life versus Mom's?

The first time I visited Mom, I cried on the other side of the glass, snotty, repeating, "He wasn't worth it, Mom, he wasn't worth it." And he wasn't. The scales in my mind had already weighed this out. Trevor's shitty, worthless existence versus Mom's.

And yet the justice system didn't use those scales to measure out the penalty.

Mom had to pay everything for that nothing piece of shit.

A transaction I've never recovered from.

And now, it could happen to me too.

Daniel has no proof—that I've found, at least—to incriminate me for any of the previous deaths. But this one, he watched me do—or attempt to do. If I bring her back, attempted murder might only give me a couple of years in prison, if it goes favorably for me. But if I let her die? I could spend the rest of my life behind bars. Just like Mom.

"No," I say simply to Daniel. "She's not worth it."

Then I lay the heels of my hands on Serena's chest, lock my elbows, and pump. *One. Two. Three.*

I register Daniel on the phone, calling for an ambulance. "Yes, someone almost drowned… Yes, the beach just outside Brisebleue. Thank you."

When he disconnects, he drops to his knees next to me.

The wind hisses through the sand like a hundred snakes. The waves roll with bottomless, insatiable energy.

Maybe Daniel thinks I've had a change of heart. But I haven't. This is pure self-interest at work, and I can't be sorry for it.

The thirty chest compressions are done. I pinch Serena's nose and lock my mouth with hers.

Two breaths, into her lungs. I feel her inflate under my hands, then wrench myself up and prepare to start chest compressions again.

"Killing people is not the solution, Lily," says Daniel. "There are better ways to save people."

"You. Don't. Get. It," I say, putting my energy into the fresh set of chest compressions, ticking the numbers off in some separate space in my head. "The world sits by while people get hurt. The world sat by while my mom—" I suck in my breath, remembering the clang of metal on skull. The way Trevor crumpled to the ground, all that wickedness snuffed out with one moment of brave violence. My mother cared. Killing Trevor was the ultimate sign of her love for me.

"I'm not going to sit by," I continue. "I'm not going to move on, or let things go. I give a shit. I. Give. A *shit*, Daniel, and if that makes me the bad guy, so fucking be it."

"Don't you see?" He's angry and earnest, and when I spare him a glance, his eyes are boring into me with all their familiar intensity. "You've made yourself into the judge."

"Yeah." I laugh bitterly. *Twenty-seven. Twenty-eight.* "I have, Daniel. But you know what? So have you. Everyone judges, all the time. You think telling the story is enough. I think that's bullshit. I *change* the story."

Thirty. I have a feeling that she's not coming back, but I fit my mouth to Serena's anyway and push two more breaths into her.

"Lily…" Daniel breathes out a ragged breath. "I *didn't* tell the story."

I come back up from the mouth-to-mouth, then put my faithful lifeguard hands on Serena's chest and start the count again.

"What are you talking about?"

"Five years ago, when I was a reporter at the *Pacific*…I got your email."

I'm about to say, *what email*, when it hits me.

"I knew I had to run that story," he continues. "*Your* story. But there was an investor in the paper who also sat on the Riovan board. My boss made me kill it. I'm sorry."

I stop the chest compressions. We stare at each other. The wind ruffles my hair.

If Daniel had investigated the Riovan five years ago—

Everything inside me wants to collapse at once, but I have a job to do, so I set my hands on Serena. Again.

"Why are you here now?" I say, furious. "Why now when you didn't have the fucking balls to do it then?"

"I couldn't let the story go," he says, fast, desperate, like he knows this is his last chance to tell me. "I kept working on it, behind the scenes. Then people started dying. By the third death, I got my hands on a staff list and saw your name. I talked to my boss again. She told me if I ran the story, she'd end my career. So I quit. I bought audio equipment and started a podcast. I used Season One to pay my way here and tell the story I was supposed to tell five years ago. You were the top of my suspect list from the start. The problem is," he pauses, "well, like I said at the hotel. I fell for you."

My heart drums a furious beat. Why does it hurt so much to hear that falling in love with me was a *problem*?

I give one final, angry shove downward on Serena's chest. *Thirty.*

Immediately, there's a coughing sound, like my anger just achieved what my constancy could not. Serena rolls to her side as seawater spurts out of her mouth. Her eyes open, dark slits, blinking in confusion.

"What happened?" she says in a wet rasp.

I look at Daniel. My insides are burning with emotions too strong to name. He looks at me.

I brought her back. There was no murder tonight. *Now what?*

Daniel lays a hand on Serena's forehead like one might a child and leans over her.

"Lily just saved your life."

"Oh." Serena's eyes slip closed again. She lies motionless on her side, but she's breathing.

"Lily…" says Daniel. I can hear the agony in that single word. "What am I supposed to fucking do now?"

I almost spit out, *Go back and fucking fix what you broke.*

But of course, he can't. And neither can I. Neither of us can fix the mistakes we made five years ago. He can't run the story when he was supposed to. I can't go back and glue Jessica back together.

And maybe…maybe I wouldn't have been able to.

My heart pounds and pounds over this new thought.

Maybe loving someone doesn't always mean you can save them.

Something opens in me. My shoulders sag as the anger floods out, leaving an empty, dark hole. All that seems to be left of me is negative space. The things I lost—the woman I lost.

Daniel is still looking at me with pleading in his eyes. What is he supposed to do? I can't answer that. No one can but him. We each have our crosses to bear. Our failures, living like old injuries in our bodies. Pain that will never quite leave.

"That's up to you," I say.

His face is tortured.

His eyes say, *If I had told the story five years ago—*

I know, I send him.

And if I hadn't emailed him? He never would have noticed a few deaths at a distant Caribbean resort.

I touch his arm, and even now, under these insane circumstances, I feel the electricity between us. The powerful energy of our potential.

"No one made me do any of this, Daniel. This was my choice."

He shakes his head, like some part of him is trying to deny that all of this is happening.

"It's OK," I say softly. I reach up and touch his cheek, surprised to find it wet with tears.

I feel my power over him in this moment. He's gutted, weak, guilty for betraying his own conscience. Could I convince him to pull the plug on the podcast? If I promise him my killing days are over? Could we live together happily ever after? Could we pretend I'd never done this? New chapter, don't look back?

In the distance, I hear the sound of an ambulance siren, and I know this is almost over. I'll be leaving the Riovan one way or another, and I won't be coming back.

"If you air the podcast," I say softly, "all I ask is that you expose the Riovan." Then I tilt my head and give him one last look. "And you should probably know...I fell for you too."

His eyes scan me.

"Lily," he says in a husky voice, and I know that my name on his lips is a goodbye. A lament for what we might have had, in some parallel life.

I lean forward and brush my lips against his—his soft, expressive lips that have tasted every inch of my body.

I should try to convince him not to air the podcast. I should be smart, and look out for myself, and keep playing the game I've been playing all along. Do my all to persuade him by whatever means necessary. He's vulnerable, and if I stand a chance at all of getting through to him, it's now. Instead, I pull away.

What are you doing, Lily? a voice shouts in my head. *This man is a threat! Your future is in the balance. Shut him down now, while you have the chance! Fight for your happily ever after with Daniel!*

But...

Is that what I really want? Happiness at any cost—even if the cost is the integrity of the man I'm falling for?

In this scenario, we'd be turning a blind eye to what I've done.

And, even though Daniel and I have lied to each other and used each other and justified the means with the ends, ultimately it's not in either of our natures to betray our moral codes. Once we've seen the truth, neither Daniel nor I can turn away. If we did, we wouldn't be...*us.*

I let out a long breath. Turn in the sand. The voice is screaming, *Stop, what are you doing,* but I take a step. Then another. I'm walking away. The sand slips through my toes, silky. The night wind tosses my hair backward.

Serena will be OK.

The Riovan will likely continue on as it always has.

I won't return.

And Daniel...

I walk faster, wrapping my arms around myself. Tears stream down my face, and I make a small, quiet gasp, because I can hardly believe what I'm doing, what I'm risking.

But I don't want to control him. I don't want anyone to compromise themselves for me—to reduce themselves. Jess felt less than. She told me as much. In the toxic story that formed in her mind, she was weak and pathetic—I was strong and beautiful. Above her. And she hated me for it, in the end. If I succeeded in convincing Daniel to betray himself for my sake, if he allowed me to be above his deepest-held principles, he would end up despising himself for it. But it wouldn't end there—eventually, he'd hate me for it too.

And that, more than anything, would destroy me.

Just moments ago, I said, *If you air the podcast*. But I should have said *when*.

Because, knowing Daniel, I know what he'll choose, don't I? I've known all along.

Fuck. The tears run faster. Am I being noble, or just a self-destructive fool?

But there's no turning back now, because I'm on the main drag of Brisebleue. The mood has changed. The DJ has stopped the music as the ambulance crawls through. People part, quiet, to watch its blinking progression toward the beach where Daniel waits with Serena. I slip through the crowd. I feel like a ghost.

Do not look back, I coach myself.

I vaguely register people talking as I pass.

"What happened?"

"Someone got hurt down at the beach."

"I'm calling it. Some drunk idiot went for a late-night swim..."

"Oh my God, I hope they're OK, whoever it is..."

It feels like I'm floating instead of walking, like I'm not really connected to the physical world. I came undone on the beach. I saved the woman I was supposed to kill. And something changed. I'm not yet sure what.

I've reached the edge of Brisebleue. The ambulance will be on the beach by now, loading Serena onto the stretcher.

There's a parallel world in which Daniel ran the story five years ago, and the Riovan shut down, and Jessica was vindicated, and I didn't kill anyone, and Daniel and I fell in love. A cruel little montage of scenes follows—Daniel and me waking up late on a lazy Sunday and squabbling over who gets what section of the paper while bacon sizzles in the skillet. We're both passionate citizens of the world in our own ways; it's easy to imagine we might get involved in city politics. Local non-profits. Argue about the candidates on the ballot, the ethics of processed meat, the character arcs in *Crime and Punishment*. We'd argue hard and love hard. It would be a great life, full of intensity and purpose...and incredible sex.

But that's not the world I got.

Not the life I lived.

Not the choices I made.

I've reached the Jeeps, all parked together just outside town in a grassy clearing, the keys still inside; there's no theft up here. I simply climb into the first vehicle, turn the key in the ignition, and rumble my way back onto the dark road that leads through the rainforest.

Above, the stars twinkle, distant and cold.

Stars are so different from fireworks, aren't they? Fireworks demand your attention with their boom and their flare—but then they leave. You have to work harder for the stars. Leave the city and the light pollution and the chaos—all so that you can see what was really there all along.

I've never wanted something as much as I want to turn the vehicle around right now.

I want to run back to Daniel, fling myself into his arms.

I want to be the Lily he can be with, without compromising who he is.

The rainforest looms like a mouth, eternally open in a black yawn. I press down on the gas, and the stars are swallowed by the canopy. The Jeep's headlamps jolt their light into the largeness of the dark. The scent of the rainforest at night is somehow even richer than during the day. Thick, floral, smothering.

I push down even harder on the accelerator.

In my heart of hearts, I know what happens next, because I know him.

He cares too much about justice and truth to stay silent.

He'll air the season.

He'll ruin me.

And I'll love him the more for it.

CHAPTER 29

BACK AT THE HOTEL, I MOVE ABOUT THE ROOM IN A DREAM STATE, booking a ticket on my phone on the first flight out, then packing my things. My Riovan-branded gear I leave on the bed.

I drive to the airport in the Riovan Jeep. They'll find a way to get their vehicle back. It's two in the morning when I park in the airport garage. No flights are going out until morning, of course, so I curl up in the backseat. At 5 a.m., I rouse myself, redo my ponytail, grab my luggage. Leaving the keys in the Jeep's front seat, I head into the blinding fluorescent light of the airport. The security line is short, and only ten people are ahead of me. I'm certain I'll be stopped by officials.

I hand the first man my passport and scan the ticket QR code on his device, my pulse racing as I remember the prison conditions on the island. The hole-in-the-ground potties. The overcrowded cells...

"Go ahead," he says with a smile, handing my passport back. "Have a safe trip home."

Really? That easy?

The duty-free shops on the way to my gate display mementos— posters and straw hats, sandals and carved earrings. I stop before one of the displays, and some achy part of me wishes this was *that* kind of trip; one I'd want to remember with a bird-shaped magnet or a set of tacky coasters.

Even while I wait in the short line of people boarding the flight to Miami, I can almost hear it—the footsteps of police, running to stop me before I leave the island. *Arrêtez, mademoiselle, arrêtez!*

But I board in peace, take up residence in my oversize seat, and am promptly offered a steaming washcloth to refresh my face and hands.

"Would you like a beverage before we take off?" says a glossy flight attendant in navy blue, leaning toward my seat with a pair of tongs to collect the hot washcloth I just used.

I upgraded to first class. I figure, if I do go to prison after Season Two drops, I'll appreciate the memory of the legroom on my final flight. The hot washcloth and the warm salted nuts are just added bonuses.

"Some white wine, please," I say. Pretty sure they don't serve that in prison either.

I sip the wine. I'm still processing so much, but one thing keeps floating to the top.

I brought Daniel to the Riovan.

My plea for help drew the attention of the man who has the power to undo me.

The irony is not lost on me.

We rattle down the runway, and when we take off I can feel the emotion held tight in my chest as I watch the island slide away, just as the sun is rising.

Here I am, soaring away from what I've done.

Not that it won't follow me. The first episode of Daniel's new season is dropping tomorrow, according to the website.

I crane to see Saint Lisieux until it's out of sight, which doesn't take long. It's a small island in a large ocean, in an even larger world. Like my life—a speck, when you stop to think about it.

The airplane ride back is nothing like the ride here.

On the way to Saint Lisieux, I was fizzing like a shaken soda can, ready to burst.

Now, I'm contemplative. Present. Sober. I don't know what I'm going to do yet; what's going to happen to my life. But that's OK, because it's not my move. It's Daniel's move. And until someone stops me, I'm moving forward.

I pull out my phone and pay the surcharge for in-flight Wi-Fi. A few taps of my fingers, and I've pulled up *Who Killed Me?*, Season One. Might as well catch up.

I pop in my earbuds and press play on *Episode One: The Death of Sammi Jones*.

Immediately, Daniel's voice washes through me. It feels like he's right next to me, telling me the story of Sammi's tragically shortened life over drinks. As I eat my salted nuts and sip my wine and choose between the vegetarian lasagne and the chicken Vesuvio for my meal, I lose my gaze out of the window and allow Daniel's voice to fill my senses. One episode melds into another, and during my layover in Miami, I just keep on going. I don't want to stop being with Daniel in this way, his voice nestled in my ear, unraveling chaos into one smooth story. I can see why my friends are into this, after all. It's not so much the lurid voyeurism involved in true crime that makes this so enjoyable. No—it's scratching the same itch that makes me enjoy completing a puzzle. Order from chaos. Finding a reason for the shit that happens.

Whatever happens to him, to me, I love that he knows the truth about me now—or most of it. There's one part I didn't tell him. Should I have? Who knows—maybe he could have helped me see the order in the chaos. But I held back, because I always hold back; of all the sources of pain in my life, this is the greatest, and most days, I can hardly bear to face it myself.

It almost makes me wish I'd told Daniel my one, final secret about Jess.

Because it's always about Jess.

CHAPTER 30

BY THE TIME I UNLOCK THE DOOR TO MY APARTMENT, I'VE LISTENED TO all of Season One, and I have only myself and the silence and the stale air.

It was good. So fucking good, the way Daniel wove all the stories together—the way you felt his genuine care and investment, and the thrill of just how far he was willing to go to get the truth.

Sammi Jones, the subject of Season One, died during the pandemic, but even though the doctors classified it as a COVID-related death, her parents insisted she never had COVID. Enter Daniel, who had come across her story on Twitter. He started by interviewing Sammi's parents, then went through all of the medical records her parents could get their hands on. Long story short, it turned out that during the supply-chain crisis, an ice-cream manufacturer couldn't get hold of a crucial ingredient and made a formula switch behind the scenes to keep production going. The replacement ingredient contained a little-known allergen, which the company did not disclose on the label. Sammi had a reaction and died from complications to her lungs.

The last episode was a tour de force. Daniel went undercover at the plant where the ingredient substitution had taken place, exposing the people who had covered up the formula change, and forged the Quality Assurance documents. Thanks to Daniel's research, Sammi's parents were able to sue the company and were granted two million dollars in damages. I googled the company in question, Cold & Sweet, and—they're out of business.

I feel irrationally proud of him.

First, I open the apartment's sticky windows, bringing in the noise of the traffic and the merest bit of a breeze. It's a hot day, and soon I'm sweating, but at least the air is circulating again. It's humid, and the parquet floors are tacky underfoot. I turn on the ceiling fan, strip down to a crop top and shorts, then dump the contents of my luggage directly into the in-unit washing machine.

As I move about unpacking other odds and ends, including my unfinished copy of *Crime and Punishment,* which I toss on the coffee table, I can feel the aftertaste of the podcast lingering like a good wine.

I move the clothes from the washer to the dryer. I pull out a frozen meal of rice pilaf and chicken and heat it up for the required two minutes, then stir, then two more minutes. I barely taste it; I'm too lost in my thoughts. I know I'm existing in a liminal space right now. A small parenthesis. Then, I lie in bed and stare at the ceiling and wait for midnight, when Episode One of my season will drop.

The season unfurls as I return to normal life, with one episode released each week. I imagine Daniel is back in the States now, editing his material and piecing together the best way to tell the story. I don't contact him, and he doesn't contact me, though I sometimes pull up his WhatsApp number and let my thumb hover, for no reason.

I go out with my friends one Saturday night in the middle of August. We start the evening at Olé Mi Arte, a new small-plates farm-to-table restaurant. From there, the plan is to hit the clubs, at which point I will quietly bow out and Uber home.

"How was your island dream job?" Nate teases as we convene outside the restaurant in our fit-to-kill garb, and I pretend to laugh.

It's after placing our order that Rachel pipes up, "Um, weird coincidence, Lil, but did you hear about all these deaths that have apparently been going down at the Riovan?"

"What?" I say, wrinkling my brow.

"Oh my God. You could have been a victim, Lil!" says Nadine. "They're calling him—or her—the Beach Body Killer, and that podcaster we're obsessed with is doing this whole series on it! The first episode is to die for. First of all, his voice is *so* sexy, and then the way he describes the sand and the water? It almost makes you want to be there, living the resort life, except…"

"Murder!" says Nate, with an exaggerated pop of his eyes that makes everyone laugh.

"Lil, it's the podcast we were all into last year," says Phoebe. She slams her palm on the table for emphasis, making the silverware bounce. "You. Have. To. Listen."

"Yeah, OK," I say.

"It's called *Who Killed Me?*, remember?" says Nate, pulling out his phone. "I know I texted you the link last year. Here, I'll send it to you again."

"You can give us the insider info so we can guess the killer!" crows Phoebe, and everyone raises their cocktail glasses, laughing and toasting to the imaginary victory of figuring out who was behind the deaths before the end of the season.

At that point, only two episodes have dropped, and my name has yet to come up.

It happens in Episode Three, unleashing a bevy of texts from my friends. *Are u OK? OMG Lily, I can't believe that guy is dragging your name into this! Call me! LMK what you need!*

No one asks the most important question: Did you do it?

But that's OK. Even if they asked? I'd lie to them.

The days slip past. I find myself talking out loud to Jessica as I move through the house doing this or that, or go to the store, or walk in the park.

"Daisies or roses?" I ask her out loud, as I contemplate the fresh flowers at Trader Joe's.

A man in running clothes turns and says, "Excuse me?"

"Sorry, nothing," I say and grab the roses—pale coral-colored things with a red edge, as though they were dipped in blood.

Taste of Heaven, to my credit, is running flawlessly without me, and I can feel myself peel away. I've hired good people; I let them do their jobs, just making a few decisions here and there. I even remove my name from the website. Better to start detaching—I don't want my plummeting reputation to bring the company down.

August is hot as a sauna. I stay inside and cook simple, small meals for myself. I consider getting a cat from a nearby shelter, which doesn't make any sense if I'm going to prison soon, but it's a good distraction nonetheless. My best hope is that, if I do end up sentenced to prison, it will only be for attempted murder, since Serena didn't actually die and there can't be hard proof for the others, but…we'll see.

"Do we like the tabby or the black one?" I ask Jessica, as I click between their little bios online. "The tabby is playful, but maybe his energy is too high for the space? And Gus is so cute. Look at that little white spot on his nose. Adorable."

Beth Ann calls, but I don't pick up. Is she listening to the podcast? I delete her voicemail without listening. The only reason I'd want to talk to her anyway is about Jessica, and I'm done beating my head against that particular wall.

My friends gradually stop texting. It's no surprise; by Episode Five, which drops on Labor Day, I'm looking pretty bad, though Vic and Sean are still active suspects, which is of course a strategic drama-building choice since by now Daniel knows that neither of them did a thing.

Episode Seven drops in mid-September. As usual, I stay up until midnight so that I can listen the second it's released.

Daniel launches in, describing the party at Island Vibes, and how he raced after me and Serena.

"The waves are wild up there, and it was dark," his voice says, deep and mesmerizing, drawing me back into the scene until it feels like I'm reliving it with him. "My heart was thundering in my chest; I was running toward what I believed to be Lily's final kill. I had to stop her. Then, I heard Lily cry out for Serena to stop, that Serena was drunk and the waves were too dangerous. My mind was racing. Could I have been wrong about Lily? Was she actually looking out for Serena? Then, as I'm running through the sand, I see Serena slip—a big wave crashed into her, and down she went, in a flash. You have no idea how powerful those waves are on the north side of the island. It sucked her under; no one could do anything, not even Lily, who was just feet away from Serena. I ran into the water. It was cold, and I almost lost my footing. I grabbed Serena under the arms and dragged her back to the beach. When we reached the sand, Serena was no longer breathing."

My heart pounds and pounds as Daniel's voice carries me forward.

"But then, Lily dropped to her knees by Serena. In a twist I never saw coming, there on the beach, I watched the woman who I thought was a killer bring Serena back to life. CPR is a violent thing. I don't know if you've ever watched someone be resuscitated, but it doesn't look gentle. I watched Lily slam life back into Serena as if her own life depended on it." He pauses. "At this point, I could tell you who the Beach Body Killer is. But I think you already know, don't you? Vote on the website, and make sure to come back next week for the Tell-All episode that will answer every question and reveal not only the killer, but the question that's been torturing me all summer. Why? Why does someone kill, and what is it inside them that drives them to take a human life—not just once, but over and over? What life story leads to that decision? *Who Killed Me?* You'll find out soon. Until then, this is your host, Daniel Lukiewicz."

There's a little ditty of transitional music, then a female voice says, "Subscribe to *Who Killed Me?* today, and be the first to hear the explosive Season Two finale! This episode is sponsored by Hank's Vegan Hot Dogs—a frankfurter so juicy, you'll never guess it's not meat—and Hannah's Closet, a non-profit that provides business-appropriate clothing to facilitate the return of ex-cons to the workforce."

And it's over.

There's a sudden blare in my ear, and I jolt upright in bed. My ringtone. I have a phone call piping straight into my earbuds.

I grab my phone to answer, and my heart goes still.

It's Daniel's number. No longer through WhatsApp, but I've looked at it enough that I recognize it right away. I answer.

"Hello?"

CHAPTER 31

"HI," HE SAYS.

I count three heartbeats before I'm capable of speech.

"I just listened to Episode Seven," I say, trying to adjust from the Daniel-in-my-ear being a recorded version to the real, in-the-moment, living, breathing man.

"Yeah," he says, drawing out the word like an exhale.

"Is that why you called?" I can't help but tease him a little. "To see if I was up-to-date?"

"I'm calling to warn you, Lily. Next week, I'm telling the world what you've done."

"I know," I say. This isn't new information.

"I wanted to give you the courtesy of a heads-up."

"What, so I can run away to Bali?"

He chuckles. "Bali, huh?" His laughter dies, and I lie back down on the bed, phone on my chest.

"I hope you're not waiting for me to tell you I appreciate the thought," I say drily.

"Of course not," he says. "And I hope you're not waiting for me to say I'm sorry."

"It's been very interesting, Daniel. I'll give it to you; you're a great storyteller. But you still haven't taken down the Riovan."

"Have a little faith," he says. "Have to save something for the finale."

"Right," I say, "since it's obvious to everyone that I'm the killer."

In the background, even as we go back and forth, my head is playing out how this will go down.

He airs the last episode.

Now, the whole English-speaking world knows I'm a killer.

Law enforcement will show up at my door. How could they not? And however much I lie and deny—which I have no qualms about doing—Daniel literally watched me attempt to murder Serena, and I confessed that night to him in no uncertain terms: *I want her dead.* I imagine Serena is more than ready to corroborate.

Final scene, I go to prison.

Epilogue, I rot there, paying for the lives of people who didn't deserve to live in the first place.

And that's a wrap, folks.

I hate this story.

If I have to go down, wouldn't it be so much better to do it for someone who *does* deserve the time of day?

I mean it as a kind of sarcastic joke in my own head, but then...

Something in me opens; a door I've kept closed.

But now I think it's always been there.

There is another way. A way for Daniel to have his killer—and a killer ending to his podcast. One that has the potential to break the internet.

Even though the idea feels new, it's not. Some subconscious part of me has been working on it. There's a reason I've been talking to Jessica in my head these past few days, isn't there? I've been preparing myself for a longer goodbye. The goodbye we were supposed to have years ago.

Maybe it's because I'm used to planning murders, but the pieces fly into place in my head almost effortlessly, as if I'd been collecting the shards of this plan for a very long time, and now I'm ready to do the easy part and fit them together.

My heart thunders so loud I feel like Daniel will hear it through my earbuds.

"Have you already finished the season finale?" I say.

"I'm still in edits, but we're close."

"What if I asked you not to air it?"

He heaves out a breath. "You know I can't—"

"I don't mean it like that," I interrupt. "I mean—what if you had the chance to record some new material?"

"Lily—what are you saying?"

"I'm going to text you a time and a place."

His voice is wary. "Please tell me what you're talking about."

"No. You might try to stop me."

"Lily…"

"Your job is to wait for my message and show up with your recording equipment. And…it might help you to be in the Cincinnati area."

"Lily, I—"

"Your first season was great, Daniel. Honestly, your second season…it's only OK. It's a bit obvious that it's me, don't you think? Where's the twist?"

"I—"

"I'm going to give you a finale that will put you into the podcaster hall of fame."

"But—"

"Do you trust me?" I say.

There's a silence. Then, "Yes."

It doesn't escape me that a man who loves truth and justice expressing trust in a killer might not make sense to anyone else. But it makes sense to me—and I know it does to him too. We understand each other at a profound level. We'd both risk it all, give everything up, for justice. We're just coming at it from two different sides. To him, it means exposing the truth. To me, it means holding the world to account. He wants to tell the story; I want to make the story.

"OK, then," I say. "Keep your phone close; I'll be in touch."

I disconnect. I'm sitting upright in bed; I hadn't noticed I'd moved from being prone. My cheeks are flushed, my body humming.

Since coming back to Cincinnati, I've been living in a bubble. I always knew it was going to pop, but I imagined Daniel would be the one to pop it—it was up to me to wait for the inevitable to happen.

Screw that.

If I have to be behind bars, it won't be on Daniel's terms, or anyone else's but my own. I'm taking back control and choosing my own ending.

Daniel can get his version of justice by telling the truth. And I can get my version of justice—the justice I should have claimed long, long ago.

I *will* go to prison before this is over.

But not for killing assholes.

No. I'll go to prison for killing the love of my life.

CHAPTER 32

THE HOSPITAL WAS MOSTLY SLEEPING.

It wasn't hard to get in here. I clipped on an old visitor's badge that no one looked at too closely to get past the front desk. Then, in the lobby restroom, I pulled the scrubs I brought over my T-shirt and leggings. On the sixth floor, I helped myself to a cleaning cart while the cleaning lady was inside a patient's room and made my way to the room I haven't set foot in for five years.

Once inside, I gently closed the door, then walked over to the bed.

"Hi," I breathed.

She's changed. But mostly what I noticed is all the ways she's the same.

The slope of her forehead. The sweep of her hair on the pillow. Her hands were crossed over her chest. Someone has done her nails recently in a blush pink. They looked great. She always did have lovely hands.

My hand was shaking as I reached out and made contact, stroking my fingers through her hair. I could almost imagine that she's sleeping.

But Jessica was not coming back.

Ever since her brain hemorrhage, she's been in a coma.

The doctors were clear from the start.

"Her coma is so deep that she will have to be on long-term life support via a mechanical ventilation machine," Dr. Banerjee explained to Beth Ann, Don, and me. It was the morning after Jessica and I had arrived in the screaming ambulance. She'd been through surgery to relieve the pressure of the blood in her brain, and now dawn was shooting its merciless light into the waiting room that smelled like burned coffee and hand sanitizer.

"But after she wakes up, she'll be able to come off it, won't she?" said Beth Ann, her eyes red, her voice thin and grating.

"I have to be completely transparent with you all right now," said Dr. Banerjee. "The damage to Jessica's brain is so extensive that even if she did wake up, she would suffer from unresponsive wakefulness syndrome for the rest of her life."

"Unresponsive…?" said Beth Ann.

"It's what people used to call a vegetative state. I'm sorry." The doctor's brown eyes were compassionate. "I know this must be incredibly hard to process."

"So what are you saying? What's the plan?" said Don, his voice rough, aggressive, though I could tell he was just trying to sound matter-of-fact.

"To be honest, she is unlikely to wake up, ever. If she does, her quality of life will be poor. Even if she wakes up, her brain function won't come back. She will always require life support." The doctor placed her hand on Beth Ann's arm. "I would recommend that you say your goodbyes and we remove her from the machines. There's no hurry, of course. You can take your time. If there's any family that would like to come in—"

Beth Ann was already shaking her head. "But surely there are…

people who just…wake up? Right? She could still be OK, even if it's a small chance?"

"If anyone can pull through this and defy statistics, it's our girl," said Don, his face contorted even though I could see the tears winking in his eyes. "She's a fighter."

"I have no doubt that she is a very strong person," said Dr. Banerjee. "But with no function in her brain, I'm sorry to say that it's not a matter of strength anymore."

"How long can you keep her alive?" said Beth Ann.

The doctor nodded thoughtfully. "Technically, we can keep her body alive indefinitely. I'm not sure if you ever spoke with Jessica about her wishes—"

"I did," I interrupted, stepping forward, my arms crossed over my body, my hands tucked into the sleeves of the sweatshirt a nurse had given me to change into. The bloody eggshell blouse was in a small plastic bag now crammed into my purse.

Beth Ann and Don looked shocked to hear me speak, like they'd forgotten I was there. I couldn't blame them; I'd been mute, a non-entity, wrapped in my shame and guilt, but now we were talking about Jessica's future, and I had to speak up.

"She wouldn't want to be like this."

"Are you her sister?" said Dr. Banerjee.

"Her—" I wanted so badly to say fiancée. "Girlfriend."

Don made a dismissive sound. "Her mother and I will be deciding what to do."

"But Jessica said—"

"What are you suggesting, Lily?" interrupted Beth Ann, her tone elevated. "That we kill my daughter?"

"Well." Dr. Banerjee's voice was soft, calm. "Removing life support is not considered—"

"We talked about it," I tried again. "I remember." Tears clouded my vision, but I wiped them away and pressed on, trying to sound mature, reasonable, someone to be taken seriously. "It was on our first date. We were asking each other weird first-date questions—like, if you had to lose a limb, which would it be—and...what was your preferred way to die. And she said, on the surgical table because then at least it wouldn't hurt, and then she said, 'But I never want to be a vegetable.' I know she said that. I remember."

"Stop!" yelled Beth Ann. "My daughter is not an *object*! You need to leave, Lily! This is our daughter, and these are our decisions!"

"Do you happen to have Jessica's wishes in writing?" Dr. Banerjee said to me gently.

I shook my head. My body was so tight it might have snapped any minute.

"Go home," said Don. "Her mother and I need some space."

Dr. Banerjee gave me a concerned look, and I could see that she was about to speak, but I didn't want her to have to defend me. It would somehow just diminish me even further.

"It's fine," I said, grabbing my purse from the vinyl couch. "I'll leave."

God. If I lived through that now, they'd have to pry me away from Jessica's side with a fucking crowbar. They'd have to knock me unconscious and drag me out. But I was only twenty-four. Still so young, and standing there next to Beth Ann and Don, I felt it. And at the end of the day? They had power of attorney and I did not. It didn't matter that I was the one living with Jessica; that I loved her and she loved me; that we owned a business together and made love and knew everything about each other, from our pet peeves to our darkest secrets. I had no power, and no way of getting it.

Over the next days, I haunted the hospital. I sent Beth Ann and Don articles about Jessica's condition. I texted them and called them and pleaded my cause—*Jessica's* cause. *I don't believe Jessica is in her body anymore. Please let her go.*

When a knock came at my apartment door two weeks later, I was stunned to be served papers. It was a restraining order. I wasn't allowed to be within one hundred yards of Jessica.

I called Beth Ann. Now it was my turn to shriek.

"What the fuck are these papers about? You mean I can't see her anymore?"

"Why would you want to?" she shouted back. "You want her to be dead!"

Over the years, sometimes I stalked Beth Ann's Facebook, which, though on private mode, she miraculously hadn't blocked me from. She'd occasionally share pictures of a birthday party they threw for Jessica in the hospital. It was gruesome, the contrast between the pale, unconscious woman I loved with the golden birthday sign above her hospital bed. The expressionless form she made against the big smiles of her parents and the nurses wearing party hats, holding up cupcakes, a mockery of a celebration.

Every now and then, I'd call Beth Ann. Always the same. Please, let her go. It's been a year. Two. Three.

What takes more strength? I asked myself at the Riovan. *To hang on? Or to let go?*

Maybe I've been making the same mistake Beth Ann and Don have been making for all these years. Hanging on. Allowing Jessica's body to keep working, and somehow, stopping her from attaining peace. Stopping *me* from attaining peace.

It's not like I didn't try to achieve it another way, though. Five years ago, stripped of power and barred from ever seeing Jessica again, I went back to the place where our downward spiral began. The place that had ruined us.

I went back to the Riovan.

Jessica and I visited the Riovan in late spring; I went back in early fall and booked two nights, which was all I could afford. I'd sent my emails to the news outlets asking for help, describing how Jess had spiraled after our "dream vacation" and ended up in emergency treatment. I didn't have the heart to type out the whole sordid ending of her life as I knew it—it felt too raw to send in an email blast—but I did say that she "attempted suicide." Even with that, I'd got nothing back. The Riovan was not going to fall; it was going to continue on as if nothing had happened. No one cared what had happened to Jessica or to me.

I walked the beaches, trying to remember every little thing about her that I could. I wished I had ashes to scatter; something physical. I sat on the jetty and imagined the scene of me proposing to her, over and over, until it almost felt like I had done it, and Jessica had said yes, and we were back here for our honeymoon.

While I was walking on the beach the second day, I overheard one of the nutritionists be an absolute bastard to a guest. "You keep eating French fries, you'll just keep being a fat slob. I thought you were here because you were ready for a change."

My heart and my gut squeezed so hard, I thought I might explode. In a cloud of rage, I went back to my room and sobbed for hours into the expensive down comforter and the beautiful sheets. Nothing was going to change here at the Riovan, but how could I accept that? How, when the same darkness that destroyed Jessica was still at work in this place?

That evening, I went out for a final swim before packing for my early morning flight. The water was frisky, but I'd always been a strong swimmer. I knew I was probably swimming too far out, but I didn't stop until the shore was a distant smear. Then, I floated on my back and watched the first stars pop out of the blue, and wished and wished that Jessica would appear to me and tell me she was OK, she was at peace, she was free.

I yelped as something encroached on my vision—a paddleboarder, skimming by just inches from me, like he hadn't seen me at all. I righted myself, treading water as he passed me, too stunned by the close call to even cry out. Then I recognized him. It was the nutritionist. Invading my space, my evening swim, my attempt at communing with Jessica.

"Fuck you," I remember breathing as I swam away. "Fuck you."

Then I heard a splash. When I turned, the paddleboard was empty, a useless life jacket sitting on the front of the board; he'd taken it off. He surfaced quite a ways from his board, his head popping up briefly before it sank back down. He was in trouble.

I crawled toward him with strong strokes. One of his arms burst up, and I reached out, confident I could grab it and pull us back to the paddleboard. And then—

You'll just keep being a fat slob.

My heart stuttered.

Had he been working here earlier this year? During our free stay in the spring, for instance? Had Jessica perhaps even consulted with him? Had she heard those exact words fall from his lips?

I pulled back my hand.

For a minute, I just treaded water, my legs scissoring, arms swirling. If he surfaces again, I'll help him, I promised myself.

He didn't. The paddleboard was already far to my right, carried sideways by the current, the oar nowhere in sight.

I swam back to shore, toweled off, and went back to my room, arms and legs aching from my long swim. I showered, packed my things, and the next morning, I left.

For days, I kept replaying what I'd done, and the more I replayed it, the better it felt.

Now he'd never call anyone a fat slob ever again.

I imagined how happy Jessica would be, that this level of toxicity had been scrubbed out of the world. That what had perhaps been said to her would not be said to some other girl, on some other day.

I did worry, though. Had anyone seen me out there? The water was in full view of the beach and the resort. Granted, not many people were swimming in the evening, and no one was as far out as us. It would be hard to spot us as anything but little black blobs. The lifeguards were no longer on duty; at that time of evening, you swam at your own risk. But still—would someone eventually come knocking at my door? "Ma'am, you're under arrest for the death of…" Shit, I didn't even know his name.

But the knock never came. Time slipped by. His disappearance didn't make the news, at least not the outlets I followed.

Still, I kept searching *Riovan drowning death*, or *Swimmer fails to save paddleboarder*, or any other number of key words that occurred to me on any given day, sometimes multiple times a day. Nothing.

Until one day, I got a result. I clicked the link, adrenaline already pulsing through me. It took me straight to the Riovan website.

> We Are Hiring! Do you have lifeguarding experience?
> Do you have a passion for keeping swimmers safe?
> Hourly wages plus room and board at the Caribbean's
> hottest wellness resort! Come be a part of our culture.
> Save a life, and change your life!

I stared and stared at the open call on the screen.

Save a life and change my life?

It all clicked. I *had* saved a life, when I let the nutritionist die. I'd saved the lives of all the people he could no longer berate. I'd failed to be vigilant with Jessica, but I could redeem myself at the Riovan. I could guard lives by saving them from the predators that had devoured my Jessica.

I felt Jessica, somehow, in the room with me, bestowing her approval on my plan.

I hit *Apply*.

Now, with the hum of the machines soft in the air and the familiar hospital smell of antiseptic around me, it's easy to imagine no time has passed. That the five years that have gone by were just a fever dream.

I draw up a chair by Jessica's side, trailing my eyes over the tube they've put through her throat, the blue geometric print on her hospital gown, the orange Do Not Resuscitate bracelet on her left wrist. The way her collarbones make such a beautiful V. I remember kissing those collarbones. A profound ache fills me. I draw her hand into mine, warm and limp, and for a moment, I let my head hang, feeling the heaviness of my breath, the heaviness of what it means to be alive.

I'm sorry, Jessica. The words gush out of my heart. *I'm sorry I wasn't your hero. I'm sorry I let my guard down when it was your turn to need saving... I'm sorry I couldn't put your pieces back together...*

But when I open my mouth, it's not apologies that come out.

"That first morning," I whisper. My voice catches. "Remember? After our first night together? I woke up before you did, and...I just looked at you. I don't think I've ever been more in the moment,

Jessica. I knew—I just *knew* I'd found something I had to hang on
to, something most people never find. I promised myself I would
build my life around you. I know I didn't say it out loud right away.
I mean…maybe it would've freaked you out. Too close too fast, you
know? Maybe I didn't even realize I was making that promise…"

Memories of that morning play before my eyes. The sheets
twisted around her perfect body. The sound of traffic, gentle behind
the glass, like the world had stepped back to give us some space. The
smell of yeast and sugar. She ran down to get doughnuts while I made
terrible coffee in her French press I didn't actually know how to use,
and she declared she would be in charge of the coffee from then on.
She claimed the chocolate doughnut and got crumbs on her nose. I
kissed them off.

"Maybe I couldn't save you," I whisper. Tears crowd my eyes,
spilling over, dripping down onto Jessica. "Maybe love doesn't
always mean we can rescue each other. But—I should have married
you, Jessica. I wanted to propose, but I kept waiting for that perfect
moment, and…I didn't do it."

My throat seizes with tears, and for a moment I'm overwhelmed
by the image of Jess and me in wedding gowns. She'd favor something
lacy, something with Cinderella vibes. I would have worn something
more streamlined, basic, with a single dramatic feature, like a plunging back, or a high slit.

A shuddering sigh vibrates through my bones as I release her
hand and pull out the engagement ring, warm in my pocket.

It's far from the perfect moment now, but I never should have
waited for perfection.

"Will you marry me?" I whisper.

Only the droning of the machines answers. I'm not expecting a
response, obviously. Or a feeling that Jess is here. Nothing like that.

It's simply the question that has been lodged in my throat for five years, choking me.

Then, I take her hand up again and try to work the simple ring with its tiny diamond chip onto her ring finger. It doesn't fit; her hand is swollen from bad circulation. I put it on her pinky. The fit is loose, but I fold her hand onto her chest so it doesn't slip off. Her forearms, facing down, hiding the ghost-silver lines. Last time I saw those wounds, they were not yet scars.

"I'm sorry you've had to endure this," I say, my hands over hers.

I bow my head and for a while sit in the same silence Jessica has been lying in for five years.

I wonder if she senses the passage of time. If she's feeling claustrophobic, like I often felt in the lifeguard chair, watching and waiting, motionless.

I hear the muffled whine of a siren. Maybe an ambulance. Maybe the police.

I lift my head and stroke my hand through her long, blond hair.

Time to change the story.

"I have to let you go, sweetheart. Remember when we were talking about our death plans? I know, it was a terrible first-date question, but you rolled with it..." I can't help a smile. "You said, do *not* let me be a vegetable. And I said, do *not* bury me in a casket. I had a terror of somehow still being alive and trapped inside, remember?" I laugh softly, but the laugh ends abruptly as a sob threatens to come out, even though now is not the time for that. "This is what you wanted. I'm sorry I didn't do it sooner. I know I'm about to have a lot of quiet time to think about all my choices. All my mistakes. But...I'm not afraid." I bend down and kiss her. Her lips are soft beneath mine. She can't kiss me back, but I don't need her to. "I love you."

Strangely, what fills me in this moment is...gratitude. I remember

Randy's words. *I've been lucky enough to have two great lives. Some people don't even get one.*

I guess I'm lucky.

I had one.

The sirens are louder now. I stand slowly. Take one last picture of Jessica in my mind; the way her hair shines in the light, the way the blue veins on her eyelids look so delicate, the soft empty warmth of the body waiting for release.

I follow the electric cord of her ventilator to the plug in the wall. And then, heaving one last breath into my lungs, I yank. The machine sighs as it powers down, and I return to my chair and hold her hand.

Her breathing stops. Her body stills. There's a new kind of silence, even deeper than the silence from before. I try to sense something—her spirit leaving her body? Some feeling of release, or freedom? A sign? But there's nothing.

I keep holding her hand even when I hear the telltale sound of running in the hall outside.

I stay seated as the door bursts open. Two cops explode into the room, and behind them, just outside the door—Daniel. I glance at the wall clock—right on time.

"Hands above your head! Step away from the patient!" shouts one of them, reaching for his gun.

I rise and lift my arms.

Maybe spirit-Jessica, if she exists, is also lifting her arms as she ascends into some sort of bliss. I don't believe it—but I hope it.

The next few minutes are chaos, as nurses and doctors surround Jessica. She's DNR, so at least I have the assurance that they won't bring her back.

One of the cops intones my rights as the other turns me around so that I'm facing the door, and Daniel. He's still standing outside the room, his eyes fixed on me, unwavering.

"Hands behind your back."

Why? Daniel sends across the frenzy of the room.

But our eye contact breaks as the handcuffs click into place, cold around my wrists, and the cop grabs me by the arm and shoves me forward, toward the door.

Just outside, I say, "Wait," because I want to answer Daniel's question, but the cops don't wait.

"Why?" This time, Daniel speaks it out loud, but I'm already past him, now craning my neck back to look at him. He's holding up his phone. I can see the recording counting out the seconds, and a strange part of me can't wait to hear how he weaves this all together in his new finale. "Why?" he cries out above the turmoil, doctors shouting, nurses running, cops shoving.

"When you really love someone—" I say, still craning, pulling against the cops' pushing.

"Move forward, ma'am," says one of the officers, but I twist with all my might, nearly shouting the last part down the hall.

"Sometimes you have to let them go."

Then, the most surprising thing happens, like sunshine breaking over me.

I smile.

I've worn a lot of smiles over the past years. Calculating smiles, sly smiles, smiles meant to tease, infuriate, or appease. But this one—*this* smile on my lips—springs forth as natural as a growing thing, a tender shoot from the soil of my grief. Like a blessing. Like freedom.

Like life from death.

EPILOGUE

THERE'S A GROANING SOUND AS THE DOORS SLIDE OPEN. THE OFFICERS on either side of me seem bored. This is just another day for them.

The sun slices in. The parking lot shimmers before me, like it's still deciding whether or not to materialize. It's summer, and the late-morning air has a humid scent that promises full-on mugginess later on.

My friend Nate is picking me up—the first of our friendship group to find Daniel's podcast all those years ago. Somehow, this makes him a fitting bookend to my time here. A four-hour drive from Cincinnati to the state penitentiary in Youngstown was a big ask, but hey—you only get picked up from prison once. Right?

I'm in the same leggings and T-shirt they booked me in, minus the scrubs. They hang a little loose; I've lost some weight. Not on purpose; prison food sucks. I've been dreaming of a nice, thick butter burger drenched in cheddar. Poke bowls piled high with fresh fish. Fried pickles.

R&D this morning—Receiving and Discharge—took almost three hours. So much paperwork. So much waiting while it was processed. Thankfully, I've got really good at waiting—even better than I already was, if I may be so bold, and I dare say I've earned that right. Finally, I got my clothes to change into. They released the money I've made working—laundry and kitchen, mainly, and the occasional bathroom duty—and finally returned my purse, wallet, and ID.

The doors are open. I could look behind me, say something sarcastic to the officers like, *Have a nice life*, but I don't.

I walk forward. Half of me expects someone to stop me. It might take me a while to really believe I'm free.

The parking lot is pretty empty. Some cars are huddled along the edges, but one car is parked in the very center, bold and alone. And on that car leans a man, silhouetted against the strong sunlight. Thick, muscled shoulders. A little hunch to them, promising intensity.

And…it's definitely not Nate.

I walk toward Daniel. He stays put. No dramatic running from either side.

When I stop in front of him, it feels like I'm in a dream, but I guess that's all right, since it's not a bad one so far. He pushes his sunglasses on top of his head. His familiar clear brown eyes take me in. I do the same, studying the difference that 1,095 days, give or take a few, make in a person.

"Where's Nate?" I finally say.

"Cincinnati. I saved him the trip."

Daniel has a couple of new gray streaks at the sides of his hair. The lines on his face are maybe a teensy bit deeper. I don't mind at all.

I nod at his wheels.

"Fancy car."

"It's a rental. I flew in from Miami."

"Nice rental."

His lips do that thing where they lift at the edge, like the tease of a smile, and he lowers his sunglasses so they're again covering his eyes.

"The podcast isn't doing so bad."

Understatement of the year: Daniel Lukiewicz truly has ascended to podcaster royalty.

I shade my eyes and squint. It really is bright out here. "I've kept up."

"Really?" He sounds surprised.

"An inmate had an illegal cell phone. I…rented some time."

He starts to ask something, then decides against it.

I grin. I know what he's imagining. The "rental fee" was nothing *that* interesting, but…let him think it was.

It's a bit surreal to be standing so close to him—close enough that I could reach out a hand and touch his arm, or his hand.

The last time I saw Daniel was at my trial. We might as well have been miles away. He was in a suit, clean-shaven. From across the ocean of space between the witness stand and the place where I sat with my lawyer, he testified against me. *Lily Lennox murdered four people and tried to murder a fifth. I saw her holding Serena underwater. After I dragged Serena out of the water, Lily confessed on the beach and then resuscitated Serena.*

Prosecution charged me not just with Jessica's death, but all the murders, since Saint Lisieux had chosen not to try me, thank God—though they did issue a ban prohibiting me from ever reentering the nation. Not that I'd ever want to return, thank you very much.

Daniel's count was slightly off, of course. He didn't know about paddleboard guy. Then again, was that really murder?

"Why would she resuscitate Serena if she wanted to kill her?" the defense asked.

"She didn't want to end up behind bars," he said and looked straight at me. "It was a purely selfish move."

I couldn't hold it against him; he was right.

I, of course, denied everything—except for unplugging Jessica. That, I was happy to own.

Still, it wasn't looking so good for me until they brought Serena up to testify.

"She saved my life," Serena said. "I know what happened."

During cross-examination, the prosecution really went to town on her, but she stubbornly insisted on her version of the story, over and over. *I was drunk. I went for a swim. Lily saved my life.* I remember that as the moment the tide of the trial turned in my favor.

Whether she legitimately believed it or was simply being strategic since she knew that I had one on her—the CleanSlim she'd given to Skylar that led to the girl's hospitalization—I'll never know. But I suspect that more than a little self-interest was at work there too.

In the end, there simply wasn't enough evidence for the deaths of years past to nail me, and between Serena's surprise testimony and a few others—Vic, who was all too eager to defend his hotel and me as an extension of it; Kenton, who gave an emotional account of the way I'd saved Mr. Tulaine; Brianna, who called me "the sweetest person in the whole place;" and even Carli Elle herself—they cleared me of all charges for the Riovan deaths. They only convicted me for Jess. Five years for Manslaughter by Non-Voluntary Passive Euthanasia. Good behavior brought that down to three.

Three years during which I did a lot of dishes, even more laundry, and read my way through the prison library, including a dozen more books on my list of one hundred. Though I never did finish *Crime and Punishment.* I spent a lot of time in the prison graveyard too. Mom died here; no one came to collect her body. She has a small headstone.

"You brought the Riovan down after all," I say to Daniel, which is as close to a *thank you* as he's going to get, considering.

After I set Jessica free, Daniel extended the season by three more episodes and told my whole story, starting with my childhood and my mom's conviction, moving through my love story with Jessica and her subsequent struggles. He interviewed friends, family, coworkers and brought it all to life. Then, in the real season finale, he exposed the Riovan's ugly underbelly, from the contracts with questionable supplement companies to the fast-and-loose pharmacy to the destructive tactics used by staff to "motivate" guests. The story spread like wildfire. People started coming forward with claims of abuse by the staff, lawsuits rained down, and the hotel folded within the year.

Maybe one day I'll show Daniel the letters I've received in prison because of his podcast; letters from women recovering from eating disorders, and their families, sharing their stories because they felt a connection with mine. A few of those letters included article clippings about other resorts where people had spoken out and made changes, because Jess and my story gave them the courage to do so. I read about how the hashtag #ChangeforJess went viral, inspiring people to rethink the overall culture, imagery, and language around wellness in gyms, schools, workplaces.

I can't say I'm proud of all that, since it was other people rallying, speaking up, making change. What I can say is that it felt like a gift—strange and unearned—that somehow, after everything, people cared.

"Yeah," Daniel says, his voice gruff. Raw. "I'd do it all again."

I shield my eyes, trying to make out his eyes behind his sunglasses. "So would I."

I wait to see if he's upset by this. But his expression doesn't change.

"So you're driving me back to Cincinnati?" I say.

"Is that where you want to go?"

I don't answer for a moment.

"It's where I'd been planning to go. I need to officially sell Taste of Heaven to Lisa. Sign the paperwork."

"You know, there's this thing called Docusign..."

OK, *smart ass.*

"Well, where are *you* going?" I say.

"Chicago. I have a lead on a story that might become Season Six."

I tilt my head. "I mean, I've always liked deep-dish pizza..."

"They have good Italian beef there too. Just saying."

OK, now I'm salivating. I clutch my purse strap. "All I have with me are the clothes on my back."

"Pretty sure there's a Target in Chicago."

"And what? I just...follow you around while you do your thing? See the sights?"

He shifts his weight. "Actually, I've been looking for a cohost. For the podcast."

What?

It takes the surprise a few seconds to move through my body.

"OK," I say slowly. "You want me to cohost the true-crime podcast that tried to pin six murders on me?"

"Well...five. And one attempted."

"Are you nuts?"

"You're smart. Passionate. Witty. You care about justice."

"I think we come at justice from *slightly* different angles."

His grin blooms slowly. "Is that a problem?"

We regard each other. There's so much I don't know. Where I'm going to sleep tonight, for example. Or, you know, what I'm going to do with my life.

But none of that seems as relevant right now as the question standing before me, muscled and confident and simmering with quiet energy.

"What about us?" I say softly, because I can't ask, *Are you still in love with me?* Not out loud. Three years and a prison sentence stand between then and now, and I can't assume anything.

"That's what I came here to find out," he says.

I reach forward and gently push up his sunglasses so I can see his eyes. I look at him and let him look at me.

Ooooh, shit. I remember this. The power of his gaze as it delves into me.

It's the gaze of someone who knows me.

Not everything, of course.

But the most important things. What I've done and why. And somehow...

He's not scared.

I lower his glasses. Nod slowly.

Then, I walk over to the passenger side of his fancy car and get in. It's hot and smells like new car inside. He climbs in too, and we close our doors in tandem, like we've been doing it that way forever.

"Where is this going, Daniel?" I say, briefly brushing his hand as he reaches for the gear shift. I can practically feel the electric zap as my skin meets his.

His gaze pierces me from the driver's seat. "Only one way to find out."

My heart thunders, but it's not adrenaline powering it this time, or fear. It's hope.

I was lucky to get one great life with Jessica.

And I'm starting to think that maybe, just maybe, I'll be lucky enough to have two.

The car roars to life.

"Ready?" Daniel says with that wolfish grin, and I don't answer him with words, but with my eyes, I send, *What are you waiting for?*

He sends back, *You.*

I send back, *I'm here. I'm ready.*

And we go.

READING GROUP GUIDE

1. Every year, Lily Lennox jets off to the Riovan wellness resort to work as a lifeguard, but she's not just there to save lives, she's there to take them too. How did you feel about reading a novel from the perspective of a female serial killer? Did anything about Lily surprise you?

2. How does Lily choose her targets every year, and how is this year different? Who does Lily end up choosing to murder, and why?

3. The novel takes place at an upscale wellness resort, modeled off places that exist today. Why is Riovan a problematic resort, and what might this setting say about the current wellness industry?

4. What happened to Lily's fiancée, Jessica, and why does Lily feel she needs to get revenge for the tragedy that occurred? Do you think revenge at this scale can be justified?

5. Not only is Lily trying to cover up her latest murder at Riovan, but she also has another obstacle in the way: Daniel Black. Who is Daniel, and why is he really at Riovan? Were you surprised by the twist in his identity?

6. This story combines elements of suspense with a swoon-worthy love story. How did you feel about Daniel and Lily's connection? Did you find yourself rooting for them to end up together or for them to take each other down? Discuss.

7. Daniel is revealed to run a successful true crime podcast. Do you listen to true crime podcasts? If so, why? How might true crime media help fuel conversations around justice?

8. Though Lily and Daniel care deeply about each other, Daniel still testifies against her in court and uses his podcast to pin her as a murderer. What did you think about this ending, and what might it say about our characters and how they feel about each other?

9. This story explores the idea of feminine rage by putting readers in the mind of a nuanced and morally gray main character. What might the novel say about how women, and people in general, feel about our current sociopolitical climate?

A CONVERSATION
WITH THE AUTHOR

This novel is such a blast! What inspired you to write this story?

First, *I* wanted to have fun. The idea of a "good for her" revenge story set on a tropical island was the first spark. When writing books, I frequently start with a simple concept like this that feels exciting to me. Then, I have to do the work of uncovering why my characters would do these (often extreme) things. Even after knowing that Lily was going to target people who hurt others via "wellness bullying," I had to wonder why she would kill. A lot of people have been hurt in similar ways but don't resort to serial killing—so why would she? I had a lot of fun coming up with a backstory that hopefully gives credibility to why she would go to such extremes. I also loved ending the story with Lily being unapologetic about what she's done.

Why do you think exploring the wellness industry is important? What do you hope readers think about as they walk away from this setting?

First, I do hope they'll think about fat-shaming. It was important to me to highlight how it's not just about the overt comments that we can quickly flag as negative but the gaslighting, such as the way that Riovan codes the word "fat" as a shameful word to be avoided. However, there's a larger problem that is at the root of fat-shaming: society's routine objectification of women's bodies. It was really important for me to take it deeper and explore not just the fat-shaming side but the beauty-shaming side and how a certain type of beauty can be coded as "dangerous" or "slutty," *especially* in young, adolescent girls; this is Lily's experience as she goes through foster care with a target on her back that spells "trouble." While working on this book, I wanted to bring home the idea that women can't win, no matter their weight or physical attributes. When women are objectified, everyone loses no matter where you sit on the spectrum of social beauty standards.

Lily and Daniel are so much fun together, and we love that their story has such a twisty end. How did you decide to end their love story the way you did, and what do you hope it says about the two main characters?

I love this question because, to be honest, I struggled a *lot* to come up with the ending. I wanted to stay true to the thriller side of the book as well as the romance side, and I had my sights set on a happy ending, but I didn't want to give them a "cheap" resolution that flung an unearned happily-ever-after at them. Let's just say there was a lot of brainstorming and mental hand-wringing (is that a thing?), which led me to what now seems obvious—for the ending to feel satisfying, Lily and Daniel each had to act according to their own moral compass and deal with the consequences. Neither could back down. I love that they're both uncompromising on their values and how they've chosen to live those out, and even though they come at justice from different angles, they have that mutual resonance and therefore respect for each other that enables them to pick up their love story in the end with no hard feelings. It was a tricky one to figure out, but I hope I pulled it off!

Why do you think Lily's story is important to tell, and what do you hope readers take away from the novel?

One of my favorite scenes to write was the scene where Lily and Jess are returning from the Riovan and have an argument about some airport M&Ms. Jess has struggled with weight-based shame her whole life; Lily has experienced beauty-based shame when she was coded as "trouble" in her vulnerable teenage years. I really wanted to highlight the way that, in this moment, they can't "see" each other's pain or make room for the experience of the other. They're too blinded by their own hurts, past and present, to come together and realize they have both experienced the same thing at the core: objectification, just in different flavors.

Changing the world is a big job. Of course I would love to see the end of the objectification of women's bodies in our culture. But will it happen in my lifetime? Not likely. It's so extremely entrenched. However, if we women can be on one another's sides and create space for all the different experiences of pain that this harmful culture brings us, no matter our body type, size, or other physical features, I think that can bring a sense of community that will make us stronger and beautiful moments of healing.

Do you have a writing routine? How do you get to the page and write an entire novel?

Yes, I do! But it's not consistent throughout the year—it's very hot and cold, in fact! I often write only one book a year—sometimes two but no more than that. The process wrings me out, and I've learned over the past decade that one to two books a year is all that my book-writing well has to give. However, once I have a concept that I'm excited about and the creative energy is flowing, I draft very fast and usually write my books from start to finish in six to eight weeks. My writing time, when I'm drafting, is always in the evening on weekdays (7–10 p.m., to be precise), since I work a full-time office job, full-time hours as a literary agent, and am a mom to three young kids (not to mention my husband occasionally likes to have my attention too?). During book-writing time, my evenings and weekends belong to that book until it's done!

ACKNOWLEDGMENTS

I had *so* much fun writing this book. Like, it was a little ridiculous.

Thank you first to my incredible editor, Thorne Ryan, without whom this book would not exist. Your editorial eye is *chef's kiss,* and I just loved working on this story with you!!

Thanks to my husband, Adam, my Chief Advisor for sexy banter (which it turns out I struggle with!). Adam, this book would not be as good if you hadn't been there every step, lending your wit and humor. I'd be like, "Babe, I think something funny needs to go *here*," and you'd take a look and, within seconds, come up with something brilliant. You make everything in my life better, and I can't wait to see what we get up to next.

My writing (not to mention my LIFE) is also tremendously aided by my top two beta readers and critique partners, Jenny Kodanko and Joy Pitcairn, who I'm also so lucky to call my besties. The way I love you guys… Well, it's too long for the acknowledgments section, so just call me later and I'll emotionally yammer at you instead. Jenny, the writing retreat we went on together in February 2024 (where I finished writing this book and burned the polenta!) was one of the highlights of my year. Let's do it again as soon as possible!

Thanks to my dad, who (among many other things) knows a lot about electricity and spent hours with me working through how to kill Michael Johnson (as I took furious notes). Also, sorry I made you an accessory to murder, Dad. Thanks to my mom, who helped me think through the very last scene and land this thing. And thanks to the Berg clan, who enthusiastically brainstormed Lily's psychology with me. You guys are the best.

Thanks to my kids, Alice, Ben, and Zac. Becoming your mom has been one of the greatest joys of my life. I love all the books you guys write. Right now, *Trapped in a Nightmare* (by Zac) and *Nightmare Forest* (by Ben) are giving me endless delight.

Thanks to all the people involved in getting this book out into the world—the team at Sourcebooks, editors Liv Turner and Shana Drehs, the team at Transworld, cover designer Irene Martinez, publicist Emma Fairey, production controller Phil Evans, editorial assistant Anna Carvanova, and my brilliant copy editor, Claire Gatzen.

Finally, thanks to my readers—I hope you have as much fun reading this one as I had writing it.

ABOUT THE AUTHOR

Sienna Sharpe is a pseudonym of Jenna Satterthwaite. Born in the Midwest, Sienna grew up in Spain, lived briefly in France, and is now happily settled in Chicago with her husband and three kids. Sienna studied classical guitar, English literature, and French and once upon a time was a singer-songwriter in the folk band Thornfield. She loves sushi, reading in her natural habitat (a.k.a. her bed), and women taking back their power.